ABOUT THE AUTHOR

JP lives in Western Sydney with his family, including one dog with back issues, another with anxiety issues and another who is an escape artist, attempting to flee from their constant love, affection and security.

Before his writing debut novel 'The Invisible Tether', JP focused on writing songs for the melancholy masses and in complete contrast, also developed vibrant and catchy children's songs.

He has worked in education, human resources, business development and communications but is often dreaming of other wordly adventures and experiences.

You can find him posting parody videos on social media, planting native bush foods in his backyard and chasing the sun through rivers and national park trails.

Jpmcdonald.com.au

THE GEMARINE CHRONICLES

BEYOND FORSAKEN WORLDS

JP MCDONALD

Cover Art by Jennifer Rackham
Gemarine Logo by Jennifer Rackham
Edited by Louise Pearce @ Refine Fiction
Developmental Editing by Emmie Hamilton
Internal by Daiana
Comic art by Ioinart
Character art by @Graph_desinglit
Title designs by Upklayak @ freepik

NOTE TO THE READER

Although I have made this world a lot more tolerant and non-judgmental than the world we are currently assigned, there are a fair few considerations I'd like you to take into account before reading this piece of work. I apologise if by some chance, you are offended by anything listed below and strongly advise you consider your wellbeing if the following pieces of content may in fact, become a trigger for you.

Depictions of, and references to death, recollections of war, extreme violence, mild gore, trauma, abuse, torture, graphic sex scenes, kink scenes, substance abuse, adult language, and manipulation.

If you are put off by graphic sex scenes then it would be best to avoid Chapter 16 and Chapter 36.

Otherwise, I really hope you enjoy your new home - Gemarine.

ALSO BY JP MCDONALD

THE INVISIBLE TETHER

DEDICATION

For the budding biologists, naturalists and conservationists who give a voice to the voiceless and for the everyday person (or alien) who makes small sacrifices to benefit their planet.

PROLOGUE

LOCATION: PERIAH
YEAR: 118 (THE PRESENT)
XAN – 24 YEARS OLD

*N*othing is flawless in a galaxy built from chaos.

A skyline streaked with ruby shards held Xan's gaze. The setting sun bathed the land before him in blood and battle. Chaos was a deep cumulonimbus cloud, threatening a severe thunderstorm.

He wasn't a meteorologist.

These days, Xan was considered a Xeno-biologist, a conservationist and quite possibly an entrepreneur. But he found himself adept in other fields of science that weren't exactly his expertise.

The art of chaos though, not so much. That was Juniper's speciality. With a sword as her brush she painted in colours of doom. Watching her dexterity, her nuanced, stylistic embellishments – it was evident she was an artist of a generation.

Behind him, the portal hummed in admiration as the rest of his companions reached the safety of the ship. They listened to his desperate plea to retreat. To ready themselves for the greatest journey yet. And now he stood without them.

Upon reflection – maybe he *did* know about chaos. Maybe in the explosion of matter that created this galaxy, a part of it was also a part of him. It was about time he embraced it.

A shaking hand clasped his Cranston ray gun.

Boots devoured the ground beneath him as he charged into the distance.

A primal scream followed.

The portal groaned at his desertion.

He would be back soon enough to finish what he had started.

CHAPTER 1

LOCATION: GEMARINE
YEAR: 108 (10 YEARS AGO)
XAN – 14 YEARS OLD

Stars had faces. Pallid though they were from the echoes of their slaughter millions of years ago.

Still, they twinkled from the confines of a beautiful grave, dazzling all who met their gaze.

If the gaze were that of a boy hurtling to the ground, thrown from an orbiting spacecraft, those faces would become distorted. Ghouls with scythe-like grins that could rip one's soul in two. The boy in question, Xan, couldn't make out the details of the star system. They were just a blur of volatile shapes as he somersaulted through the sky.

But starry eyes only bear witness and seldom interfere with galactic phenomena. So as Xan pleaded to those indiscriminate trails of twinkling light, they simply observed, as they had always done, and always would do, letting him thud onto the surface of Gemarine.

Xan was sprawled across the flaxen grass. It was taller than the dry fields of wheat on Earth, ready for the harvest. It encased him like a

1

fickle fence, swaying gently as a comfortable breeze billowed around him. Bioluminescence flickered inside the tendrils, pulsating fervently in the darkness.

Xan's hand instinctively shot to his throat, scratching at it in a nervous panic as he realised his predicament. He was outside the spacecraft in an alien world.

I need breathable air.

Rigid fingers clawed the ground.

His heart was a fist pounding against the prison bars of his chest.

Lucidity returned to his mind and he remembered at once that he'd studied Gemarine for a year. The air on this planet was breathable. He was safe.

Nausea overcame him; that human instinct to fear the unknown.

He smoothed through clumps of dark hair matted to his scalp. It was damp with perspiration – or was it blood? Raising trembling fingers in front of his face, he could not discern a crimson kiss. The acrid smell of smoke was the incense of death, burning through the reverie of a pleasant arrival in Topaz City.

An enemy ship had disrupted the planned pleasantries, trailing them as they entered the Gemarinian atmosphere. The laser fire came quickly. Quicker than the disappointment of a welcome plan made obsolete.

Xan gazed up at the purple and aqua hues swirling like an aurora above him, but the smoke from the crashed ship skulked like a sentient shadow across his view. Twin moons stared down at him, leering, the chill of night summoning gooseflesh on his skin. The ship that had held him was now a hulking mass of distorted metal sculptures, curated by bad luck and an alien wilderness.

The bodies of Franje, the pilot, and Derrison, the being who inducted him, were torn to shreds from sharpened glass and laser burns. Flowers of flayed flesh arranged in disrupted soil. An arm sleeved with the triangular insignia of Gemarine twitched periodically, like buzzing wires searching to connect to their circle of life once more. He hadn't known Franje well, but Derrison had visited him countless times in the lead-up to Xan's departure, and the shock of their mangled corpses struck at his heart.

The journey was made full of promise and wonder, not of dire expectations. Although Xan knew about life and death and the grey areas in between, he had not yet witnessed a broken body, shedding its essence into nothingness.

He wasn't aware of the moment changing him, but young individuals with hope sparkling like gemstones in their eyes seldom identify the occlusions that threaten to eradicate their innocence.

The enemy ship was nowhere to be seen. After it had brought Xan's ship down, it veered off into the void of space, flanked by the twin moons of Gemarine – beacons for unknown explorers.

He rose from the ground, dusted himself off, and checked for any noticeable blemishes. Xan was relieved. He was relatively unscathed. There was a sizeable cut across his right arm and an ache in his lower back. The moment before the ship went down, Derrison's eyes had gone wild with foresight as he unbuckled, sprinted to Xan, and fastened a device to his wrist. A shimmering forcefield had materialised, surrounding Xan with electromagnetic protection.

Xan smashed through the window – splintered glass twirling, like frozen snowflakes in a dance of death around him as he rocketed out into the planet's atmosphere. Just before he hit the ground, the forcefield surged and flickered, exhaling its final wispy breath. Without its protection, he landed heavily on his back, throwing out an arm to cushion the fall.

The ship collided with the planet, crumpling in an explosion of glass, metal and blood.

The knowledge that he was now stranded, alone in the wilds of a new world, worked its way like neurotransmitters throughout his body. The relief from earlier dissipated as the severity of his situation took hold.

The skin on his arms glowed under the light of both moons and he raised them, placing shaking hands on the back of his head. His arms quivered like jelly as he sucked in breath after breath, shutting his ashen grey eyes tight in an attempt to bring calm to his frazzled state.

Xan didn't often let himself be taken so willingly into fear's embrace, and this time would be no different. Although it may have taken a little longer, the focus on his breathing, the spotlight on just one of his senses, gave his brain a chance to welcome a departed friend: clarity.

When Xan had regained some control, he forced himself to approach the ship. Wary the enemy could return to finish the job, he would gather remaining supplies into a transportable pack and move away from the area. The overcast sky was a true co-conspirator, harbouring the secret of ambush, allowing the attacker to fade from view. Each time he turned his head toward it, he shuddered, remembering it could pull the veil back, revealing him at any time. If he moved toward a covering of trees to set up camp, at least he would be hidden.

Although he was young by Earth standards, he possessed a special mind: one that absorbed information quickly and deduced logical routes, finding interest in science and the life that surrounded him.

The structures of logic and form were dominant, but he also had a compassionate streak for animals, and bettering the environment. The mantra he used as a budding scientist on Earth was: *The path is true if it is walked with empathetic footsteps.*

The phrase kept him grounded, kept him focused on exploring science as a means to help – to find solutions.

Right now, though, the environment was an alien world he had no experience with. He needed to focus his goal on understanding it, and reaching the city.

Where would empathy fit into the truth of this path?

Twisted hulking trunks of spiralled wood loomed ahead. The spires beyond the trees peered at the shimmering luminescence of the distant city. The city was a promise of grandeur; the route there, however, was soaked in squalor and hardship. The scent of crushed bark, the essence of vanilla and the hint of fresh chamomile wafted toward him. In a desolate alien environment, it brought him comfort knowing there were similarities here. The air's chill was not a desperate wail into the night; it was muted, merely awakening the receptors on his skin. He wondered about the weather as the sun rose. Would this planet stink with humidity or would it fluctuate seasonally?

He swallowed, steeling himself against his plight as he reached the wrecked ship and started to sift through the inventory at hand.

The silence of the field was a caution to his senses. Xan knew that intuition was not something scientifically proven, but an acute awareness prepared his heart to heed a warning.

He saw the eyes first, before the complete outline of the creature. Glowing amber, bulbous and threatening.

"Hello, who's that?" His voice was a silky cobweb trembling in the wind.

A spiked tail rose out of the long grass, menacing. A creature on all fours stalked with slow, purposeful intent. It was the prowl of a predator, and with the ferocious stammering of his heart, Xan assumed the role of prey.

This world was not like his, but it would still stand to reason that wild creatures should not be crossed. It must have smelt blood. As he surveyed the tears to his bodysuit, red droplets dripped from frayed threads; a vibrant red rose petal swallowed by the soil at his feet.

"I have no quarrel with you. I possess no threat." He slowly pulled out the blade given to him by Derrison while aboard the craft, as standard-issue Cranston ray guns were no use to him without understanding how they worked. "But I will use this if I have to." He grimaced at the thought of hurting a creature. It went against everything he was. A budding biologist; a caring conservationist.

The creature didn't understand. How could it? With each step forward, it purred with a low intensity, four canines at the ready – desperate, it seemed – to kill.

The ground rumbled and a soft groan cut across the quiet. The soil trembled once more, then Xan was violently thrown backwards as the surface shifted underneath him. The bioluminescence faded and red and brown dirt erupted like a fountain, raining fragments around them both.

A large, horned beast emerged from beneath the ground, teeth bared in a hideous snarl, eyes black like the coat of a reaper. But instead of chasing Xan, it fixed its attention on the smaller creature who had been stalking it a moment ago.

Xan hastily crawled the first few metres on the crumbling dirt, but regained traction with his boots and launched into a run, flailing with spindly arms and legs, toward the forest of twisted trees.

He reached the shelter of the forest and paused, placing a shaking palm on the closest trunk, watching from afar.

The smaller creature fought valiantly. It reared up on hind legs, displaying black tapered claws sharpened to acute points, slashing as the horned beast dived for it. Its agility was on show, evading the aggressive thrust from the larger brute with ease. It lashed its spiked tail across one of the beast's independently moving conical eye turrets. Barbs pierced the hazy black iris, red blood casting shade across its periphery. A roar of indignation cracked across the expanse.

Although blinded in one eye, the horned beast swung out its own heavy, leathery tail. The smaller creature was caught in the age-old war of life; brawn against brains, agility over size.

At that moment, evolution appeared to fail it.

The horned beast's tail made contact with a sickening, dull thud. The smaller creature yelped, high-pitched and frantic, as it flipped end over end across the dirt.

As the hazy air settled, Xan watched it lie broken and panting. Its silence spoke louder than any whimper of pain.

The horned beast roared triumphantly for a moment, then stumbled on its stumpy legs, its ruined eye causing instability. Once steady enough, it lumbered forward inch by inch to enact the final kill.

Large amber eyes found Xan, who watched from a safe distance. The creature was defeated, yet not ready to resign itself to death. The way it looked at him with something akin to hope filled Xan with empathy for this beautiful creature. Beauty could be severe and deadly. It had marked him as prey not less than several minutes ago. But he understood that animal instinct evades retribution.

All lifeforms deserve a certain degree of reverence and what better way to revere than to save?

He let the sturdy pack slip from his grasp and it thumped onto the red surface, blowing a puff of dust that enveloped him like an aura. The Cranston ray gun was menacing in his right hand, clasped with a white-knuckled grip. His eyes flicked from one button to the next, trying frantically to discern what was what, as the thumping of the horned beast's feet grew closer to the hapless creature on the ground. Xan squeezed an orange button. The gun buzzed and vibrated with mild annoyance. A charging bar materialised on the side of the gun. A spectrum of colour turned from pale orange to blazing red, and then a shot careered into the distant forest, severing a row of innocent trees.

A striking jolt tore through Xan's body, pain rearing at the apex of his shoulder from the kickback of the gun. He stumbled back against a wooden soldier, its branches rifles marking Xan's chosen path.

Steadying himself, Xan burst forth, screaming in a high-pitched wail, his voice breaking in a primitive, and undignified manner. Gun pointed at the horned beast and with wide eyes full of terror, he squeezed the trigger. A bolt of vibrant cerise surged from the weapon, burning a hole through the open mouth of the beast, who was seconds from engulfing the helpless creature. The kinetic energy as Xan moved forward subdued the kickback, so as his innocence slipped away and courage swelled, the beast wavered, and fell to its side.

Xan reached the other creature, and it lay on a nest of upturned soil, its hind leg caked with rich blood. It snarled as Xan approached, and he reconsidered what to do.

How can I show this creature I just want to help?

The horned beast lay on its side, smoke emanating from the venom of the ray gun. Satisfied it would not cause harm to anything again, Xan turned on his heels and ran back to the discarded pack to search for medical supplies.

Regeneration gel should do it.

Xan approached the injured creature, stooping low to the ground, bundling himself in close and small, showing he was no threat. He hummed a lullaby from his childhood; a soothing stepwise melody with legato notes. Maybe it was the tonality or the adagio tempo, but the creature's snarl was lost. Although the front canines remained, the two locked eyes and, quite possibly, the essence of that moment permeated their defence systems and broke down the walls that separated both species.

For Xan, first contact had already been made when Derrison approached him in his family home in Hong Kong over a year ago. But transcendent contact of sorts was something he hadn't anticipated. Although the creature was wary of Xan, it turned its face away, fluffy with different shades of grey fur, focusing on cleaning its wound. A blue forked tongue had nearly licked off all the blood as it pinned back long pointed ears, sullen with concern.

Xan bent down and let it sniff his hand. He waited patiently until, thankfully, it appeared the creature would not taste his supple flesh. He opened the tube of regeneration gel and lathered his finger first.

He breathed in deeply and murmured, "Here goes," and smeared the gel across the wound.

The creature groaned at his touch, the cool sensation of the gel on its gaping wound most likely bizarre. Xan cooed, doing his best to administer the same level of care he once did to his pet cat, Mei, when she used to tangle with rose bushes. The creature was growing more and more comfortable with his presence. It tucked away the formidable canines and settled for tightly pursed lips with the occasional flicker of its forked tongue. Xan wrapped the wound in what appeared to be a bandage fused with a material he didn't recognise.

Stooping low once more, Xan said with a resonant calm, "Now, I'm going to pick you up and take you over there." He motioned his head toward the intact part of the fuselage. "I don't know why I'm talking to you, but hopefully you can respond to tone or vibration and understand my desire to help."

As he bent down, he felt the creature tense, but once he secured his arms around it and began the walk bound to one another, it just felt right.

Fate is an unknown force in our lives, whether it has weight that stifles or whether it gives us purpose that infuses the soul.

He carried the creature into the hollow of the crashed ship and said, "I guess we'll camp in here tonight, rather than take our chances in the forest. It would be great if you'd consider not eating me during the night."

CHAPTER 2

Juniper didn't dream of the world she was born into. Like many others on Gemarine, she was happy to leave the idea of Earth behind and focus on the countless opportunities, rather than mourn a loss so far removed from her reality.

She was taken as a two-year-old and brought to live with a clan of other Humans who had longed for a daughter of their own. These Humans had truly embraced the way of Gemarine, which meant that Juniper grew up sharing their ideals.

For most species, it was difficult to adjust at first.

Aranthers were easily pleased, copulating in orgies with any species that inhabited their planet. The Humans and Sytheracts, however, who had spent some time on their own planets, took longer to adjust to the Gemarinian ways.

Gemarine was home to three distinct lifeforms. Whether it was the luck of the stars or a path set out by the Celestials, the Aranthers,

10

Sytheracts and Humans were all compatible in the physical sense. That is, they could interbreed because their differences were only subtle in nature. The elfin-like ears and pale complexion of the Sytheracts, the Aranthers with brightly coloured skin of various hues and 'additions' endemic to various tribes; the Humans so bland and symmetrical in comparison.

But not all Humans were bland. Ten years ago, the raggedy kid they dubbed, 'King of the Wilds' moved in with the clan below hers.

Juniper had relished taking Xan under her bionic exoarm. Of course, it hadn't been bionic back then. Because they were the same age, Madame Bleu's staff recommended her mentorship to teach him the ways of Gemarine. They were inseparable, and over the years they shared more than simple moments and memories. There was a guiding hand in their interactions, like they were always destined for much more.

The spherical robot cleaner, RC9, spun around Juniper's ankles, squeaking as if to apologise for getting too close.

"It's okay, my boy." She knelt and stroked its shiny dome as beady digital eyes blinked and straightened as if finding a smile. She wondered if its AI capabilities were enough to discern feelings – the same type of feelings she saw glistening in Xan's eyes whenever an intimate moment crept up between them.

As RC9 spun and wheeled away, she chuckled, imagining that Xan questioned her own capacity to feel or emote, as he often searched for life inside her jade eyes. She shook off the Xan haze and focused on getting ready to leave for work instead.

Being an integral part of the soldier program had high demands. Over the years there had been attacks that threatened the safety of Gemarine. Highly ranked and decorated, it was Juniper's job to snuff out enemy threats before their presence was known within the atmosphere. She would plot against an enemy, discussing combat tactics to ensure no unpermitted species crossed that invisible line.

If anyone dared cross a line protected by Juniper, then they were either completely brain dead or simply unaware of her legacy. The list of prestigious feats on the battlefield easily outnumbered her twenty-four years of age.

She didn't suffer fools. Even if the paperwork from her crew wasn't to her standards, she used her aggression for the right purpose. It was a reason why the job energised her. But it also took something from Juniper: her arm, when she was just nineteen. A war hero, adorned with patches on her uniform and accolades fixed to her ego.

When a part of you dies, another is forged, she had whispered to herself, as she lay upon the recovery bed after the incident, as the smell of singed flesh crept into her nostrils. Later that night after losing her arm, she had called Xan to help her forget. He had dropped everything and gone to her.

Advanced technology meant that Juniper's exoarm was an improvement – much stronger than bone with additional enhancements to make life easier. Any other Gemarinian would have fitted a type of pseudo skin on top as a disguise, but she preferred the raw look of metallic boronium, shimmering with the blue of an arctic lake. Her exohand was different though; a glove-like exoskeleton with nerve endings that allowed her to touch, grip things with precision and operate weapons at a lethal capacity. The additional military-issued fittings accentuated that lethal component.

It wasn't the only thing she'd altered her appearance with, though the other enhancements were purely elective cosmetic procedures. Eyes of green shone like a hazy jade stone, and her hair tossed and turned between waves of deep, endless space and curled spirals of vivid purple. A part of her hair above her left ear was shaved close to the skin and the voluptuous curls were brushed over onto the other side, creating a part, like a dense shrub in the throws of an Earthen spring. White hexagonal cosme-tatts glowed on the left side of her neck, hiding hideous battle scars.

Juniper's clan lived on the 97th floor of a huge high-rise complex. Each clan possessed an entire floor and the closer one lived to the top, the higher their working status. Juniper's clan were among the most elite soldiers within Gemarinian society, but Gemarine being a place of civil peace and equality, there wasn't all that much discrepancy between the levels. Her assigned section of the 'level' was what people of Earth would call a studio apartment. It was one large open room with curved cornices and stark white walls. The furniture was sparse and Juniper preferred it to the chaotic mess of tokenistic items her fellow clan members hoarded. A pewter grey couch, a holo station with her personal holos on loop, and a weapon closet stocked to the brim with all manner of ray guns and hyperblasters; she needed nothing more than that. Natural light streamed in from floor-to-ceiling UV-controlled windows that lined the exterior.

Juniper looked out into the morning. The red-eyed sun fluttered its eyelashes, casting rays across the city as sleek black buildings stiffened like a charcoal forest after the kiss of flame. The exterior of the building was clad in reflective glass, catching the cleanliness of the street-level urban paths and hovering transpos as they zoomed along the edges of the gutter, levitating several stories in the air at their maximum hovering capacity. Elegant angular, medium-sized ships hummed peacefully, decorating the sky during the morning migration.

There were large screens adorning certain sections of the apartment showing various natural scenes from planets that Xan had taken her to. Fond memories of stealing away on his ship every so often to frolic in streams of thaw-water cascading from mountain tops capped with snow and ice. If there were anyone in the universe worthy of the tag 'favourite', it would be him. Too bad romantic love wasn't a concept on Gemarine because maybe Juniper would already be in love with him. But her Earthen days had not been long enough for her to be branded with those societal expectations as she built a new life on a new world.

Xan, though, often battled the memories and expectations of Earth versus what Juniper tried to instil in him as a Gemarinian. He was more at ease now and less enamoured by feelings; those pesky and putrid things.

Juniper had fucked Xan many times now – alone and at Fusion with others – and he was less tethered to the Human idea that sex meant love and happily ever after. She laughed at the thought while she trailed her black skin-tight suit up her athletic calves, zipping it up across her breasts to just below the base of her throat. She slipped her boots on and fastened a clip at the top that released the air pressure, so they fit snug to the contours of her feet. Tying her hair haphazardly in a high ponytail, the thickness became a fountain, with curly strands dripping down to settle upon her shoulders.

Stealing a glance at herself in the video reflection, Juniper pursed her thick lips, which were scarlet red and bright against the light brown of her skin. She turned swiftly, grabbing a Cranston ray gun and magnetising it to her right hip, and fixed her Multi-Purpose Device firmly to her wrist. Aside from the dialectachip implanted upon their planet induction to interpret and sometimes translate the dialects of the different species, MPDs were the most common piece of tech on Gemarine. A large, chunky bracelet, the device held credits, ID and clearances to gain entry into the places she needed to. It also acted like a personal online library full of information when she was stuck for a useless fact or a tactical manoeuvre she needed at work.

The door slid away and she stepped into her personal motitube. She flicked her wrist at the sensor. "Juniper 63457 – take me to ground level." She spoke with clarity and conviction.

"As you wish," the AI voice beamed pleasantly into the small domed space. A mechanical strap fastened around her waist automatically. The gravity was depleted inside the tube and she rocketed downwards. The tube was made out of a clear bioplastic material, so an overwhelming rush of the colour spectrum flooded her vision as she fell in a controlled manner, nearly one hundred levels to the comfort of solid ground.

Juniper emerged onto the street, where countless other beings popped out of motitubes and strode across the pearly white footpath. Robot cleaners like RC9 were hard at work, ensuring the presentation was always immaculate. A teenage male Sytheract on a hoverboard sailed way too close to her head. Upon realising she was a high-ranking soldier by the inscription below the insignia on her sleeve, he squealed, "Sorry," in a high, panic-stricken submission and sped off before she could voice her thoughts.

Little shit burger. If I ever see him again, I'm gonna crack that hoverboard in half and shove it up his ass.

Curls bounced atop her head as she shook it in disappointment, dialling up a transpo on her MPD to get her off the street and to the safety of her headquarters.

After a short ride, humming along in perfect quiet in the back of the transpo, Juniper checked her reflection quickly before stepping out into Soldier Headquarters.

The building was steadfast with fortified stone the colour of a sabulous shoreline after it had been ravaged by an overzealous wave. The famous insignia cast in a fading bronze mould scrutinised all who walked underneath, as if they were not worthy of its inscription set below the apex triangle encasing the fallen Pinnacle Star: 'Contentment through unity, peace through protection'.

Juniper rolled her eyes as she scanned her MPD at the unassuming glass door. Although she was a true advocate for the Gemarinian way of life, she had her doubts about the validity of unity and what it really stood for. Madame Bleu was their leader, armed with a pack of mindless cronies called the 'inner circle'. She preached all this bullshit about togetherness, fighting as one for the cause, but after countless battles and a severed arm, she didn't quite accept that if Madame Bleu believed in unity and equality, then why the fuck were her hands so clean?

This particular rebellious streak in her was concerning, especially if she were to mouth off within the walls of the headquarters. So for once in her young life, she bit her tongue and reserved such distasteful musings for Xan and his crew, when she was perhaps under the influence of drugs or alcohol.

Marvest, a blue-hued Aranther with thick brows that shadowed large, bulging eyes greeted her as per usual with a dismissive wave of a clawed hand.

"Marvest, you gorgeous picture of perfection, how goes it?"

"You kill me, Juni." He exhaled with an easy smirk, seeing through her charm. "I'm playing my part and I'm playing it well."

"Yes you are, Marvest, and looking good doing it," she called, pointing and winking as she crossed the barrier to her assigned motitube.

Marvest rolled his eyes, and two forced puffs of air gushed out of the nostril slits just above his mouth. A nervous tick whenever Juniper laid on the charm.

After zooming through to the correct level, Juniper breezed into the room to address her crew members. She was in command of a small crew of three and they all gawked at her in equal parts awe and anticipation as she stood in front of them. An exofinger brushed a purple curl away from her face with a furious flick. "What are the delightful activities we have in store for today?"

An Aranther called Benius, with two large fangs, puffed his swollen cheeks and called out, "Um, there have been no sightings of the Cryptoborgs overnight anywhere near our airspace. No further information obtained from the one we have in holding." Juniper tapped an exofinger on the desk in front of her, contorting her face to express complete boredom as he continued. "There's an unresponsive ship in the Senmore Section of the universal route, so there's a possibility that we might want to explore some of the options there, if we are equipped to do so."

Juniper folded her arms and pursed her thick lips in considered thought. Suddenly, things didn't seem so boring. The Senmore Section was known for its dangerous passage and more often than not, a simple passing ship with a traveller and a pilot might get nabbed.

"Benius, bring the fucking heat. Don't sit there and beat around the bush by giving me tentative and wispy assessments."

His eyes flicked nervously to the other crew members, Serarra and Jimeny, who had their heads down, desperate to avoid the stare of humiliation, unwilling to validate his worries or Juniper's taunts.

"Be decisive, get straight to the point and give me a proper recommendation with some clarity and gravitas." She flexed her biceps inches away from his bug-eyed stare.

"Um, my apologies…" Benius faltered as Juniper exaggerated her exhale and slumped her shoulders, letting the hunky metallic arm hang low at her side, emphasising her disappointment.

"Errr, yes. I will prep the ship and supplies for exploration of the Senmore Section," he spluttered.

Juniper put her exohand on his shoulder, squeezing with boronium-induced strength, and bore her hazy jade eyes into his bulging yellow ones.

"Great fucking idea." Her monotonous voice and deadpan expression spoke louder than anger.

She looked at the other two frozen in fear. "Go and help him now!" she hollered.

Serarra jumped up first, the spikes of her silver mohawk bouncing up and down like gnashing teeth as she ran toward the docking area, and Jimeny's bulky frame lumbered behind. Juniper leant back on the desk and crossed her arms. She sighed loudly, ensuring they could hear, but then smiled behind the facade of leadership. A free spirit with the weight of being revered, she let a chuckle escape as she watched her little minion puppets flail at her command.

She stuffed an A3 nutri-chew into her mouth. It oozed sweet and salty goodness packed with the antioxidants, plant protein and minerals she needed to replenish her for an exploration. It tantalised the taste buds in ways that meals of the olden times or celebratory feasts could not.

Juniper moved away from the desk, rounding the captain's chair, and softened into a comfortable recline. Considering the danger of the Senmore, she knew they needed to be careful. But a war ship was not a thing to be fucked with, and any dead-eyed Cryptoborgs that wanted to mess with Juniper needed to bring someone extra special. Memories of their blue blood splattered on red dirt and stained across her cheeks. The acidic stench of exposed flesh pried tears from her eyes but no remorse from her heart. Juniper was the best soldier Gemarine had ever seen and she refused to let the floating ship graveyard of the Senmore deter her from doing her job.

CHAPTER 3

LOCATION: ZEPHTAR
YEAR: 118
LILIANNA – 22 YEARS OLD

As a Sytheract, Lilianna felt more of an affinity with the Humans over any other species on Gemarine. Actually, that was a lie. Her affinity for the creatures that came from exploring the wilds of other worlds was where she felt most at home. Still, she scrolled through the data clouds, deep diving into the histories of all the species now in the company of Gemarine. The wealth data fascinated her, and she understood not only a lot of what had lived on Earth, Dracia, and of course Sytheria, but the subtle nuances of cultural and social traditions. Wistfully, she dreamed of walking the cobbled streets of Aventine Hill in Rome, studying the elusive Thylacine in Australia or exploring the glaciers of the Wyndry Tribe in Dracia.

Lilianna was incredibly lucky that Xan had chosen her to accompany him and his beautiful creature sidekick on their missions.

The best job in the universe was hers.

On this specific mission, she was forced to bring Massy along instead of her fearless boss. Finally, Xan had relented on her completing solo missions, but "only if Massy trails along with you."

Not really solo then.

But when there were opportunities to demonstrate her trustworthiness, she would strive to overachieve. That was why she had everything ready way ahead of time, stored in specific areas of her pack. It was better to be overprepared.

Massy was often insufferable, but navigated the stars like a sentient asteroid darting through space with surprising agility, so it was hard to complain.

"Approaching Planet Zephtar, in the Beta Quadrant. You all set, love?" Massy's voice was croaky from the reconditioned air circulating throughout the *Attenborough* – the ship named after Xan's favourite naturalist on Earth.

Lilianna rolled her golden eyes that sparkled with the burst of a shooting star and tucked a stray strand of blonde hair behind her cuspated ears, a unique trait of the Sytheract species. "When have I not been set, Massy? I know our target is elusive but I have all the equipment to make sure we can find one at least."

"Alright, alright. I'm just giving you the news, you know? Nothing to get your little panties in a twist about."

Lilianna turned to Massy with a dagger-like glare that slowly turned to a grimace amidst her disgust. "My panties should be the furthest thing from your mind."

Massy laughed. His long black hair atop his head was knotted like a *Pyther* nest, which was usually filled with spindly twisted plant roots wrenched from the swamp planet of Thykos. A crown of black and yellow circles decorated his forehead. It was a unique Aranther mark of birth from the lineage of the Darshan Tribe, and his were bold and set deep like scars on a battle-worn warrior.

"If you ever joined us at Fusion, then maybe I wouldn't have to think about them. I would know." He raised his thin eyebrows, a twinkle in his dark wooden eyes.

"I'll go when I'm ready." She crossed her arms over her chest and sighed so delicately, Massy would never have heard it.

Lilianna wasn't like the rest of the species on Gemarine. She didn't see fusing – or sex, as some Humans called it – as anything trivial. She was fascinated by Human books that spoke of love and passion. Of course, she knew all about romantic love, as when a Sytheract found a mate or soul bond, they were monogamous with one another for life. She often dreamed of a world where she would know what that felt like. To her, *that* was the real idea of fusion – the fusing of souls to complement, to sway together like waves in a shifting current.

For all its wonders and promises of perfection, Gemarine felt soulless at times. *United in soullessness*, she thought, and sighed deeply, craving more, but resigning herself to what was.

"You do you, love. We wouldn't want you any other way." Massy smiled genuinely and reached across the space between them and flicked her on the upper arm with a long nailed forefinger.

Lilianna stifled a giggle, shrugging away and play-frowning as she looked out the window.

The *Attenborough* touched down with a jolting thump. She searched through the viewing window at the arid landscape beyond, dotted with a flicker of green among drab shades of brown.

A groan of annoyance came from the back of the ship. Lilianna almost groaned herself, remembering that Ryker was there. She tolerated Massy playing the part of simpleton goofball. Although she preferred intelligence and presence, he was a harmless nuisance at best.

Lilianna tried to see the best in everyone; she made excuses for the darkness in others by casting too much light upon their strengths. Ryker, however, was a plague upon positivity.

Everything he did was enhanced with a sour attitude. Skulking around with spindly arms and legs, downcast and mopey, with a raven fringe clawing across his eyes. A passion for creatures was non-existent. Which made her question – why was he even a part of this crew? She knew the answer, though. Xan accepted him as a favour to Madame Bleu. The same Madame Bleu who was the caretaker of this world; who stood upon the stage at the Pinnacle Star festival and other celebrations declaring, "Contentment through unity, peace through protection." She'd heard it recited in groups with a cult-like quality, and seen it plastered underneath the insignia atop Soldier Headquarters and where Madame Bleu and the inner circle resided.

So the favour was a political one, she guessed. A favour for keeping the biobase functional, perhaps? The place that Xan had built to house all the endangered creatures. The place where he brought each species back from the brink – a purpose she took on as her own.

She no longer stared wistfully at archived videos of soul-bonded Sytheracts. She cared not for the late nights on Gemarine fuelled by hormones and drugs. She remained focused on reversing the effects of forsaken hope, caring for the creatures and silencing extinction.

Ryker huffed again, purposefully audible so as to syphon a reaction. Despite his mechanical skills maintaining the ship, she much preferred that he wasn't seen or heard. *Just like the way a space jump happens; I don't need to know the formula or how it works, I just want it to function properly and get me to my destination.* Ryker operated as part of the *Attenborough*, but she was in a better mood when he stayed out of her way.

Massy yelled toward the back, "A little too rough for you, my boy?"

Lilianna turned and Ryker sneered with his thin pale lips, and narrow, ink-splattered eyes. "The custom Dillionators won't last very long, if landings continue to be so rough." His voice bubbled with acid.

"That's why you're on the ship, isn't it, Mr Fix It?" Massy winked at Lilianna.

Lilianna smiled effortlessly, brushing wavy blonde hair across the back of her neck and letting it fall in a bunch over her left shoulder.

The scowl Ryker gave could have set the whole planet ablaze, but he turned sharply, his long, oily black hair flicking like a horse's mane, muttering an incantation of hate under his breath.

"Do you really need to encourage his darkness to infect the ship even more?" Lilianna bristled with hatred.

Massy raised his eyebrows and jerked his head back. "Whoa, I don't think I've ever heard you say a bad word about anyone."

"I just…" she stammered. "He just irks me." Her lips twisted in annoyance. Massy unbuckled and got out of his seat and waited for Lilianna to finish. "Like, I guess I just don't appreciate people who are really negative and bring others down. Massy, he doesn't even try to be polite."

Massy shrugged his broad shoulders. "I don't know. He's hot and cold with me, too. Besides, Xan's the man and he thinks Ryker is solid."

Lilianna thought about Xan and her heart twinkled like faraway stars in the Nolious Galaxy, known for the brightest sparks and space trails in the universe. She trusted him more than anyone else on Gemarine. In fact, throughout the entire collection of galaxies they explored, there was no one else she would trust with her life. But she simply didn't understand why he had agreed to help Ryker.

A political thing shouldn't interfere with our conservation mission. But then again, she had never delved into the relationship intricacies between Xan and Madame Bleu, who had allowed him to build the department and the biobase. Madame Bleu must have asked for something in return. *Maybe Ryker was part of the deal and now we're all stuck with him.*

"Is it the blue pill for *this* atmosphere?" Massy asked Lilianna, with an array of colourful pills strewn across the control board.

"Yes, Massy. Honestly, what would you do without me?"

"Die. I would one hundred per cent just die. So, I love your work." He bowed with the grace of a divine Celestial, popping a pill into his mouth as he straightened.

The primary hatch released and they both filed out into the air-locked section. Then the secondary hatch opened and the blue pills released the required amount of resistance into their bodies, combating the atmospheric conditions.

"Now, I know you wouldn't have read the briefing notes, but I'll quickly explain what we're looking for."

Massy chuckled as his cracked and tired boots thumped onto the dry flustered surface, kicking small cobalt rocks across the vast landscape. "Fuck, there's nothing here. Is our target an insect or what?"

Lilianna massaged her temples, wisps of long hair curling around her with a mild gust of wind. "The target is similar to a turtle on Earth, if you've heard of that." Massy's eyes shifted from side to side, indicating he had no clue. Lilianna clenched her jaw and decided to describe it for him instead. "It's about the size of my fist, and it has a hardened bright blue shell, so it blends into these rocks around here. Its skin, though, is a pale brown and it extends its neck out of the shell, usually out of curiosity when high-pitched noises are produced."

"So you want me to squawk like a Dragon Bird, will that help?" Massy started to flap his arms and scream in the highest of pitches available to an Aranther.

Lilianna placed slender fingers into her pricked ears to block the sound, pursing thin lips and scrunching her eyes tight. "No, Massy!" She produced a small device that clipped onto her MPD and pressed a large green button. "This is all we need."

"I don't hear anything at all."

"That's because the frequency that the Truntalisk— which is its name, of course—hears is way more acute than what we can perceive."

"Simple terms for the non-nerds of the world please," Massy requested as he swaggered beside her, adopting his best 'cool' walk as the sun radiated against his tanned skin.

Lilianna pinched the bridge of her nose and inhaled deeply, remembering his piloting skills were unmatched – his intelligence, however, languished in the bottom percentile. "Basically, we can't hear things that the *Truntalisk* can."

"You learn something everyday, don't you?" He nodded as if satisfied with himself.

"Well, you do when you hang around me for a day."

A breeze picked up swirling aurelion dirt and the diluted scent of hydrogen sulphide around them. The scent thankfully didn't linger, but the heat did. Zipped up tight in their suits, Lilianna wasn't looking forward to the intensity of the hike. However, it was never about her. It was always about finding the creatures and trying to give them a second chance. She put one foot in front of the next in search of the *Truntalisk* and its impending salvation.

CHAPTER 4

Something coarse and wet caressed his cheek, like a serpent slithering over submerged rocks damp with moss. Xan opened his eyes and was face to face with the creature from the previous night. The decision to dine upon him was thankfully abandoned – unless licking was a means of consumption by this creature, in which case, it would take a while.

In the light of the morning, the creature appeared to be smiling with huge eyes the colour of honey with flecks of burnt coffee, its midnight blue forked tongue retreating back into its mouth. Not being from Gemarine, Xan was unsure what this creature was, but it reminded him of a mixture between a fennec fox and a dwarf tiger. Vibrant blue and black stripes lined its body, trailing toward a light grey spiked tail that curled with feline curiosity. Elongated ears pricked up and sagged with the apparent changes in its demeanour.

"Alright, alright, you. I guess it's comforting that my skin isn't salacious to your taste buds, right?"

26

Sitting down, it craned its neck, eyes glistening with a peaceful calm, as if reassuring him the menu was, indeed, Xan-less.

"Well, let's have a look outside and see why Gemarine is the Mecca of all worlds."

Xan pushed himself up with a groan, bruising evident on parts of his body after being thrown from a spacecraft the night before. The gash on his arm showed signs of scabbing over and didn't require any extra attention. Otherwise, he was alive and functioning well enough. He looked at the creature as it tried to stand. The regeneration gel had helped a great deal, but it wasn't without a limp, which hindered its grace as it stumbled down the hatch and out into the feeble light.

The bioluminescent grass was a dusty yellow in the daytime, and the twisted trees of the forest ahead looked less striking and daunting caught by the sun, but a feeling of dread wound inside him like an old clock. He loved nature and hiking with his family on Earth. Lantau Island was a common destination for him, running through the wooden columns of the wisdom path inscribed with the calligraphy of the Heart Sutra – carrying on to the Nei Lak Shan Country Trail. Always with the Tian Tan Buddha looming behind, hand raised, offering courage and protection from negativity. A lone hike in a world he knew nothing about struck the bell of fear that echoed in the chamber of his soul.

I must turn away from the consumption of fear; I must empty myself of all I've known.

He looked down upon the creature and smiled. "I guess I won't be alone. We can be new, together."

As he stood on the hatch of the ship, he could just make out the faint shimmer of the city beyond the forest. Xan surveyed the path ahead. There were sparse areas of darkness and of rusty sand, deep pockets of emerald parcels and huge boulders crumpled in defeat.

The moisture in the air hung low in a light fog, so the path ahead was not incredibly clear. Even though the temperature of the morning was brisk, he had the feeling it would heat up throughout the day as the sky glowed with violet and cerulean surges. The prominent scent was of dry grain, nutty and wholesome. The tiniest hint of a ginger flower twirled around him, and in a confusing moment Xan felt as though he were walking along the border of Hong Kong and the new territories where it grew in abundance.

It would be a long journey, but he didn't have a choice. A new 'clan' awaited his arrival and he was going to make sure he got there. He remembered the night of his thirteenth birthday, staring out the window at the jacaranda tree in his front yard. Its vibrant purple flowers had shed upon the pavement below, like the first covering of snow, as if winter could finally laugh with colourful exuberance.

LOCATION: EARTH
YEAR: 2031

As a single flower fell, it billowed toward the ground, but instead of gathering speed for its final descent, it simply paused in the air. Suspended in decay. Xan's eyes narrowed, focal points confirming his disbelief. He jumped up from the edge of his bed, his pale green cotton blanket tossed with a reticent cool. Fever was in his footsteps as he ran through the corridor, combusting throughout his body and quickening his heart rate. His disbelief doubled as his parents stood motionless at the kitchen sink, washing bamboo chopsticks, frozen in the monotony of responsibility.

Thoughts whirled and he was poised to pinch himself to see if that method would reap results. But the door burst open and Derrison was there, clad in a fitted black bodysuit silhouetted by the lights of a spacecraft. The same ship he would use as a shelter on the first night of his new life.

After Derrison calmed Xan down, they sat together at the round dinner table. Remnants of dumplings clinging to the tablecloth, the smell of jasmine tea still heavy in the room. Coarse stubble clamped to Derrison's jawline, a calm repose in eyes that mirrored the blue willow china decorating the family room. His proposal was simple: come with us or your family will die, along with the world.

Xan questioned, "I'm sorry, but what kind of choice is that?"

"It's a choice no one should ever have to make, but often fate makes fools of good-natured acts." The genuine empathy in Derrison's voice was evident. "Your act in the future will end up destroying the world. We are trying to ensure that Earth remains, and from our calculations, if you are taken from this timeline – all will be well."

Xan's heart hammered, the walls were closing in. "How do you know I'm going to destroy the world? I'm...no threat!" His voice cracked, endemic to puberty and stress.

Derrison sighed with pity. "We know about time, young man, as you can see." He pointed to the digital clock, stuck at 10:33 pm, then at the more compelling evidence of his frozen parents. "If this were a joke, how would we even pull off something like this?"

Xan sank back in the wooden chair, almost golden with the syrup of varnish. Unable to speak, Derrison then continued, "There will be more time to think. I'll visit you often just to check in and to support this process."

Before Derrison departed and time resumed, he was given a contact lens and a small earpiece to wear, which would show him a virtual tour of Gemarine's main cityscape, Topaz City, and answer any questions he had. All he had to do was speak the question into the air and an answer would come.

Derrison left him behind that evening, but thoughts lay close to him in his bed. The pillow dried his tears, but nothing else would comfort him. How could he be responsible for the death of the world? He recalled 'good-natured acts'. Already, Xan was in the high-achievers club at his school, had a scholarship to study at Oxford through the green initiative program, was developing sustainability modules to present to the young leaders forum in Singapore. His good-natured acts, it seemed, would falter.

Wondering why was never a wise investment. He needed to diversify his portfolio with disbelief, instead.

A year had not been long enough to say goodbye to his parents, to his friends. But it was all he had. A sacrifice so they could live was much better than the alternative.

"Are you coming with me or do you have a home to go back to?" he asked the creature, mind now focused on the present.

Its tail, without spikes protruding this time, reached up and coiled around Xan's wrist.

"I guess that means yes."

The pack was on Xan's scrawny shoulders, but a new friendship was forming in his heart. He and the creature walked off into the forest of twisted trees.

CHAPTER 5

LOCATION: GEMARINE
YEAR: 108 (10 YEARS AGO)
XAN – 14 YEARS OLD

Among the cover of the trees, Xan studied some of the items in his pack. The furry creature remained on all fours beside him, inquisitive eyes examining him as well as the gadgets he inspected.

He shook a device not much larger than a mobile phone. It had a bizarre connection clip but he didn't understand where or what it needed to clip into. However, a red laser halo surrounded his entire head like a cloud then faded away. The machine registered a beep and a gender-neutral AI flashed up with a welcome message.

"You have been scanned and registered as a Human. Welcome, this is your Multi-Purpose Device or MPD for short, and I am your personal assistant, Phineas. Please fasten me to your wrist."

Xan moved the device to his wrist and two claws emerged, clamping down and fixing to him with a slight pinch.

"How can I help you today?" Phineas chimed as pleasantly as an AI could.

Shaking off the painful pinch he wondered, *Could it be this easy?* "Ummm, could you place a call to someone in the emergency department or a rescue team perhaps?"

"Apologies, Human, a communication chip has not been installed on this device, therefore communication does not become activated until you register within the city walls."

His shoulders sagged and he kicked the dusty, creased ground with the toe of his boot. A solitary rock rolled end over end, diverting the creature's fascinated gaze upon it. With a spring from its front legs, it launched at the poor rock, batting it across the dirt. A game was invented: Creature vs Rock. Who would win?

"Well, what will you be able to help me with exactly?" Xan asked Phineas.

"The information stored on this device will provide you with any answer pertaining to Gemarine and its inhabitants. I was meant to answer some questions that your host could not upon your entry into the atmosphere."

Xan glimpsed the city in the distance, and a thought struck him. "Do you have a navigation system?"

"I can operate in a navigational capacity for you. Where do you wish to go?"

"Can you tell me exactly where I am now and how long it will take to get into the city?" Xan watched as the creature lost interest in the rock, deeming it an unworthy opponent. Shadows like deformed limbs cast from the twisted trees, littering the ground around them as the sun settled lower in the sky.

Three bars shot across the small display of the MPD, bright even in the golden light of the day. It was a loading signal, letting Xan know it was doing its computery thing.

"You are currently based in the Wilds of Gemarine. Little is documented about the Wilds. It is said to be desolate and dangerous, usually a place where the insolents of Gemarine experience exile. However, the route into the city can be calculated if you wish."

The computer seemed to rush over the exile part, which made Xan a little concerned. *Isn't this planet meant to be something like a utopia? Why are people getting exiled?* As if answering his own thought, he remembered countless regimes on Earth, conflicting views that drove people to take sides, the divisions that had started to become clear after all the problems Earth had faced in the twenty-first century.

It made him remember that Humans – or simply, species in general – were complex creatures with endless possibilities for problems. Even in utopian societies, an acidic disease could snake its way underground, corroding foundations until they collapsed in on themselves.

"I require an answer, Human," Phineas said, startling Xan out of his thoughts.

"Yes, yes please. And my name is Xan, so just call me that," he said flatly.

"Nice to meet you, Xan. Travelling on foot means that you will reach Topaz City centre in approximately four days' time. However, the battery on the MPD is solar-fuelled, so it is best to conserve power when you can." Phineas was pleasant enough, as well as informative, at least.

Xan's heart sank. "Okay, I'll try to power this down. Can you be available in the background if I make a wrong turn?"

"I will power down and return when you call upon me," Phineas stated, and then went silent – presumably, powering down.

Now, what am I going to do for food?

The rations would not last, and even though the risotto ball-like masses of deliciousness were, well, delicious – he didn't have enough to suitably cover the amount of time he would be hiking. *Would I need to start hunting for food? Where would I even start?*

The creature purred next to him as he absently stroked its head. *Maybe I'm not the one who'll be hunting.* "What should I call you?"

Its amber eyes twinkled in the sunlight, innocence and devotion written on a whisky-stained scroll encased by time.

He thought of Chu, his best friend on Earth. Or, former best friend. She would soon forget he existed and she would go on and live her life – whatever that may be.

Memories came upon him suddenly.

The local library was stacked with so many books, docking stations and computer screens where he chose to study for hours on end. He saw Chu now in his mind's eye, sitting in the chair opposite him with pigtails in her hair, scrunching up wads of paper and hurling them in his direction. Sleeping on arms splayed out on the light, varnished desk, listening to music together, one earphone in her ear, one in his, watching movies on her phone while he tinkered away learning the wonders of biology. Chu did it all just to share his space.

An assignment on Chinese mythology had brought them together. They were tasked with studying the Qilin. Thought to possess good luck with its peaceful predispositions, it also appeared whenever a new, benevolent ruler would assume control over the land. It was the one bit of schoolwork she enjoyed. With encouragement from her parents, she was more artistic than academic. Her books were filled with drawings of the Qilin or the 'Chinese unicorn', much was her obsession with it.

Xan's impending departure had hurt Chu terribly. He wasn't sure he'd made the right choice by informing her one week in advance. There were tears, tantrums and desperation in trying to stop him from leaving. But integrity ensured he did it anyway, rather than leave on a whim. The last time he saw her, her brown eyes flowed with tears of an interrupted future; dreams that washed onto her rosy cheeks. Xan reached out to Chu, brushing his hand against hers but she yanked it back and ran from him, down past the flower market and toward Prince Edward MTR station. The kumquat trees that lined the streets were meant for good fortune, so he closed his eyes and hoped that fortune would accompany her throughout the days of her life.

The creature craned its neck.

"I don't know your gender but I know your heart. That matters greatly. I'm going to call you Qilin. It's after someone I loved very much." Xan clapped his hands and Qilin jumped up, startled. "Since you're named after a mythological creature that brought good luck, I'd totally love some of that right now so we can get to the city in one piece."

Qilin licked Xan's cheek, almost as a mark of acceptance.

"It's settled then."

Xan and Qilin set off into the unknown. There was no set path in the Wilds of Gemarine, but Qilin's keen scent and Xan's wits were all they had to scupper and stumble, save for the occasional directive from Phineas showcasing his navigational awareness.

The Wilds were often frequented by creatures caught between varying degrees of ferociousness and curiosity. There were moments where Qilin would halt, ears pricked, discerning whether the crack of a branch was simply it falling from a height or if danger lurked.

The deeper they ventured into the cove of twisted trees, the darker and colder Gemarine appeared. Xan was not prepared for such a chaotic welcome.

Derrison had briefed him that first night, of course, but they had both been preparing on and off for about a year. Time would freeze, and Xan would know that if he looked out the window, Franje would be waving from the ship, and Derrison would saunter out with his blonde hair bobbing with each easy step.

They went over Gemarinian customs, city social rules, the lack of judgement, the whole sex thing, the drug culture, and the overarching freedom of self, so he was expecting the regular welcome that everybody got. Not once did he need to research 'Hiking in the Wilds with a…'

He stopped and peered at Qilin. *What are you?* At that moment, he realised it was a friend. In fact, the only one he had in the known universe. It reflected his gaze, inquisitive, simmering with a polite question, *What can I do for you?*

Xan's thin lips curled into a smile of his own and he opened up the MPD. "Phineas, can you scan this creature and give me a brief profile please?" he asked the AI.

"Scanning now." A jet of red laser shot out and scanned across the area, settling on Qilin, narrowing down and encapsulating it. Qilin leapt in the air playfully, swatting with sharp, gnarled claws. Growling and murmuring in high pitches, it snapped its teeth around the technology it didn't recognise.

"Scanning complete," Phineas announced.

Xan was excited to learn more about his new friend.

"This creature, known as the *Mika Tikaani*, is classed as rare and thought to be extinct. They were driven to the brink of extinction from the disruption of their habitats from the *Rinovader*, or large, horned beasts. They can be solitary omnivores, preferring to hunt for smaller critters, however their prey, *Flabbers*, which can be compared to rabbits or squirrels on Earth, are rampant in the Wilds and are a good source of protein for beasts and Humans if required. Not much is known about the *Mika Tikaani* because they are elusive when approached and ferocious when cornered or put under stress. Legends from the ancient scrolls depict the *Mika Tikaani* as a creature that is wise, loyal and holds considerable power. Their power is unknown, but often the creature is pictured with a golden aura, which indicates it might be able to shift matter in a way that Humans or citizens of Gemarine cannot." There was a slight pause, then, "Scanning once more to determine gender."

The red halo circled across the *Mika Tikaani* at Xan's heels and Qilin rolled around on the floor, licking at the air as the laser encircled it.

"A rare creature with power, hey," Xan said in monotone.

"This *Mika Tikaani* is a female," the AI said simply.

Qilin, no longer fussing, sat calmly on her behind. Her front legs were straight, paws flexed, bright blue and light charcoal fur criss-crossed in DNA crochet toward her deadly claws. She craned her neck and her fangs protruded as if she were about to sneeze, lowering her ears to accommodate.

Xan knelt in front of her, her exhale kissing his nose, the scent of myrrh upon her breath. He closed his eyes and pushed his forehead to hers. Qilin nestled into the creases on his forehead, as she became a dominant thread in his rich life tapestry, blending into the textures and colours around her. Xan felt her almost sigh with contentment. He extended a hand and rubbed the back of her ears, trailing down her spine, moving his fingers in between the thin fur lovingly.

"I'll need to look after you then." He shivered in the failing light as a chill stung them both. "I mean, we will need to look after one another."

He was bold and loved the idea of exploring, but fear of the unknown gripped him. Qilin felt it too, as she raised her paw and placed it on his hand, giving comfort, and not for the first time, Xan saw something deeper within her eyes, a deeper sense of cognition perhaps? Empathy, even? But either way, it buoyed and concerned him at the same time.

CHAPTER 6

LOCATION: GEMARINE
YEAR: 118
LILIANNA – 22 YEARS OLD

Lilianna stood outside the doors to Xan's lab after leaving Massy and Ryker in the docking bay to clean the *Attenborough*. The *Truntalisk* was soundly sleeping in its spherical pod, hovering right beside her.

She hesitated at the door and took a deep breath. Xan was everything to her. On a planet that didn't recognise the furtive feelings of love and longing, she sure recognised them within herself. As far as she knew, no one else felt this way on Gemarine.

Xan had been indoctrinated into the Gemarine way of life, mostly through Juniper's influence. As she thought about Juniper, she felt a wave of conflicting emotions. On one hand she respected her strength, almost revered her; that nonchalance, her 'I don't give a fuck' attitude. But then again, a droplet of envy contaminated the well from which she drank, leaving her parched at the bond that Juniper and Xan shared. A bond that came from growing up together, learning about Gemarine together, experiencing all the pitfalls and pains of self-discovery together.

A part of Lilianna wished she hadn't been restricted to Level 33; wished she had access to the upper levels, but something in her processing had made it so she hadn't met Xan until around four years ago. She had known about him; everyone did. The boy who survived the Wilds. Or rather, 'King of the Wilds' – so said the sensationalised media campaign. The headline was across all their MPDs in an instant. Then, when he was processed, Xan shared the same learning halls she did. Except he was in classes that reflected his age bracket.

Xan was the closest thing to a superstar on Gemarine. On her home planet, Sytheria, she remembered various scientists and their robot counterparts reaching a status like that, but they never created the fanfare that Xan did. Surviving the Wilds was something that had never been documented previously, let alone by a fourteen-year-old Human. It was always assumed that once exiled, citizens were banished to the Wilds, death so gaunt and famished would swallow them whole.

Lilianna was startled by the sound of scratching on the other side of the door. Qilin must have felt her presence. She felt silly all of a sudden and waved her MPD against the port. The doors shot open and, sure enough, Qilin was there with a goofy look that reminded her of a warm greeting. The beautiful creature cooed at her arrival, leaping up and licking the side of her face with that dark blue tongue.

"Alright, Qilin, alright. I missed you too." Lilianna giggled through bursts of genuine joy.

She looked around the lab, a smattering of modern, sterile and new age all rolled into one. Prominent, white trimmings fused with metallic tech contraptions bolted to each lasthforth wooden desk. The colour was a beautiful light oak mixed with an ancient pine, all milled from the Warfastions on the planet Brooderus. The lasthforth trees grew one metre in height a month, which made it perfectly sustainable and profitable for the Warfastions, who shared a trade agreement with the Gemarinians.

She could see Xan through the glass, goggles on and staring at a computer screen with that deep scowl of his, holographics prancing like unicorns around him. Her heart soared into the blackness of space, pricked by the point of a star, drawing blood and encircling her. She ignored the absence of her stomach and waved. Perhaps he didn't see Lilianna behind the flashing holographics. She let her arm fall by her side, shoulders slumped and fingers bent in dejection. Qilin howled, and Lilianna jumped, trying desperately to silence her.

Her cheeks flushed, burning with the heat of a summer sun as Xan looked up and spotted her. His sideways smile narrowed his dark grey eyes into a sultry stare. Xan's tongue lashed his top lip briefly before he spoke and his voice gently hummed with measured excitement.

"There she is!" He flung the tech goggles across the desk and swiped across the holographs, which made them shimmer and retreat to the stark white corners of the room as if fear struck out at them.

The lights dimmed as Xan stepped through the automatic doors. Qilin jumped up around the height of his waist, and he chuckled while smooshing her grey furry face.

Lilianna welled up with pride every time she saw the interactions between them, as if witnessing something special. She knew the story of how they came upon one another. Everyone did. But to be a part of what they shared, even if seemingly insignificant, was a great privilege. One day it would be stored in galaxational records, for generations of space dwellers to marvel over, and no doubt it would encourage them to value creatures too; to do everything they could to avoid contributing to the extinction of a species, like so many across time and space did. Their interaction would spur action and that was beyond important.

Qilin slipped around the back of Xan's legs, clipping at his heels, playful exuberance still rife within her. This allowed Xan to take Lilianna in his arms – a place she always felt safe, like a forest dwelling surrounded by a fortress of green. A place she longed to stay for more than a fleeting moment.

Xan pulled back and Lilianna smiled with her usual warmth, heated by an unspoken passion within. "Ah I missed you, love." His deep voice, breathy but strong, was laced with honesty.

Lilianna shifted uncomfortably, brushing a blonde strand of hair behind her pointy ear. "I…errr… Yeah, you would have loved to come. Shame you couldn't."

"I know, right? The pitfalls of running a department with Dr Ranjit and reporting to Bleu the Buzzkill." Xan scratched the back of his head, his bicep flexing inside the skin-tight bodysuit. His eyes shifted to the pod next to Lilianna.

"You brought him back!" His voice changed. It was childlike, surging from deep and assured waves, to vibrant colour and full of excitement.

The pod opened as Xan waved his MPD against it. Qilin jumped up, resting her front paws on the edge, cocking her head as she absorbed the sight of the male *Truntalisk*.

Xan bent down, carefully searching the creature who had retreated into its shell, most likely at the sight of Qilin's large, honey eyes beaming like a deathray into its cracked, scaly face.

Lilianna's confidence soared. "I'm so pleased we were able to bring him here to unite with the female. There was always a slim chance we might find the male, but yeah, I'm so happy. As always, I reported on measurements, filed all the notes on the galaxy cloud and documented the process about how we found him."

"Lili, you always impress me." Xan swivelled his neck and beamed up at her, his gaze like warm tea swirling with fragrant and calming herbs.

Her pride was a star bursting with light, but she fought against the notion of pleasing him. Nothing else made her feel complete like the way he valued her knowledge, her passion and her skill with creatures.

Xan turned back to the *Truntalisk*. "This is one of your greatest accomplishments to date. Honestly, their predicament was beyond dire, so the fact that we can start to increase their numbers…it's perfect." He straightened, placing a warm hand on her inner arm, stroking her gently with his thumb.

Lilianna inhaled sharply and held her breath. "Thank you so much," she finally whispered.

Qilin jumped up, knocking her to the ground, and licked her cheek. Lilianna giggled, but Xan's deep and commanding voice returned.

"Qilin, cut it out, this is a workplace," Xan shouted, as the hint of a smile twitched against his cheeks.

Qilin's ears flopped down, and she loped across to her little oasis in the far corner of the lab room.

"Sorry, boss. I'll get to storage now and put the *Truntalisk* safely in the enclosure."

Xan started walking away, strong shoulders straining against the bodysuit. He halted, and turned back around, his twinkling eyes hidden by a scowl. "Call me boss again, Lilianna, I dare you."

Lilianna rocked back. A carefree cloud rained on her. "Never again, boss." She brought both hands to her mouth to hide her giggle.

Xan cracked his knuckles and launched toward her in a playful fight. Soon they were running around the lab, Qilin snapping at their heels, Lilianna squealing in delight. She let Xan catch her and wrap her in a strong embrace, and then he threw her onto the couch near Qilin's oasis. The black suit highlighted the ripples of his muscles as he towered over her, chest rising and falling with quick breaths from the short burst of cardio. A coquettish grin appeared and not for the first time Lilianna wondered if Xan would consider her, and only her.

She bit her bottom lip. She couldn't help pushing against complacency and draw a deeper mark that hinted at exposing blood, exposing something deeper within her.

"We're a family first, Lili, and work comes second. Don't be a cheeky little shit again!" He wagged his finger, his chest catching up with his breath. "It's actually so unlike you," he laughed, "but I like it."

Lilianna was quiet and reserved around most people, but there were moments where a playful side found its way to the surface. Being around Xan made her nervous, but she liked it when he challenged her. In fact, she liked who she was when she was around him. Only he did that. No one else.

The MPD on Xan's wrist pulsed red, flickering in and out. Lilianna stood up slowly as Xan, with a bemused expression, read that Juniper was calling him.

"This is bizarre." He swiped across to answer. The line was terrible but it was clear enough to hear there was trouble afoot.

An explosion.

A high-pitched yelp.

Juniper's voice: "Xan, I need—"

Static.

"—under attack, I—"

Static.

"—Senmore Section—"

Static.

"—Val—"

Static.

"—help—"

Static.

"—need you—"

Lilianna and Xan exchanged a look, concern bleeding from a wound incited by fear and love.

"I have to go," Xan said with finality, worry lines growing between his eyes as he scratched at his shoulder.

"*We* have to go," Lilianna insisted, dialling Massy and Ryker from her MPD immediately. "I'll ready the *Attenborough*."

Qilin howled for the closest thing she had to a mother. Juniper was in trouble, and it was up to them to find out what had happened.

CHAPTER 7

Dead ships floated like suspended snowflakes on ice planets. Bulky scraps of metallic shards danced in a silent ballet, pirouettes turning to silhouettes against the deathly void of space. Frozen bodies somersaulted, forgotten; technical gymnasts in an endless routine encased in the moment of their demise.

Juniper was aware even through her thick skin and the cold compression in her veins, that this graveyard was a merchant for souls, staking claim to the unfortunate who dared toe the line between the territory of the Cryptoborgs and Gemarinians.

The Senmore Section was the dead airspace where there was an unwritten rule not to cross. Some ships and bodies were centuries old, stuck in a gravitational loop. Others, though, like the ship they approached, were recently wrecked. The decade-old D-230 spacecraft had been lulled into a deep sleep – a huge hole blown through its side, crew members still twisting throughout the far reaches of space.

Juniper had come to investigate, not to rescue.

"No lifeforms on board, Captain Juniper."

"No shit, Benius," she scorned through gnashed teeth. She didn't have a particularly good feeling about the mission and her fear came out in misdirected aggression and intimidation. "Activate the Solu Shields then, kid."

Benius, an Aranther with sweat glands as effective as a leaky faucet, released the Solu Shields with a timid finger. The baritone hum of an electronic choir sounded, and the highest-level shield forcefield coated the ship in its comforting embrace.

"Pull up alongside the D-230, will you? And Jimeny – run the diagnostic report and syphon the camera footage on double speed." Juniper scratched at the exohand with her real nail absent-mindedly as she scanned the ship for any signs of concern.

Jimeny stood up, blue skin silky with perspiration. "Camera feed has downloaded. Routing to holographs to show five mins before the hole was blown into the ship."

The camera shook as the D-230 sped through space dodging debris and wrecked ships. The screen showed silver hair cropped in a buzzcut, the kiss of deep darkness to his skin, and a Sytheract cosme-tatt in the shape of a diamond glittered in violet bursts on the side of his neck.

"That's Captain Larrsen," Juniper breathed.

But he's meant to be in the Diaticus System on relocation missions. Why would he have come through the Senmore? This doesn't make any sense.

Captain Larrsen was speaking directly to the onboard camera. "We're being pursued by a ship of unknown origin." As the camera switched to the external feed, the pursuing obsidian-black ship was almost camouflaged within the void of darkness. Its front bore a semi-circular arc of sharp pincers. Bursts of orange lava trailed along its tail, burning through its centre and along the edges, accentuating its menace among the stars.

Juniper gasped.

45

It couldn't be.

This was a ship described in records from long ago. A ship that belonged to the original enemies of the Gemarinians – the Valkor. She only knew because Xan had banged on about it for years. There was a stalwart assumption that he'd lied about his fall from the sky as well as the description of the ship that sent him there. Or rather, he was too young, too unaware of ship identities and didn't understand what he'd seen.

But she knew he didn't fuck around; he was a straight shooter with trust that leaked from his perfect pores. She should have known better.

He would throw it in her face during researching and educational seminars at the learning centre.

"This was the one, Juniper."

"Xan, you're delusional at the best of times, but yes, the Valkor were out to get you," she would tease, her dusty green eyes rolling in an over-exaggerated manner.

Since then, there hadn't been any sighting of one throughout the galaxy, let alone close to Gemarinian airspace. But her eyes didn't deceive. Whether it was in real time or not, she knew it was a Valkor ship.

Benius's voice was a brumal blast. "That looks like a—"

"Shut up, Benius," whispered Jimeny and Serarra at the same time.

Juniper regained her composure and looked over at them. "What do you think, Benius? Go on," she prompted with encouragement.

"It's a Valkor ship," he finished, his striking yellow eyes now wide, pried open by fear's claws.

Juniper breathed in deeply, solidifying her wavering strength. "It looks like it to me, Beni ol' pal." She moved her exohand to the top of her ponytail and tightened it, then nervously fiddled with her fingers.

Jimeny and Serarra exchange worried looks. They were nowhere near prepared for the Valkor. The stories they'd been told about them were encased in lore, sure, but she could sense the crew would be frightened by the possibility of an encounter on this day.

The Valkor were one of the first species permitted to share Gemarine. As Madame Bleu led the colonisation of the first city, Topaz City, she tasked General Heronicus, the leader of the Valkor, to build another city in the far south called Rosanthor, where walls of ice rose like cliffs of stone. Madame Bleu knew the Valkor had a rich tradition of land defence, so she predominantly employed them as her fortification warriors. It was said that the General did not take too kindly to being used and deployed in harsh conditions, so he revolted.

Heronicus summoned his troops and stormed Topaz City, slaughtering hundreds of Gemarinians during the inception of their colonisation. The specifics on how Madame Bleu eradicated the Valkor were unknown, just that she made a play, threatened their home planet perhaps, and then they were gone.

They were a memory twisting like a floating follicle in the Senmore. Nothing heard, nothing seen, until now.

The camera played on with Captain Larrsen addressing the lens directly. "I am concerned they knew about our mission. They knew we were coming and they drove us into the Senmore. This is something bigger than any Cryptoborg could muster. I think that this is—" At that moment a brilliant flash cut their power, the ship lost all functionality, the camera flickered in and out.

The panic in his voice now evident, a being with resignation to manage, he continued, "We are now drifting, the ship has encircled us twice – it must have disrupted all our controls. If you receive this message, flee immediately. This is the end for us. Beware. There is someone in the Gemarine squadron who has betrayed us – make sure you—"

The front angle showed the Valkor ship blast a powerful ray into the D-230 and the feed was disrupted.

Silence.

Juniper was hardly ever afraid. She knew what she could do up against the Cryptoborgs, up against all the other known enemies of the galaxy. She had studied all the others extensively.

But the Valkor was an ancient threat. A threat she'd never thought to take the time to understand. If Xan were here, he would have scoured the sparse galaxational records to divulge any weakness. Finding it from a tiny detail about the way they slept or something trivial like that. Mr Anthropology, Mr Creature Collector, Mr Science Guy, himself. But Xan was not here to bail her out. She suddenly felt incredibly stupid for accepting this mission, and the need to heed Larrsen's advice, "Flee immediately," rang loud inside her mind.

"Okay, let's get out of here." She pointed an exofinger and whirled around.

Juniper was a soldier of war; a warrior of her people, known for many famous feats of courage on the battlefield. Retreat was seldom her strategy, but a warrior knew the price of life more than any. At that moment she recognised that without knowledge of her enemy, the warrior within her craving a foe's blood to line her path like a red carpet needed to be subdued.

With all the self-control she could muster, she bit her tongue and watched members of the crew prepare their retreat.

The engines were silenced like a muzzled beast. Just out of sight, from the dark shadows of space came a beam of light aimed at their ship – the *Junkpunch*.

The Valkor were still there.

A trap had been sprung.

They were caught.

A surge shot through the *Junkpunch*. An eruption of chaos as the crew were thrown to the ground. Juniper stabbed her boronium exofingers into the control board and it steadied her against gravity.

"Controls are down, Captain Juniper, controls are down." Benius's voice quivered, mirroring his hands.

Juniper steeled herself. "Benius, what is the status of the shield?"

"It's down, it's down! I can't see the Valkor ship, where is it?" A manic state was overcoming him, his pale skin almost translucent now.

"Sit the fuck down, Benius. Remember your training." Juniper strode over to Benius, shook him by the shirt and shoved him back into the seat. His breathing was erratic, eyes spinning wildly.

Nausea roiled low in Juniper's belly, but she was not going to lose her mind. Kneeling in front of him, she collected herself and in a weird moment thought of how Lilianna might approach this. Out of anyone in her life she was surprised to think of her in a dire situation, but Benius needed calm, and positivity, so that's who she tried to emulate.

"Look at me," she almost whispered, as she took both his hands.

He stopped looking around, his gaze finally settling on her. There was admiration in his starlit eyes, an awe that couldn't be masked. Juniper placed her warm hand on his arm, gently squeezing it, knowing it would ground him. Knowing she evoked more within him than anyone else could. Eyes can sometimes utter words that a mouth cannot.

"We are going to be okay, Ben. Serarra will pull the lever, encase us inside the pod and we will get away once the shot is launched." She stood and raised her voice as Benius blinked twice and set his jaw, regaining his composure.

"Look alive, people," she shouted across the deck.

The Valkor ship finally came into full view, looming across the front view port, staring them down with fierce intent.

"Everyone take a green pill so we can withstand the vacuum of space for at least an hour if anything happens to us. Zip yourselves into suit number five and let's prepare."

"What's suit number five do again?" Serarra asked, her long eyelashes fluttering in the midst of solemn stares.

Jimeny began in a rhinal tone, "It contains a combination of microfibre and stem cell nanobots – that will set upon you to repair non-lethal damage if you are—"

"It makes you a boss bitch – that's all you need to know," Juniper interrupted with a simper.

Jimeny shrugged in defeat, while Juniper's humour appeared to lighten Serarra's anxieties slightly.

Sometimes you need to know science to find a solution but then other times you just need a smile. Balance is key.

They all did what they were told as the ship came closer to the starboard side.

A message flashed up on the screen: *Prepare for boarding. Do not resist.*

Jimeny cried out, "Captain Juniper, their weapon systems are offline, they're intent on boarding us."

Juniper watched with anger building as the Valkor ship locked onto the *Junkpunch*. A long reinforced metallic barrier shot out across the divide, clamping in place. Clicks, ticks, tocks and grinding gears told them all they needed to know. The bridge was in place and the Valkor would soon be there. High-pitched alarms rang out; the stale air was drenched with fear. The rusty doors buzzed and they opened with a customary *whoosh*.

Juniper yelled, "Get your weapons out now. Lock onto battle mode." She positioned herself behind part of the control panel, so she could still see the ship doors.

Two large figures burst through, clad in modern, pristine armour shining with black and white hexagons. Bronze helmets with two horn-like spikes shimmered under the flickering lights of the *Junkpunch*. Their voices were distorted and mechanically deep. "Holster your weapons immediately and come with us."

Juniper wanted to stand up and fight, but the only person she was fighting was herself. She needed to think rationally. This wasn't about pride anymore; her ego was damaged enough. If she wanted her and her crew to survive, she needed to repel the instinct that had crafted battlefield fables in her honour.

"Why are you here? What is the point of boarding our ship?" Juniper yelled.

The mechanical voice buzzed with the intake of their breath before they spoke. "Our purpose is to turn the wheels of fate, spinning toward what was always meant to be."

What the fuck is this robot bitch on about? This isn't slam poetry night at the Bokidor bar.

Juniper was shielding herself behind a sturdy column connecting the control deck to the ceiling. Moving her head to the side slightly so they would hear her, she shouted, "Stop talking in riddles and give it to me straight."

A silence hung as if they couldn't comprehend what she had said, confirmed by their response. "We know not of 'straight givings', but we must reiterate that fate is our guiding light. We have come aboard to find our livelihoods once more."

Juniper laughed with force. "Your livelihoods? Last time I checked, we had some discarded pills and chew packets but nope, your livelihood ain't here." Moisture trickled down her neck despite the masquerade of banter. "Time to leave and look for it elsewhere. Bye!" she said sweetly.

A moment of silence hung in the air before the metallic swathe of body armour jangled as they rushed in her direction.

Juniper went completely cold. The humour in her tone was gone from moments ago, now bathed in the dark memories of combat. "Stop moving or I will be forced to protect this ship using whatever means necessary!" she screamed, as wails of war echoed in her mind, igniting the vicious vixen within.

Their footfall ceased. "We know what 'means' you often take, Captain Juniper. You are a force to be reckoned with," the taller one taunted.

Juniper wiped her sweaty palm against her thigh and regripped her Cranston ray gun. *They've heard of me?* What Captain Larrsen warned them of was so very apparent now. Her mind was racing, and she was taken aback at the time it took her to formulate a response.

"Well since you've heard of me, you know what I'm capable of. Consider your next move wisely," she warned through grinding teeth.

BENIUS
18 YEARS OLD

Benius cowered behind the control desk, watching Juniper. His hands were shaking, the weapon tremoring with them. He wanted so very much to make her proud. Noticing that she wiped her palm against her thigh, it was obvious the situation was dire.

What could he do to help? He eyed the lever at the opposite end of the ship. The lever activated a defence system that would identify internal targets if the ship was breached and eliminate them. It was two automated Cranston ray guns that dropped from the ceiling, *so it isn't going to be perfect but it would definitely help*, he thought.

This was his moment. A moment that would ensure Juniper respected him.

JUNIPER
24 YEARS OLD

Juniper saw in Benius's eyes a thought, a dangerous flicker of heroism. She went to say, *Don't you fucking dare*, but he slunk out of her line of vision just as her eyes widened. He was going for the lever, but it was too dangerous.

She yelled, drawing the Valkor's attention to her, "Tell me what you want!"

"We want you to come with us." The larger of the two stood imposing with arms slightly apart from their sides.

"Why?" Juniper questioned.

"Because you're special," the mechanical voice behind the helmet droned.

"That's not enough."

BENIUS
18 YEARS OLD

Benius nearly got there.

His arm was outstretched, the desperate hero story so close to being written. The other Valkor who wasn't engaged in the conversation turned to see the tips of his fingers twitching, reaching. A burst of laser fled in Benius's direction.

Benius felt intense heat through his arm, then burnt flesh hung where his elbow should have been. The smell of seared skin floated into his nostrils. He cried out, hoarse and desperate, as Juniper sent a bolt of her own in the direction of the Valkor who'd shot him. They went down immediately after being struck through the chest, armour incinerated by the valuable captain-issued laser gun smoking with satisfaction. The other Valkor ducked as shots from Jimeny and Serarra followed as soon as Benius fell.

Juniper found her way around to the opposite side of the control panel to get a better shot, but the Valkor had two deflector shields surrounding them, so it was almost impossible to fire a shot off. Jimeny stood and fired at the Valkor but the deflector shield rebounded the shot straight into his neck.

He didn't have time to scream.

But silence couldn't take away the deafening valiance he held in death.

Juniper cursed.

Benius screeched in terrible pain on the floor, writhing and twisting. Serarra was on bended knee, trying to calm him, to lather his whole arm with the regen gel. But it wouldn't work. His arm was gone for good; Juniper would know that better than anyone.

JUNIPER
24 YEARS OLD

Juniper found a moment of clarity among the cries of pain, the lasers fizzing in various directions and the smokey haze that had settled around her, an acrid aroma offending her senses.

She opened her MPD and sent a message to Xan.

"Xan, I need you to know we're under attack. They've boarded our ship and it doesn't look good. I'm in the Senmore Section and I think they're Valkor. Please don't help; let the soldier units know. I just need you to know what happened and that..."

She faltered. What would be the last thing she could say to her best friend?

A shot fired above her head crashed into a wire-filled metallic casing. Golden discharges of electricity rained down on Juniper, singeing some of the purple highlights through her hair.

The Valkor saw that Juniper was otherwise occupied and stumbled forward in the direction of her crew members who were ripe for the taking. They took three large, swift strides to reach them. The Valkor swung a metallic hand, connecting with Serarra in the side of the head, sending her crashing across the floor in a crumpled heap. She didn't move as blood blossomed through her silver hair.

They then picked up Benius by the throat, and he squirmed in defiance. It was the only thing he could do.

"Come out, Juniper, or this one dies."

Benius breathed heavily without screeching anymore as his legs dangled in the air, the sadness in his eyes resigned to his fate. Juniper stepped out, her arms aloft.

"No!" Benius's voice was a rusted tool cutting into thick wood.

"Slide the laser across the floor to me." The Valkor's deep voice was calm.

Juniper did as she was told, as Benius tried to kick out with all he could give in that moment. His last moment.

The Valkor produced an ionised plasma blade, crackling with the desire to decimate. Cupreous sparks of flame were tattooed across Benius's final glance before the blade plunged into his chest. His face twisted in agony as the burning sensation pierced his heart and the steel of the blade cooled his descent into oblivion.

Juniper screamed, launching herself forward to confront the Valkor. Their helmet visor was a sable screen for callousness. They tossed Benius onto the ground like a dysfunctional piece of tech, placated by the ease of the dispatchment.

Juniper tensed her jaw, knuckles clinched. The rancour within contorted her face as she screamed curses, advancing with gun drawn toward the Valkor. But in the face of such aggression, they calmly pushed a button on their suit, dispersing a cloud of gas into Juniper's path.

The gas tickled her nostrils as it wormed its way inside. It took mere seconds to take effect. Her vision distorted and she dropped to the ground. The veil of darkness concealed the pervading devotion of consciousness.

CHAPTER 8

LOCATION: GEMARINE
YEAR: 108 (10 YEARS AGO)
XAN – 14 YEARS OLD

The sun was low in the sky in the afternoon of the third day. They had traversed the twisted tree forest in relative peace. Their stomachs were satiated by Qilin's *Flabber* hunting skills and Phineas the AI's contribution to which wild berries were safe for consumption. A red rash pulsed on the inside of his forearm, bitten by an unknown insect-like creature in the night. He was too slow with his MPD to figure out what it was, but Phineas confirmed the rash would not be the end of all things for him; it would only be a mild to medium irritation. It wasn't wrong.

Qilin comforted him with a low purr at night, a drone that lulled Xan into a peaceful slumber. It also seemingly sent vibrations through the land, emitting an energy that warded off unwanted intruders.

He couldn't put a finger on why Qilin, a rare *Mika Tikaani*, had decided to follow and tether herself to him, but he certainly didn't complain.

He searched the MPD for answers on the social arrangements for the *Mika Tikaani* but there was nothing to be found. As he discovered throughout the journey, it was a species that had very little information, which he thought odd.

Xan lay on a bed of crispy fallen leaves and large, plump flowers that he had gathered during the day. Propping a hand behind his head as he reclined, Xan summoned Phineas and asked about the various creatures that inhabited Gemarine. To his dismay, not a great deal was known. Right then, he vowed to learn more. If stumbling across a *Mika Tikaani* proved anything, it would be a worthy examination of the planet's xeno-biology. Although having studied Gemarine and the inner workings of Topaz City, it didn't exactly prepare him for this excursion into the Wilds. He knew the three species, the customs, the societal dos and don'ts but nothing about the wilderness and its potential creatures. There was a definite gap in the market, and when he finally reached the city gates, he would be able to propose a project focused on documenting and conserving these creatures. As Qilin walked beside him, matching his pace, he stroked her behind the ears and she looked up. The curves across her mouth appeared to slide upwards, cheeks swelling in a pseudo smile. The poster child for xeno-conservation was smiling at Xan. *What a bizarre and wonderful creature.*

As the hot afternoon sun licked them with a sweltering tongue, Qilin and Xan came upon a glorious pool fed by a small waterfall, trickling over circular grey stones. The water shimmered in swirls of delicate faded blue and teal, with an abundance of canary and verdant green plants adorning the area. Light caught on the surface of the water twinkled like thousands of crystal facets emerging from the dark. Flower pods on the end of branches from withered, ancient bulbous trees, exhaled a mist of cool vapour, as if the moisture within their plump bodies required release every few minutes.

Xan moved to the water's edge, extending his wrist with the MPD attached close enough to gather a reading to determine if the water was safe to drink. At Phineas' confirmation he cupped both hands, splashing it on his face, and funnelled the cool liquid down his throat.

"You know what?" Xan turned to Qilin with a serious expression. "I think I'm going to have a swim. It's too inviting and it's too damn hot right now." Qilin ignored his statement and flicked her blue forked tongue as she lapped at the water.

Xan stepped onto more solid ground and stripped off, grateful that no one was around. Qilin wouldn't police the indecent exposure, at least he didn't think she would. So, he let his pale skin soak up the sun as he swam, refreshed by the water in the Wilds of Gemarine.

Xan was nearly under the waterfall when Qilin yelped in a way he'd never heard before. He looked at her, puzzled for a moment then turned, wading toward the cumulation of bubbles at the waterfall's base. Droplets sprayed his face as he writhed at the base of the falls. He wiped his brow, feeling lively and refreshed, and turned to the bank with a gigantic smile to share with Qilin. But his smile faded and the cool, refreshing feeling of the water morphed into a feeling of cold unease. Qilin flitted chaotically at the water's edge, squealing in that high-pitched fashion. Masked by the surge of the small waterfall, he hadn't registered the sound, but now it was all he could hear. The spikes on her tail stood tall and fierce. The robust forequarters of her legs were rigidly planted, her enlarged scapula striking as she stood tall and menacing. All canines were bared, and her ears stood on end as she peered into the water around Xan. Something wasn't right.

Expanding ripples in the water's surface now undulated toward him. He thought it odd, as the waterfall trickled steadily the other way, like the gears of a timepiece coaxed by energy.

Xan's muscles tensed and his mouth went dry as he stared at the crystal-clear water below. Smooth, mossy rocks blinked up at him, luring him with their innocent disposition. Tufts of kelp swayed to the gentle song of serenity. A shadow loomed and like a partial eclipse, obscured the beauty of the moment. Xan's heart flapped in terror as he lowered his head into the water for a better look. Focused eyes discerned the details of the shadow. A distinct, slimy grey tail flickered out from behind one of the bottom-dwelling rocks then darted off toward the waterfall where the swirling torrent made it difficult to see.

Wrenching his head up out of the water, panic set in. Xan kicked off hard in an attempt to swim to Qilin, who was edging toward the water, then retreating and going back again. Her panicked whimpers added texture to the symphony of splashing droplets.

Xan's arms flailed with desperation, crafting frantic strokes toward the banks to safety. He gulped down water, spluttering as he stupidly yelled for help.

Xan didn't get far before searing pain wrapped around his leg. As he swivelled his head, he glimpsed the large creature: a mane of bright green cartilaginous frills framed its slimy, elongated grey face. Gills pulsing, fangs bared with malicious intent, pulling him down with burning red clawed hands. Xan's scream transferred underwater and immediately his lungs started to fill, heart rate increasing as he struggled against the force of the creature pulling him down into the depths.

The creature faced him and latched its large fangs onto Xan's chest, intent on gorging on his heart. Again, he opened his mouth in a scream as the creature's lips closed around the small wound. Xan's fingers grabbed hold of its frills, pulling and tearing membranes in a blind panic. The creature's neck pulsated as it sucked, feasting on one of Xan's most vital organs, ignoring the counterattack. Xan's dark blood escaped its mouth as it twirled in the water like a stray leaf caught in the undertow.

Lungs are not meant to take on so much water; they are branches that billow and fill as inhaled air circulates. A build-up of fluid in the lungs results in a pulmonary oedema. Treatment may include getting the fuck out of the water. But as the creature consumed Xan's blood and dragged him down, things didn't look promising at all.

Marbled, grey rock encased the pool, making the blue of the water dazzle. With the onset of fear and impending doom, one discovers clarity. The clarity of a discerning eye that stares into the face of the harbinger of death. The clarity of acceptance, as all that makes one Human is a forgotten soliloquy uttered to the empty auditorium of the mind. The clarity of finality, as dreams break like a cradle and sing a sweet lullaby before darkness comes.

An almighty roar cut through the underwater wall, surprising the slimy grey asshole enough to let go and back away from Xan. Although Xan's vision was hazy, he saw the creature catapulted into the air, at the same time as he, too, was thrust out of the water. Xan was dumped on the western bank, carried by the arms of the wind, spinning with the chaotic control of a mini tornado. On all fours he spluttered and heaved, hoping desperately to breathe again.

As gulps of air filled those beautiful alveoli, filtered by Mr and Mrs Bronchi and Bronchioles, he couldn't believe what he saw. Qilin walked across the surface of the water to where the fanged creature hung suspended and watched as it twisted and turned, writhing in agony as it appeared to be suffocating in the air. Droplets clung desperately to Qilin's paws, then retreated back into the pool with only the slightest disturbance. Her once amber eyes shone a deathly blood red. There was rage. There was truculence. There was power.

As the creature tried to escape, Qilin roared with a ferociousness Xan had never heard before.

Suddenly, the creature caught fire, bursting into red and orange flames. A shrill scream pierced through the cloak of confusion. It was truly haunting. The desperate, dying pleas of an alien ravaged by an unexplained force. The creature burned to black, shrivelling into a husk. Its ashes floated on the wind and settled upon the surface of the water. Black flecks seeped into the bright blue and bobbed like discarded seed pods carried on a gentle stream.

Qilin galloped across the glassy surface of the water toward an astonished Xan and sat by his side, and she licked at his chest as a way to stem the bleeding. Xan grimaced while she cleaned the wounds on his chest, a shaking hand stroking the fur on the top of her head.

Beyond Forsaken Worlds

A purple flower sprouted next to Qilin's paw, turning from seedling to a blossom in seconds. Qilin paused the wound cleansing and snapped it off at the stem with her teeth, nudging it toward Xan and peering at him with a look he could only describe as concern. Not for the first time, Xan thought Qilin possessed a depth of empathy that many Humans did not, and wondered again on the origin of this creature.

Xan clasped the flower, his hands still restless, and his breathing ragged. Qilin pushed the hand holding the flower toward the open wound with her nose, pinning it against the fresh blood on his chest. As the flower contacted the skin, a sharp pain zapped through Xan and he cried out. The skin sizzled as the flower cauterised the wound, stemming the blood flow. The smell of toasted flesh wafted toward his nostrils, oddly mixed with the sweet notes of the flower – like ylang-ylang and cherry blossom.

Qilin's eyes had shifted to honey once more. In that moment she was calm and attentive, looking hopeful. By now, he had caught his breath and his thoughts swarmed, as did the oxygen around his brain. Synapses flickered like tributaries of lightning within the topography of his mind.

He reached out to her, hands still trembling with the expulsion of adrenalin and the loss of core fluids. Rubbing through her coat of blue and black fur, he found words difficult to come by. Not that she would understand them anyway. *Or would she?*

Qilin purred reassuringly and nestled into his neck. The gesture let Xan's muscles relax and his head loll onto her strong shoulders. It was a relieving comfort to be in the embrace of his saviour. It wouldn't take away the horrific experience that was now fused into his memory, but the embrace gave him hope. Hope that he would never have to walk alone. The memory of his footprints would be trapped in contoured sands, adjacent to four paws forever falling into step together.

What have I just witnessed? Qilin can seemingly alter the elements in some peculiar way. But how and why hasn't she shown this power before? Is every Mika Tikaani *the same?*

61

"Thank you, girl, thank you for saving me," Xan whispered with laboured breath as he watched the ashes of the creature dissolve into the sedimentary bank.

Xan took some time to recover, then got dressed once more, hoisted the pack onto his shoulders and set off with Qilin at his heels. He thought back to the first time they encountered one another when he had saved Qilin from the horned beast.

Why didn't she exhibit this elemental power then? What's different this time?

Xan didn't know what would happen when they reached the city gates, but he vowed he would never give up Qilin. Their bond went deeper than just four days on the road together. This was something written in the stars, signed by fate. But there was also a curiosity within him to understand her potential, to study her – as a friend and not solely as a specimen. If there were more like her, he would ensure she could thrive in a colony once more.

One step at a time though. Let's just make it to Topaz City intact, shall we?

CHAPTER 9

Massy's eyebrows were drawn together, birthmarks crinkled as he leant forward inspecting the void through the pilot porthole. He was navigating the system with caution, gripping the yolk controls tight. Recognising the dire situation Juniper was in, he had switched the thrusters on, darting in and out of the debris at the fastest speed he could, while still maintaining altitude stability. Xan stood at the back of the large piloting area; Lilianna peeled in close to him against his shoulder. Her left hand fumbled nervously along the inside of his arm, until her fingers entwined with his. Xan squeezed, so their hands were now locked but he avoided making eye contact with her. There was no need for a smile or whispered gratitude, he was just honoured she stood with him.

Words are often tainted simply by the distance between the heart and the mouth. In this moment, presence itself retains eminence, while the art of speaking falls redundant.

Lilianna's presence still couldn't quell his restless heart as they searched for Juniper. For signs that she was still alive.

She didn't make calls like that. Well, only once. And he had found her and saved her then. This time, he didn't even have access to the full message. It was a collection of broken words. What was clear to him was her desperation.

He played back the recording again as they followed the tracking beacon on her MPD through the ship graveyard.

An explosion.
A high-pitched yelp.
Juniper's voice: "Xan, I need—"
Static.
"—under attack, I—"
Static.
"—Senmore Section—"
Static.
"—Val—"
Static.
"—help—"
Static.
"—need you—"

Lilianna sighed beside Xan, her eyes trailing upwards, their arms now linked as she leant against his body.

"We're going to find her shortly, Xan." She reached across and patted his arm awkwardly. "It will be—"

"There's the *Junkpunch*!" Massy pointed, his long fingernails scraping against the pressure pane.

Xan disengaged from Lilianna, letting his arm fall by his side as he moved with purpose to stand beside Massy, peering out into the ship graveyard. Juniper's ship was the latest addition to the dreary location. There was a large hole blasted in its side. Small remnants of the contents within encircled the ship in an endless orbit.

"Should we pull up alongside and retrieve the data?" Massy inquired. Xan ignored him briefly. "Ryker, get up here please."

"I'm already here, sir." Ryker's eyes were hidden behind the tangled mess of oily black hair strewn around his face. He had the pointed ears of his Sytheract mother but the tanned complexion of his human father. One of the original interspecies babies born on Gemarine.

"Can you please sort out the data migration for us now." Xan's command was forceful, a tone this particular crew wasn't used to.

Ryker pulled back his hair, tying it into a knot at the top of his head, his rigid collarbones prominent as he bent over the dashboard and typed code into the computer. Sweat beaded on his forehead. "Sir, I kind of didn't want to say anything. But I'm just wondering…why are we here?"

Lilianna stepped forward protectively. "We're here because one of our friends is in trouble."

"But this is the Senmore Section. I have…ah…concerns we aren't going to get out of here," Ryker complained, wrinkles creased below his scalp. Xan hadn't seen him so afraid before.

"If Madame Bleu knew about this," he piped up, but immediately looked sheepish at the mention of her name, as it invoked not only gravitas, but a tether to why he was a part of the crew.

"Ryker, you knew when you came aboard that this was off the books, why would you bring her up?" Lilianna scowled in disgust.

Xan raised his voice. "Enough, both of you."

The silence that followed was a fist to the throat.

"Ryker, do whatever you feel is right after this. I'm sorry I put you in danger. Truly." He bowed toward Ryker, whose shoulders sagged as he avoided Xan's eyes. Ryker turned his back on Lilianna, and in silence continued working on the feed, Lilianna's glower burning into the darkness of his hair.

"What in the black void is this?" whispered Ryker as an image materialised on the screen.

A being in a bronze helmet, a silver spike protruding from each side like devil's horns, green eyes large and demanding bore through the metallic confines. Ryker warned, "This is a live feed."

Massy reeled back from his chair. "What the fuck?" he breathed.

Lilianna caught herself, but Xan noticed a putrid fear building up within her, cowering behind her gold eyes. There was good reason to be afraid. No one had seen one of these beings in a long, long time.

Xan rose in stature, acknowledging who – and what – this was. "Where is she?"

"Xan, I presume?" Xan's dialectachip translated the Valkor tongue to something discernible.

"Yes, but answer my question first." Qilin growled beside Xan, narrowing her honey eyes to slits as Xan flexed his hands.

The Valkor took notice of Qilin. "Quite a sight, the *Mika Tikaani*. Haven't seen one for quite a while."

"Stop fucking ignoring my question and tell me where she is." Both Xan's fists were now bunched, his red cheeks flushed with anger.

"Which she, exactly? I have two here."

The camera panned across a dimly lit room. Dark circular stains ingrained deep into the surface of the walls. Rusted surgical blades stared with hunger at flesh primed for consumption. A taste would not suffice when a succulent meal was on offer. Juniper was chained to a wall, gagged and bloody. Her ringlet curls were laden with the weight of moisture, sagging to just below her shoulders. The chain squeaked as she bucked and fought against the restraints. Parts of her suit were shredded near the torso, dark skin glistening with the tears of torture. One of her female crew members with short grey hair was also bound, a mask of dried blood plastered to her face. The dejection in her was rife, as her shoulders slumped in defeat, eyes wild and desperate.

Xan didn't waver at the sight of Juniper's condition. She shook with a fierce energy, trying to yell but not succeeding due to the gag clamped across her mouth. Xan wanted to exude the same energy and found it came naturally to him.

"Don't you fucking touch—"

"Look son, give it a rest," the Valkor interrupted in a condescending tone, resonant and musical. "You have no bargaining power. I know you want her back. I'll give her back, no issue at all. I'll send you the coordinates to where we are, so you can come aboard our ship for a small conversation and then she is yours."

Massy breathed through the side of his mouth: "This seems like a trap."

Xan ignored him. "Send the coordinates. I'll be seeing you soon." He signalled to Ryker to cease the transmission and at that, he severed the connection.

Massy searched the coordinates and started muttering to himself. Ryker looked over his shoulder, nervously cracking his fingers.

"Xan, it's on the other side of the Senmore – are you sure you want to do this?" Massy warned.

"I'm more certain than I've ever been. It shouldn't concern you, though. I want you to follow orders. You drop me off and get out of here. They clearly want me for something and I'll see what it is. But all of you aren't involved in this."

Lilianna protested but he raised a hand. "I couldn't live with myself if something happened to you." He gazed deep into her eyes for a second and then turned toward the rest of the crew. "It's not your fight."

Massy shrugged. "Alright, you don't have to tell me twice." He pushed the yolk down and turned sharply to avoid a floating piece of broken fuselage. "On we go then. Transpo service engaged."

The *Attenborough* coursed forward and Xan took his leave, heading toward his quarters to prepare himself with armour and weapons. Lilianna followed close at his heels.

"Don't do this. Let me come with you," she begged.

He stared straight ahead, striding with purpose. Distractions weren't welcome while he was busy converting the fear to hatred.

Lilianna ran a few extra steps and jumped in front of him. "Stop," she said forcefully. Her open palms flattened against his chest, golden eyes peering up at him with concern. "I want to come with you."

He took a deep breath in, considering for a brief moment. The warmth of emotion he would usually feel was no longer inhibiting his actions. When he confronted the Valkor, he would need to be cold, and be willing to make tough choices to ensure Juniper made it through unscathed. Xan pushed past Lilianna and continued on. "I'm doing this alone, Lilianna. Don't follow me." His voice was flat and final.

LILIANNA
22 YEARS OLD

Lilianna watched Xan walk around the bend. Furious, she turned and nearly bumped into Qilin as she stalked after him.

"Sorry, girl." Lilianna bent down and stroked her head. Qilin purred with a soothing drone.

"Why is everything so hard?" she complained. Qilin whimpered with a gentle squeak, placing one paw on Lilianna's bended knee in a comforting gesture. It unnerved Lilianna, yet consoled her at the same time. They treated the *Mika Tikaani* as a glorified pet but there was something more to her. *I wonder how much she actually understands?*

Dualities were everywhere. A resonant calm in the face of dread, denial as an antidote to acceptance. So why wouldn't another present itself to Lilianna? A comfort in knowing there was more to understand, to unlock – but being wary that sometimes things were hidden for a reason.

MASSY
24 YEARS OLD

Massy navigated through the debris with finesse. He was near enough the greatest flyer in the galaxy and he knew it, but self-preservation was important to him, and although he would often do a lot for Xan, he wasn't sticking around to see this one through.

"I guess we have to stay and wait," Ryker said, scratching at his wrists as if a rash had crept onto his skin.

Massy scoffed. "You can if you want, but I'm out."

"You are?" Ryker sounded surprised.

"You shouldn't be made to feel bad for wanting to save your own skin, kid."

Ryker shifted uncomfortably.

"Why do you think those in the inner circle are still around? They don't go out on suicide missions to save a hot piece of ass for one. And two, they understand that shit isn't a game. You want to live the best life you can, then do a job, earn your credits, have a good old party and repeat."

Ryker searched past the stars to a twinkling beacon ahead. The coordinates looked to be a menacing ship.

Massy saw something within Ryker falter as his mouth tightened to a thin line. His words must have rung true.

He was no hero. He was a survivor, just like Massy.

XAN
24 YEARS OLD

Xan steadied himself in front of the video screen pulsing back his mirror image. He was tired, worn, and the sickness in his stare almost consumed his entire being. People often didn't use a regeneration pod until in their thirties. That was when Humans began their descent into a waning metabolism, developed wrinkles that spanned the face like the rings of a severed tree. Other species fluctuated between forty and fifty years before combating similar issues. The Sytheract skin, notably youthful and taut, lasted the longest. He was considering the regen pod when he returned; he felt old and haggard even though he was only twenty-four.

This was not about age, though, nor the nails of time carving imperfections into his dimpled face. He set his defined jawline with determination, and felt the spark within him – which usually filled him with excitement and passion – dim as the light that Juniper kept tethered to his soul diminished.

In a way, he might never understand or comprehend how their bond stretched beyond life and death and preservation. Xan knew she would easily do the same for him. Fates entwined the moment Madame Bleu had made her his mentor and neighbour.

He straightened his posture, the silver sheen of his armour glinting as the light caught its surface. The smell of rust and sweat stung the recycled air.

Qilin circled his feet, as if reminding him that his tether to souls extended past Juniper, to her, to Lilianna, to the whole damn crew. *Each one of them gives me purpose and they deserve to be led, to be protected.*

Massy's voice floated over the speakers. "We're approaching the coordinates. A large ship on the edge of both systems. I'll dock and leave immediately and get help from others when we're back in range or away from the signal blockers."

Xan flicked off the reflective video screen and ground his teeth, clenching his jaw and grunting, as if steeling himself for a fight. He needed to forge a weapon from the heat of his love, wielded by the hand of vengeance. Xan wasn't used to the weight of the armour and his purposeful footsteps laboured as he approached the control room.

He stared out at the giant ship through the viewing pane, and he was in awe. Orange highlights beamed across its dynamic wingspan, allowing its intimidating dark body to bask in the gravitas of its size. Embarrassment coursed through him at the realisation that it was fifty times the size of the *Attenborough*. Size did matter in this case. The outer glass caught the Senmore graveyard in its reflection, as if foretelling their glorious death.

With heavy boots, he jumped off the hatch and onto the metallic surface of the enemy ship. No one greeted him in the docking area. He inched forward past two large, gunmetal grey pillars, sturdy and strong. The wind from the *Attenborough*'s thrusters blew dark strands of hair across his forehead as it left him alone inside the enemy vessel. Rather than watch the crew disappear into the distance, his passive stare turned icy as he carried onward with Qilin close by his side, to the automatic door buzzing with energy.

He inspected the forcefield, but felt a presence lurking behind him, noticed a shape dart from one pillar to the next out the corner of his eye. Readying a hand to his Cranston ray gun, he drew and charged it with determined speed, spinning around to face the culprit.

Lilianna raised her hands and yelled, "No, Xan, stop!" Her voice was almost as foreign as his frightening movement would have appeared to her.

Xan's rigid stance fell slack, but looked to Qilin beside him, eyes narrowing. "You knew, you little shit."

Qilin basically shrugged and turned away, walking toward the door with her head held high, and her tail swaying pompously. Despite Xan being adamant this was his fight, Lilianna's presence would keep him watchful, grounded and even more determined.

Lilianna smiled with the warmth of a new day. "I was never going to leave you to go alone." She inched forward as Xan holstered his weapon. She took his hand, interlacing her fingers with his, locked with the keys of their flesh. Her eyes offered calm, but what he saw surprised him; a deeper connection he hadn't realised or hadn't acknowledged until that moment. Jaw slackened, and heart stupefied, his legs weakened.

"I'm with you 'til the end," she whispered with a voice that held on the wind. She peered up at him in expectation.

Before he could register the feeling, Qilin nipped at both their fingers. Xan yelped at the jolt of pain and ripped his hand away, his forehead wrinkling in annoyance.

"Seriously, you're toeing the line, missy," he warned, but Qilin motioned with her neck to the doors and he knew she was anxious and unwilling to waste any more time.

LILIANNA
22 YEARS OLD

Lilianna took a moment to steady herself and focus back on the task at hand. The way she felt with Xan, knowing he could also sense the energy between them, had excited her, despite their dire mission. Nerves had stung her like thorns raking over skin, but the importance of that moment steadied her.

She couldn't believe she was bold enough to say those words – *I'm with you 'til the end*. It was a declaration and a promise, one she was ready to commit to, but Qilin rightfully brought them both back to their senses. Their moment had passed and she, too, would need to summon a force within to face the enemy.

XAN
24 YEARS OLD

Xan discarded whatever feeling it was that crept beneath his skin, instead flexing his fists and tensing his muscles. He needed to be ready, needed to find courage for Juniper, and he needed to face a situation that might very well be his end. The three of them walked forward, steps echoing around the cavernous docking bay. It smelt of Busotil — a type of low energy fuel with only 10 per cent hydrogen, 40 per cent boron and a combination of bambalon and trixxium, used for smaller ships. It was thick in the air, and it permeated the usually filtered, metallic, recycled oxygen that flowed through large accommocrafts such as this one. They were usually mini mobile cities that kept large numbers of species aboard at any one time as a temporary housing convoy from one planetary home to the next.

They reached the shimmering forcefield with swirling purple hues blending to mauve and spectrums in between. It appeared to be the only way through. It was large and wide, like a warehouse door but pulsing with burning purple light. Xan yanked a hair from his head with an unabashed wince and tossed it into the swirling mass. Upon contact it singed and turned to ash almost instantly.

He motioned to Qilin to stop moving forward but she was already seated on her rear, propped up on her two front legs waiting for their next move. The three of them stared at the forcefield.

Xan quipped, "I suppose there's no doorbell?" A smirk slipped from his face, and he stole a sideways glance at Lilianna who giggled nervously despite the tense situation.

Then came a dull whir and the forcefield trembled. The power source was wrenched from its grasp and the purple light receded. The way was open. White walls lined the narrow corridor, while the gleaming metallic pathway wound away around a bend. They followed the curving path until a chunky door came into view. Xan sighed in anticipation of yet another obstacle, but the door opened without a hitch and they passed through.

Dread simmered within Xan, making its way to the surface. Tiny droplets of perspiration traced the curve of his jawline to the veins in his neck.

Why are the doors opening so easily?

The sound of the locks releasing as they made their way forward reminded Xan of another time, a less stressful time, when he was still on Earth.

Whenever his mother needed soy sauce, Xan would run next door to borrow from his neighbour, Mrs Yin Choo. She used to live in Australia, but after Gorden Grey accidentally prompted the rising of a clone army, she had booked a one-way trip to hermitville in Hong Kong for a fresh start.

A single dark eye magnified by extra-thick lenses would peer out at him while simultaneously flicking around the periphery of the hallway. He remembered a long gold chain suspended across the gap in the door. Xan always wondered why there were at least five clicks, metallic scrapes and crunches from her side of the door, before she half-emerged.

When paranoia surfaced initially, it was like a chip in glass. One could get on with their life while it was contained as a tiny speck. But over many years, cracks could spread until the entire piece of glass might shatter at any moment. And when that paranoia festers within, one can never ever go back. As her own paranoia grew with news of a clone army, Mrs Yin Choo only added locks, more security. She never took them away.

As Xan, Qilin and Lilianna passed through the high-tech security system with the ease of wading through a shallow pond, there was nothing but concern as a piece of Xan's own paranoia attempted to take over.

Mrs Yin Choo would eventually feel comfortable enough to open the door and let him in without as much scrutiny. Now, the Valkor were letting him in without obstacles. There had to be a reason.

What was it?

CHAPTER 10

Xan had reached all the necessary Gem-quals and now had the chance to access all parts of Topaz City. Since most start the process of 'qualification' at the age of ten, he was older than the others, having arrived on the planet when he was fourteen. Lilianna had reached all of hers the previous year, and they opened many doors to adult adventures, where things were regarded as a little more risqué to the more conservative Sytheracts or Humans. As a result of her moral code and personal feelings on promiscuous adventures, she reserved her intimate interactions with Gemarinians of equal belief, or at least in the confines of a more one-on-one experience.

Xan had called her for a drink to celebrate his Gem-qual milestone after they had been working together for five months. She had thoroughly enjoyed being under his tutelage during that time, and as soon as the job offer came through from the transition department, it ended up being a star made in the constellations. In her job interview, she had spoken passionately about her research of various planets that neglected creatures, flora and insects in the search for more capitalistic or urban worshipping practices. At one point, scientists estimated that Earth had one hundred million species, but each year they would lose at least one hundred thousand through extinction. Usually, it was caused through direct human involvement. It was a disaster.

Lilianna had researched a particular creature called the *Rusputer* from Gorblact – which was approximately four-hundred light years away from Gemarine. She highlighted that their decline was extremely concerning and she desperately wanted to locate them and do something to fix it. The *Rusputer* was a small, feathered rodent-like creature, with barnacles on its six legs, helping it to syphon moisture from surrounding condensation pools.

To her surprise, in just her second week, Xan had called her into his lab.

"Lilianna, I don't know how this will make you feel, but I've managed to secure a mission to Gorblact to see if we can find the Rusputer.*"*

She felt herself flush and her pale, silky skin drew colour. She hoped he wouldn't notice. Lilianna sat disbelieving, while Xan waited patiently for any response at all.

"Oh, Xan, I…" She welled up with the possibility of finding something she had dreamed of. And, to her utter embarrassment, she started to cry.

Xan's expression shifted from excitement to concern. He knelt before her, then warm, calloused hands gripped her knees and rolled slowly up her thighs. She inhaled sharply, and the tears stopped. He then placed his arms around her, and it was the first time her heart had sung a joyful melody, operatic and dominant, vibrating throughout her body. She didn't know it then, but love had trapped her in a silky web, spun just before morning kissed its brittle strands. Intertwining threads would build over time until she would eventually recognise her predicament.

She gathered herself momentarily. "Xan, I, my goodness, I didn't realise my emotions would overcome me like that. Please, forgive me."

Xan shrugged but his warmth was a perpetual flame. "To know that you care this much is why I know we will do wonderful things together."

He held her hands in his, and she focused on the way his thumb moved across her skin, caressing.

After two weeks of rough nights, setting traps, failing and starting all over again, they finally uncovered three Rusputers and took them back to the Gemarine biobase. The intention was always to establish a breeding program, accelerate growth to healthy numbers and then release back into the wild.

This was the first time she would be meeting the famous Juniper, his best friend, sister and lover all rolled into one. She'd been a witness to the holo calls Juniper made to him — sometimes thoroughly inappropriate ones. He would take the holo vids with her on his days off work, visiting and exploring new places together. It was evident that their bond was something Lilianna would never hold a beacon to. Admittedly, knowing that she could never reach that kind of relationship with Xan upset her deeply. She looked up to him as a pioneer and teacher, but the way he charmed the blood from her veins, making her feel valued and accepted was something else, and although Gemarine was filled with a diverse crowd, he stood out.

Lilianna planned to get to the Inebriation Level before the others, just so she might have time alone with Xan. She rode up the motitube and entered the main area of the level. Panoramic views of the urbanscape were laid out before her. Skyscrapers dominated the skyline; sleek dark elder trees in an urban forest. Air traffic of smaller flying crafts littered the sky. They spread out into the distance like insects traversing the interstices of an abundant tunnel nest. The sun cast rays across the upper levels, throwing beautiful shades of violet, pale orange and decadent scarlet into the bar. Even though she was much more comfortable sitting beside a flowing stream or studying the hollowed-out trunk of a silverwood giant, even she could admit it was a sight to behold.

The main bar served alcoholic beverages and an assortment of drugs. An Aranther with a mullet-hawk, fluoro-pink eyes and bulging biceps entertained patrons with tricks and a dashing smile as a bonus. Situated across from the band playing on various synthetic instruments, ranging from the gritty bass of the Babadock to the smooth, sine-waved Valeriot, were various rooms designed for different purposes. Themed holo-experience rooms ranged from natural wilderness, dungeons, deep space, tech spec with virtual reality and so much more. One simply needed to search the information database and it pointed to a room that satisfied all their requirements. The rooms could be used for aesthetic backgrounds for business meetings, sexual encounters, special occasions or, if they had a bank of credits, simply a chance to experience scenery, if they were unable to get off world.

It took Lilianna no time to find Xan at the bar, sitting closely to a girl she hadn't seen before. She was a stunning, dark-skinned, lithe woman, effortlessly beautiful, laughing with thick lips and eyelashes that rolled like gentle waves with each graceful movement of her body.

Xan turned and spotted Lilianna's gaze transfixed on Juniper and waved, which made her compose herself, feigning her search for him, then responding by accelerating through the crowd toward him. She smiled a lopsided smile, nonchalant and carefree to anyone who saw, but she was uncomfortable, and only she knew it. Her boots shuffled across the sticky floor, stepping over the automatic cleaners that moved with agility around ankles and boots.

Xan reached out and took her into his embrace briefly.

"Hey, you, I fucking love it when you decide to come out." He shouted above the noise, his smile like gemstones caught by the sunlight.

Lilianna stood with one hand fixed to her hip, while the other scratched nervously at the back of her head.

"Yeah, well, I wouldn't miss it, would I?"

"Let's get you a drink." His hand slipped around her waist and he pulled her toward the bar.

"You've met Juniper, haven't you?"

Juniper stepped forward, and the green in her eyes almost sparkled as her lips merged into a confident smile.

"No, I haven't. I've heard a lot about you." She bowed in the traditional Gemarine greeting. But before she had bent far enough, Juniper put strong arms around her and pressed their bodies together.

"Lilianna." She dragged out each syllable. As she pulled back, Juniper's eyes glowed with wonder. "Wow, you are something else." Lilianna noticed her exohand as she brought it up to her face and caressed her cheek. She flushed with embarrassment.

"Xan never explained how beautiful you were, my goodness."

Lilianna was thrown by her compliments and open flirtatiousness, and she looked at Xan with raised brows, signalling him for help. He just shrugged, as if to imply she would need to fend for herself.

"Oh, I…that's really nice of you to say. But no, I think you are in a… different category to me." Lilianna turned her eyes to the floor, shining with spilt drink.

Juniper almost cut her off. "Stop with that nonsense." Her tone was brash and dismissive. "I'm so happy to finally meet you, anyway. Let's get a drink." She linked arms with Lilianna and they strode toward the bar in close proximity.

"What do you drink?" Juniper readied the credit transfer on her MPD.

"Oh, just the fermented Boly juice."

"Oh, honey, that is sad. On a night like tonight, you aren't having fucking Boly juice."

Juniper turned to the bar. No one was close to their section, but she caught the eye of a bartender on the right-hand side. She motioned with her head, biting her bottom lip and raising her eyebrows in a provocative way. The Aranther bartender immediately took notice and slid over to them.

"Haven't I seen you at Fusion a couple of times?" They directed their attention to Juniper and ignored Lilianna.

"If you have to question it, then maybe not, because the way I fuck is memorable enough my face would be imprinted on your brain." She flicked her hair over her shoulder and then slammed her fist on the table. "Now get us both two Bundles of Delight, and do it at half price for not coming over sooner."

Lilianna was shocked at her direct nature, but equally intrigued. Once they'd composed themself, the bartender slunk back from the bar to make both drinks. "As you wish," they uttered before doing so, clearly under her spell.

Lilianna whispered, "I can't have a Bundle of Delight! That's filled with like, three or four shots of alcohol."

"Lilianna, this is a celebration and I insist you let loose a little bit." Juniper almost towered over her, peering down with a devilish smirk. "Besides, I think Xan will really like it." Juniper placed her warm hand across Lilianna's back, and she shivered with surprised delight at such an intimate touch from a stranger. Juniper pointed to Xan who was now laughing with Massy, and Lilianna realised how much she not only desired to please him, but felt compelled to impress Juniper as well.

"Yeah, sure, I'll have one with you," Lilianna conceded.

Juniper laughed dismissively. "You had no choice in the matter."

Lilianna pulled her hair behind her ear, in the nervous way she did, and realised Juniper's charm was contagious. Maybe she liked her forcefulness or she admired such confidence, but she felt like melted ice in her hands.

"There you go, beautiful." The bartender handed both drinks to Juniper, and she flashed her MPD at them.

"I'll be at Fusion tonight, so if you see me around, ask me if I want to play and we will see what happens." She turned without waiting for their reaction, craning her neck in the direction that she expected Lilianna to follow – which, of course, she did, snapping at her heels like a pet companion.

"Oh wow, Bundle of Delight for you, Lilianna. Looks like you're up for a big night!" Xan teased.

She took her first sip and stifled a shudder. "I guess so." She forced a smile.

"Yes, I get it, Juniper – somehow the male in every species is always lesser than the female or non-binary." Massy's voice was heavy with sarcasm as he rolled his dark chestnut eyes.

"I appreciate you conceding defeat." Juniper shook her drink in the air at him and flashed a dazzling smile. "Take this radiant beauty for instance." She placed her arm around Lilianna. "She is as delicious as they come, but her mind burns with an intelligence that enables her to run absolute rings around someone like you." Her face twisted as if his very existence were grotesque.

Lilianna giggled as Massy pouted and placed a hand over his heart as if pierced by an arrow.

"Some of us can't have it all. Some of us are just sexy specimens." Massy pursed his lips into a kiss and winked at them both.

"You wish, pal! Some have a lot more than others, that's for sure." Juniper's voice was deep, but Lilianna took note of the way she scanned for Xan and the way she nibbled her forefinger absent-mindedly as he came across from the bar to join them again.

"Drinks for all," he said as he popped several frosted glasses down on the table in front of them.

"It's your special day! You weren't meant to pay for anything," Massy said, frustration in his tone.

"It would be a special day when you start sharing around your credits," Juniper quipped. Massy looked a little sour at the comment.

"Let's just have fun tonight," Xan said dismissively.

"Are you coming to Fusion? If so, we should get going soon," Juniper sang, ignoring Massy and directing the question to Lilianna instead. She felt her cheeks flush under Juniper's hungry stare.

Massy pushed forward answering as if Juniper asked him instead. "I can't make it tonight. I've got to attend some bullshit flight course in the morning. But, bitch, I've seen you there often enough – cheers for ignoring me by the way," said Massy.

"Cheers to that." She laughed. "How about you, honey?" Juniper's hand rested on Lilianna's thigh briefly, and she tried to keep her face neutral. It seemed as though Juniper knew what Lilianna was feeling but she wasn't quite ready to process the excitement that ran through her.

"Um, no, I don't really do that. I'm sorry." She shifted uncomfortably in her seat, noticing how small and feeble her voice sounded, even to her own ears.

At Juniper's visible disappointment, Xan explained, "We chatted about it before, right, Lili?" She smiled and nodded, and placed her hands into her lap now that Juniper's were curled around her drink. "It's more about the Gemarine way; it isn't for everyone. I know I found it really difficult to adapt and understand that sex was only a physical thing; that the whole family structure wasn't anything like I had known."

Juniper announced proudly, "I definitely showed you the way." They shared a "Cheers," but Lilianna felt the intimacy between them, as if they knew in a few minutes they would be on their way to Fusion, exploring more than just the drink menu.

Lilianna spoke up, the alcohol giving aid to the strength in her voice. "The Gemarine way isn't really *my* way. And I guess there are others that feel…the same as me."

"You know what, I stand by you, doing your thing," Juniper said. "It's much harder in any world to make a stand and defy what the masses do, so I respect you for that. It doesn't mean I wouldn't want you to come with us tonight, but I know you'll do that when or if you're ready."

Lilianna nodded, still embarrassed, but thankful Juniper didn't breathe down her neck about it and that she seemed to have a softer side. Surprised that Juniper was her ally on that particular battlefield, Lilianna heard her say, "The Gemarine way is sometimes fucking bullshit, to be honest."

Massy piped up, "How so? I think we're pretty damn lucky."

"Surely, Lilianna, you can lay down some wisdom here?" Juniper gestured with her exohand, giving Lilianna the floor.

"Well, I guess, it's like we are all…thrown here from different worlds and expected to thrive when the cultural differences can be…really stark. Sometimes those little things make such a difference, you know?"

Massy raised a finger. "I wouldn't know about—"

"So help me, black hole of the Daygobare System, if you finish that sentence with 'little things' I'm actually going to squeeze that 'thing' into oblivion with my exohand," Juniper warned.

Massy lowered his finger and averted his gaze. "Never mind then," he said sheepishly.

"Please continue, my dear." Juniper gestured to Lilianna, smiling sweetly to the point of excess.

Lilianna chuckled. "I don't know, I guess the Gemarine way caters to confidence and, like, a certain sense of apathy. What about introverted people? What about the people who are emotionally charged? What is their value?"

"Ooooh, so proud of my girl." Juniper beamed, and although she appeared sarcastic, it then became clear she was not as she offered her thoughts to back up her point. "Confidence and cockiness is so celebrated, but you're right. I've heard about all the wonderful work you do, but because you aren't front and centre, lauding yourself, it's not written on our MPDs as distributed news. So, even though I'm living that confidence-fuelled life, I certainly see the pitfalls."

Xan raised his glass in agreement and sipped quietly.

Massy argued, "Yeah, but that's the thing, they carefully consider who comes here, I think. It's all for a purpose. So, in a way, the quieter people have a place in this society and contribute to the amazing lifestyle we're able to enjoy."

"Damn, Massy – why don't you stick your tongue inside Madame Bleu's asshole a little more," Juniper spat.

"I fucking would, though. She would taste delicious."

Xan grimaced. "Well, maybe you can get on her exclusive list when she needs a good rimming."

"Fucking sign me up, boss." Massy flicked his tongue out, pretending his glass was Madame Bleu's asshole.

"I see enough of you doing this at Fusion, waltzing around there with a shit-eating grin," Juniper said, flashing her teeth in a wide smile.

"You can talk! Caked in a steady glaze of cum from head to toe," Massy teased.

"It's good for the skin." She patted her smooth cheeks. "Better than eating shit, anyway." Juniper winked to send the taunt home.

"Alright, you two," Xan laughed, "you're both fucking crazy."

"Speaking of which, good looking, it's time to head out," Juniper said, diverting her full attention back to Xan.

Lilianna caught a glimpse of Juniper's hand sliding against the inside of Xan's thigh as she kissed him softly and seductively on the mouth right in front of them.

"Mmmm yes, yes it is," Xan announced, after Juniper's tongue was firmly back inside her mouth.

There was movement around the table, and Massy called out, "Alright, you two fuck bags, enjoy it all. I'll see you out there next weekend probably."

Juniper hugged Lilianna and whispered in her ear, "I know you don't want to tonight, but one night you should think about joining us."

She smiled. It was a tantalising dare, and it lingered in Lilianna's thoughts for a long time. When she lost sight of them both and sat in the transpo to her level, she couldn't recognise what she felt for Juniper. But a deviant part awoke inside of her, and although it might have been like a microscopic cell at that point, cells are still the basic building blocks of all living things. Was it time she embraced living?

CHAPTER 11

LOCATION: THE SENMORE SECTION
YEAR: 118
LILIANNA – 22 YEARS OLD

Lilianna fixed her gun into the side of her bodysuit as she watched Xan stride ahead; her caution could not materialise and confine him to a protective bassinet. Even Qilin, as loyal and fixed to him as she was, stalked the corridors, flicking uneasy glances to the left and right. White panels gleamed and cameras squeaked in the corners above.

Xan halted in front of one of the cameras.

"What are we doing? Where is she?" he yelled, throwing his arms wide and letting them smack against his sides, fists balled.

Lilianna stopped moving, her long, spindly fingers clasped around her wrist, and scratched nervously. She pursed her lips, considering what to say, but nothing came out. Qilin turned around and sat on top of her feet like the pair of fluffy warming boots she wore when the icy winter season tore across Topaz City.

Lilianna absent-mindedly reached down and stroked behind her ears, and a low purr came from out of the side of Qilin's mouth, reverberating throughout her body.

Xan arched a leg up and kicked across one of the white panels, and it crumpled with some resistance to the force of his blow.

"I said, where is she!?" he bellowed, his eyes wide, spraying an angry mist of saliva.

Almost instantly, a serene voice floated across the speaker system. "Please, calm down. A representative will be deployed to your position shortly."

"About fucking time," he shouted again with a deep growl. Perspiration slid across a vein pulsing at his temple and trailed down toward his jugular.

Lilianna had never seen him like this. Her love was a fire, and his sweet nature was a dainty breath of oxygen allowing it to burn, but the passion in him now was a wild wind that could scorch a planet. Her tongue swept across her lips as she considered what it would be like to be the focus of such raw passion, but as she heard movement in the corridor, she quickly remembered where she was and the situation they were in, and she felt ashamed.

Three Valkor approached, even from far away their cold black armour strapped to their frames was bulky and fierce. They had large hands that could crush Lilianna's skull as if it were fragile, cracked glass. With helmets abandoned, their foreheads protruded like balconies surveying a broken galaxy, dark hooded eyes and hook-like noses as they stared straight ahead with menace and intent.

"Nice of you to fucking—"

The closest Valkor cracked Xan across the mouth with the hilt of his weapon and he stumbled back, thumping into the already damaged white panel, dazed and confused.

Lilianna let out a desperate cry and lunged forward to cradle him. She had a heart for compassion and hands to heal, rather than the resolve to yield a harbinger of death. Qilin let out a ferocious roar and attacked the Valkor who had hit Xan, launching at his exposed neck. Incisors bared, she tore the trachea from his throat. Blood splashed across the white walls in wet, forceful bursts. The sound of a snarl, beastly and callous. The malevolent gleam in the eye of a predator as its victim stewed in a vat of gore.

Xan regained some composure and moved to support Qilin but he stumbled. As the Valkor's leg twitched for the final time, a female Valkor smashed Qilin across the head with an open palm and the trachea dropped from her jaws as she was thrust backwards into a wall. She flopped onto the metal floor motionless.

Lilianna ran toward Qilin and slid across the pools of blood on the floor to her side. At Lilianna's cradling touch, the *Mika Tikaani* breathed a ginger sigh, whimpering in pain. Just ahead, Xan launched himself at the Valkor, knocking her to the ground with clenched fists born from the seed of wrath. But the third Valkor overpowered him. One great punch that drew blood from Xan's nose made Lilianna feel as though she could see ripples of victory span across the hostile river before her. But powerful oceans of malice feed all rivers and tributaries, rendering a ripple a mere nuisance. Xan was a diminishing vexation as the Valkor swiftly attacked the nerve point of his arm, and in an instant, he appeared to lose all feeling until it dangled useless at his side. With a wailing, guttural scream Xan hung his head, defeated, as the Valkor roughly bound his hands in front of him and shoved him against the wall.

Qilin clambered back on all fours and the creature's eyes began to turn to a blazing red. Lilianna had seen it once before and knew what would happen. Dust converged in front of Qilin's eyes, suspended like a marionette awaiting the flick of the puppeteer's wrist.

But Xan yelled, "Qilin, don't do this, don't do this! I need you." His desperation was wrapped in a sense of foreboding, lamenting a loss that hadn't yet come to pass.

Qilin shrank back. Instead of her fur standing on end, the bristles relaxed, curved and reclined across her skin folds. Crimson eyes encased themselves in amber once more. Lilianna relaxed too, not knowing how many more times Qilin could switch before she might never return.

The Valkor yanked Xan to his feet, brutally dragging him by the hair as he turned to Qilin and Lilianna.

Lilianna cowered in the corner and held Qilin close as the other Valkor approached. "Please don't hurt us," she pleaded, tears now staining her defined pale cheeks.

The Valkor stopped and looked down upon them both. Power in stature and power in predicament. Lilianna shielded her face by turning away and flinging her body across Qilin, awaiting a blow that never came.

"If you stand up and carry this creature, I'll let you walk ahead." The Valkor spoke with a deep, but surprisingly soothing tone.

Lilianna wearily opened her eyes, previously sealed shut with dread. "I...I...yes, I will, I will," she stammered, confused.

Scooping Qilin up in her arms, Lilianna felt slick, wet Valkor claret matted throughout the tufts of her fur, and her sharpened jaws glistened with scarlet flesh fibres.

"Put this on her." The Valkor motioned. It was a muzzle of sorts, and she obliged, clamping it down across Qilin's jaw, whose eyes narrowed with disapproval.

"Now walk ahead of me," he commanded. The sapphire in his eyes set him apart from the other Valkor.

Xan was still yelling into the corridor. "If any of them are hurt, I'm going to end you." His hoarse voice trailed off as she lost sight of him around a bend.

Lilianna didn't know why, but this Valkor didn't seem to have the same amount of hatred or brutality as the others. Granted, he was involved in their capture, but it was as if he pitied them rather than wanted them to suffer.

"I just wanted to say," she searched for the right words, "that I'm thankful you didn't use violence on us just then." Lilianna swallowed without turning around. "The easy option was that but, well it means—"

"Don't thank me. It's nothing." His voice was gruff with frustration.

Lilianna tried to look behind, but—

"No turning back," he snapped.

"I'm sorry." She regained composure and said, "My name is Lilianna and I'm—"

"Listen, don't take my mercy for an invitation to converse. Just walk."

"I was just going to ask if he," Lilianna pointed up ahead as Xan was dragged through imposing black doors, "will be okay."

"Do you think I have any say in what happens?" His voice was deflated, as if his status wasn't recognised as noble within the Valkor hierarchy. "When I hand you over, consider that the end of our road."

"What is at the end of the road?" Lilianna cried out with a diminutive rasp, the walls closing in around her as they neared the end of the corridor and the penultimate black doors that had swallowed Xan.

"When our paths diverge, may you find peace as you cross into the ether." Forced enlightenment tinged his tone, as if the words were recited from a text he once believed but now gathered dust somewhere.

"Wait, I don't want any ether excursion." Lilianna's heart thumped against Qilin's body in her arms, a cold realisation spreading through her that ether likely meant death.

He remained silent. The longer the space between words stretched out, the more fear of the unknown gripped her.

Lilianna paused and quickly turned, facing the Valkor. Her eyes bulged with panic. "Just tell me what they're going to do to us!"

He shoved her forward. "Calm yourself and keep walking, Sytheract." Lilianna tripped on her feet initially, wincing from worry as Qilin's low growl vibrated against her own chest.

The black glass doors opened and the Valkor shoved her inside. Heavy, calloused hands grabbed her as Qilin was yanked from her arms. The cold was now a freezing burn coursing through her. Tears were blades, ripping through her tear-ducts and bursting down her cheeks. Shallow, misty breaths congealed before the discernment of misery settled upon the scene. Qilin was shoved into a see-through bioplastic cage, fist-sized airholes punctured at the sides, boronium trimmings glinting with artificial light. Qilin conceded in a crouch, seething in the muzzle.

Those large Valkor hands bruised her biceps as they pressed into her, twisting and jostling until her bound arms were raised above her head and suspended from a hook in the ceiling.

Her eyes flicked around the room. Qilin in her cage, Xan fastened with shimmering sturdy black metal to a stark white chair, Juniper in chains bound to the wall, her dark skin glistening with blood across her exposed arm. Rips in her suit revealed gashes that had healed quickly – most likely laser burns. Her green eyes were framed by an undying scowl of hatred. A body lay at her feet, unmoving, in a pool of fluid glistening with death's acquiescence.

Lilianna called out, "Juniper are you okay?"

"Honey, I'm always fine," she said with a tired smile. "Now, Lilianna." Her face changed, and a grave weariness melted across her features. "Just breathe. Don't panic. Most of their wrath has been wasted on me and Serarra. Tell them what you know and everything will be okay."

The doors clicked shut, and frazzled, Lilianna spat out, "But I don't know anything."

"Exactly," Juniper breathed, wincing as one of her wounds pinched her.

The menacing leader of the Valkor stepped into view.

CHAPTER 12

LOCATION: GEMARINE
YEAR: 108 (10 YEARS AGO)
XAN – 14 YEARS OLD

Wind howled with horror. It was not a sorrowful song that set the hearts ablaze with melancholy embers. It was shrill and it rattled the soul.

Moments before, the ambience of the final forest bordering the city walls felt placid, almost welcoming. But wilderness was unpredictable on any planet.

Xan and Qilin skipped down slick rocks lined with moss into a valley collecting trickles of water into rushing puddles that some might call a seasonal stream.

As rain like sharpened needles scraped across their faces, Xan spotted the small mouth of a cave. He turned and ran toward it, noticing Qilin's reluctance to follow. As Xan reached the cave entrance, Qilin walked tentatively with weary concern, but followed him regardless. It was as if she understood that protection meant the same in perilous situations and ominous ones. She sat beside him as they peered into its entrance.

Like a firefly caught in a web of darkness, the faintest glow flickered ahead. Qilin sniffed the red sand, collecting fine particles on her nose until she stopped, purring in apparent satisfaction. Her tail curled upwards and the bristling spikes stood on end. *A sign of adrenalin perhaps?* Xan mused.

He bent down, inspecting her discovery. A foreign footprint encased in rusty sand. The imprint of life in the Wilds. Not the usual code of DNA, but in grains of sand one often found the legacy of species past. Xan hoped that if he followed the human-like footsteps into the recesses of the cave, it would lead to an encounter with an ally.

Qilin continued to sniff the sand, inching into the darkness, coaxing Xan forward with her. The only ally he could see was taking him into pitch black with the hint of hope glimmering ahead like a timid beacon.

As they traipsed forward, Xan considered why there were fresh footprints from a humanoid in the Wilds. During his hours of study, he had discovered two cities were colonised: Topaz and Rosanthor. Many more were planned in the coming years but at that moment the two cities were sufficient enough to contain the population. Rosanthor was an icy fortress, built for defensive fortification and only the hardy, winter-loving folk were able to thrive in the south.

Either way, it didn't answer the question about why there were Gemarinians in the Wilds. It made him wonder about the nature of 'utopia'. Walking toward the gates of a new world – the delicate promises of a new life – he couldn't help but consider, was this a terrible choice? Was there something sinister lurking beneath the utopian ideals of Gemarine?

He certainly hoped not.

Thoughts about something baleful lurking turned his attention to the shadows surrounding him and the sinister threat they posed to his current state of being.

Qilin's amber eyes glowed softly, illuminating the tiny space ahead, so at least the shadows didn't swallow him whole, famished though they were.

As the speck expanded, the dank smell of the cave teeming with moss and lichen withered away, replaced by cured meats and fermented fruit mixed with spices like star anise and cinnamon. Sure enough, when the scene opened up before him, salted chunks of jerky meat hung across a clear wire strung between rusted metal poles. The firefly light from a distance was an old computer, unlike anything Xan had seen before. Judging by its weathered nature, it must have been vintage in comparison to what Topaz City possessed in the present day. Rags of clothes, torn pillows and furniture that had seen better days were collected in a heap in the corner.

That was all the evidence he needed of Gemarinian life in the Wilds. But why were they living in such disarray? And most importantly, could they even help Xan?

Qilin had a hold of a cushion in her jaws, throwing it up and pouncing on it, sending a puff of dust floating into the air like powdered snow at the turn of winter solstice.

His eyes followed the dusty mist as it found its way into the shadows' embrace to a type of ancient artefact displayed on a large smooth rock.

It was a perfect disc, thick and metallic and about the size of a ceramic plate. Xan wondered whether it was made out of copper or just stained with dirt and marred by the decay of time. In the centre of the disc was a carved hollow space in the shape of a column with a pointed peak. The object itself was missing.

Xan gazed at the floor once more and took in the jagged fissures in the soil around him. Tools discarded in the sand, sections cordoned off by frayed threads and containers full of dried mud littered the area. Other small artefacts and broken shards came into view, functional items of the past.

This was an archaeological dig of some kind and the inhabitants of the cave were cataloguing what seemed like prized possessions of the original guardians of this planet.

But who were they? Why hadn't he read anything in his induction research? Wouldn't that have been important to know?

"Hey, Phineas," Xan's croaky voice echoed in the cave as he turned on the MPD, "I'm wondering, is there any information about who first inhabited Gemarine?"

"Hello, Human Xan, there are four thousand and eighty-three ancient texts on the data cloud with references to the first inhabitants. Would you like me to dictate all of them?" the AI asked.

Xan fidgeted, impatient. "Can you just summarise for me?"

If Phineas understood an impatient tone, he certainly didn't let it affect his competence. "Gemarinians refer to the first inhabitants of this planet as 'Celestials'. They used this planet as their base from which to monitor the wider galaxy."

Unbelievable! Divine creatures used this planet as their home.

"How did they fall into ruin?" Xan wondered, stroking his chin.

"That information is not accessible on the data cloud," Phineas reported flatly.

Xan considered this for a moment, and his train of thought turned sceptical. "Do you mean that the information is either redacted or restricted?"

Phineas replied, "I repeat, the information is not accessible on the data cloud."

The repetition of the AI's response likely meant a block had been placed on accessing information about the Celestials. This revelation worried Xan. He had left everything behind. His family, friends, his future. His humanity. Trusting an alien guy with some fancy technology. What if he'd sacrificed everything and been lied to?

He decided to focus on what he had before him. "Phineas, scan this artefact and tell me what it is please?"

A moment passed before Phineas replied, "May I direct your attention to the image loaded on your MPD."

Xan focused on the device on his wrist. The image presented four immaculate beings standing atop cliffs gnawed by the morning frost. Three beings held the circular artefact to a pit of flame, surrounded by three crystals jutting out of the sand. The fourth being stood further from the group with a—

"Is that…a *Mika Tikaani* in this image?" Xan blurted out excitedly.

"It is, indeed, Human Xan. The Celestials believed them to be wonderful companions."

Xan laid eyes on his own *Mika Tikaani* now curled up in the sand, resting a weary head on her tail, spikes retracted, of course.

"They most certainly are." He then focused his attention on the other parts of the image. "But why wouldn't you have told me that earlier?"

"You did not ask me to access this information."

Xan nodded, accepting the AI's predicament then quickly focusing on the image once more.

"So, is this some sort of ritual that the Celestials are conducting?"

"As far as the information about the Celestials goes, I have stated previously that there are only rumours and hearsay. Many have said there is an ancient text that provides details and clarity about their involvement in the galaxy." Xan nodded, keen to learn more. "This was a painted image found in a cave structure quite like the one we are in now. This painting is rumoured to depict an energy transference ceremony, where the energy from the beings is transferred into the crystals you see below. The ancient artefact you see in the painting and here before you, is a housing for one of the crystals. It is indeed quite a revered and valuable cultural artefact."

Xan considered the possibilities of energy transference and wondered how this could be managed. How could matter shift into rock? It didn't make sense. But then again, the wonders of the universe were only just starting to open up to him and there was a lot more he needed to learn.

He looked around the cave and wondered what other secrets the red sand held.

Just like the Gemarinians and their pursuit of celestial knowledge, maybe he would never know.

What he did know, however, was that he needed to take advice from Qilin who slept soundly on the sand, safe from the elements outside.

CHAPTER 13

LOCATION: THE SENMORE SECTION
YEAR: 118
JUNIPER – 24 YEARS OLD

Juniper rested the back of her head against the wall. Anger surged at the sight of Qilin, Xan and Lilianna shackled because of her. The decision to call Xan to bid farewell, to warn them from following her had backfired. Now they, too, faced torture and even death, because of a weak moment when she wanted to hear Xan's voice, or to hear Qilin squeak with excitement.

"Welcome, Xan. So lovely to have you on this ship." The Valkor general beamed, revealing yellowed teeth beneath a nose shaped like a grapple hook.

Xan scowled at the apparent leader of the Valkor. "Are we really doing this? These feigned pleasantries while you have all of us shackled like slaves." He spat on the floor. Blood and saliva crept toward the Valkor's boots.

The Valkor's thin lips curled into a smile, doused with evil intentions. "I thought you were meant to be the level-headed one, Xan. I guess that

98

makes…" He stooped toward Lilianna suspended with her arms above her head. She grimaced, inhaling sharply, her eyes distress beacons calling for help.

"Don't fucking touch her." Xan's deep growl was laced in dark devotion.

The Valkor placed a long, bent and calloused finger to Lilianna's lips. She squirmed, closing her eyes tight, flicking her head from one side to the other in a desperate attempt to get away. He wiped delicately across her cracked lips, gathering her scent on his finger, then licked it feverishly, tasting her.

"Mmmm, how I've longed to taste a Sytheract for decades. You are delicious." His hooded gaze brimmed with mild satisfaction.

Lilianna winced, staring with a hint of defiance in her eyes, but resignation and powerlessness was written in her body, shackled and small.

"Listen," Xan demanded with the now familiar grunt of forcefulness in his voice. "Why did you bring us here?"

Juniper piped up. "Yes, Almighty One, tell them why we are here," she chided, shifting against the wall stained red with blood. "The story is a lovely one, Xan, strap yourself in—oh, oh wait, you already are." She readjusted herself, losing the sarcastic smile completely. "Like I fucking told you, you pea-brained fuck. We don't know any of the bullshit and we aren't interested in helping—"

"Always talking way too much," the Valkor interrupted, fashioning his scarred hand into a puppet, mimicking a flapping mouth. "The moment I set you free will be such a burden released. I can't stand wasting another moment with you."

Juniper shrugged as best she could. "Do you think I give a fuck?"

The Valkor turned, directing his attention toward Xan, as if bored with Juniper's response. "Now let me explain it to the people with a heart and maybe they will see things a different way."

No one saw Juniper roll her eyes, but as he resumed his speech she thought, *How precious to say I have no heart when none of my crew remain.*

One dead at my feet, the other two confined to death on a broken ship. One day he will learn the wrath of my heart and realise his grave mistake.

Xan breathed, "What is it, what is this story that's brought you out of the shadows?"

The Valkor turned his back on Xan and spoke to the frosted glass wall behind him, almost as if revealing vulnerability was a burden too much to bear.

"Years ago, we were driven into the darkness, away from our planet into a collection of several housing vessels spanning the galaxy." He stretched his arms out wide, indicating the vessel's size. "We were fortunate enough to have received word from someone who had broken out of Gemarine, wanting to warn us of our impending doom."

"What does Gemarine have to do with anything? You were the ones always trying to take from them. In the datascrolls of recent history, the Valkor decided to slaughter Gemarinians in the city because of a land dispute!" Xan recalled.

"This is the lie that has been burned into the minds of everyone on Gemarine. I'm not criticising you now, because that is all you've known. But it is a fabrication of events." He looked over his shoulder at Xan, the black of his armour, the creases on his large forehead, the scar across his right cheek all defined by a surge of hatred. "The datascrolls are a subjective version of history. A fictional masterpiece I think not; a collection of propaganda to incite the obliteration of an entire race, it is."

Xan said, "Well I don't believe you. This whole charade has proven that you aren't the victims here. Look at us right now." He rattled his hands against his bonds, biceps bulging with contempt.

"You're right, you know." The Valkor's voice softened and he turned around slowly, the silky tunic beneath his armour flowing with grace at his movement. "Over the years, indignation boils and it changes who you are. I am not who I was back then. Betrayal is set deep in the scars on my body but also in the blood that fuels my heart."

He moved toward Lilianna and she cowered from him, but he loosened her chains and brought her down carefully, still bound, her hands now lying in her lap. It was clear to Juniper that Lilianna didn't know how to react, but before she had her chance, the Valkor general turned away again.

"But my mission for you, that Juniper so desperately insists you won't be a part of, involves uncovering the truth so you will see it for yourself. Once you accept that, there will be no doubting what I've told you."

Xan frowned. "So, what is it you want from us?"

"Patience, Xan, you will find out."

Juniper grunted. "Fuck, do I have to sit through this saga again? Honestly, get to the point."

The Valkor ignored her.

"We decided to forgo our Gemarine citizenship and escape the planet, as well as our own home world because Madame Bleu was planning to destroy everything." He paused briefly as if to let that sink in, but Xan and Lilianna didn't react at all. "She has been doing it for a long time now, to many other worlds. It's her formula. Kill the inhabitants of a planet and steal its resources to better *her* world. And it worked for such a long time before you all made it to Gemarine." He threw his hands haphazardly in the direction of Xan who was still tightly bound, bloodied and scowling. "That slimy, spineless inner circle understands. They're the only ones who know every little detail. But they let it happen. They are complicit in the genocide." His fists now bunched, creases deepening on his forehead as he strained to contain the anger. The Valkor turned back and faced the glass. "She runs things carefully, so that all her other worker bots or the regular mindless citizens of Gemarine contribute to her continued domination of the galaxy without knowing the intricacies. The Valkor used to be another race permitted to walk upon Gemarine, but upon our exile, all those who knew of this were expunged, except for Yedash who escaped and warned us all." He shifted toward Qilin's cage at his feet, but looked wistfully beyond the wall, seemingly reaching into his mind for a painful memory. Qilin bared her teeth, readying the spikes on her tail to strike if he got too close, but he didn't even appear to notice or care. "About five ships were sent into space. Five of thousands. Madame Bleu heard about the planned escapes, her two offsiders arrived in the vicinity of the planet and blasted it into smithereens. The Senmore Section is where our planet once was. Now each meteor floating in space is part of who we were, who I was, after she blew our planet up. She killed over ninety per cent of our population. Including every beautiful creature we had. Wiped out of existence just like that."

Xan remained silent.

Juniper thought, *Great idea from Valkor McGee, bringing up the creatures to really sell his plight to Xan.* Her tired voice rose from the bloodied floor. "But that's not the most interesting part, everyone. Apparently, all our planets met the same fate as Ralis. They're all dead and mined for specific resources to help power Gemarine."

The Valkor didn't interrupt this time, even though her words were heavy with sarcasm.

She continued, "So Earth is dead, Sytheria is dead, and Dracia is dead too. But here is the kicker...he has no proof."

"Please disregard Miss Juniper's tone. She is still angry about a little bit of torture and kidnapping."

Juniper flexed her upper arms, about to tear the walls down with her wrath, but he held up his hand. "Please, just let me get this over with. You and I both know the stakes. Let Xan and his pretty little plaything hear them too."

Juniper went from boiling to simmering, seething with a scowl. "Get it over with then, you over-dramatic cunt."

Lilianna flushed at the mention of her being Xan's plaything, but seemed to swallow the embarrassment down, because in that moment even if curiosity were a fragrance, it would be too pungent for the aroma to be pleasant.

The Valkor continued, "I don't have proof. But the power station at Gemarine will give you all the proof you need."

"I'm sorry, but why do we need proof?" Xan's voice rose in anger. "Why should we do anything for you, considering our treatment?"

"I'm not saying to do it for me. You all had families on your home planet once and the very fact you agreed to come to Gemarine was because the way Madame Bleu put it to you, your involvement would have terminated your planet in some way. What if I told you it was the opposite?"

Lilianna's croaky voice spilled into the air for the first time. "Wait, so you're saying that we were lied to and taken from our worlds in order to ensure they would eventually die?"

"That is exactly what I'm saying. Everyone on Gemarine was taken from their planet for a reason. A reason that would benefit Madame Bleu. Maybe one of you developed a way to make sure your planet thrived for generations, maybe you were a warlord fighting off invasive species, maybe you simply bonded with a person who was a leader, and you nurtured their success. I don't know what scenario would have been the correct one."

"So, multiple timelines are confirmed to be a...thing?" Even Xan was confused, which meant something.

"You have seen time manipulation with your own eyes and I bet you never thought that possible." The Valkor waved an arm, appearing frustrated at Xan's lack of acceptance.

Xan looked off into the distance, most likely thinking of that moment in Hong Kong with Derrison, which he had explained to Juniper multiple times – the fascination, the nervousness, but more than anything, the desire to know more.

"But is it confirmed?" Xan pushed.

"You would need all three crystals to explore the different timelines. So, in answer to your question, no one in the known universe has seen this completed." The general was quick to add, raising a finger in defiance of logic, "But I put it to you, to prove this theory wrong before you dismiss it altogether."

Xan sighed. Juniper started to see a change in him, the silence helping to manoeuvre his thoughts. That same desire to explore, to understand the world, and it appeared to be fuelling his decisions here.

The general changed tact before Xan could verbally accept; it appeared he had seen the shift too.

"From sources on the inside, I know that you, Xan, were extremely well sought after by Madame Bleu."

The general studied Xan, whose creases on his brow had not diminished. "Why would she want me?"

"Think about it. In the last ten years you've been on Gemarine, has anyone been brought back older than fourteen years old? You were one of the oldest inductees ever."

Xan knew this to be true. Lilianna was brought over when she was nine and that was considered old. But fourteen was nearly unheard of.

"I know she tried when you were younger, but it was like the universe was fighting her and, well, we thought we had taken you out all those years ago when we shot down your ship."

"That was you?" Xan burst out.

"We thought you were the key to her plans somehow and when we realised you were still alive, decided to study you from afar instead."

Xan's face twisted in horror and Juniper tried to recall any moments where she had felt watched. Aside from Fusion, she drew a blank.

"So, I've just been monitored all my life?"

Juniper interrupted, "These guys are fucking creepers. This is proof! They probably sat in bushes stroking themselves while watching you, Xan."

The Valkor general seethed and his voice was flat against the small space. "Do not trivialise what we have done, Juniper. You do not know the lengths we have gone to ensure the right solution is reached."

"Oh, I know the lengths, alright. Maybe the length of the chains you bind us with? Or the length of this cell or the length of the trail of blood from an innocent crew member of mine." Juniper's voice was a tired rasp brimming with hatred. But behind the hatred was a deep sadness. Despite the quips and sarcasm, her heart ached for the lives lost and for the way she'd dragged Xan into a mess he shouldn't have known.

"Regrettable decisions can still wield results," the Valkor general uttered flatly. "Xan, despite the circumstances, I believe this task will give you purpose and you will see that all I'm trying to do is prevent extinctions. Isn't that what you do?!"

Xan said, "So, what am I supposed to do?"

"The first step is to go back to Gemarine, search through the power station and test all three power sources and see for yourself. They will each contain a specific resource that cannot be found on any other planet – you can test if it's from a dead world, and suffice to say, they all will be." He paused, his lips pursed. "The second part will be more difficult."

Juniper roused once more. "Honestly, Xan, why are you even entertaining this lunatic?"

"If this is true, it's bigger than all of us, Juniper." Xan shifted and a part of her lamented a small feeling of betrayal.

"Exactly, I—"

Xan cut the Valkor off. "That doesn't mean I'm not going to fuck you up as soon as I get out of these chains."

The Valkor laughed unreservedly. "I didn't realise how much Miss Juniper has rubbed off on you over all these years. Too bad you didn't rub up against this specimen more often."

Lilianna flushed again, casting her fearful eyes to the floor.

"Could you just stop objectifying her constantly. It's pretty rapey, if I'm being honest," Xan spat as the Valkor directed his hungry gaze on poor Lilianna.

"Look, fine – torturing, murdering – it could have been done differently, but time is not something we have. Not now anyway."

"What does that mean?" Xan puffed.

"It means exactly that. A squadron of Gemarinian soldiers will be here soon enough so I should leave."

He turned to Qilin, confined to her cage, and made his way slowly toward her.

She was lying flat, her head resting on her paws uninterested, but at his advancement she sprang up on all fours, sensing something wasn't right.

"That is why I must do this."

The Valkor pulled a vial containing a bright blue liquid from his breast pocket and shook it fiercely.

"What is that?" Xan tensed, alarmed as the Valkor walked toward his creature companion.

The general stopped at the bioplastic cage, and pulled out an injecting device, metallic and menacing. He pushed the blue vial into the cartridge holder and it beamed bright, ready for use. The Valkor turned to Xan as it pulsed threateningly in his grip. "I wish there was a better way. But with her around…" He flicked his head at Juniper, who didn't know if his heart was untainted by the calloused hands of time. She could sense what he was capable of in desperate moments though, where his bitter memories would overcome any slither of virtue. "I can't trust you without some kind of insurance."

Xan gazed at a being lacking any shred of remorse; of someone who had lost it all. The general bent down over the cage, holding the injecting device against a small opening where Qilin's hind legs were.

She spun her head around and red eyes flashed again as Xan's piercing scream filled the containment room. But once Qilin understood Xan's desperation, she let the power subside within her and although fear most certainly would be gripping her, a resigned glance communicated what words could not.

Juniper deduced it was Qilin trying to tell Xan it would be okay. That they would meet again. But Juniper knew Xan better than anyone else and without his girl, he would be untethered. A ship without navigation drifting the sea of space, waves of darkness permeating his soul.

Juniper knew what was coming before it occurred. She didn't want to look into Qilin's solemn face as the injection went into her side. There was a chaotic flinch, muscles recoiling as the blue liquid in the canister emptied into her. Juniper certainly didn't want to hear Xan cry out and watch him nearly break his wrists from struggling to save her. She didn't want to see Qilin's eyes turn black and her body flop lifelessly onto the floor of the cage without anything left to give. She didn't want to watch Lilianna's tears erode the beauty of her high cheek bones and silky skin. But she experienced it all and beneath all of that, the anger twitched and seethed. This was her true family and they were being torn apart in front of her.

"What did you do?" Xan wailed, his fists striking the wall beside him again and again as far as his chains would allow. Graffiti sprayed in a mist of blood.

The Valkor opened the door of the cage and reached in, amidst the voiceover that beamed across the ship, and caressed Qilin's body, still rising and falling with breaths of defiance. "General Heronicus, your courier vessel will leave in T-minus five minutes."

Heronicus picked up Qilin's cage and placed it on his shoulder to bear the weight. "She is heavy, gosh."

"You are fucking dead!" Xan rattled the chains as he screamed. It was guttural, like the primitive generations of Earth all risen as one in a desperate cry before the end.

"Xan, I warned you not to follow Juniper's path, she—"

"Don't you fucking dare talk shit now. Tell us what you did," Juniper seethed as Xan shook with fury. Lilianna's tears pooled in her lap, her shoulders shaking with pain.

Heronicus smiled, and it was almost reassuring. "I've placed her in a coma with the blue liquid and you have forty-eight hours to meet me at specific coordinates. There, I'll give her the purple liquid which will instantly wake her up. Your MPD will tell you the coordinates when you return to Gemarine." The doors opened, but he paused and looked at them one last time. "If you don't get to me in forty-eight hours, she will die. And it would be an utter shame to send such a powerful creature into the wasteland of memories, a place that is merely an echo of what we could have had. It stunts your heart because you will never make more." He wistfully looked off into the distance again, but then he sent his determined gaze upon Xan one last time.

"Meet me there, Xan, or you lose her forever." The tunic beneath the armour flared as he turned, flashing across the glass before he vanished.

Xan shouted, "Bring her back. Qilin!"

Juniper tried to talk to him. "Xan…Xan, we'll get her back, it's okay."

Her soothing tone was lost to the desperate fury in his screams. She had never seen him like this. In the ten years she had known him, this was the most he had broken in front of her.

Lilianna was still crying, but her eyes were wide with fear, reacting to what she now saw in Xan. Her superior at work, a man she no doubt revered, was coming apart in front of her. Juniper knew she needed to bring him back.

A mechanical click sounded and suddenly, the bonds loosened and they were free.

Juniper couldn't help but reach out for the body of Serarra at her feet before she sought freedom. Bending down, she swept her eyelids closed, shielding that penetrating final glance from the guilt of living. The pool of blood infiltrated the clarity of Juniper's memory of her. The beauty in her dark, tanned skin, the courage in her desire to learn, her unwavering footsteps that followed Juniper wherever she walked.

Lilianna wiped her eyes and slowly stood, but Xan, in his manic haste, threw the bonds across the room. They smashed into the wall and clattered to the ground as he ran out the open door. As Juniper tended to Serarra's body and Lilianna wiped away tears with the back of her hand, Xan sealed the doors shut without saying another word and stormed off.

Juniper and Lilianna looked at one another, realising they were locked in the room together and Xan was free on a ship most likely teeming with Valkor.

But the red in his stare was fierce. Juniper knew what that meant after a decade of sparring together, from her training as a soldier and war hero. Xan untethered and full of rage loose on the vessel – every Valkor should be deeply concerned.

CHAPTER 14

Juniper rounded the corner in the agricultural section of the learning centre. Although it was in the middle of the urban sprawl, they had a large expanse of land where they studied crops, plants and insects that helped successfully cultivate various fruit trees. For instance, there was a type of insect like a bee, called a *Rover* that pollinated the majority of the flowering trees. It was so much like a bee that it allowed Gemarine farmers to utilise several crops from Earth, enabling Humans to experience tastes of their childhood and culture. So, they kept a colony close by.

The second flying pollinator was called the *Philix*. It wasn't as prolific as the *Rover* because it exclusively pollinated one of the most delicious fruit trees on the planet. The fruit was called Lushes and it had the sweetness of a blueberry, with a sour burst of citrus, complemented by the aftertaste of fresh mint. There was a large aviary of these creatures and Juniper could hear shouts and scuffles as she approached the large door, frosted glass obscuring what was inside.

She scanned her MPD against the locked door and waltzed in. Xan was on the ground and two large Aranthers, one male and one non-binary, towered above him. Xan's beige linen uniform was scrunched in their grip, one eye was swollen and black-rimmed. They all turned as she entered.

Her eye was drawn to the opaque wings of the *Philix* lying next to Xan, lifeless, colourful feathers strewn across the ground surrounded by several large rocks.

"What the fuck is happening here?" Juniper's voice was a hacksaw through bone.

"This little stain of a Human is messing with our business," spat the bigger of the two Aranthers with a bright red mohawk.

"And what business would that be?"

"None of *your* business," replied the other with large eyes and gold goggles to enhance their vision.

Xan twisted loose from Mohawk's grip and rolled away, crawling on his knees along the ploughed ground to Juniper's side. Juniper looked him up and down disapprovingly before continuing.

"Well, this stain right here," she thumbed at Xan, "he's my business, so technically it is." She walked forward with purpose, piercing them with a threatening glare.

Both Aranthers appeared less sure of themselves as a look of unease passed between them.

"Look, it's not our fault he's fucking useless and can't keep his button nose out of what we're doing," Goggles protested.

Juniper remained composed. "I hypothesise that what you were doing was not particularly on par with what Gemarine would deem…hmm… acceptable behaviour."

They tried to speak but Juniper held up a finger, raising her sharp voice. "And as a result, you can receive the 737 punishment from a soldier-in-training." Juniper's smile was cunning, she couldn't hide her masochistic delight at being able to put both Aranthers in deep freeze, then thaw them out over the course of days.

Their shoulders slumped, their eyes flicked around as if searching for assistance.

"No way, on what authority?" Mohawk cried.

"My fucking authority," she yelled with finality.

Juniper launched at both of them with dominant force, bending low and shouldering Goggles in the stomach, then spinning and aiming a weighty kick to Mohawk's nether regions.

With a groan, Mohawk dropped to his knees, sucking in air and wincing. Goggles had recovered and bounded toward her, arms raised. "I'm going to kill you," they bellowed.

A large arm with blossoming maroon scales swiped over Juniper's head as she bent low with the agility of an athlete, striking a blow to their kidneys with her palm. They doubled over, propping themselves up with a shaking arm.

"Enjoy pissing blood for a week, you mindless fuck." Juniper spun mid-air and kicked them in the side of the head, inducing a restless sleep.

Landing heavily on her feet, one hand poised on the ground, her other arm hanging out for balance, she taunted Mohawk, "So when you locate your balls, do you want to try me or what?"

"Fuck you, bitch," he spluttered and coughed.

"Probably shouldn't have chosen a male gender with the ol' cock and balls. Seems like too much extra baggage for an oaf like you. Make sure your friend doesn't make the same mistake, yeah?"

He charged, but didn't get far. She met him with a twirling kick to the chest that sent his mass sprawling across the ground. Dust swarmed as she rolled, positioning herself behind his shoulder and grabbing his neck in a sleeper hold. "And three, two, one...sleep time, baby."

Mohawk's body went limp and she let him slide into her lap.

She stroked the side of his face and looked at Xan. "The little munchkin looks so cute when he's sleeping, don't you think?"

She rolled her eyes and jumped up, letting his head smack the ground with a thud.

Xan stared at her awestruck, a certain tinge of pink colouring his ears in embarrassment.

"Thanks, I suppose," he uttered sheepishly, looking down, unable to meet her eyes.

Juniper smiled with restraint like a bud primed to flower, the sweetness trapped inside. "C'mon, Xan, I'll always have your back."

Though her knuckles bled from the fight, she clasped his cheeks anyway, inspecting the damage inflicted on him. A blackened halo crowned his left eye and a gash underneath seeped tears of blood. Her heart mourned at seeing him this way.

His presence shifted when skin met skin, as her gaze simply settled deep into his dark grey eyes. The weight of the moment seemed to push them together and strengthen their bond.

Xan turned his face away briefly. "I feel like an idiot." His shoulders sagged and Juniper immediately felt as though he were desperate to leave the scene.

Juniper took her hands away from his face, resting them against her sides, then nudged him forward. "Let's get out of here then, before they come to."

As they walked out the door and into the fields of westler grain, she implored him, "Why do you feel like an idiot?"

"Because I, like, can't protect myself. I'm fucking useless." He was dragging his feet against the pavement, head down, watching his footsteps intently as if they were the pinnacle of beauty.

Had she crossed an imaginary line by defending him? When she saw her friend in need, she simply stepped in. There wasn't a second thought. But Xan wasn't one to start fights; he was quite a gentle soul. Although he had shown resilience and fortitude when hiking through the Wilds, aggression wasn't something one would find, even in the cobwebbed sections of his mind. "What happened?" she asked curiously.

"They were throwing stones at the *Philix* and I just got so mad. Whenever anyone hurts a creature, I just can't take it. So, I ran up to them, swinging fists but, well, looks like they got the best of me." He kicked a stone, head still lusting after those sexy feet of his.

"Where is the shame in that? You were trying to protect something that can't protect itself."

"Like what you just did with me?" His gaze shifted to her for a short moment and she recognised insecurity.

"Xan, you know I train for this kind of shit. Besides, Qilin is normally around you any other time except at the learning centre so no one usually fucks with you."

"Yeah, well, at the learning centre is when I came across these... disgusting, filthy—"

"Fuckbags? Shit stains on the underwear of life?" Juniper provided him with wonderful names and descriptions.

He laughed. "Yes, as you so eloquently put it."

A silence settled. Xan seemed to be thinking long and hard about something. "I know this is annoying," he said finally, "but can you please, maybe, train me or whatever?"

"Another thing I have to teach you?" She giggled, and he growled with annoyance. But she returned with an air of determination, "Of course, Xan. Every week on Freeday One, early evening, we can go to Level 75 where I do my training. It's a date."

"Thank you." Xan looked relieved, puffing out a large breath.

LOCATION: GEMARINE
YEAR: 110 (8 YEARS AGO)
JUNIPER – 16 YEARS OLD

Level 75 was deserted this evening. There was a gathering in the city circle to celebrate the 10th anniversary of 'The Severance War', where they'd fought off one of the first Cryptoborg invasions.

As Juniper walked through after disembarking from the personal motitube, she spotted Xan leaning up against the wall, scanning through his MPD. His face was pensive, lips bunched as if concentrating a little too hard. Still, he rocked a casual cool stance with ease. Qilin stalked in circles in a corner appearing restless, bouncing and snapping at little insects that were now regretting their ascent to the higher levels.

Juniper's footfall wasn't loud, but Qilin flicked her head up almost immediately and bolted toward her. She dropped to her knees producing an endearing smile that was reserved only for the *Mika Tikaani*.

Qilin leapt up and licked Juniper's cheeks and bit into her neck playfully.

Xan looked up from his MPD and couldn't hide the smile that emerged onto his face. Juniper wrinkled her nose playfully, careful not to let Xan's excitement migrate into the dangerous territory of romance.

"Well, look who showed up," he drawled, his voice dry like fickle tinder.

"Are you joking? I'm five minutes late, you little nerd bitch," Juniper snapped, as she tied her curly black and purple hair in a ponytail, readying herself for the duel to come.

"You're just afraid now, as I'm getting better than you." His eyebrow cocked and he flexed his growing bicep in jest. Juniper huffed in amusement, disguising the worry that he had possibly grown into a worthy opponent.

She roared with a hearty laugh. "Xan, the day you beat me is the day I retire to the birthing division."

"Prepare your loins then, 'cause I've been practising with holograph programs and I'm taking you down," Xan said, puffing out his chest with confidence.

Juniper stood with her arms loose at her sides, her feet in a casual stance. She gave Xan a half smile, the only indication she was ready to begin. He took the first step toward her, but she showed no mercy, throwing a flurry of punches while he defended each one with a precision she knew could only come from practice and familiarity.

Each thump of a thwarted punch, each slap of a defended kick echoed throughout the level. The colours of the setting sun leaked through the windows and allowed a burst of orange, purple and red to permeate the space, spilling vibrant splashes onto the soulless white walls and grey floors.

This light is doing wonders for Xan. It makes him look like a sun god. A sun god I want to burn me to a crisp, Juniper thought, allowing herself the momentary distraction of the colours that painted pure attraction across his skin.

One second of lustful distraction was enough to forgo thwarting his fist that barrelled in her direction. She shifted her weight onto her back leg, intending to aim a kick to his chest, but Xan pressed his body in tight to hers, holding her thigh in place next to his side. Juniper grabbed onto his bicep in an attempt to balance herself and was met with hard muscle underneath taut skin.

Xan slammed her onto the floor, the weight of his body pressing through her middle. Juniper's face opened in shock as she took in his strong grip, of the way his body moulded to hers. He let her go abruptly and positioned his hands on either side of her, effectively pinning her to the ground.

Juniper took in the sight of his strong shoulders that begged to be held onto, the veins in his forearms straining as he held most of his weight off her. Finally, she looked into his grey eyes, noting the flash of pleasure he had in obtaining this dominant position over her.

His face was mere inches away and she was acutely aware of how his chest rubbed against hers with every inhale, how their breath mingled with each exhale. She could smell the remnants of soap on his skin along with the musk of sweat, and an ache of longing started to take hold. Juniper knew she could have easily escaped the cage of his arms, but she widened her legs further, allowing him to nestle against her core.

Heat flooded through her along with a need only he could satisfy in that moment. Desire started deep in her centre and radiated out through her legs, spreading to her fingertips. Juniper bit her bottom lip in an attempt to stop the flow of energy. Xan's eyes zeroed in on that action and she felt him grow hard against her. She loved knowing he felt dominant over her, that she was able to give him that power and confidence.

Xan pushed himself forward at the same time Juniper opened her mouth, willing his lips to find hers. They clashed together, their tongues colliding in a fury of tension that spilled over the breakwall of their fortified passion. She reached up and massaged her fingers against his scalp, burying them in his hair of finely spun silk. He tasted of sweet honey mixed with a wooded glen on summer's eve and it was so fucking good.

Juniper took it in and savoured his taste, getting lost in his touch as his strong hands found the back of her neck with the grip of a man who tendered the soil – rough and meticulous. She knew he wanted more than this tasty appetiser. With the banquet table within reach, it was time for the delectable delights. Juniper rolled him onto his back with their mouths still locked together and clawed at his chest, relishing the way his muscles felt beneath her. Another part of her flickered with more excitement, but before she could enjoy the feeling, he forcibly flipped her onto her back, assuming control once more. He dug into her, kissing her like sharpened steel raking over taut flesh. She fucking loved the feeling of being taken over, of having someone who could match her strength and then some. A breathy moan escaped her, recognising Xan's wild streak. She was about to attempt to tame the beast.

Just as Juniper reached down to undo his pants, something rough and wet grazed their cheeks. She had forgotten about Qilin in their lust-fuelled fighting, and she giggled hysterically as the *Mika Tikaani* stuck her blue forked tongue out and lapped at them again.

Juniper and Xan shared one last passionate look then burst out laughing as Qilin pounced on them, wanting to partake in the only type of wrestling she could understand.

Juniper drew a very hard line at bestiality.

CHAPTER 15

LOCATION: THE SENMORE SECTION
YEAR: 118
JUNIPER – 24 YEARS OLD

Banging against the glass didn't work. There was no point hoping for Xan to come back; he was all emotion and rage. Juniper turned her back against the doors, sliding downwards until she slumped on the floor. She grabbed at strands of curly hair as she let out a frustrated sigh.

Lilianna paced the length of the small cell splattered with blood as chains creaked, demanding control once more. "Oh my gosh, what is he doing? Why did he just leave us here?" she shrieked.

Juniper wiped blood from her cheek, inspecting the ruby as it dripped from her exofingers. "I guess, it's his way of keeping us safe," she said with a hint of annoyance.

Lilianna's voice was high-pitched, stained with worry and rapid quavers. "What for? The general is gone. It's over."

Juniper pushed herself up and moved, taking Lilianna's hands in hers. The need to quell Lilianna's frantic nature was number one priority because it annoyed her. Weakness was never a drink she ingested willingly, and she declined to purchase it for others. But aside from the annoyance, she very much wanted to bring calm to Lilianna, wanted to teach her resolve, teach her that to stand strong, she must first strengthen the heart.

Lilianna stopped pacing and looked into Juniper's eyes. "Just take a moment with me, Lili." Her voice found serenity, while the corner of her mouth dribbled with the blood of torture.

LILIANNA
22 YEARS OLD

Lilianna stared at Juniper with admiration, quite possibly with reverence. Juniper had been tortured, witnessed the deaths of her beloved crew, yet Lilianna couldn't muster the strength from enduring the unconsenting touch and leering eyes of the general, watching Xan break and abandon them in a confined space. It was all too much. Her bottom lip quivered and she fought against her own instincts to drop to her knees and let her emotions consume her.

JUNIPER
24 YEARS OLD

Lilianna's cheeks were pale, made worse by the artificial light casting its radiance across the cell. Juniper continued, "Keep looking at me and breathe in deeply, just do as I do." She took a deep breath, her exhale tickling the tip of Lilianna's nose. Juniper breathed in deeply again, her chest expanding, the sweat and blood mixed in a trail of liquid that dripped between her breasts. Lilianna quickly averted her gaze and stared into her eyes again, this time participating in the experiment.

Once Lilianna calmed, Juniper said, "Listen, honey, I don't think he's protecting us from anything on this ship; he's protecting us from him."

Lilianna let go of her hands and she scratched at the back of her neck. "What do you mean?"

"I mean that, we both know how much Qilin means to him. There is nothing in this world he loves more, including both you and me. Whatever we discover will not be pretty and you should—"

Before she could finish, there was a commotion down the hall. They both pressed their faces against the tinted glass doors, straining to see.

Massy and Ryker came into view, their thick boots slamming against the metallic floor. Juniper and Lilianna both knocked against the glass with fervent purpose and the two rescuers turned to them. Massy was clearly relieved and smiling as he tried to work out how to open the doors. Ryker wiped his black fringe away from his eye to rest behind his ear.

As the doors slid open, Massy went to hug Juniper, but she shrugged him off immediately, so he was forced to wrap his arms around Lilianna instead. "Oh, girl, I'm so glad you're okay."

Juniper spoke in hushed tones to Ryker as she forced him to move into the hallway. "Where is Xan? Did you find him?"

Ryker was quiet and gruff. "No, we expected him to be with you."

"Fuck," Juniper spat and took off at a run.

Ryker called after her. "You need this?"

She turned back and held her hand aloft, but he wasn't good at throwing with his scrawny arms. He bent down and slid the weapon across the floor. Juniper scoffed as she knelt and retrieved it, swiftly standing and setting off down the hallway.

LILIANNA
22 YEARS OLD

Massy still held Lilianna close, her legs so weak, if he let go her entire world would collapse. He gripped her shoulders and shook her gently. "Hey, girl – are you okay?"

"I'm just a little...dazed." Her words were a creeping fog across a panoramic expanse.

"Yeah, it seems that way." He turned to Ryker. "Hey, son, get over 'ere and give us a hand, will you? She's pretty out of it. Worse than me after that cocktail of stimulants I did last weekend." His eyes glowed with a devilish hue.

Ryker didn't appear to be impressed either at the joke or about having to help Lilianna, but he crept across the floor and held out his arm, flanking her other side as they tore themselves away from the torture room. A body they didn't recognise lay flat and motionless on the floor, surrounded by dark viscous blood.

"Is she dead or—" Ryker's voice was small.

"Ryker, look at her, mate, she's long gone," Massy said with condescending callousness.

Ryker's face went even whiter than before as he ingested the sight of gruesome death, at the hands of an extinct alien threat.

Lilianna cringed at being so close to them both, especially Ryker. She felt unclean. The Valkor general's leering gazes, the way his fingers grazed her skin, the torture chamber she was bound within, the blood trailing across the floor. It was all too much. She needed to be cleansed, she needed to breathe, she needed to forget.

They passed a room on the left, but something made her want to stop and go back. "Wait," she said, breathless but curious.

They stopped and she looked inside.

Two Valkor soldiers lay dead in a heap, blood rolling into dark pools fed from wounds across their slashed necks. Her stomach chose to riot, bile lurching into her throat; she didn't want to believe who caused that damage.

JUNIPER
24 YEARS OLD

Juniper searched many rooms off the main hallway, some containing furnishings with nothing else, while others wore the bloodstained uniform of wrath, manufactured and designed by Xan.

She didn't study the bodies, there was no need. Rage was a story she knew well. These killings weren't savoured – he killed to satiate his pain.

It isn't satiating pain, it's merely masking it.

The control room was larger than she anticipated. The window fed into deep space, looking out at limpid stars and distant moments that burned delicately into the present.

Juniper laid eyes upon the killer, but not before the whimpers reached her ears. The music of mercy – a frail voice begging, followed by the strident scream of a desperate man. *Her* desperate man.

"Where did he go? Tell me or I'll gut you." A curved blade, markings across the hilt, dripped blood onto the cheek of the killer wielding it high above the next victim.

"I don't know, I told you. I'm no one. I don't know these things, I—"

Xan sliced across the begging Valkor's cheek, then plunged the dagger deep into his right shoulder with a wild pleasure in his eyes. The Valkor cried out in agony.

Juniper finally found her voice. "Whoa, Xan. Fuck. It's okay I'm here. We are going to get her back. It's okay."

Trance disturbed, Xan's neck twisted toward the sound of Juniper's voice feigning calm, her arms outstretched, reminding him of the warmth of her embrace. He flinched as if considering her words, but his eyes were cold. A world of ice, crisp and dark, haunted the beauty she knew so well.

"Xan, please," she begged, as the high-pitched cries from the pained Valkor flooded the air around them.

"You want me to stop after what they did to you? After what he took from all of us?" Xan shouted. Shouting was just a way for the voice to expel emotion. Unrefined hatred moved in decibels.

LILIANNA
22 YEARS OLD

Lilianna burst into the control room with Massy and Ryker on her heels, adrenalin driving her forward. Xan stood shirtless with a curved knife in his hand. Flecks of dark red and black marked his face, while his biceps and sculpted chest were painted in Valkor blood. It was a mark of his demise; a mark of furore in its most detrimental form.

Her eyes quickly took in the sight of the Valkor and realised it was the same one who had treated her well earlier in the ordeal. "Xan!" she screamed, aghast. "What are you doing?"

Juniper held out her hands to him and Lilianna knew she was hoping for him to come back from the edge on his own, but Xan was taking too long. Pushing past Juniper, Lilianna discarded the cautionary approach and voiced her shame instead. "Xan, think about what you've done."

Juniper exhaled loudly, dropping her arms in defeat.

Xan caught Lilianna's eyes for a fleeting moment and must have seen her horror, must have realised he had lost her respect. She hoped that in the mortification so evident in her tone and in her stance, he would feel it too.

Xan dropped the dagger and backed away, leaving Lilianna to tend to the Valkor's injuries. "I'm so sorry," she whispered to the Valkor. "He's not himself. He's not normally like this."

"He's slaughtered everyone on this ship." The Valkor's voice was stripped raw and stricken with grief. "My friends…they're all dead." A trembling hand wiped across sapphire eyes dotted with flecks of pink. Tears made them brighter, a contrast in melancholic symbolism. Moving his large hand through already dishevelled auburn locks, it grazed across his cheek and smeared blood underneath his chin as he settled on his shoulder, pushing inward to stem the wound.

Lilianna wrapped his uninjured arm around her shoulders and helped him stand. "What's your name?"

His voice still weak with fear. "Dallis."

They turned away from Xan and Juniper and walked away together. "Let's get you patched up, Dallis. Come with me."

JUNIPER
24 YEARS OLD

Juniper thrust herself forward and caught Xan as he crumpled into her arms. He was silent, his stare vacant. She placed her hands on his cheeks and whispered, "Honey, it's okay. I've got you. I've always got you."

Xan's eyes shimmered, but he was still not quite there. Juniper pushed his head into her chest and let him remain as close to her heart as she would allow.

Lilianna was speaking in hushed tones with the injured Valkor and helping him to stand. Juniper couldn't believe what shit Lilianna had just pulled.

Firstly, bitch, don't push past me when I have things handled.

Secondly, handling a delicate situation by evoking self-hatred and shame in the affected person is a terrible long-term strategy.

Thirdly, great idea to discard your friend for a piece of shit Valkor you've known for three seconds.

Fourthly, fuck you times thirty-seven.

Juniper did her best to focus on Xan's comfort and squash her momentary hatred of Lilianna into a tiny puff of air that she could breathe out and forget ever existed. But she knew it wouldn't be easy and she'd need to teach that judgemental little bitch a lesson.

"Massy," Juniper yelled across the cavernous control centre. "Ready the *Attenborough*. It's time to get out of here."

By then, crews from a fleet of D-230s had gathered, staring dumbfounded at Xan and the injured Valkor who was using Lilianna to walk.

Juniper bellowed, "What the fuck are you idiots gawking at? Get this injured Valkor onto one of the D-230s over there." The little insect minions finally started moving.

She turned to Ryker. "Ryker, c'mon, buddy. We need you to do more than just stand here gaping at the world. Go and help Lilianna now, hurry up."

Ryker fixed his jaw with a quick snap and stumbled on boots that seemed far too big for him, but with purpose he arrived next to Lilianna, helping to shoulder the load of the Valkor, an extinct species that wasn't so extinct anymore.

When the world was quiet and Juniper and Xan were alone, she felt his tears slide down the curves of her neck. She had seen him in every position imaginable but never like this. He had done this for her before – held her as she broke. But Juniper never envisioned a moment where she would go against her true nature and be the one giving comfort.

The bizarre thing was, she didn't mind. Although it wasn't something that formed part of her everyday, in grave circumstances her heart thawed, and it beat for the right person, an illusion of someone who knew how to love.

The chill in her heart thrummed throughout her entire body. Plunging downwards, she felt that pang of disappointment in Lilianna. Although the Sytheract girl was clearly smitten with Xan, at the first sign of darkness she had turned away, feigning concern for a Valkor she hardly knew so she didn't have to confront something real.

Considering she was meant to be the compassionate one, it didn't sit right. As the silence between her and Xan grew like a cloud of vapour across a desolate plain, she knew she had to speak to Lilianna. Sometimes lessons learned were grains of sand accumulating upon the dunes of the world, but other times they were a desert storm.

CHAPTER 16

Juniper stood at the counter with Xan. They had farewelled Lilianna, much to Juniper's disappointment, but fate had provided a perfect opportunity for her and Xan to share yet another first together.

"For your first night, I think we should transfer some extra credits and get the premium level," Juniper said.

Xan was already beyond excited at being at Fusion. The stories Juniper told him made him react more often than not and he wanted a chance to experience it for himself.

On the premium level, the lights were dim, veiled in a violet hue. Slivers of white light spun inside the main area like dying stars caught beside a black hole. Flashes of skin caught Xan's eye and his pulse quickened. Even in the main bar, people were deep in the throes of passion. He scanned the expansive area; a circular bar in the middle of the room held a collection of scantily clad bartenders, strippers hung from poles reaching up into the high ceiling, flinging neon lingerie to people waiting for drinks. A steady beat pulsed filling up the room, creating a giddy atmosphere, thick with energy and joy.

It was music Xan didn't care for; computerised junk composed by algorithm most likely. But then again, not many people were brought up on Earth knowing what music with emotion was, and what memories it could evoke. Here, though, Gemarinians made their own memories with flailing limbs and sordid flesh.

Large screens displayed paintings and frescoes from Earth, murals of beings entangled in rapture. It was an odd choice, a contrast to all the clean lines and the modern feel of the rest of the room.

"So, this is Fusion, Xan." Juniper extended her arms and twirled around twice. She was a floating oar lost in a sea of naked bodies. Although she had yet to derobe, she was still the most dazzling thing in the room.

She continued to walk backwards through the throng of gathered evening participants to the bar, as Xan smiled and looked around to find a seat for them both.

Juniper came back with two strong drinks. She sat beside him and handed over a tall, frosted glass. Beads of condensation carefully caressed its sides, sliding tentatively toward his fingers curled around its girth.

"Cheers to us, love." Xan watched her take a sip of her drink – the way her lips perfectly formed around the rim of the glass made his heart race; her eyes boring into his were diamond studs drilling into the weight of expectation surrounding the evening. Xan shifted his body closer to hers, feeling the hum of electricity buzzing between them. He wanted nothing more than to take her then and there, but he refrained. Instead, he casually sipped at his drink, tasting the fresh botanicals of mint with a hint of lavender and the comforting embrace of berries. The aftertaste of chilli hinted at a scorching evening ahead.

"I bought this for you, too. It's on me, if you want to indulge." She held out a dull orange pill with raised eyebrows and a smirk that dared Xan to resist.

"Is that the..."

"Only the best enhancements for you, my birthday boy." She shuffled closer, placing a hand on the inside of his leg. Immediately his skin sizzled.

Xan was wary of the pill; he hadn't had one before and didn't know what to expect from enhancements. But one couldn't buy better with the money Juniper would have spent.

This one, according to her, would be able to mirror her pleasure receptors and send them back through his body so he could feel double the pleasure. It was a linking device of nanotech bio transceivers that allowed for neural chemical changes.

He didn't answer, unsure of taking substances cultivated in a lab.

"Listen, I know you. I'll be with you the whole time. Just finish this drink and see how you feel. If you don't want it, we can save it for another time." Her smile was as easy as her tone: casual, confident in her own skin.

She stopped staring into Xan and leant back, basking in the scene before them. Her hand remained on his leg. He gazed around; one of the strippers was now straddling a bartender as he poured drinks for customers. Pink light flashed on her bare breasts and the bartender's forked tongue curled around her erect nipples.

Juniper's hand moved slightly higher and squeezed the rippling muscles in Xan's thigh. They each took a swig of their drinks as they surveyed the room around them. His eyes lingered on the far-right corner where an Aranther was fastened to a circular spinning wheel. His hands, feet and neck were bound and he was completely naked. One Human male knelt in front of him, pleasuring him in his mouth, while a Sytheract male and a female prodded him with mild laser batons on his rear and around his nipples.

Juniper moved her hand further up Xan's thigh and massaged the bulge between his legs, indicating a yearning for more. Xan tore his eyes away from the scene in the corner and fixed upon her instead as she bit her bottom lip. He had felt those lips over every inch of his body throughout the past several years, but with the violet light mixed with the sultry dark shade of her lipstick, he couldn't deny himself any longer.

He forcefully grabbed the back of her neck, his fingers digging into a knot of her purple hair. She gasped and winced before closing her eyes and producing a wicked smile. She loved that, just as he loved to exert his command over her. There was something about their sexual dynamic that transcended regular life. On the battlefield, she annihilated anyone who dared approach her. But in the kingdom housing their bodies, Xan was king and he would ravage her.

He rewarded her by pulling her close, skin to skin, and kissing her as if he were descending into a crater thick with lava, bubbling to an eruption. She drew back and licked her lips, savouring his sweetness.

"Give me the fucking pill, Juniper," Xan commanded, his voice low and raspy. He watched in anticipation as she reached down and drew out two orange pills. Xan went to pick one up, but she pulled back, wagging a finger at him.

"No, no, no, you naughty boy."

Xan's heart pounded against his chest. She liked to play around with control, but she would be dominated tonight and he needed her to know that.

"I want the fucking pill now." He tightened his grip on her hair. Her wilful smile widened and her appetite for him grew wilder.

"Okay, sir." But defiance shone like a spotlight in her eyes. Xan loosened his grip and before he knew what was happening, she placed both pills in her mouth and sipped her drink. A smug smile scarred the beauty of her face.

"What the fuck," Xan started, but she grabbed his jaw and squeezed it, forcing it open, then she stood and straddled his lap, spitting one pill and the drink slowly into his mouth.

They swallowed and she flicked her tongue against his, teasing him, then drew back slightly. With a smirk, she unzipped her top and exposed her breasts, pushing them toward his face. Xan opened his mouth hungrily, softly scraping his teeth against her nipples in the way he knew drove her wild. She groaned against his ear and the sound spurred him further, devouring the flavour of her, savouring the shuddering vibrations she involuntarily produced.

"See how that guy is fucking her?" she whispered, nibbling on his earlobe. "Do you want to fuck me like that?"

Xan could hardly think straight as he focused his gaze on the couple in the corner. The Sytheract female's blonde bob swayed across her shoulders as the man's muscles rippled under his dark skin, aggressively taking her from behind. Her red lipstick was smudged across her cheeks. Mascara trailed underneath both hazel eyes. "Yes," he breathed. That was exactly what he wanted to do to her.

Juniper pushed him back onto the couch and left him there alone as she sauntered up to the couple. Xan watched with renewed desire as Juniper approached the female first, cautious but amorous. Her guiding hand twirling around the Sytheract's areolas while the aggressive thrusts of the male behind jerked her body forward. As the female licked her bottom lip, a sign for Juniper to continue, she grabbed her blonde hair and shoved her tongue into a mouth salivating for the beauty before her. The man's look of ecstasy intensified and Juniper turned her attention to him. She stalked slowly around the blonde Sytheract, taking in his strong arms gripping the folds of her silky skin. Moisture glistened on them both as he drove deep inside her. Juniper licked her lips and launched herself at his mouth. Fighting against his tongue, Juniper grabbed his occupied hand and diverted his attention to her wetness, making sure Xan could see it all.

Juniper said something to them that Xan couldn't hear over the thumping bass drum, amidst the sawtooth synths, then watched as the three of them returned to where he sat.

Juniper inched her bodysuit down until it was a puddle on the floor and leisurely bent forward, placing her hands on the back of the couch on either side of Xan's head. Her breasts were level with his mouth and he took no time in unleashing his tongue across the right nipple, sucking with low intensity. As the man entered her from behind, Juniper shuddered, then Xan's lips shifted to her left nipple, erect as if begging to be examined by his tongue. Hands unzipped his pants and he looked down at the blonde Sytheract beside him on the couch, leaning over and fighting to take his considerable length in her mouth. He groaned as he bumped the back of her throat. She was a good girl, it seemed.

The orange pills took their effect and Xan began to feel every ripple of ecstasy coursing through Juniper as the man drilled harder and deeper, heightening her sensations. Juniper repositioned her grip from the back of the couch shifting to Xan's right thigh and bent over more, allowing the man behind her to reach new depths. Juniper's eyes never left Xan's as if daring him to reach out and claim her.

The blonde female wiped her mouth as she rose off the couch, her hungry gaze finding Xan's. He was teetering between wanting to accept Juniper's dare in a display of rough dominance or allow the blonde to finish what she started. Xan no longer had a choice, as she positioned herself on top of him, letting her forehead rest against his as he settled into her. Their lips found one another's like rolling waves disappearing beneath a promontory. As she rocked her hips back and forth, grinding him further into her, Xan gently cupped her breasts until his fingers came to a point, teasing her nipple. She kissed him, moaning into his mouth as sweat danced off her and he absorbed it into his body.

Juniper appeared not to appreciate the lacklustre energy the blonde had for Xan, so she grabbed the Sytheract by her shoulders and assisted her until she convulsed, reaching her peak. Before the blonde caught her breath or could even say farewell, an Aranther male and the dark-skinned man carried her off to another section of the room to entertain each other.

Xan focused his attention back on Juniper and twisted her hair in a fist, pulling her up for a punishing kiss. She dug her nails into his back and asked, "Did you like seeing him inside me, Xan?"

He ignored her taunts and pushed her down onto the couch. She continued, "I loved having another man inside me, you know."

Xan slapped her across the face, a faint red mark smeared across her cheek. Satisfaction burned within him as she smiled, knowing the deviant inside her craved this treatment.

"Spread your legs for me," he commanded, his voice deep and gruff.

Instead of obeying, she looked at him with defiance and he knew he'd have to be more forceful. He brought his face against hers then whispered into her ear, "I'll show you what it's like to have a real man inside you. Now spread your legs."

Her breathing hitched at his words and desire reflected in her eyes as she spread wide, her fingers pointing to where she wanted him. "Show me, sir."

As he entered, Juniper winced, grasping his back and pulling him close. Her hips surged forward and her nails raked against his spine. A silent plea for him to go harder, faster. Xan gasped at the pain, then held a hand against her throat as he met her demands, giving her what she begged for.

Juniper grunted into his open mouth with each thrust, as the orange pill fizzed and ignited throughout their bodies. The nerves infused and twisted inside them, sending shock pulses to their pleasure centres and rocketing to all the outer fibres of their bodies. Soon, they both could not contain their cries of raw pleasure as raptures of ecstasy drew broad and defined strokes on a pure white canvas, aching for colour.

The plethora of different species at Fusion flanked them, hands from all kinds squeezed and groped Juniper, while fingers explored Xan's body. Strong hands caressed muscles that strained as he took up residence and became landlord in Juniper's pleasure house. Despite the limbs splayed around them and the lips and tongues that brushed against them, they only had eyes for one another in that moment.

Juniper tightened her arms around Xan and brought him flush against her. Their bodies were clad in primal desire, slick with sweat. Her eyes bore into him as she pressed her forehead to his, her mouth open, crying out frantically, as she ground her hips against his, allowing him to hurt her, to break through the barrier to erupting.

Juniper started to come undone as her legs twitched beneath him and her eyes rolled. He fought to concentrate on holding back but the pill threw her pleasure right back into him and he was losing control.

The walls crumbled as Juniper begged for him to fill her. She started to convulse, followed by a guttural scream of intense satisfaction. He held her tighter as her pleasure shot through him then immediately was a master of his bodily functions no longer, releasing into her with a beastly roar.

Xan and Juniper lay motionless, breathing heavily as bodies writhed beside them. He opened his eyes, waiting to see the hazy jade in her stare. Juniper's eyes might have betrayed her as they appeared to twinkle with adoration. She reached out and kissed him, almost to confirm it. He kissed her back, more forcefully than he should have. Sometimes it was hard for him to forget love; to remember that she didn't subscribe to that.

Xan carefully helped her to her feet and they both swayed, light-headed and weak at the knees. They pushed through endless bodies to the shower level, giggling with one another and unable to say anything of value.

As they shared a shower, he washed her back, kissing her neck delicately.

"See how the intensity is different here?" she called over her shoulder.

"You're right," he breathed into her ear.

"That's why I keep coming back."

Xan laughed warmly. He wasn't jealous she had these moments with strangers, but a part of him wanted her to say something more.

Juniper turned to face him and moved so that the haze in her eyes blended into the steam that crawled around their faces. She was up against him now.

"Don't let this fuck with you, but…" She briefly avoided his gaze, the internal debate rife within her. "That was an intensity I have never felt before." She kissed him quickly on the cheek. "I'm glad it was with you."

Juniper spun back around and flicked her hair into his face. "Now, wash my hair, bitch. Thank you."

Xan smiled. It didn't fuck with his head but it fucked with his heart just a little bit.

CHAPTER 17

LOCATION: THE ATTENBOROUGH
YEAR: 118
XAN – 24 YEARS OLD

The *Attenborough* felt empty to Xan, or was the emptiness that spread out inside of him all encompassing? Although Massy was there at the controls, ranting and raving to fill the void of awkwardness, it didn't soothe, it merely disguised Xan's aching heart.

He turned to his left at the place now vacant and wondered where Qilin was. Whether he would be able to save her. Xan didn't know life without her; his footsteps were hers and their hearts beat as one.

The anger had subsided and there was now the reality of what he had done in response to such loss. He wore a robe covering his chest and abdominals, stained with the blood of faceless beings he had slaughtered without reason, without mercy.

Xan shuddered from the cold in the ship, but also with the memory of splitting flesh, of cries of anguish, of begging, of tasting the blood on his tongue as it spurt onto his face, eyes wide with searing rage. Shaking his head, he fought the onset of throwing up, but it made Juniper stir just above him. Her hand was resting on his shoulder as she conversed with Ryker, but she must have noticed Xan's movements and bent down.

"Hey, love, how are you feeling?"

His voice croaked. It was frail like the dust that collected on a windowsill waiting to be brushed away. "Juniper, fuck, I'm so sorry, I am—"

"Don't you apologise to me, Xan. I know you. I know this was something else entirely." Her loyalty was forged by the ceaselessness of time, and it was so evidently strong in the defined beat of her song.

"I don't know where it came from, but also, I don't know what to do – with the Valkor situation and with living with what I've just done." There was a desperation in his voice, seeking wisdom from a hardened warrior who had blood on more than her hands.

"There is no choice, Xan. We'll do as he says. We'll meet him and we will get her back. Regardless of the lie I think he tells, I seek the truth of your heart, and it's no secret that Qilin is your truth." Her eyes became unfocused as if a memory clouded the skies of the present. "If we don't find her then you might remain broken and I won't have that." Juniper's body tensed with defensive aggression.

He smiled. The pieces slowly shifted closer to the whole. "Honestly, thank you. After all these years, you still surprise me."

Juniper smiled back with that strength behind everything she did. "I'm going to get a hydration bottle for us, just to give us a little bit more pep after all that bullshit." Juniper patted him on the shoulder and set off toward Massy, who was singing a traditional folk ballad from the Animus region of Dracia.

LILIANNA
22 YEARS OLD

Lilianna sat with Dallis, the injured Valkor, as he was attended to by a medic bot. Ryker sat in the corner, arms crossed and glum.

"Lilianna, can we have a quick chat, please?" Juniper smiled sweetly, flicking her long eyelashes like large nets cast into the ether to pull her in.

Lilianna was wary. Juniper didn't usually put on that voice unless there was something wrong. *I wonder how Xan is.*

"Where are your quarters?"

"Just down the hall here, I—"

"Let's go there," Juniper said flatly.

Their footsteps tinkered along the grey floor, Juniper's dominant and purposeful, while Lilianna's were tentative and careful. The lack of conversation made Lilianna sweat.

The door opened and they walked in, and as the door shut, Juniper faced up to Lilianna who immediately backed up against the door.

"How would you describe yourself?" Juniper asked casually, but without letting her move.

"Um, what's this about, Juniper?" Her shoulders sagged, her hands twitching with nerves.

"Answer the question."

"I don't know. Why are you treating me like one of your crew?"

"Oh, the crew I no longer have anymore because they were all slaughtered by one of your buddies in there?"

"He didn't do—"

"Were you fucking there, Lili?" Her voice was a cannon blast. "Did you see how many of them came in and tortured me, cut me, tried to drown me. Oh, and then gutted Serarra right in front of me, bleeding, crying, screaming for me to save her."

Lilianna stared at the ground and didn't say anything.

"I didn't think so." Her now calm voice was tinged with frustration.

"Now, since you can't answer that question, I want you to be truthful with me. What does Xan mean to you?"

Lilianna raised her eyebrows at Juniper and fidgeted in her stance. Juniper's arms were crossed over her chest and she pouted, waiting for a reply.

Lilianna's eyes moved to the floor again and her hand reached up to tuck a strand of hair behind her ears.

"Well, it's hard to really talk about that out loud. I've never discussed how I feel about him with anyone."

Juniper relaxed her arms and they fell by her sides. She walked across the room to the bedside table and flicked through some crystals Lilianna had collected. Juniper must have figured the open space might allow Lilianna's feelings to flow.

"It's difficult, I suppose, if you haven't really…admitted things to yourself."

As Juniper's back was turned, Lilianna spoke. "I…I guess I feel a great deal for him."

"Yes, that much is obvious, go on."

Lilianna's heart rate was high and the hammering in her chest vibrated all the way through to her temples. "I don't know."

"Lilianna, one thing you know about me is that I'm not jealous. I'm not bound to anyone by love or affection. I don't talk with the language of the heart so pour your feelings across this floor – it certainly won't change how I feel about you."

Lilianna was still unsure about pouring out her deepest emotional secrets to the most emotionless being in the galaxy. "I guess, I guess I feel very strongly for him. I might say that I…that I…love him."

Juniper walked toward Lilianna once more. "Interesting." The tone in her voice suggested condescension and the gleam of her eyes hinted at something sinister. "Everything I've ever read about love talks about it being unconditional, being deep and divine and transcendent."

"I guess so." Lilianna's heart was flapping like neonate wings against the squall.

"If that's the case, why the fuck did you turn away the very moment you saw darkness in him?" Juniper's voice was suddenly intense and powerful.

Lilianna backed away, shrinking against the wall. "I didn't turn away from him, I—"

"Don't you bullshit me, Lilianna." Juniper levelled a finger at her. "You got fucking scared seeing him like that and you tried to cover it up by feigning you cared for this Valkor."

Lilianna's hands started to shake. "I was scared, I'm sorry…I've never seen him like that." Tears began to fall.

Juniper immediately reached out and held her close. Lilianna resisted for the briefest of moments, then allowed herself to be held. Juniper's open palms reached up toward the sides of Lilianna's cheeks, and she pressed their foreheads together.

Juniper's voice was a stray droplet after a heavy downpour. "I'm sorry you were scared. But if you love him. Truly love him. You embrace the light, you embrace the darkness, you heal his pain, you protect him from stones cast – you *don't* turn away at the first sign that he is a flawed being." Juniper's stare was a warning. "That is not okay."

Lilianna broke the stare, casting her gaze downwards. "I'm sorry, I'm not as strong as you." Her gaze returned, aiming a pleading look from the golden orbs of her eyes into Juniper. "Help me to be stronger."

"Why do you think I'm here, honey?"

Lilianna let Juniper brush her hair back from her eyes and not for the first time, she was conflicted about how Juniper made her feel.

"Listen, if you say you love him, then you need to accept this darkness. Step up, Lili. Gather yourself but step up really soon. You're better than this."

Juniper opened the door and walked out, leaving Lilianna to take a deep breath in as her hands continue to shake.

JUNIPER
24 YEARS OLD

As Juniper walked past the mediroom, grabbing the hydration bottles and heading toward Xan, realisation dawned that if she knew so much about love to lecture someone else about it, then maybe she did have a heart. Maybe she did feel love for Xan. But it wasn't Earth love or any traditional love; it was her own version. It scared her to acknowledge it. To acknowledge it made it real.

Her status as a war hero would now be tainted. The crew she was tasked with training were all dead. The purpose she lived for and thrived upon was wrenched from her. The thing she buried inside her now crawled to the surface, cracking through glaciers built to withstand torrid summer days. But now the heat was too stark to ignore.

CHAPTER 18

LOCATION: GEMARINE
YEAR: 108 (10 YEARS AGO)
XAN – 14 YEARS OLD

Qilin padded ahead of Xan as they approached the outer edge of the forest. The thick wall of black and twisted trees thinned out, and the ground had turned a viscous mud underfoot, until dry, barren land stretched out before them. Red sand swirled in the tiniest breeze, settling as dust on their boots and paws; an imprint of an ancient moment guiding them on.

The city lights looked dazzling from where they stood, but the unyielding landscape beckoned them to cross with a devious smile. Xan's legs were heavy in the sand, while Qilin danced and flitted her spikey tail at lizard-like creatures that scurried off at the sight of anyone larger than themselves, their scales iridescent in the waning light of both moons.

Xan was sure that travelling in the evening would be a better idea, but the cold soon turned bitter, leaching into his soul and extracting all hope from within. Magnificent and formidable statues loomed ahead and as he trudged closer, he laid eyes upon a large head, separated from the body, half cracked and in pieces buried in the sand. The body was immense, power in their presence and confidence in their stance. Crystalline necklaces trailed down in beads to hands that held gemstones depicted with a glowing aura in chiselled stone.

Xan searched the horizon bathed in the dusty red haze enveloping other statues that had succeeded in withstanding the elements and the punishing hands of time. However, as the cold continued to worsen, he knew he needed to stop for the evening. So, against the feet of the first statue he lay, Qilin curled up next to him. A fitful sleep ensued and dreams of these beings materialised in his mind, when they thrived on this world many moons ago.

The city gates were there in front of him, and he stumbled the last few metres and dropped to his knees in the sand. Xan's cheeks were grimy with dirt, chest heaving from exhaustion. He called out as loud as he could, but it came out like the last bit of moisture wrought from a vine – so feeble and small. "Help me!"

Qilin sat by his side waiting patiently, even licking his cheek to give him comfort. Xan was truly spent. The sand blowing around his face, seeping into each and every orifice, his lips worn and cracked, blistered from the heat of the day and the dry chill at night. His voice rang out again, hoarse in the swirling wind. A camera squeaked, a hydraulic hissed. An acknowledgement of life on the other side.

"Please, let me in," he cried desperately. "My name is Xan Au, I was meant to come here days ago but my ship crashed!"

The silence clung to him like the torn shreds of his bodysuit. Then after some time had passed hearing nothing but the beating of Qilin's loyal heart, a high-pitched alarm pulsed and the refined white gates began to peel back. Beaming lights punctured through the expanding cracks, silhouetting several beings in bulky costumes. Xan flicked his arm up, shielding his eyes, and squinted at the fluorescent artificial light dilating his pupils. Qilin flexed, standing at the ready, waiting to defend him. But as the sentient shadows slithered into the light – no longer faceless beings – a robotic voice spoke calmly through a loudspeaker overhead.

`"No need to fear, Xan Au, Child of Earth."`

The reassuring words spoken by a calm female AI voice echoed in his head. Black tore across those blinding lights and consumed him. His body relinquished the fear and fear was all that was driving him.

He felt hot and cold in random bursts underneath his skin. Vision hazy, he smelt lavender and pine, even tasted hints of it at the back of his throat. It wasn't dry anymore, though; groggy as he was, he felt almost refreshed. Spherical nodes were notched across parts of his battered body as he lay on a clean, fresh white cot. There were little transparent casings that kept him boxed in, presumably to stop him from rolling onto the sparkly floor and sullying the pristine medical environment.

As the transparent casing lowered slowly, a robotic hand prodded his flesh, testing his human malleability. The robot appeared to be satisfied, as it turned and zipped across the waxed floor on squeaky wheels to gather something. Xan groaned as he attempted to sit up, trying to get a glance of what it was. Squeaky's body swivelled unnaturally, its head lingering in the opposite direction as it rolled right back to him. Beads of pixels for eyes, white as frothy cream. Metallic pincer-hands held a small piece of food. A chewy, gelatinous ball was shoved into his mouth. Xan had read about these in his induction material, so he accepted the 'food', but before he had a chance to eat on his own, the robot's hands seized his jaw in a strong grip and clamped up and down to initiate mastication.

`"Swallow, please."` It started to repeat the instruction and, with what Xan could imagine was a worried expression on his own face, he finally relented and swallowed the chew.

As soon as Xan showed evidence of swallowing the robot moved to the electrode readings on a holo screen in the corner of the room.

Everything was white. So blinding, intensely white. Like innocence herself had taken a big sparkling dump on every square inch of the room. Xan sat bolt upright and yelled, "Qilin, where the fuck is—"

A cape fluttered around a slender woman as she burst into the room. "Whoa, whoa, my dear child." She came to a halt at his bedside and reached out to rub Xan's back. A tuft of grey hair like the crest of a wave broke atop her head. She strained through a smile depicting warmth like one of those old videos of a fireplace. It wasn't actually warmth, just a facade. It didn't give Xan comfort at all.

"Where is the creature I came in here with?"

She bent down so she was eye level with him, hand now on his shoulder.

"Xan, isn't it?" she asked curiously.

"Yes." He nodded, realising his hands were shaking.

"You've been through a lot and no doubt that creature being around may have—"

Xan didn't let her finish. "I don't know who you are or what you did with her. But we are a package deal. If she isn't brought to me within five minutes, I'm leaving…whatever this place is."

The woman laughed, and it wasn't kind. She yanked her hand away from his shoulder. "My dear child, I have not been spoken to like that in quite a while." Her face was hard, cheeks taut. "I am Madame Bleu. I'm sure you've heard of me in your induction material."

Xan swallowed and felt a pang of regret and embarrassment. But then remembered why he had spoken to her that way and chose not to back down. "Look, I apologise for my…shouting, but I have not had the 'induction' I had hoped for and as I said, my creature friend is gone and I want her back with me."

"Very well." Madame Bleu stepped back from his bedside and spoke into her MPD. "Bring in the creature. Do it quickly," she demanded with impatience as she tapped her foot on the crisp surface. "Just warning you, Xan, she had to be sedated."

Xan went to object to Qilin's treatment, but she held up a hand and a scowl creased her face, making her, for the first time, look old. "Mind your manners, boy. Do not interrupt me again." Her words were spoken slowly and quietly.

Silence consumed him, his heart hammered as he recognised that the warmth was no longer even a masquerade. She was not gentle or compassionate and he knew then, he would need to keep his guard up around her.

Someone entered the room. A species he hadn't seen before carried a cage, and inside the cage was Qilin, sleeping peacefully. He wondered though, if she had been feeling serenity as they sedated her. *Doubtful.* The cage was placed at the foot of the bed and the bizarre-looking…guy… departed with a dutiful bow. Madame Bleu hardly even acknowledged his presence.

"As you can see, your creature is perfectly unharmed." She gestured with her hands, exaggerating the formality by twisting her wrists. "We can discuss at a further point in time, after your recovery, just how we will communicate to the Gemarine community that a *Mika Tikaani* will be the pet of a young Human." She scoffed. "Preposterous. But I suppose you, Xan, have already won the hearts of the Gemarinians out there by surviving the dangerous trek from the Wilds into Topaz City. Quite the story." She raised her eyebrows in amused admiration.

"I'd appreciate your support in this matter." Xan made sure his manners were a little more refined this time.

Madame Bleu clapped her hands, startling Xan. "I digress." Her mouth formed a smile once more and her eyes twinkled with a plan about to take place. "Now, to ensure you will find Gemarine a…hospitable place. I've assigned you a guide, if you will. She will introduce you to your clan, help settle you into your level, and just be on hand to teach you all the nuances of this culture."

Xan was excited now, itching to explore what the city had to offer, to really experience his new life. "That's great to hear." He spoke with as much appreciation his tired voice could muster. "When will I meet her?"

She flashed her teeth and dialled her MPD. "Oh, Miss Juniper, would you mind coming in now? Thanks so much." Madame Bleu's voice was sweeter than innocence herself.

CHAPTER 19

LOCATION: GEMARINE
YEAR: 118
XAN – 24 YEARS OLD

Xan was the first off the *Attenborough*. Boots thumped down the ramp, as a despondent shadow loomed behind him, waiting to pounce. *But it's already pounced. It's become me.* Now it just waited as an extension of himself until he would call upon it once more to do his bidding. *Sometimes love makes us turn to violence. Sometimes we must shed our skin and use it as protection, so no harm is done. Sometimes we must fight and maim and obliterate so the lesson is learned and the things we love are safe. Sometimes you only learn this when something you love is taken away.*

The greeting he received was not as he expected. Bots, hulking and rusted, scanned him for a plethora of diseases – flashing lasers into his downcast eyes, metallic probes scratching against his blood-caked skin. Gemarinians in masks and bio suits appeared, guiding him forcefully by his slackened arms, leading him away to where Madame Bleu would be, scolding and judgemental.

He looked over his shoulder, glimpsing the rest of the crew going through the very same treatment. Before Xan could register the next move, he was thrust into a room and the masked crew slammed the door shut.

Red pulses flashed in a steady rhythm like an alarm; always a negative connotation. Robotic arms shot down from the ceiling, scratching and ripping off his clothes. Now naked and without another garment in sight, liquid sprayed down from the ceiling. He licked his lips and tasted antiseptic; the manufactured quality of sterility. It was bitter and putrid and it made him gag.

The rough treatment lasted only a minute, but he was knocked around like a boulder in a quakestorm. A green light thrummed across the floor and a voice strained with zeros and ones instructed him, "Follow the green beam into the next containment area."

One foot in front of the next; the rigmarole ensued as his memories burned hotter than the lasers that pierced his eyes. Lives he had wasted in pursuit of vengeance, lives that meant nothing as fury obfuscated all reason. Was it love that made him repent now? Or was love just the masquerade of malice? He reached for the drab grey garments made from vegetable waste, folded in a pile on the floor. It was a level-based outfit that Gemarinians sometimes wore in the comfort of their own surroundings. Xan put them on. They were ill-fitting and loose, light and scratchy on the skin. The skin that housed the heart of a broken man without his companion. He breathed in deep.

Mine is not the heart of a monster, I will atone for this. But I won't let any man or creature take from me again. I know now what I must never do again, but it should be clear to those who may take from me in the future. Don't cross me.

Xan pushed the bright blue button on the door in front of him and walked into a spacious area, goosebumps materialising on his skin – an artificial cold hummed gently from frosty air vents. Mirrored glass was ahead of him, and sooner or later the person who organised this whole charade would be smarting on the other side, tapping her foot with impatience.

There were circular seating pods positioned haphazardly around the area and he chose one to sit upon, twiddling his thumbs on the edge of the cushioned seat, waiting for something to happen. *This is fucking overkill.* Annoyance flowed like a turbulent river throughout his body. There was a ticking clock in his mind, the clock that counted down to the death of his creature companion. Reprimands were cause and effect and if everything the Valkor said turned out to be true, why should he care what Madame Bleu had to say? All he would care about was what he thought of himself. But the ticking clock was incessant and instead of reprimands, regrets and righting wrongs – he would concentrate on healing himself once Qilin was back in his arms.

A door opened behind him and Lilianna walked through, golden eyes dulled with disillusionment. Shuffling across the space to a pod close by, her shoulders were sagged and her voice was timid and restrained.

"These clothes, hey?" She pinched the oversized shirt and let it flow back, smiling politely.

"They aren't the nicest against our skin. Maybe an Aranther would deal with them better, with their tough skin, but certainly not our kind."

Massy burst through the door. "Our kind? Don't let them hear you speak with separatist views."

"That's not what he meant, Massy. You weren't here for context," Lilianna said crossly as she plonked down onto a pod, glancing at Xan sheepishly.

"Are you on a propaganda campaign for Gemarine or something, Massy?" Juniper yelled from across the other side of the room, her black hair loose, curls of vibrant purple bouncing either side of her prominent cheek bones.

Xan still hadn't acknowledged anyone; it seemed they were all trying to pretend as if nothing had happened, carrying on without addressing it. It worked better for him, although he noticed Lilianna look at Juniper and make an obvious show of getting up and moving to the pod right next to him to cover the empty space between them.

"Oh God, spare me your bullshit. I'm just warning my boss not to get himself into hot water," Massy reasoned, settling onto a pod furthest from Juniper.

Ryker entered the room. "More hot water than we're already in?" Judgemental eyes levelled at Xan, as if imploring him to explain why he put the whole crew in such danger.

Lilianna stood, stepping in front of him. "Ryker, you knew the stakes." Her eyes hovered over Xan's, as if wanting to impress him with her protective nature. Xan just breathed in deep and massaged his temples with rigid fingers.

"Massy and I didn't know we'd be sending rescue ships to...to a slaughterhouse." Ryker's eyes welled.

Xan recognised the emotion in Ryker's eyes because he knew Ryker looked up to him. Revered his calm, calculating mind under pressure and thought him to be a fair leader.

But it was clear that he felt betrayed. Xan stood up and moved past Lilianna toward Ryker, but he backed away, dark hair hanging low, shadowing the tears in his eyes desperately seeking to be unshackled. It was as he imagined Lilianna might be, if he reached out to her too. The change in her was evident, albeit masked by a counterfeit performance of civility, he smelt her fear as she hovered nervously as if not knowing whether to squeeze his shoulder or kick him in the balls and run.

Juniper and Massy were debating something, but Xan made a conscious effort to address Ryker in hushed tones so that even Lilianna couldn't hear him.

"Listen, mate," he whispered. "I'm really sorry. I lost control."

Ryker's voice wavered. "You never lose control, Xan. That's not your thing. That's why I...work for you." He swept his hair across the top of his head in the way he always did, but his eyes were on display now and it was difficult for Xan to take in Ryker's judgement without self-disappointment hampering him once more.

"I did in this instance and there are many things that I would change if I could. It was not a reaction I expected to have." Xan sighed and scratched his shoulder absent-mindedly. "I want to do better and I will figure out a way to manage myself when the people I love are threatened."

"I just don't know what to say. It hurts when a mentor falls over." His voice was freshly fallen snow, delicate but bitterly cold.

Xan felt that sting, but instead of backing down he stood taller. "Perfection is something we seek too frequently, and it is a cloud that obfuscates our ability to accept the self. It pushes us to be something we're not, to raise expectations so we're always striving but never appreciating what we have accomplished. I am not that. I am flawed and I accept this. In fact, I accept you for your flaws and I have never, ever judged you."

Ryker's gaze moved to his bare feet.

Xan's voice changed from mild disappointment to an assertive command. "Next time I fall over, I expect you to be the first to offer your hand to help me up."

He moved away, leaving Ryker fumbling with his fingers, evidently contemplating his ability to exist without the need to judge. He huffed and slunk into the chair furthest away from everyone.

Xan was upset at himself for showing such weakness, but if the regret seeped throughout his blood, he would die from an internal wound. He needed to take lessons from Juniper and build from disappointment, build from hardship and redefine himself.

He felt Lilianna hovering beside him. "Have you come to share your disappointment in me too?"

She picked at her fingernails and was about to speak when the reflective glass screen faded, revealing Madame Bleu standing there, weathered lines carved into a face sheathed in a woody scowl, peppered with wisdom and ruthlessness. At the sight of her, Xan's heart recoiled. She had destroyed the lives of so many. Eradicated entire planets, if the Valkor were to be believed. In that moment, he hated being so close to her.

152

"I don't know where to begin with you all. But I shall expect that, Xan, since you crafted this rescue mission, you will be the one to provide me with the information I seek." Her hair was a perfectly sculpted light blue puff like an immobile cloud.

Xan cleared his throat. "Madame, I can tell you with all authority that the rest of the members in this room played no part in this. I acted alone and—"

"It was actually at my request that Xan used his resources to come and find me." Xan whipped his head around as Juniper interrupted from the back of the room. "I was worried for my crew and I thought that calling someone I trusted might ensure their safety." She now stood in front of her seating pod, shoulders squared, a slight kink in her left knee, looking as relaxed as she dared.

Madame Bleu scoffed. "Miss Juniper, if I wanted your opinion, I would have asked for it. And as for your decision to contact a…creature wrangler, no less, a civilian with no training in proper combat most likely led to the death of your entire crew."

At the mention of her crew, Juniper's smirk straightened and her brow creased.

"If you think you are going to sit there and assume no responsibility for the death of three valued members of our society and chalk it up to fate, then you have another thing coming. Shut the fuck up."

The speech barb was hefty, and it winded Juniper. She sat back down on her seating pod and seemed to swallow the memory of her crew's deaths. Her eyes wavered briefly, and she bit her lip so hard it bled. She would grieve later, Xan was certain, but her persona wouldn't allow showing that weakness to a group of people, so she nodded and kept her mouth shut.

Xan turned back to Madame Bleu. "I don't think that is appropriate, Madame, she—"

"If you want me to repeat that same sentiment to you, I will gladly do so. Ignore your feeble need to defend this pathetic excuse for a soldier and tell me what you discovered upon arriving on the putrid Valkor ship," Madame Bleu howled with indignation, her bright red, modified lips pursed and plump.

Xan hesitated. The gravity of the question was a punch in the stomach. A sickness spread within him. General Heronicus had warned of Madame Bleu's cunning ways. Of her ultimate deception to deprive other worlds of resources, sending them to the brink of destruction. And here she stood asking what he knew. There was no perspiration on her brow; she stood with an almost cocky disposition that would repel even the most daring of assassins.

Xan swallowed, thinking of Qilin and how the seconds that ticked by brought her closer to her demise. It was all about finding her again. That was his priority. Nothing outweighed that. So, he lied and he did it easily.

"They took Juniper captive so that I would bring my crew to locate her. Their main purpose was to announce their re-emergence from the shadows into the light. But they truly wanted…Ryker." The surprise in Madame Bleu's face could not be hidden. "I had an inkling that may have been the case, so I ordered him to get reinforcements so he would be protected. Only Lilianna and I were bound on the ship."

Lilianna looked at the ground and Xan wondered whether she could be convincing enough if interrogated.

Ryker gasped at the same time as Madame Bleu, and Xan turned his head, finding his gaze. Xan hoped that Ryker saw a tiny ripple of desperation in the dark pools of his eyes.

"They wanted Ryker?" Her voice undulated as if it were an incredulous suggestion.

"Madame, they expected him to be of great importance to you, being your blood relation and all. When they realised he hadn't even come, they let us go, but I…" Xan swallowed hard. "I found it imperative to eliminate as many Valkor as I could for the benefit and safety of Gemarine before rescue came."

Madame Bleu stood silent, claw-like fingers drumming on the inside of her arm. Flicking her head quickly, she directed her attention to Massy.

"Pilot boy," she shouted, startling him. Then realising who he was, quickly corrected herself. "Oh, it's Massy, isn't it?"

He nodded slowly and seemed to shrink in size. Xan realised then that Madame Bleu recognised him from an accident years before. Massy had been close to being exiled but miraculously escaped the most severe punishment. Four of his fellow pilots perished in a training run and the rumour was, it was his recklessness that cost so many lives. The fear of exile was most likely why Massy was so compliant.

"So, what did you make of the whole arrangement?" Madame Bleu scratched at her cheek with a pointer finger.

"Madame, might I just say, I made it very clear to Xan that I was uncomfortable. But once I saw the risk and the gravity of what was happening, I opted out and Xan did not reprimand me or really even bat an eyelid, to his credit." Massy glanced briefly at Xan and then resumed eye contact. "Ryker and I were in agreement that we did not want to risk our lives for a personal assignment."

Xan glanced over his shoulder and saw Juniper roll her eyes at Massy, clearly unimpressed.

"The fact that you, Xan, wrangled this crew in the first place for a personal mission to save a damsel in distress is completely outside of the confines of *our* agreement. Each mission should be logged, justified, categorised and it all needs to have purpose," said Madame Bleu.

Juniper pointed her finger, interrupting. "Might I just interject briefly and say that, hey, my life has a smidge of purpose and that's a pretty decent justification. You know, saving a friend?"

"Juniper, watch your tone with me." Madame Bleu snapped. "The way you so brazenly drifted into the Senmore and sacrificed your crew is frankly astounding. Someone of your calibre should have known better in the first place."

"Again, Madame, despite your indictment of my actions – I was responding to a distress call from Captain Larrsen's ship. How was I to know it was all a ploy to get to *your* nephew?" Her last words were tinged with hate.

Ryker stepped forward. "I don't think it's right that everything is blamed on me. I have no idea how this happened. In fact, it's the first I've heard of it."

"No, Ryker, buddy, no one is saying it's your fault," Massy reasoned.

Juniper added, "Exactly, that's not what I meant. I'm saying, for some reason these Valkor wanted to get to you, Madame, and all of a sudden, we're the ones on trial? I think if I were being frank about things, well... you wouldn't particularly want to know what I think..." She trailed off, biting her lip and adjusting her exoarm.

"Oh, is that right? Well, how about you sit the fuck out of the soldier program for a healthy few months. It's not like you have anyone left in your crew to defend Gemarine with, anyway," Madame Bleu yelled from behind the glass, her face drooping and distorted as if melted wax shaped her hatred. "Escort her out immediately."

Juniper shrugged and waited for the guards to enter. "Fucking brilliant, I haven't had a holiday in years." The guards bustled in, dragging her away as she smirked at Xan and disappeared behind the door.

"Xan and the rest of your crew, I think you've earned yourself a lengthy break as well."

Xan protested. "We have a mission scheduled in the morning and it's dire. The *Perutonian Ridge Crested Joloulos* is only visible in the atmosphere for ten days of the year. If we don't go then we might not see them."

"Xan, might I remind you, I don't give two fucks about your collection of strange creatures. I agreed to let you do this because your fame meant that I had to tread carefully. Give you what you want and look good for the people," she mocked. "But now I suspect it will be different. You're just a weirdo science nerd who owns a sanctuary. Big fucking deal. You fly around the galaxy like you own it, so consequences must be thrust upon you when you abuse your power." She narrowed her eyes, her voice threatening in its delicacy. "I can take everything from you in an instant."

RYKER
21 YEARS OLD

Xan was fighting a losing battle, his chest heaving, an outpouring of emotion starting to choke him. Ryker watched him struggle and didn't know what to do. On one hand, he felt betrayed that all the lessons were a lie; all the care and compassion was lost when he chose violence. But from what he understood, the Valkor had taken Qilin and that information had not been shared with Massy or Madame Bleu. It was something he had overheard from Lilianna in the mediroom. If there was one thing he was sure of, it was that Qilin was a good soul and a soul that complemented Xan. Maybe since she'd been taken, he had lost himself. *Grief tends to make monsters out of us all.*

Ryker stepped forward. "Madame, this is actually really important."

"You are defending him after what he put you through?"

"I don't agree with his choices, Madame, but I care about the *Perutonian Ridge Crested Joloulos*. It was said to shed feathers that adorned the Celestials of the Golden Age. It was one we had prioritised as a gift to you. That of which, we weren't supposed to mention."

Madame Bleu considered his words, her confident facade fading as her eyes twinkled with the youth of a distant star. Lines of age and the burden of power creased her forehead, shattering the illusion. But just for a moment those eyes faltered, and Ryker knew his words were like magic.

Ryker, not known for his charisma or charm, offered it on bended knee, a gracious lie that would give them a chance to bring Qilin home.

"Ryker, I appreciate your honesty. This creature intrigues me, so I will permit this expedition. But I wish to be kept abreast of all developments."

Xan nodded. "I will organise a personal briefing upon my return."

"When you do get back, I will see to it that you are confined to your lab for a period of time. This is not over, Xan." A light seemed to flick off inside her. She was instantly bored. "For now, it is late, so get out of my sight. Each of you will report to me in three days' time or you will find residence in the Wilds."

Lilianna whispered, "Exile?" Her voice was a barren lake-bed, exposed to the tyranny of the sun.

Madame Bleu continued with scorn on her face and primacy in her tone. "Massy, Sytheract girl, Xan and Ryker – I want you to know that Gemarine will not be exposed again. I will make sure of that."

They all turned to leave but Madame Bleu's voice cut through their retreat. "Xan, where is that creature that is always attached to your heel? I almost don't recognise you without it mimicking your shadow."

Xan swallowed. "Madame, I'm not taking her on a rescue mission. You know I'd do anything to keep her from harm."

She shrugged, frowning as apathy seized her face. The flick of her olive cape floated for an instant and snapped back to the floor, slithering behind her as she exited the viewing platform.

The crew walked out of the interrogation room and into Topaz City bathed in artificial blue light.

CHAPTER 20

LOCATION: GEMARINE
YEAR: 116 (2 YEARS AGO)
RYKER – 19 YEARS OLD

"Hello, sir, um…pleasure to ah…meet you." Ryker bowed because it was customary to do so, but it felt over the top. Regardless of his status as both Gemgen – one of the few generations to have been born on Gemarine – and Madame Bleu's only blood relative, he despised formalities. In fact, he was apathetic to life at the best of times. This was far from the best of times so one could imagine his state of mind.

Xan produced a beaming smile. "The group holo call with Zondini and Madame Bleu requesting your work interview wasn't even a day ago and you're here already. How very odd," he mused out loud.

"Oh, I'm sorry, I didn't mean to cause any…um…stress or—"

"Don't be silly, mate," Xan said dismissively, swatting his hand through the air. He turned to one of the lab cabinets and reached for an orange vial. "So, what makes you want to get involved with xeno-conservation and the biobase?"

159

Ryker shifted uncomfortably, the formal cape that flapped around his ankles felt utterly ridiculous and he loathed that Madame Bleu made him wear it. He took in Xan, the only real famous person on Gemarine. The combed dark hair, short sides neat and tidy, smokey eyes like the dying breath of a decommissioned ship's exhaust, the faint hint of stubble more defined across his top lip. The media had made such a big deal about him for years. Still to the present day he was the subject of positive stories about his xeno-conservation feats. Even in regular conversation on the streets and in mechanic groups, he would overhear all the thirsty first timers at Fusion raving about fucking him or watching him fuck. Every damn Gemarinian wanted a piece of him.

From the initial look of him up close, there was definitely something aesthetically pleasing, but special? *I think not.*

Xan smiled. Dashing white teeth, straight and gleaming shone through a lopsided smile.

I guess there is charm in his smile, Ryker conceded. *How do I play this? I don't really care if he takes me on or not. If it's not him, then it's another lowlife who's employing me as a favour to Madame Bleu.*

"I guess I just like ships, sir, and want to work with moving parts."

Silence spread thin across the lab as Xan examined the vial under a scope, then flicked the data to the holo projection. Ryker assumed he'd send him packing.

Instead, Xan laughed and shrugged. "Well at least you're honest. I rate that." Ryker couldn't help but let the hint of a grin show as his forehead crinkled in disbelief. "I don't really need another Xeno-biologist, I suppose. If you like working with parts – then just keep your head down, maintain the *Attenborough* well and you won't have any problems with me." The warmth of his smile reached Ryker like a midsummer bonfire beckoning from a distance.

Ryker still hadn't wiped the disbelief from his face. All his life, he'd been yelled at, spoken to like a second-rate species pushed into a corner.

Yet here was the most famous person on Gemarine, besides Madame Bleu, and he was just…chill. It was weird.

"Okay then," Ryker conceded, then with brewing curiously asked, "what's an *Attenborough* by the way?"

Xan laughed. "Oh, it's the name of my ship. There was this famous naturalist on Earth, Sir David Attenborough, who did a lot of work documenting all different kinds of creatures so that Humans might value them and their habitats a little more." The smile began to fade, as if there were a painful truth behind the memory of his idol.

Ryker tried to think of something appropriate to say. "That is quite a noble thing to dedicate your life to." As soon as he said it, he realised that was exactly what Xan was doing.

Xan quickly changed the subject. "What's your experience, by the way?"

"Not much real ship experience, but I've been tinkering away on refractor engines from the war, restoring them."

"That sounds like a fun project."

"It is," Ryker said flatly, unsure of where to go with the conversation. It was hard enough stringing three sentences together without wanting to crawl back into the peaceful shell of introversion.

"Alright, well it's fine you're not really a talker. Go check out the *Attenborough*'s core and see what needs doing in there. If you have a list by tomorrow, we can get approval for parts and you can learn on the job. Sound okay?"

"Ah, yeah." He was about to say, "I appreciate it," but Xan sped off, moving toward an enclosed part of the *Attenborough* carrying a cage with some creature buzzing inside.

Ryker watched him until he was out of sight, not really knowing what to make of him. At best, he was intrigued, although he didn't particularly care about which creature they saved from the brink of death. Maybe he could just put his head down, work quietly and save himself from a life of tyranny and neglect.

CHAPTER 21

Xan walked up ahead with Ryker, talking in hushed tones to him. Lilianna wondered why all of a sudden Ryker was the golden child.

Was Xan just thanking him for not exposing the lie about the Valkor targeting Ryker? Or buying Ryker's loyalty somehow?

What would Xan be able to offer Ryker that Madame Bleu couldn't?

Ryker looked around nervously, spotting Lilianna and her prying eyes. Still, Lilianna couldn't exactly read lips and despite her straining, she still couldn't discern their conversation. It didn't help that Massy was talking mindlessly as they walked. It meant she might never satisfy her curiosity.

"Well, that was intense. Totally didn't expect Madame herself to be ripping us a new asshole." Massy scoffed, knotted black hair up in a bun. The yellow and black circles on his forehead distinct atop his eyes that shimmered with mischief. "You were awfully quiet, though."

Ryker spun back around, and his raven hair flicked like a coat in the breeze. He narrowed his eyes at Lilianna, then shrank into the darkness, sliding along the path to his level away from the rest of the crew.

"Lilianna, I said you were quiet." Massy raised his voice, still with an air of playfulness.

Lilianna tried to interpret Xan's demeanour as she half-heartedly answered Massy. "I guess when Madame knows me as a random Sytheract, I don't think there's much point in me saying anything." She huffed, the disappointment in her voice too coarse to dilute.

Xan didn't look any worse than he had before. His footsteps were more rapid perhaps, as if the faster he strode the swifter the night would end.

"You should be taking lessons in being charming from yours truly." Massy beat his chest twice with one closed fist, his eyelids fluttered flirtatiously, mocking.

She couldn't help but scoff. "Oh, Massy, I'll be sure to make your acquaintance when desperation overcomes me."

"Speaking of desperation – do you want to make the most of this evening, m'lady?" He bowed low, then raised himself up quickly, jerking his eyebrows up and down so the circular birthmarks contracted and expanded.

Lilianna glanced ahead at Xan waiting for a transpo he must have dialled on his MPD. "Massy, I'm not going to Fusion with you," she said, rolling her eyes.

"Who said Fusion?" His palms upturned, feigned innocence on his face. "But now that you mention it." A disgusting smirk infested his face, and the wink he produced took him from tolerable idiot to creep.

Lilianna kissed him on the cheek, hiding her disgust with a friendly gesture. "Goodnight, you goof, get some rest. By the way, thanks for coming back to help us...eventually."

She barely heard him say, "I thought the heroes get some love at least." He stamped a foot on the ground, loud enough for the crack to resonate off the other buildings lining the footpath.

"Fusion isn't love," she yelled behind her as she jogged across the smooth manufactured path, focused on catching Xan.

"Xan, wait!" she called.

He turned around, a flicker of embarrassment crinkled in his acknowledgement of her. "Where are you going?" she produced breathlessly.

"I need Juniper's help to go find this evidence," he murmured, ruffling his hair as he searched the horizon for the transpo.

"Why wouldn't you ask me?" Her voice was small, a flower quivering as it awaited autumn's kiss of death.

"I…I just thought you might have needed some time away…from me." He avoided her gaze.

She moved forward nervously, but reached out, heart beating down the sturdy walls of her chest. Her hand settled on the inside of his arm, and she immediately felt his pulse strong and defined but his skin was clammy. He was evidently tense and eager to find Qilin. "I'm sorry, Xan, I didn't know what to do when I saw you like that. I shouldn't have been afraid and I shouldn't have let you deal with that by yourself."

He shifted uncomfortably, but allowed her hand to linger longer than it should have. "It's nothing, Lili, I'm just embarrassed and I'm shameful and…just…sorry you had to see that. Sorry that even happened." He added the last line hastily, the smoke in his eyes sprinkled with water, dousing flame.

"No, it's something that I accept you for." She was determined to find strength in her voice for this. "I will always accept you, whatever you show or whenever you might make a mistake." She brought her free hand to his other arm, facing him front on, the stare between them uninhibited, unobstructed.

"Well, it was just inappropriate, especially you working with me, to see me like that." He looked down.

Lilianna wrenched her hands away instantly, almost as if her skin were irradiated. Why did he mention inappropriate and work-related? Was she not more to him than that?

She was hurt. After all the time they spent together, after countless overnight missions, lingering stares, flirty banter – how was she still considered just his work protégé?

A scowl rose like an eruption from her overactive core. She was about to turn sour. But she caught the worry lines violently corrupting the hopeful stream of Xan's eyes into a sea of darkness.

The absence of Qilin at his feet was almost as stark as if he hadn't been wearing boots. Almost as if his toes had been severed. His orientation was off without her to steady him. Lilianna swallowed the pressure building and reminded herself that she could overthink every minuscule moment later.

The next phase wasn't about her, it was about Qilin. And she wanted to help get her back. "I don't care about that stuff, Xan. That…work stuff. Anyway, I want to help." She straightened, standing as tall as her frame would allow. "What do you need me to do?"

Xan hesitated as if considering that the task might be too grave for her to participate.

"I'm going to Juniper's level now to convince her to help me. Come with me now and all three of us will figure this out together."

JUNIPER
24 YEARS OLD

Juniper was already several drinks down when Xan showed up.

She opened the door with mixed emotions. Part of her wanted to hold his body tight, while the other part wanted to shove him out the door, knowing what he would ask of her next. She turned without saying a word and flopped down on the couch.

Xan stared at the empty flasks lying on the counter and his body tensed. "Are you going to come with me?"

Juniper sighed, lying back and resting her head on a golden pillow. Her legs were crossed and her arms were above her head. "I just feel broken if I'm being honest. I get reamed by that fucking psycho Madame bitch and I'm just exhausted from having the most harrowing experience of my life."

Xan was silent for a moment, then shifted on the spot. "Sometimes I think you completely get me and then other times I'm grounded by how you want to zip yourself up in a cocoon and forget the real world."

She turned to him sharply, her eyes as frosty as a winter blizzard. "The real world? This is it, Xan." The words came out doused in bitterness. "There might not even be any truth to this conspiracy, yet you want me to be happy about cruising through space satisfying curiosity? Do you neglect to think about me sometimes? I lost my crew. They didn't fucking deserve that." The weight of tears pushed against the barrier of her eyes, and she swallowed the regret and sadness with difficulty. "I have a stone heart most of the time, but I feel every crack that forms, every divot created by a barb of cruelty – you of all people should understand that."

Xan grew in stature as folded arms turned to aggressive finger-pointing. "Why are you debating right now – this is Qilin! She is family. We can deal with all the other bullshit later."

"Other bullshit," she whispered. She stared at the ceiling and huffed. "Just fuck off and give me time."

"We don't have time, Juniper." Xan's voice rose in intensity.

Juniper couldn't believe her best friend, lathered in the soapy scent of selfishness, was stinking up the room. She wanted to open a window and haul him off the edge – with a tether attached of course. Just to scare some common courtesy into the pile of mush he considered a brain.

Where was the empathy he was famous for? Was it stored up for all the extinct creatures that leapt across the galaxy? When a fellow Human needed some compassion, did he require a booster, similar to serotonin?

If she kicked him in the junk would that boost some empathy back into his body?

Juniper flung herself forward and stood, wobbling slightly before striding past Xan. She adopted a cool tone, making it sound foreign coming from her mouth. "Just please give me some space. I'll contact you in a bit." Her strong exoarm yanked the door open, then she held an open palm toward the hallway, directing him to leave.

Xan stared with an open mouth and she lowered her eyes, avoiding the betrayal laced within his gaze. He turned swiftly, swearing under his breath. She slammed the door, returned to the couch and took a hefty swig of dark liquid, hoping it would bring her a feeling of repose.

LILIANNA
22 YEARS OLD

Lilianna absent-mindedly scanned her MPD while ruminating on thoughts about why Xan was probably on his knees begging for Juniper but was so great at rejecting her own demonstrations of devotion to him. Lilianna had to basically invite herself along to help on this mission – so why was she not considered as valuable as Juniper?

You're not a war hero, Lilianna. This is preparation for a war.

Xan stormed into his level, shoving the door back with forearms rigid with hatred. Lilianna jumped up from the couch like a feline startled out of peaceful slumber.

"Let's just go, Lili, I'm not going to wait for her." His voice was gruff and covered in anger as he rummaged through drawers and closets searching for items to take with him.

"Wait, what do you mean?" She slowly moved forward, entwining her fingers nervously.

Xan's digits roamed the bottom of the drawers for some kind of tool perhaps, but spat his response back. "She's too exhausted to help or something, I don't know, just—"

Lilianna was shocked but she interjected calmly, trying to halt Xan's manic search for sanity, it seemed. "Just wait here."

"What, you think you're going to convince her to come?" He stood stiff, looking at her now with the gaze of a distant storm, the brink of fury arrested by rolling clouds.

She turned to the door then looked back at him. "Just wait, please. It will be okay." The confidence in her voice was a technique to soothe him but it was unnatural, like it was two sizes too big or something. Somehow, she believed in herself to get this done, to make up for turning away before. A redemption song drifted above frequencies they couldn't perceive. She would seek to reach out and make that melody her own.

JUNIPER
24 YEARS OLD

Juniper swung the door in aggressively. "I thought I told you to give me—" She faltered as Lilianna stood in front of her, oddly tall, arms folded, eyebrow arched.

"Oh, Lilianna, what do you want?" Juniper said dismissively. Was this really Xan's best ploy? Sending in someone who minutes ago was questioning her own loyalties.

"Are you joking right now?" Lilianna cocked her head to the side.

"What?" Juniper breathed fire. "Watch your tone with me—"

Lilianna burst into the room, interrupting Juniper yet again. "There you are having a huge dig at me when this is a massive crunch moment and you're sitting on your hands." She caught her mistake and flushed, correcting quickly, "Hand, I mean."

Juniper didn't bother highlighting her mistake. "I never said I wouldn't come; I'm just taking stock right now."

Lilianna tensed her fists, swallowing hard. "Seriously, you love him too, so stop running around acting like you have no heart." Her voice was rising, coated with a hint of nervousness. "If Qilin dies because you needed space, then he will *never* forgive you, so take five seconds now to realise how fucked your life will be without him and decide what you want to do."

Juniper sighed, anger subsiding as the corner of her mouth trembled. Tears fell from her eyes unexpectedly and Lilianna was clearly caught off guard. She watched droplets dive into Juniper's outfit, sorrow hidden once more.

"I lost my crew." Her voice came out weak and small. "I fucked up." Her usually strong knees buckled and she crumpled on the floor, unable to maintain eye contact. The bravado, pride and anger, was a wall that fell into decay. Now the contents of her stronger painful emotions were laid bare. Strength wasn't usually associated with pain, but emotions were surprising depending on the moments that galvanised them.

Lilianna stepped forward and reached out instinctively, grabbing hold of her shoulders as she bent down, finding her level.

"You're the strongest person I know. Put all of the stuff aside about doing it for Xan. Let's fight to make amends. Let's fight for the souls that were taken from you, certainly not by any fault of your own." Juniper's eyes met Lilianna's, interested in what she had to say. "Let's just find out if all this is real. We save Qilin in the process and we have the ability to right a wrong that we may have contributed to."

Juniper couldn't believe she'd broken down in front of Lilianna, and better still, she was the one consoling her and bringing her in line.

Life works in mysterious ways.

"Okay," Juniper said, face drawn resolute after the weakness broke her open. "Okay, I'm with you."

Lilianna repeated the stark warning Juniper had thrust upon her. "Sometimes you need someone to give you the honest truth."

Juniper laughed through the very last of sniffled tears. "Yes, very good. Using my own sentiments on me. Classic dick move."

Lilianna helped her up with a warm smile and an equally caring caress.

"Don't talk about this with anyone please. I trust you and that is hard for me to do." Juniper averted her gaze now, but was regaining the essence of herself once more.

Lilianna nodded. "I've got you."

LILIANNA
22 YEARS OLD

Lilianna sauntered through the door, at least that's what she thought a saunter might look like, having never particularly been a saunterer.

Xan frowned. "Let me guess, she couldn't—"

Juniper breezed through after her. "Couldn't what?"

He looked surprised. "You're coming?"

"Wipe that dumb fuck look off your face. I would never abandon you." She crossed her arms and pouted at him, then carefully turned her eyes down to the floor. "I'm more than just a little broken, though."

"I'll repair you, I swear to the stars. I'll fix everything I promise…but it will take time and I'll give you that after we find out the truth and save Qilin."

Her exoarm dropped to her side, and her other hand clung to her bicep, squeezing as if uncomfortable. "I know you will." She gestured to Lilianna smiling stupidly, watching on. "You have both of us to help, and we would travel beyond forsaken worlds to find what you need, to build a new life with you and make everything right again, for everyone."

Her words were sifting sands in a barren land, unseen and unheard. Instead, he strode forward and met Juniper. Fingers curled around her cheek and he arched her head up to face him, her jade eyes now radiant, fresh with wet tears. They met his intense gaze, sprinkled with the dust of passion. Xan's lips found Juniper's and she parted hers, melding their passion for one another. He broke off, wet with her essence on his lips, pressing his forehead to hers. They breathed in unison for precious seconds, an unspoken truce dilating the intensity of their stare.

Lilianna was about to shift away; it was an intimate moment that she shouldn't be a part of. She turned, but Xan reached out for her hand before she moved away. As he pulled her in close, she stumbled but his strong arms caught and steadied her. Before she knew what was happening his lips were on hers too. She let her eyes close and a moan escape her. He tasted of sweet honey and cinnamon. Lilianna almost opened her mouth, hungry for more but he pulled back until their foreheads touched in that same intimate gesture. Juniper smiled beside her.

Lilianna didn't really know what to make of it all, but her heart was submerged in the ocean of Xan's aura.

Was it a kiss of friendship, like a more meaningful thank you?

She didn't know, but at that moment, Lilianna felt she was more than a co-worker for the first time ever. All of those times he had shielded himself from her in the name of being the boss. Well, he could eat that now. A decadent dessert with frosting that read *Lilianna has been validated.*

Xan's actions and the gaze he had levelled on her meant that in the story he was writing, she wore an opulent dress on a palatial level, not just a torn uniform in a dank windowless basement.

"C'mon then, we can all fuck later." Juniper laughed as Lilianna flushed, and not for the first time. "Off to the power grid we go," she sang, skipping toward the door like she was a cast member of a musical.

"It's not as easy as that. I'll have to get my testing kit, and we'll need a ship." Xan scratched his chin thoughtfully.

Juniper summoned her commanding prowess. "Okay, Lilianna, you have access to the lab. You can go there first – get a mobile kit and meet

Xan at the power station." She turned to Xan and pointed in his direction. "Xan, go straight there and I'll get us a ship. Simple."

"We're splitting up?" Lilianna coughed, the inside of her mouth was a barren watercourse. Fear was the sun in the midst of a drought. This was the beginning of a war. Who was she to be involved in something like this? Although she had jumped up and down in front of Xan practically begging to be included, now the time to act was upon her. Doubt was rampant. Her nerves were alive Would she die before she had a chance to really live?

Surprisingly, Juniper was the one to offer encouragement. "We both know you aren't built for war, but you are built with a heart for purpose. And there really is no greater purpose, is there?"

Lilianna thought about this. *The purpose of her people? The purpose of correcting mistakes?* But Juniper was often painted by artists who focused on the wrong details. They might paint her naked, legs splayed and inviting. They might paint her bloodstained and war-torn, or even fierce, foul-mouthed and lonely. But here, she spoke of purpose. Despite the gallery of paintings that depicted public perception, she waved the brush not with strength, but with passion and love. That was the purpose she hinted at.

Lilianna was wary but she steadied herself, smoothing out the creases in her outfit, taking a big breath in. "Okay, okay. It's only lab equipment. I can do it."

"I mean, you bring a test kit, I steal a ship. Levels, girl," Juniper teased.

It seemed difficult for Xan to smile, but an etching of one was sketched across his face.

Juniper clapped her hands. "Alright, my loves, let's do this."

They all smiled at one another. Their smiles were steeped in sadness and exhaustion, but they were doing this together and it meant more because of that.

CHAPTER 22

Xan and Lilianna had just taken the orange pill. On Yarmandor, it was a little tough to breathe because of the sulphur-thick atmosphere; even with the pill it felt like they were ascending a mountain in high altitude.

The smell was pungent, like rotten eyes and trash soup.

Delicious, thought Lilianna as her stomach churned in annoyance.

Although the pill had an element of scent suppression, the aroma still snuck through, like one of Massy's innuendos on the ship – it was a predictable occurrence and ever-present. But they needed to fight through the pain of stink to win their prize. Her eyes watered as she scoped the sky around them: bright orange with pulsing waves of green vapour crashing against one another, sending cracks of thunder around the planet.

She flicked her hand across her face several times, then slapped her own cheek accidentally, squinting in hatred. "These bugs are horrendous,

173

Xan." Lilianna continued swatting as the *Panremoes* swarmed around her, nibbling at her pale flesh like a tasty treat.

"You forgot to engage the distrillian spray, didn't you?" Xan lectured, as they stammered up a steep incline, the yellow of the sulphur like solar flares enveloping them in a constant glow. "It has high concentrations of magnesium and citronella. It's a concoction the biobase team and I developed, based on combating a species on Earth called mosquitoes. It really does help," Xan relayed, skin as supple as ever.

Lilianna was annoyed at herself for giving the *Panremoes* a free meal and looking like a novice in front of her boss. "I'm sorry, I mustn't have realised I—"

"It's alright, don't stress." He swatted the air with disregard, not to shoo away the insects. "You'll find your way when you've been on a couple more expeditions. You'll know what to pack and what to leave behind," he said soothingly. Xan passed her a small vial of spray. "I packed one for you just in case." He smiled revealing his perfect teeth and his perfect eyes twinkled on his stupid, perfect face. Her imperfect heart faltered, and she cursed him for what he evoked in her.

"Close your eyes." His smile turned to concentration as he held up the bottle before her.

She did as he suggested, feeling the cool mist kiss her face like salty air fresh from the ocean.

"Turn around, I'll get the back of your neck," he said, but stopped abruptly. "Oh, there's something on your neck, hold on." He pressed his palm gently into the small of her back and she inhaled sharply. Xan carefully gathered a small creature, reptilian in its nature, from the surface of her neck – fingers caressing her soft skin as he did. It was a gesture focused on the insect, and he placed it into a breathable specimen jar he had strapped to the belt on his suit. Qilin sniffed at the jar, then licked Xan's hand as if to congratulate him on the find.

Lilianna's knees weakened at Xan's touch. Any accidental brush of his shoulder against hers, any lingering rub of their upper arms was a drug.

The energy from his skin ignited her. He was a naturally charming and flirtatious person, so she knew that his actions never hinted at a depth where emotions bristled and formed desire and love. But she sure felt that hot flush every time. Her pale skin betrayed her. And if he were perceptive enough, he would have realised by now that he could bed her in a second if she were anything like Juniper, or anyone else on Gemarine for that matter.

But she was very clear about her beliefs. They'd had that conversation many times. Not because Xan would have been overly curious, but mainly due to long rides out in the galaxy, when they had covered a wide range of topics. So, he knew never to cross that boundary. But her body sure said yes enough. In fact, it bellowed it from a mountain top, so every sentient lifeform knew about her burning loins. But ultimately, it was his heart that needed to engage with hers and there hadn't even been an audible whisper.

"It's a *Putilian*!" Xan exclaimed, fascinated eyes wide with wonder. "Wow! You know that they can lower their core temperature and survive without eating for approximately one whole year?"

"No, but hey, you're the extinction executioner." She laughed, alluding to an MPD newsflash that detailed his latest conservation effort at the biobase. The headline: 'Extinction Executioner: an Oracle for the galaxies most vulnerable'.

He laughed too. "The photo manipulation of me with the scythe was ridiculous."

Lilianna scoffed. "Oh, you weren't complaining when you saved it as a holo and strung it up in the lab waiting area for everyone to gawk at."

"Look, I'm just plain old Xan to you though and I like it that way."

"You're not plain old Xan, you're my boss."

"I really hope you don't start being all formal with that boss nonsense."

"Mmm okay, boss."

Xan rolled his eyes and promptly changed the subject. "Let's continue on, we really have to push to get to the Loomarian Zone to set up camp."

Qilin bounded ahead on the path, always ultra-excited to explore with her human brother.

They were cute. How endearing it was seeing them both on the MPD express comms all those years ago, but truly knowing them was a privilege. Their bond went beyond that of the three species that flitted around Gemarine. But then again, Qilin was also just very special and sweet, which was way more than anyone could say about the best Gemarinians stalking their residential levels. Xan was conducting a study around some of the apparent extraordinary things Qilin could do, but Lilianna hadn't seen anything other than a plain beautiful, loyal soul.

I wonder why value is placed on extraordinary feats, when there are others who create symbiosis together, keeping ecosystems afloat, yet they would be neglected in a heartbeat. The tragedy of life is that the brightest feathers are marvelled at more than the purposeful, aerodynamic ones.

They reached the Loomarian Zone and Xan set up the containment sphere in the valley. It was coming into night and shadows were cast from gnarled dead branches and cone-shaped lava tubes. The illumination was turning a haze of neon green, as the vapours in the sky took prominence when the black of night awoke. Outside the windows of their containment sphere, a yellow fog surrounded them as it swelled into the sky to die in the blackness. Lilianna breathed in the oxygen within the sphere as if it were filled with a sweet scent, thankful to be rid of the sting at the back of her throat from the sulphur.

"How good is it to breathe properly again?" Lilianna huffed, sitting cross-legged on the ground, and invited Qilin closer to her for a pat.

"I've calculated that getting out of here tomorrow gives us enough time to get into the regeneration chamber for at least an hour and it will repair some of the damage that might have crept its way across our skin particles or seeped into our trachea or bronchial sacs. The pill can only contain so much of the sulphur, often a little bit of wear and tear occurs," Xan finished with a weary smile.

"Oh, that's lovely. Goodness, sometimes I forget how crazy we are to do this stuff." She chuckled, shaking her head.

"What do you mean?" Xan tilted his head to the side.

"We are literally risking our lives for insects or little creatures that no one else cares about," she reasoned.

"Ah, but this is all part of ensuring everyone *does* care or at least starts to recognise the importance of different species."

"But this particular one, Xan? The air in their chamber needs to be... crazy."

Xan walked toward the corner and began unzipping his uniform. Lilianna immediately averted her gaze across to Qilin, who was now sleeping opposite her. "Like, I get symbiosis and all that. It's important. But this seems like such a bizarre catch."

"Yeah, but air quality or their specific atmosphere should not preclude them from being saved, you know?"

She brought her eyes back to him as he fiddled with a lighter shirt, his upper body exposed, chiselled and tantalising. Nervousness enveloped her and she wanted to look away but at the same time eat him up.

"Right, Lilianna?"

She realised she hadn't responded as her jaw was basically upon the floor, a puddle of saliva forming, enough for Qilin to splash in. Lilianna flushed. "Um...yeah, of course, I'm just saying it's hard." She cursed herself for the use of that word.

Xan pulled the shirt over his head and started to take off his pants, changing into a more comfortable bamboo-type of cotton infusion. She couldn't stare any longer and walked across to Qilin, patting her as she studied the wall.

"Difficult tasks don't discount the need for intervention or action." He pulled up the pants, but they were snug, the outline of everything evident, and she knew right then sleep would be hard.

Dammit, stop thinking that word.

The first overnight camp would be exactly that, with her tossing and turning, trying to ignore the call of her body and respect the louder call of her heart.

In fact, she was finding it more and more difficult to follow the path she had always believed was hers. She was unique in the world she lived in, her views and actions deemed unconventional. And it wasn't like she was a prude; she had sexual desires but she didn't want them to mean nothing. That's what she valued about her home planet and of the tales of Earth, there seemed to be something more to those interactions. On Gemarine it felt transactional.

Either way, she had a soft spot for Xan and she wondered if she would ever be able to look at him without a lustful lens.

"Are you going to get changed into something more comfortable or what?" Xan asked, snuggled in his corner, arms resting behind his head.

She shrugged. "I'll do it when I'm ready."

"I'll make sure to avert my gaze." He laughed teasingly.

"Shut up," she blushed, "I'm no prude, I'm just not going to waltz into Fusion like it's a buffet and, I don't know…fill my plate with everything on offer."

Xan laughed with warmth. "I respect you, girl. Don't you worry, Qilin and I will sit here and read. We shall not peek, isn't that right, Qilin?"

Xan poked Qilin in the side of the belly, tickling her. She snorted and rolled over on her side, inviting a proper belly scratch.

Lilianna started to undress as she turned away from Xan. Her bare chest faced the outer walls and she could almost see her heart beat as it hammered against her pale skin.

She lowered the rest of her suit and quickly put on her comfortable outfit. Her nerves spun and her breathing increased. But as she slipped the material on, it felt silky and smooth against her skin, creating a soothing effect. Lilianna spun around quickly and Xan was reading a book on his MPD extension and seemingly hadn't seen anything at all. She was relieved but also wished she had caught him taking a peek.

XAN
22 YEARS OLD

Luckily for Xan, Lilianna hadn't seen his eyes fixed upon the smooth lines of her back, the flowing rivulets of blonde hair that she swept across her shoulder, the valley of her neck exposed to bury his lips into. The moon was the prey of his envy – a long reach capable of caressing her supple skin, glowing at its touch. Xan's breath quickened, imagining all the ways they could press themselves against one another and turn the rest of the night into something memorable.

CHAPTER 23

LOCATION: GEMARINE
YEAR: 118
JUNIPER – 24 YEARS OLD

Juniper had a small pack clasped to her back. These packs weren't comfortable or fashion statements. They were clinical and sturdy, stark white reflecting the bulbous lights in the dark street. The pack only contained the three things she required and it seemed a little overkill to carry that uncomfortable hunk of annoyance, but it added to her disguise. She was the thief in the night, but she needed to look like a queen of the night – just with a big-ass pack.

Was it a little wrong she was doing things this way? Maybe. But what other choice did she have? She had taken back her crew's MPDs for a reason. The reason was to honour a tradition of the soldiers. At their service scheduled for next quarter they would gather to commemorate the fallen. She, as their commanding officer, would move with shuffled steps to the aisles of remembrance. A newly erected slate-grey stone would be perched among the others like a severed tree in the forest of the dead.

She would seek their names and clip their MPDs to a vacant slot in the stone. Retiring the MPD and the data trace of the soldier.

Did her using these MPDs to steal a piece of equipment soil that tradition? Soil their service and their memory? It might.

But she also knew that all their last moments were in devotion to Juniper. Not to Madame Bleu, not to Gemarine, but to Juniper. They would have followed her anywhere and died by her words, and her command. She thought of Benius, that nervous little dingus staring up at her with wide eyes. He'd had so much promise underneath the inexperience of youth. His last moments proved what bravery lurked beneath those starry eyes. Jimeny with a mind like an MPD, a master of the controls of any device, and poor Serarra.

As the Valkor general held the last remaining crew member with a curved needle knife to her throat, he asked Juniper again. "Tell me what you know or she dies."

Juniper yelled through tears that streamed down her face, unashamed, dancing in the air like nobody was watching.

Serarra knew with a glance that Juniper would not betray her. The reaction of her mentor was not of desperation, but of knowing that no matter what she tried to say, Serarra would die. The resignation of death besieged her, the stone in the aisle of remembrance materialised in her mind. Her name, freshly carved next to the others who fell before her. The last thought that settled upon her was the pride of dying at the feet of the greatest soldier to serve Gemarine. A soldier who would change their world and more worlds beyond them in time.

She smiled almost peacefully and with a breathy whisper said, "It's okay." And the Valkor sliced from ear to ear, tearing across her throat, the gushing red river of slaughter spilling at Juniper's feet.

The memory of Serarra's death hadn't stopped haunting Juniper's waking moments and although she had been cleansed, it was as if Serarra's blood were attached to her, stained on her fractured soul. But it was a stain that reminded her that whatever this was, it was more than her. And as Xan and Lilianna had made very clear — it was not about helping that cunt of a Valkor. It was about making things right again. *So if the army or Madame Bleu herself discover this blatant neglect of the soldier's code, so be it. I'll fucking waste the lot of them and start my own army and the code will be: fuck codes, do what you want.*

The transpo pulled up a block down from the forces of Gemarine. Juniper got out, swished her spritely black and purple hair behind her shoulder and flashed her sparkling jade eyes at the milky blue Aranther transpo driver. "Take another twenty credits for loyalty to confidentiality, honey." They scanned her MPD without taking their eyes off her.

"Appreciate that," they stammered, taken by her beauty and confidence.

"And the next time I see you at Fusion, I'm yours for the night." She blew them a kiss and they nodded in agreement, jaw slack and surely wondering why luck had bestowed itself on them that night.

Juniper waited until the transpo blew away into the mist of neon lights ahead. Turning in the opposite direction where the streets were bathed in shadow, she submerged herself. *I'd actually probably still fuck the shit out of them even if I was just playing a game.* She thought of the transpo driver and their smooth blue skin, and licked her lips. Carnal thoughts clouded her decent ones due to the combination of danger and craving physical release after going so long without.

It didn't help that Xan was basically a beautiful meat stick dangled in front of her and every second moment she just wanted to chew on him. *Am I fucking dog? Hot damn. I'm a weird bitch.* She couldn't forget about Lilianna, who was extremely alluring, and despite them having a bizarre friendship, the want to explore her wouldn't go away.

She shook her head. *Fucking hell, Juniper. Focus.*

This was a prime example of why the Gemarinian way encouraged sex to cleanse the mind. If she went three days without any physical stimulation at all — she was not at her peak. During the war they had set up fuck stations and recommended for charity's sake to utilise them at least once a day. She recalled lying in a muddy trench with a fellow soldier or two, blood-soaked and surrounded by long-dead corpses. Regardless of the situation it helped them to focus, to expend energy and aggression through the right channels.

She reached the doors of Soldier Headquarters and saw Marvest. *Fucking shit balls.* She needed to get through without Marvest noticing her.

Juniper flipped around hastily with her back flat against the wall, hood firmly lowered over her forehead, concealing that voluptuous bounty of hair. *It's so late, no one would be scoping these levels right now. I can fool the little numbskull.*

She dialled Marvest. The hood ensured the shadows kissed her face.

Marvest appeared on her MPD holo. "Who's this?"

"Serarra," she choked out in a dainty vocal disguise.

"Oh, Serarra, why are you calling so late? And are you trapped in a damn bunker? It's so dark, I can hardly see your beautiful face," he said, laying on the charm.

Juniper fought the urge to roll her eyes. *I wonder if this charm angle actually gets him laid more?*

"Sorry, Marv, I was getting some work done on the eighteenth level and as you can see, there's something wrong with the energy conserve recognising me. It's super annoying. Can you please come up and get the lights back on?"

"I could try and locate the warden. Abandoning this post isn't really acceptable." His head scanned in the direction of the warden space and his clawed hands gestured as if hampered by rules that were not his fault.

"Okay, thanks. Do what you can, please. Call me a child, but I'm not fond of being alone in the dark." Juniper added the last bit as an added incentive for his daddyness to get him moving.

Marvest walked off around the corner to locate Warden Barnible.

Taking her cue, she scanned the MPD at the door and shimmied through after it flashed green. She had the grace of a trained dancer and the poise and determination of an assassin.

She glanced up at the low voices coming from the warden's space, shadows splaying out onto the grey tiled floor. Juniper's breath matched her footwork – fast, frantic and chaotic. A small squeak across the floor alarmed her and she looked up, eyes wide with fright. But the shadow of Marvest didn't manifest his physical form so she sped the last few metres, crashing into the motitube. Dialling Level 5, it took off instantly with a jolt, catapulting her toward the ceiling. Marvest came into view then and look puzzled, as she was transported to where the service ships waited for her.

The tube door opened with a *whoosh* and she stepped out into the expansive hangar. Ships of varying sizes slept before of her: the Wingdoms, the Subset 3000s, the 4000s, the Battalion 5s, Longdong Silvers – *Wait, is that the made-up name for it with everyone at the barracks?* She shrugged. *Honestly, we're juvenile dickbeans sometimes.*

All the newer ships gleamed in the darkness. They were sharp and decisive through the air, but she turned her attention toward the medium-sized ships that were a little more beat-up. If she thieved a rust bucket it would mean the pursuit that would surely come might be a little less deadly.

Although no one usually worked at this time of night, a sense of dread still crept through her veins in much the same way she crept through the hangar, tethering herself to the darkness like an anchor to the ocean floor.

Steeled by war and covert missions, the beat of her heart still thrummed with vigour. Her breath caught in the well of her throat. It didn't matter how many times she went through this, the adrenalin still burned, fuelled by focus. It was only the fight that would change, if it indeed it needed to come to that. Luckily for her there was no fight, only a flight to come. There were several smaller scratched-up ships to select from, frowning with the ache of better days passed. A particularly tired and worn Comet 8 winked at her from the corner of the hangar, her eyes less resigned to retirement than the others.

Juniper's piloting ability heeded no fanfare. Out of all those holo medallions glinting on her wall, none of them said, "Thanks, you're a decent pilot." But she could handle herself in a Comet 8, she figured. Anything larger would make her question the wisdom of her choice. The bells and whistles didn't litter the Comet's controls but it was good under the hood, and better yet, a solid A to B option, which was all she needed.

A creaking door as it hinged open, a wobbly ramp as her footfall bounded toward the controls. She sat down at the pilot's chair, hazy with dust and surprisingly comfortably cushioned. She reclined with a sigh of satisfaction.

The noise of the engine filled the hangar, the roar of a beast calling to the rest of its troupe. It was a signal of death, alerting every alpha in the area to tear her to shreds.

The hangar doors began to slowly open, reacting to her ship as it hovered, ready to move forward. Sweat beaded on her brow as they opened inch by inch, squeaking into the silence.

The darkness confronted her in an endless sprawl. Stars twinkled, a runway to follow; the path to redemption. And as the sweat frosted on her shoulders, relief relaxed her muscles – no Gemarinians lingered beyond the doors to capture her. A smirk dominated her face as she sped out into the city, rounding in an arc and surveying her castle, her kingdom. The place where she was the alpha, the top soldier, the person that no one fucked with. Her reputation would be ruined solely from the decimation of her crew, but this. This meant banishment. Exile. Into the Wilds she would go. And no one came back from there.

Well, that isn't exactly true. Xan was the only person to have survived.

Xan. I'd do anything for that godlike do-gooder shit-head, she realised as she hovered over the city, inputting the coordinates. As it had been for the last ten years of her life, at the end of the day, she peeled back the accolades and the things that didn't really mean anything. It was Juniper, Xan and Qilin. They were her home, so home she would go.

CHAPTER 24

LOCATION: YARMANDOR
YEAR: 116 (2 YEARS AGO)
LILIANNA – 20 YEARS OLD

Lilianna wasn't looking forward to going back outside again, but *I can't stay in my little bubble of suppressed desire forever.*

Her tired eyes felt red raw – like wriggling iron worms nestled peacefully under the cover of her eyelids. The pills didn't combat the sulphur as well as what she had expected. Xan's eyes, however, were vitreous orbs holding the horizon's gaze, effective and unscathed. The ridiculous goggles he'd fashioned the previous day served him well. Although he looked like an insect, he wouldn't need half as much time in the regen chamber as Lilianna would.

She recalled their conversations into the early hours of the morning. Xan was excited about the footage that would be captured on the trail cams, lyrically describing the new species he wanted to find in the Grouter System after they were back from Yarmandor. Laughing at memories of when Massy had his finger bitten clean off by an *Angel Boronus*. Remembering Massy absent-mindedly stroking the little reptilian's head while a retractable set of teeth had shot out and taken his digit as its own.

She marvelled at how, even though her eyes stung and hurt, her cheeks ached more from the laughter they'd shared.

"C'mon, little love," Xan announced. "It's time. There was movement on the trail camera stream about sixteen minutes ago, so we gotta go catch the *Oppatous*."

He threw her the pill and this time, as soon as it went down, she held out her hand for some goggles.

"Oh, the pretty little lady doesn't care about ruining her appearance today?"

She groaned. "Please, bossman, I'd like to follow safety protocol, if you don't mind."

Xan threw her the goggles, then bent down and gave Qilin her injection, all the while grinning at their exchange. They waited until the MPD beeped, signifying they were okay to venture outside.

The xanthic fog was still thick around them, especially in the valley. The ground was a mess of rocks and they crunched and cracked as the trio traipsed across them. Boulders lined the clifftops, peering down like elder overlords, surveying the fate of their lands. They hardly saw a living thing, except for the various insects, so Lilianna started to get doubtful they would find what they were searching for.

Xan dismantled the trail cam fixed to a large rock face, stuffing it inside his pack. He placed the pack on the ground against the rock and took out the containment chamber. "Let's go without packs from here."

She nodded, already tired from the walk, but careful not to show any signs of weakness. Xan still had a bounce in his step – *How does he maintain such a high level of vibrancy? I want what he's having.*

There was a puff of dust ahead and Qilin pounced numerous times. She was in pursuit of something that was disturbing the path that curved around the bend.

Xan scampered after her as best he could, and Lilianna straggled behind. Before them, a cloud of dust had formed, and Xan pushed through it uninhibited. Lilianna mimicked him, shoulders broad with a fearless gaze.

The fog cleared as they broke through, revealing Qilin with the *Oppatous* in her mouth, holding it like a lioness would hold her cub. There was a degree of care taken in her approach, but the *Oppatous* continued to wiggle and squirm, squealing at the disruption. It was a rodent-like creature with dark grey fur and tufts of bare skin. *This one in particular is certainly not the cutest thing to look at.*

Xan carefully took the creature out of Qilin's mouth and placed it into the containment chamber. It didn't have any teeth to bite with. It had prominent gums though, as it usually fed upon microscopic bacteria that grew on rocks, or small flying insects.

Its beady eyes reminded her of Ryker and she stifled a giggle as she fought against voicing that thought.

"What're you laughing at?" Xan cocked an eyebrow, a half smile raking across his face.

"Never mind." She brushed him off. "Can we get moving now, though?" she said, looking around impatiently.

"You don't like this urine-coloured fog planet?" Xan laughed.

"Not particularly." She squinted behind the bulging goggles. "I don't exactly love looking like a bug-eyed freak."

"I'll make sure not to take you to another planet filled with sulphur and swarms of freaky bugs then," he drolled, twisting the corner of his mouth.

"I think that's a solo expedition for Massy." They both laughed.

As they reached their discarded packs, Qilin growled and cozied up against Xan. The lines on his face crinkled and he became suddenly grave. Where a moment ago humour reigned supreme, anxiety now held a sickle to its throat. "Lilianna, get behind me," he warned, his voice no longer light and playful.

They scanned the rocks and their peripherals but nothing appeared. Xan reached for his pack, digging inside to locate something. She never saw him pull anything out, but felt intense pressure against her ankles and she stared down in horror.

Pincers locked onto Lilianna's boots and clamped down. A harrowing scream from a creature tore across the dense fog. Xan reacted within seconds, grabbing at Lilianna's arms and pulling her toward him. Her high-pitched, terror-stricken shriek mixed with the deep grunts of Xan's desperation. His wide eyes focused downwards, kicking out violently at the large, furry pincers that were wrapped around her ankles, yanking her down toward the creature's burrow.

The claws retreated as Xan's boot struck a decisive blow in between its joints. A huge crack split the air like the first cry of thunder before it found voracity.

Xan fell back with Lilianna in his arms. There was no time for a cute moment between them as he shoved her off, her body rolling a few metres away, caking her in layers of dust. She flicked her golden hair away from her eyes in time to see a huge arachnid-crustacean hybrid rise from under the ground. Sand and dust flew all around Qilin and Xan, bursting like a fountain. The creature used its legs as spears, thrusting forward as Qilin and Xan used their agility to evade punctures drilling into the ground.

Qilin bounded with a quickened pace up the creases in its legs and swung her tail at one of its many eyes. The creature reared back, stunned, as one of the prominent spikes in the *Mika Tikaani*'s tail pierced its cornea. Blood burst like a flower unfurling for the sun. Wet droplets hissed as they were absorbed into the dirt. Xan grabbed a sturdy rock and slammed it into one of the pincers, cracking it in half. Instead of faltering, the creature used one of its other limbs and pinned Xan up against a rock wall. Xan flexed his muscles, straining to keep the pincers from snapping shut and severing him in two.

Lilianna screamed out, helpless. The poetry of impermanence written in the scene before her; the rhythm of Xan's staggered breathing, the sorrowful lament of tears that trembled in his eyes, the cacophony of the creature's malicious intent. Her voice turned to a whimper – premature petals that fell, shaken by a rising gale.

Claws scraped across the flat, brittle ground. A roar of a guardian, possessive and devout ripped across the environment. Qilin burst into view, her eyes burning embers, raging; a demonic plague set to be unleashed.

Xan was slick with sweat. His goggles were smashed and lay discarded on the ground. A victim of one of the creature's razor pincers. Tears streamed down his face as he confronted his mortality. But recognition burned within his stare, as he glimpsed Qilin's pulsing red eyes. A low growl rose in intensity; a crescendo of veracity, of fierce rage.

A nostalgic acknowledgement swept across his eyes as if he knew what was coming. The ground shook, the fog swirled, spinning into a ferocious tornado. It spun around Xan with the DNA of true chaos, lifting him from the pincer's grip as the creature became disoriented from the sudden weather phenomenon. Xan flew through the air and landed in a heap close to Lilianna. She gasped at the sickening thud as his body hit the ground. Her pale cheeks simmered to a pink hue from the ache in her stomach; the sinking feeling that the person she cared about the most might not plant a smile in the wasteland of her emotions, might not gaze in earnest at the panorama of her true desires.

He hadn't moved, even reflexively, so terror shifted in tumultuous arcs upon her face. The emotional duress caused her physically to falter. As she rushed to his side – not only to administer aid, but to soothe her restless fear – she stumbled clumsily.

Lilianna didn't take her eyes from Qilin though, as the terrifying alien creature snapped its pincers toward the little thief that stole its meal. But in an instant, shards of rock shot up from the terrain, spearing each of its legs, cracking its shell into pale orange pieces, impaling it to the ground from whence it first emerged.

Black blood oozed from within, staining the ground with a halo of darkness. Screams of pain filled the air, high-pitched, tortuous and wretched. Its breath was shallow, eyes darting in fear. The fear of recognising it was prey, the fear that predators seldom know. But when the moment came, was it resignation built from memories and experience or did denial occlude that death would finally come?

Qilin stood proudly on all fours, chest extended, fixed glare burning red – directing all her concentration at the creature.

Xan stirred beneath Lilianna and she helped him sit up. "Qilin, is she—"

Then he saw Qilin and his words faded. She was okay.

XAN
22 YEARS OLD

Lilianna reached for Xan's hand and it became his safety net. A rumble sounded, and it rippled across the soundscape. Embers fizzed and flames sprouted from the sand. Growing in strength, the scorching heat climbed up the alien creature's legs like a strangling vine. Its skin bubbled and popped, and then the fire burst and roared with its own life and soon the creature succumbed. The blackness of its blood had become its tomb. And its tomb would turn to ash, forever speckled within a golden fog, floating on an unforgiving world.

Qilin's eyes lost the deep red glow, and like the fire, they diminished. She flicked her head with regal ease, turning around to face Lilianna and Xan. It was as if she sighed with relief, noting their safety. With her head held high, Qilin shook her blue and black coat, ridding the dust from her back. She crouched low, gliding across the ground. The muscles in her strong legs rippled with every movement.

Qilin then moved toward Xan, the blue in her fur shimmering as if sunlight cast its solar dust upon her. Xan stared with diffidence, with a hint of shame and regret, as if he'd forced her to act. It concerned him that such a display of power would deplete her strength and leave her vulnerable. It might even have an expiration date. When it would expire was unknown, but fears that no being liked to touch, or give rise to, are the ones that lay waste to denial; the ones that follow a retreating path to the edge of a cliff.

Lilianna appeared too shaken to react, only watching as Qilin approached her first, licking her cheek with a careful caress, in complete contrast to the powerful being that had thwarted a terrifying creature.

The smell of ash leaked through the stinging sulphur, an apology in Qilin's eyes was lathered with honey and brass. Her forehead brushed against Xan's and they inhaled the presence of one another, letting it strengthen their bond, letting it fuse their souls. He lay his arms across her neck, his fingers digging into her fur, firm enough to be rough, but that roughness was love, from the intangible to a physical manifestation. His eyes closed as his head hit her shoulder and they remained wrapped in a bizarre embrace of human and alien creature until Lilianna shuffled over, patting Xan's back as if to say, *You've done this for long enough.*

Xan dusted himself off, stared at the charred body of the creature, then sighed, limping to get his pack and check on the *Oppatous.*

"It looks like he's still alive at least," he said, relieved as his shoulders slackened.

"Xan, I don't even know what to say. What did Qilin just—"

"Stop. There's no point in discussing it now because I'm still going through tests." He was short with her, and she stepped back with a hurt expression. Xan softened his tone. "I've mentioned to you once before about how I believe her to be more than she is. Well, you've now seen it with your own eyes, there is something more to her."

"What are you doing about it?" she inquired, leaning forward, interest piqued.

"I've been studying her for years, developing tests, recording data. But this is the first time since I met her that it's happened again."

"What do you think made her act out?"

"I think it's when her life is threatened," Xan said simply.

Lilianna shook her head. "But, it was you. You would have died. Not her."

Xan scrunched his face up and massaged his temples. "I really don't know right now. But my eyes hurt, my body is broken – I'd love to get the fuck out of here. I'm well and truly on the Lilianna train of hating this place."

She laughed nervously and took another look at Qilin, now sitting peacefully at her side, licking her paw as if nothing had happened.

"I'm also keen to see the readings on what just happened."

"What do you mean?"

"She's wearing sensors and she has done so on every field trip we've been on, in case this happened. I'm finally going to understand *why* it happens."

CHAPTER 25

Xan made sure he tipped the transpo driver for confidentiality like Juniper suggested. He didn't have any wigs or costumes that he used for sexual play like she did, but it also wasn't particularly necessary since he wasn't banned from expeditions, yet. There was a risk of Juniper being tracked by one of Madame Bleu's inner circle, so she'd stowed some in her pack just in case. She was the rebellious one, so it would be more prudent to have extra eyes on her.

He realised that having an MPD meant it was quite simple to pull up where he'd been and what he had been doing, so one of Juniper's dead crew member's devices was strapped to his wrist instead.

General Heronicus's threats rang in his memory; his voice was a solar flare, distant and explosive. Sometimes looking behind was the only way he could walk forward with certainty. As he explored the reams of mentally stored pictures of the past, he fell upon Qilin unconscious in the cage. It both enraged him and focused him.

Everything Xan was doing now was for her. She had sacrificed her safety for him countless times, but now it was his turn to repay her. It was selfish bringing Juniper out of the black hole of grief. It was irresponsible to allow Lilianna – a novice in dire situations – to wander off alone to enact part of the plan. Skeletal wings of guilt unfurled from his shoulder blades, readying to fly him headlong into the sun. But seeking forgiveness from his two closest companions was worth momentary shame, for it meant his energy was devoted to bringing Qilin back. Later there would be time to repent.

The power station was a beast in itself, a structure one would expect to be scarred with grime, sodden with soot. But it stood in the middle of a derelict industrial quarter, brilliant and white in among the drab abandoned buildings drunk on the fumes of yesteryear when they, too, had been gleaming, worthy and useful. Conical shafts reached toward the observant twin moons, discerning the spectacle before them: Xan, a pseudo-famous xeno-conservationist nerd, trying to break into a facility powering the whole planet.

Xan inspected the heavy guard from where he stood, which ultimately stoked a negative intuition within.

He scanned the shadowed street, the orbs of lights that decorated the city was absent here, almost as if what was hiding inside didn't want to be found. No other guards lined the perimeter around the station; it was only within that he experienced the feeling of dread.

I feel so small, so minuscule in this madness. I'm a babysitter for insects and animals – what the fuck am I doing here?

But he quickly shook his head, remembering the big amber eyes of the *Mika Tikaani*, replaced by the desperation in the insidious glare of the Valkor general.

The Valkor had sent directions to his MPD, which he had forwarded through to the one now on his wrist. The instructions were almost a revelation – an underground tunnel and a guide perhaps? It was all a little unbelievable. But then again, mere days ago, none of this would have seemed feasible.

Xan neared the building opposite, spotting abundant cracks in the mortar as flakes of grey paint scuttled into the breeze. Stairs slick with moisture led down into an ominous basement. His footsteps echoed off the walls in the narrow alleyway and puddles gleamed in the night with a combined glow from both moons, reflecting the Gemarine night sky.

The stairs led to a heavy-set metallic door locked with a keypad. On Gemarine, doors were always opened with an MPD, so staring at this primitive form of tech made Xan completely aware of his potential obsolescence. At a moment's notice, he could so easily be deemed surplus to requirements if Madame Bleu found out about this betrayal. His life would become a speck on the galaxational timeline. In fact, it already was, wasn't it? What was he in this mess of a galaxy, but a dilapidated vessel floating in a sea of dying stars?

Although the insignificance of his life seemed grave in that moment, he reflected on why he ran the biobase. Why he fought so hard against extinction. A meaningless speck on a timeline, still comprised of moments so rare and beautiful, unique and life-altering. Moments were worth preserving. Extinction was worth exterminating. There was a legacy in that, a way in which to ensure his vessel didn't float by aimlessly. It made waves and ripples that expanded into the far reaches of the galaxy, ensuring other lifeforms did more than sit idly by and admire a pretty view. They would engage in fortifying it forevermore.

The breeze in the alleyway picked up, skimming water off the puddles and making the icy chill that had solidified in his veins a little more prominent. He whipped his face around, eyes flicking, the condensation in his rapid breath building a halo around his head. Angelic he was not. Angels didn't fear. They cruised the skies, harp melodies fluttering like long eyelashes eradicating doubtful stares. But there were no melodies to soothe him, his hands shaking as he reached out to the keypad and entered the numerical code 825467.

A blue light flashed across the panel and the door released inward with a huff. He pushed inside tentatively but was desperate to get out of the open. Nerves tingling within, the smell of damp was rife and he drowned in it. Rusted pipes dripped onto the rough, textured floor.

This wasn't anything like the Gemarine he knew. The abandonment of the streets swept inside this building in particular. Hollow and dark, a hue of grey enveloped every place where his eyes landed. Cobwebs, scratches, creases and cracks touched everything within reach as if time had wanted to forget this place.

Xan followed the path that turned to the left until he became boxed in. The walls narrowed, coaxing him with a gentle hand further down a steep decline. The musty, cooler chill crept around his body and he shivered at its touch.

Finally, a blue light shone ahead as the narrow walls opened onto a larger area. The soft lights illuminated a storeroom of sorts. But there were hunky metallic boxes strewn haphazardly, gathering dust.

How often did people come around here?

What was going on in this abandoned building?

Approaching the door at the end of the corridor he got a sense that this was the end of the line. Beyond was the power station. Beyond, destiny beckoned him.

His gaze traced across the heavy wooden door. The polished surface gleamed. *That's odd. The coating on the wood looks new.*

Shaking off his puzzlement, he searched for the keyhole mentioned in his instructions. It was as if the further he went into the Gemarine underworld, the further he went back in time. Numerical keypads, keys and locks. Whoever had devised this entryway, was conscious of avoiding technology.

In the top right-hand corner he spotted the key buried deep into the lock already. An untrained eye would have mistaken it for a protruding nail. But Xan had noticed the metallic key blooming with three petals, twisted in its rusted radiance atop its length.

Before he twisted the key, he glanced up at a grey screen flickering. The size of an adult human hand tucked into the cornice. It played the scene of an empty hallway in between bursts of static. A nest of black-and-white ants crawling.

It took him a few hefty seconds to understand what it was: the hallway beyond the door. Otherwise, how else would 'they' be able to frequent the power station if they might open the door into the path of patrolling guards?

Moments passed and he still hadn't turned the key and landed on the other side. It was as if he couldn't quite trust that flickering screen.

Faith and hope were often the cards he played. In the game of life, even if one held a trump card or two, they were never quite guaranteed pockets of gold. The key turned. Harsh artificial light seared his eyes. The path was vacant. Golden.

He had memorised where he needed to go. He crouched, cramped as he walked. There was always the threat of his own extinction. Usually quite adept at empathetic gestures, he had never felt a deeper kinship to the creatures he saved as he did now. A guard could round the corner, a robotic laser beam could shoot from the roof. Xan wouldn't know how or when danger would present; there were a multitude of ways. Nevertheless, he felt compelled to keep low to the ground, on guard, making himself as small as can be. Hope and faith were fickle associates in the pursuit of victory.

The low hum of a generator pulsed ahead. Xan's gaze sliced through the windows to get his bearings, eager to know which path to take to avoid the guards. A heavily fortified area was further to the left, set up like the type of checkpoint Gemarinians needed the clearance scan of an MPD to get through. Four guards of varying genders and species spoke among themselves, unaware of the threat behind them.

Satisfied that no one else patrolled the area where the generator growled, he followed the sound, leaving the guards to converse and let a makeshift agent on a mission find his way unobstructed.

The groans of the generator grew louder as he approached the door housing the answers he was there to find. He couldn't help but gawk at the scene beneath him through a large viewing window. He stood on a mezzanine level, looking down on huge copper pipes twisting like coiled snakes stirred into a frenzy by a delectable, docile prey. They all fed into one gigantic vat, dials flashing, steam shooting out the sides, churning energy and powering the grid for Topaz City.

Guards came into view patrolling the top-layer corridor, encased by a criss-crossed metal fence about shoulder-height. Xan ducked down, abandoning his gawk fest and shifted his mindset to the growling and the answers that lay behind that red-rimmed rusty door.

The door swung wide, exhaling a groan as it did. Three distinct chambers lay ahead, grates pulled back, revealing a deep vat filled at various levels of geological substances. Each labelled from the home planets of all the species that inhabited Gemarine.

Well, that's a fucking bad sign. He scowled at the vats, each with their own pipe that led down into what he'd seen through the window a moment ago.

Spinning his pack to face forward, he rifled through it, finding gloves and sealed canisters that would keep the samples from contamination. He was doing this a little old school, but he didn't have the luxury of rolling through the facility with robotic lab equipment on his heels. Stalking forward, his powdered latex gloves snapped against his wrist. Xan reached for the samples, clasping them in the palm of his hand. The moment stalled him as he studied the mined sediment sealed in the conical tube. He was the architect of the future, holding scaled sketches of a world in muddled shades of grey. Building atop demolished civilisations? He held tight to hope that this was not the case. That Gemarine was self-sufficient and could function without the ashes of genocide.

Xan placed the tubes into a cool storage container in his pack. Intense concentration ensued until he had both tubes stored carefully. As he moved his attention to the final vat, he heard shuffling on the other side of the door, the slithers of light coming into the room disturbed by heavy boots at the doorway. The door swung back and he froze.

CHAPTER 26

LOCATION: GEMARINE
YEAR: 118
LILIANNA – 22 YEARS OLD

It was just her luck that Lilianna had snagged an overly chatty transpo driver. Comfortable in silence and her own thoughts, this was an abuse of her time.

Aside from her obvious indiscretions as a polite individual, it was important at that moment she try very hard not to evoke suspicion. So she nodded enthusiastically, feigned a giggle or two, channelling Juniper, and most likely, failed miserably.

When the time came, she paid extra credits, blowing a kiss from under her hood. But her golden eyes still shone like moons beneath the delicate veil of twilight. She hoped those extra credits would ensure her eyes were instead a moonless night, dark and forgotten.

Lilianna reached the lab door and held up her own MPD. One of Juniper's crew would not have been permitted into this area, so it was her only choice. The fact that Madame Bleu had referred to her as 'unnamed

Sytheract girl' gave her the best chance to get away with this. Mischief calls for anonymity. Lilianna was a whisper in a hurricane.

The lab lights blinked at her, yawning at the disturbance. She walked through into a white wonderland of sterilised equipment gleaming on shelves, windows sparkling clean. Incomplete holo notes still floated in the air scrawled in Xan's illegible hand. Days of emotional stress, physical demands and being way out of her comfort zone meant she was not only out of sorts within, but outwardly appeared dull, swallowed by fatigue.

Lilianna strode past the space Xan usually occupied, and the small area in the corner that housed a comfortable bed for Qilin, a tube dispenser for her water and a custom *Mika Tikaani* regen chamber for if she ever got injured on assignment.

She sighed, a sadness encircling her. *I hope she isn't in pain.*

She glanced at the MPD; time mocked her with its countdown: only twelve hours left to meet the general.

They had been awake for a long time. She couldn't even remember the last time she let herself be carried away in dreams, imagining scenarios of playing tour guide to Xan on her home planet. Showing him the habitat of the flightless *Flurgre*, the gem-ridden caves of Ithantiscist, the ceremonial celebration of the soul bond with flowing red silk garbs that tethered hands together forevermore. He might see then, that he could use his arms for more than a passionate embrace, his heart for more than a spark to ignite a lustful rendezvous. Instead, his heart would be a seed in the garden of his soul, emerging from the soil, expanding, blossoming, reaching with everything it had to that source of light.

She frowned. Dreams were one thing, but they were desperate ways to escape the truth. Simple lies to convince oneself that hope should not be abandoned. It was cruel, really.

In the reality of the moment she caught her reflection in the glass around the lab; dark rings of gloom cradled her bright eyes; they had somehow diminished like a world had swallowed its sun. Her ragged blonde hair tied back messily. Wispy strands had haloed across the top of her head as she'd flipped the hood down across her shoulders. Her cheek bones, sunken, wonderless, haggard; the shell of the girl who had once stood in the same spot consumed by the excitement and desire to do good. She frowned again. Keeping her lips pursed and her gaze poised was no use.

She spotted the mobile test kits in the corner of the lab and shuffled over, then grabbed one and hauled it onto her back. It was already in backpack form but bulky and rectangular, like a shell she could retreat into at any moment.

As she turned to leave, the doors flew open and a compliance officer from Madame Bleu's entourage strolled in. She recognised him as Zondini. Slick violet hair combed back tightly, a curved, pointed nose, and accusing blue eyes scorched her like a flame.

He was startled to see her and was on the backfoot immediately.

"Who are you?" His gloved hand went to his belt, where his Cranston ray gun was holstered.

"I'm the lab assistant. What is this all about?" she stammered, nerves pulsing through her, fear evident in the frantic melody of her voice.

Immediately he went on the defensive, but his hand rested against his side still cautiously close to the Cranston ray gun. "What are you doing here so late? Who gave you authority?"

Lilianna took a deep breath and steadied herself. Suffering from anxiety meant regular social settings were like a battlefield, to be defeated and bloodied by jovial conversations. Never mind a situation where, if handled incorrectly, her life would cease, and the lives of others hung in the balance.

"I work nights, sometimes. As a lab assistant I need to...I don't know, basically try and impress my boss." She shrugged, and her golden eyes fizzed at him, then faded as she looked at her toes. If Zondini looked at her hands he would see them tremble like morsels of dirt farewelling a ship from its surface.

Zondini grunted like a valve releasing the tension a little at the peak of its low-pitched climax. "Your boss works you hard, then."

The beat of Lilianna's heart levelled slightly. "Yes, well, when I'm running my own lab I know I won't ask these kinds of things from my assistants." She smiled, channelling her inner Juniper. "I'm guessing your boss is similar?" She rushed the last part, though, failing to hit the sweet note of sultry her flirtatious friend always found.

"You could say that." His voice, even and measured.

Lilianna looked over at the bev-store in the corner of the room and pointed. "Did you want to mix a drink before I head out? It could take the edge off both of us."

Zondini looked cross as he considered her request.

She gave it a little more to send it home harder. "Or, I suppose, if you're worried about getting caught, it's probably not worth it." Sighing with disappointment, almost switching off an excitement meter within.

"No, no," he rushed out, holding up a hand encased in its fabric sheath. "One can't hurt."

Lilianna smiled, but she wondered whether this was a smart move. Should she take the time to build rapport to ensure a path to freedom? Or waste time, hoping that Juniper and Xan would wait for her?

A few months ago she stood in this exact spot working quietly. Xan was over her right shoulder and had just finished talking in hushed tones with Ranjit.

She felt his presence before she turned and gazed into the misty grey of his eyes.

"Have you thought about a creature you'd like to try and…find?" he said.

Lilianna swiped across the zoom holos of the microbiomes. They switched off and her thoughts turned to the plight of the Truntalisk *on Zephtar.*

"I'm happy to find the creatures you think are most import—"

"That's not what I asked." Xan's voice was sharp; a hint of anger in the tone juxtaposed with a taunting smile.

Lilianna looked away and bit her lip. She was embarrassed to speak her mind. What if the Truntalisk *wasn't the calibre of creature Xan normally went after? Furthermore, was she even ready? She started to shake her head as if to concede her research had been non-existent, when Xan broke the silence, his tone now fatherly and warm.*

"You know, I wouldn't ask you unless I thought you were ready. I've seen you researching the* Truntalisk *and I think it's time for you to lead something of your own."

She spoke way too fast. "It might not be what you would do, but I really think…"

"Stop." *He rested his hand against her arm.* "Aim for the* Truntalisk *after a couple of smaller trips, but just know, I think you're ready. You've been ready for a long time. Now, I want to see what Lilianna can really do when she's the one calling the shots."

"Grab a seat," Lilianna said excitedly. "I'm happy to alter my schedule and to do so with someone of your pedigree is…well, a lovely change, to be honest."

Stepping forward, he grabbed the chair and it squeaked unapologetically across the waxed lab floor. He didn't take his eyes off her as they creased with his smirk.

"So, what's this boss of yours like?"

Okay, so now you can't snoop around when I'm here, I guess you'll uncover my thoughts, maybe try to trip me up.

"To be honest, he's normally quite fair, but I guess he wants me to improve." She puffed her cheeks out, dejected, as if cursing the time it took a lowly lab technician to ascend. "There's a lot of work to do after everything the last few days." Lilianna poured red liquid into a glass filled with ice.

"What happened the last few days?" He leant forward, gloved hands clasped together.

Blue liquid splashed over ice and cascaded into the red, creating swirls of dark purple. She took a metal mixer and swished it around. "Oh, my boss got caught up in some rescue attempt trying to be a hero. I guess there's a fine line between being bold and being unhinged." Mint leaves sprinkled into the glass, topped with carbonation liquid garnished with a pinch of lemon zest. A foreign powder sank to the bottom of one glass.

"Being a hero doesn't always mean flexing muscles like a brute. Sometimes a quiet approach, or a quiet disposition is enough to change the game."

She felt his eyes trail her movements, as if basking in her introversion and putting a value on her, acknowledging she was something more. He had no idea what she was capable of. Lilianna herself didn't really know. But it was time to grow. There was no steady progression of character-building, no baby steps in finding out how much of herself she would sacrifice for someone else – for a noble cause, even.

What am I capable of, really? she thought as she poured the drink for Zondini and then one for herself. She pushed his frosted glass across the desk, and it bumped softly into the gloved palm of his hand. "Here's to climbing the ladder…quietly." She smirked, a dare in her eyes.

"To the quiet achievers, who will rule the world with an iron mind, not an iron fist." He took a sip, smiling with as much warmth she thought he could muster with the scorn that hung in his dead eyes.

Drinking the purple liquid, the mint leaves stuck to her lips, refreshing the sting of the alcohol.

Holding back a wince she managed, "I think it's quite refreshing, if I'm being honest."

Taking another healthy sip, Zondini swished the liquid inside his mouth.

Such a heathen at heart. All these fancy clothes and velvet gloves can't hide the fact that he's just a mindless minion.

"It's quite good." He nodded, pursing his lips in satisfaction. "What's the drink called?"

Ignoring his question, she instead produced a statement. "It's quite hot." Lilianna fanned herself with her hands, then unzipped her suit a touch. The discarded hood lay slack against her shoulders. She placed the drink against her neck, letting the icy glass cool her, or give that impression anyway. *How does Juniper do this and make it sexy?* She was cooking in one pan, working with bland, white meat. A fancy meal required multiple elements. Sweet to contrast the sour, bitterness to play against the salty; textures to enhance the palette. A star chef though she was not, Zondini's mouth hung open, salivating for the singular supple item on the menu. *The gendered males are so easy, comets above!*

"Oh, sorry," she giggled and put the glass down, "that's totally not the name of the drink." Lilianna laughed and he followed her, movements slow with glassy eyes.

"It's called 'The Sweet Goodnight'," she concluded.

"I wonder why that is." His eyes were flickering, hands limp, words slurred. This would be the moment.

"Do you want to go to Fusion with me?" She moved to the other side of the desk, her hand finding his leg. As she did, it felt like a part of her soul had become infected with an incurable disease.

"Fusion? Ah yes, yes that's good." His body sagged against the desk, eyes fighting gravity.

"Well c'mon then," Lilianna said excitedly, fighting against her own internal gravity as she dragged him upwards.

Zondini sagged in Lilianna's arms, wearing a slack smile. The weight of the backpack and a limp male body pressed against her almost made her crash to the ground. But she held steady. Her days of shouldering samples and carrying creatures in cages had built up her strength.

"Whoa, this will be fun," he slurred, vacant eyes flickering in a dopey haze.

"Yes, yes c'mon," Lilianna said impatiently, straining to steady him. "Let's get to the motitube, quickly."

They reached the motitube with great difficulty, his knees giving way more than once as the two of them fumbled through the darkened hallways of the xeno-conservation levels. The motitube sucked them down to the bottom and when the cool evening air caressed Lilianna's flushed cheeks, she linked arms with Zondini. Passers-by hurried on, casting curious glances as they stumbled across the pavement, Lilianna feigning inebriation. Her laughter cut like an alarm in the still silence of the night.

Zondini's black ship, all angles, sheen and slick, gleamed in a parking bay ahead. Lilianna gasped and steered him the other way, dialling up another transpo to avoid the cameras in his ship. Not that he could suitably steer in his condition.

They filed into the transpo. "Fusion please," she said flatly.

The transpo driver, an Aranther with a faded scar across his left eye – a war wound, now a reminder of otherworldly tension – scowled. "Jeez, will he even be able to…ah…enjoy himself?" He slowly smiled with playful wickedness.

Lilianna baulked. "Oh, him – he's fine," she protested, elongating 'fine' to enhance her nonchalance.

Zondini pouted and squinted at the driver. "Boyo, I'm real good. Don't you worry about big ol' Zondini."

The scar creased, the playful nature settled into acknowledgement of minding his thoughts. "Oh, my bad. You enjoy your big ol' self." He swung around and off they went.

Lilianna pulled up her hood in the back of the transpo as she watched the lights outside dazzle, her nervous breath fogging the window.

Zondini sidled up to her. She felt him before she turned to his slackened face. Violet strands of hair stuck out from the perfect slick he'd presented earlier.

"So, girl, let's start things up here."

Sickness spread throughout her like a rushing flood between the weathered rock walls of a gorge.

She kept her hood up as she walked into Fusion, wishing she could pull a blanket over her heart as flashes of the car ride invaded her mind.

She resisted him as long as she could, but ultimately relented. The slack-jawed kiss from his toxic lips was wet, as an eager tongue sought to roam the inside of her mouth. His hands fumbled across the inside of her leg, groping at her breasts, and all the while she had giggled, pretended this was a game. But the game for the trophy of her soul was not a game she wanted to play.

The sickness wouldn't abate as she looked at this place with fresh eyes. Lasers pulsed across the level in relative darkness, but glow body paint flashed on naked bodies so close she could see the beads of sweat running down the corridor of muscled shoulders, groups of men servicing one another, aggression, passion, submission and even tenderness.

Thoughts turned to Xan, of the times he'd asked her to accompany him. *Wouldn't it have been better to experience this with him? Rather than this...fool?*

She recoiled as Zondini's eyes met hers and he pushed forward for a kiss that was more like he spat across her face. Smiling, hidden hatred boiled, tears steamed and threatened to trickle like condensation down her heart of glass. Her breaths stale from rising bile, memories and regrets accelerating her pulse. Hands shaking, she sat him down, whispering into his ear, "I'll be back with a drink, babe."

His eyes were half closed as he responded, "Yeah, babe, drink me up."

Oh, my comets, he's losing it. Lilianna slunk away and scanned the room for the closest doppelganger.

There. Golden eyes, lips and breasts fuller, dressed with too many holes; demure escaping through one of them perhaps. But that was the best option. *I guess a more...promiscuous version of me.*

"Hey," Lilianna said, "how many credits will it take for you to give that guy a good time? It's his promotion day so I wanted to give him a good experience."

"Oh girl, he looks yum." The Sytheract licked her lips and seemed almost to forget about the credit. Then she said, "But everything has a price so…like…I guess two hundred will do it." Her eyebrows arched, waiting for an answer.

Lilianna held up the MPD and typed onto her screen and, without looking up, muttered hastily, "I'll give you four hundred if you forget me."

"Babe, you *so* have a deal." The Sytheract girl held out her dainty wrist to accept the transfer. "Hun, I'll keep my mouth shut about you, but can I say – you are not someone easily forgotten." She batted her eyelashes with provocation. "Please find me next time you're here. I wouldn't mind a little taste." She looked Lilianna up and down, as if imagining the night they would have together.

Lilianna forced a giggle. *I look exactly like her. Is she into herself that much?*

Zondini had rested his head back and closed his eyes, which sent her feet into a frenzy as she ran over, worried he was too far gone.

She touched him on the leg and he shot up. "Huh?" he snapped, confused. Then he recognised Lilianna, and a toothy smile returned to his dopey, half-paralysed face. "Oh yes, sexy time, we have?"

Narrowing her eyes, trying to understand him, she shrugged. "I'm getting the drink I ordered." She bent across him, and as she gave him a quick kiss, pushed a small dose of slow-release adrenalin into his leg. She didn't want him to pass out while a girl looking like her fucked him senseless all night. It was important she had an alibi in case Madame Bleu ever came snooping. If she were caught drugging a member of the inner circle, Lilianna was certain her fate would be worse than exile.

Lilianna moved behind him and toward the door, and the other Sytheract girl took her place, fixing him a drink and sitting on his lap.

Lilianna couldn't smile with satisfaction; she'd lost a part of herself that night. When one sacrifices a part of themselves to save the lives of a cohort, a scar remains, yet a feather is added to the cap in one's soul. It serves one well beyond any flickering iteration of who they *thought* they were.

UNKNOWN
UNKNOWN AGE

Not far from the exit, the hooded girl with the golden eyes stood, watching a couple intently. She looked too much like Lilianna for it not to be her, but she appeared sadder than usual, not as anxious, and just a little broken. Then she seemed satisfied enough and turned toward the exit. He never expected to see her at Fusion. Why was she here and where was she going in such a hurry?

CHAPTER 27

LOCATION: GEMARINE
YEAR: 118
XAN – 24 YEARS OLD

Several thoughts ran through Xan's head at that moment the guard had sprung him. Stupidity was often reserved for those who hadn't scoured clouds of information, or scorched their eyes from studying the MPD so frequently. But he sure felt stupid now.

Could it really be called a plan if it isn't planned?

If he'd been thorough, maybe he might have waited until Juniper had come back, signalling him as the stolen ship touched down on the shadowed street beyond. The industrial graveyard was a perfect place to bury the scent of their criminal activity. But instead, he'd burst through the door, curiosity stoking an ember until he alone set everything ablaze without a watchful eye to douse an inferno. The regrets seeped through him like a noxious gas. He was too emotional this time and it eroded the immoveable stone that was his brain.

He could see all the guard's features. An androgynous Sytheract, with twinkling cosmetic fangs bathed in blue light when their mouth opened wide in surprise. Tendrils behind their ears flared out, coiled and frilled, at the perception of a threat. Their eyes shone with a placid fear, but as they registered Xan crouched and submissive, the gleam of a predator was in their stare. They pushed forward, laser drawn, about to utter victorious words stained with presumption.

But she came, and she was swift and severe. The burning in the Sytheract's eyes sizzled to smoke as Juniper burst into the room, her skin blending to shadow, muscles flexed and deadly as they tightened around their neck, swiftly snapping it with a muffled crunch. The Sytheract slipped through Juniper's arms, flopping to the ground in a heap – victorious only in acquainting themself with death.

Xan's and Juniper's eyes met. They shared a moment of clarity, mixed with sorrow and salvation, diffusing in the air, sour and pungent. Relief exhaled from within as he nodded and smiled with nothing but sadness. She did the same. Words were pebbles in an endless ocean. All that mattered was the current that always brought them closer to one another.

They both stared at the body, each filled with guilt. Xan's stomach lurched as his conscience berated him like a child scorned.

JUNIPER
24 YEARS OLD

Juniper clenched her fists and closed her eyes, trying to absolve herself with the mantra that she lived her life by; Xan is number one. A death by her steady hand in the pit of war seldom cast shade across the pastures of her mind. But a patrol guard doing their rounds didn't sit right with her. As Juniper took stock of where she was and the man she protected, it dawned on her. *Maybe this is war. A war that isn't written in braille with flecks of dotted blood, nor told through the melancholy melody of a soldier's wailing cry. When there is division on what is the perceived path of righteousness. Mixed with the unrelenting determination to follow the path to its end. That is war.*

"So it begins," she breathed, steadying herself against the hardening of her heart. She knew this feeling well.

The essence of thankfulness evaporated, and Xan and Juniper quickly recognised the situation was dire.

"Did you get what you needed?" Juniper croaked, arms that brought death moments ago now limp against her sides.

"I've got everything I need, but now, ah…what are we going to do?" Xan gestured to the body on the ground, his hands shaking.

"Let's drag them into the underground space and figure out what to do next." She shrugged. "It's the only thing we can do for now."

"Right." Xan fixed a determined gaze, positioning himself to help, and lifted the body with Juniper, shuffling back into the hall, moving with great difficulty toward the door Xan entered from. On this side it was disguised as an off-white and basic panel, so they nearly missed it.

Juniper stole a quick glance at Xan. A man unfamiliar with using his hands for anything other than saving, had killed, had maimed, had carried a carcass. She wanted to shield him from it all — to have lent him her hands so that every time his fingers caressed a forlorn creature they would not be sullied by the memory of his own desperation. Juniper wasn't sure if redemption was something she could bestow upon him. But as each future door opened, she vowed to walk ahead of him, taking laser fire to her flesh, seared and scoured so that a morsel of his decency would be preserved.

XAN
24 YEARS OLD

As they got closer to the door, panting with the weight of the body, the door swung back. Despite the convenient nature of the timing, their panic and fatigue pushed them through, plonking the body on the floor, hoping whoever had opened the door into the basement was an ally.

They dropped to their knees around the body as dust kicked up, swirling like a fog in a harbour of punctured vessels.

Juniper and Xan peered upwards as the dust settled. They were surrounded by a group of different species, scowling, each in bizarre, mismatched clothing, torn suits. Wrinkles prominent, scars written deep in the lines of their faces telling fables without happy endings.

Regen chambers could be found on almost every level in Topaz City, so Gemarinians scooted across slick city streets devoid of scars, nurturing them on the inside instead. Used to seeing skin taut and supple, laying eyes upon these abominations was daunting and surprising.

One of them stepped forward, a commanding presence enveloping her. She didn't appear menacing with her palms upturned and a mist of serenity caught in the lines on her face. There was a crown of twisted twigs atop knotted black and grey dreadlocks, her thin lips curled into a curious smile.

"Xan and Juniper, I take it?" She spoke with confidence, as if she were a long-lost clan member of theirs, extending her soiled hand to help pick them up. Her skin was coarse, as if dusted by a salty ocean breeze. Bowing to Juniper, she hesitated as she caught Xan's glance.

"Forgive me, but we…saw…what went down on the Valkor ship and my feelings about you," she spat, glaring at Xan, "ain't all that rosy." She straightened and squared her bony shoulders.

Xan's scalp prickled and he suddenly felt a shiver. "How do you know about that?"

"We've a lot to yarn about, but not enough time." She adjusted her garments, pale skin visible through frayed tears, scars like battle medallions, a part of her. Salvaged bits and pieces from army uniforms of old sewed together, creating something barely acceptable. "The name's Miami, and I'm what you'd call Leader of the Exiled."

"The Exiled?" Xan asked, frowning.

Miami turned away from him, disgust written clear in her wistful, hazel eyes that squinted as she recoiled and shifted closer to Juniper. "Yeah, but as I said, we don't 'ave time to explain all the gory details. We 'ave to fix this mess." Her voice was stern, almost patronising. Flicking her attention to a dark Aranther brooding in the corner, fangs on display. "Balfour, get over 'ere."

Balfour was a large Aranther from the Plaxxon Tribe, the hint of muscles snaked over his heavy-set frame, dark skin, porous and dry, flaked across his arms. He approached, looking the dead guard over. Not a glimmer of sadness tickled his face. Tears didn't cascade from the deep brown pools in his eyes. He considered a solution without the weight of emotion to constrict him.

Miami barked, "Take the body to the face scanner and get it done – by the looks, maybe Voilani can take its place?"

"Yes, Mother, yes I'll get it done." Eyes lowered in reverence of her. He dragged the body away, heaving while a couple of other stragglers followed.

Miami turned to Xan as if reading his thoughts. "'Mother' refers to a more…matriarchal set up 'ere in the underground. They see me as maternal, not big bad ruler." Eyes lingered on his. "Down 'ere we thrive on love, togetherness, unity. It keeps us alive. Rather than cry for freedom, our exile brought us together and gave us something to cherish."

Xan nodded. *Through the lament of liberty, they are bound by loss. The very thing that broke them is their healing solution.* He recognised her presence as something revered here, but she was wary of him, a spectator to a grave moment in his life when vengeance took hold, breathing life into his body as he carved a path of death. *How could she have seen it? Who else knows?* Thoughts turned sour; anger spiced the broth in the usually calm kitchen. *She judges me for the one moment I raged for a friend, for my family. By the scars that tattoo her body, has she done the same? When her maternal instinct was laid bare.*

216

"I know there isn't much time, but Lilianna isn't here yet, so please, if you could explain who you are and what you're doing with the body of that guard – we'd really appreciate it." Xan tried to sound as calm and as non-threatening as possible.

Miami saw past him, looking at Juniper as if she would prefer to explain it to her, but Juniper snapped, "I was going to ask, *what the fuck is going on*, but that's why you should give him the lowdown, because he's the eloquent one, not me."

Miami turned, hesitating.

"Look." Xan tried to muster the courage to defend himself without anything but words this time. "I don't know what you've seen or how much you know about me, but I…have made some terrible choices lately. I'm just hoping when I can test these substances," he gestured to his pack, "I'll be able to make amends."

Miami nodded, expression softening, as he pleaded for judgement exemption, for the time being. "I don't like to repeat myself, so listen carefully. I lead these Exiles." She huffed with a hint of annoyance, a deep breath swelled her chest and she cleared her throat. "The Exiles are made up of generations of Gemarinians who once lived within society, banished into the Wilds. Some were the children of noble parents of the olden age, some have been 'ere before me and some…well, landed on the doorstep over the last few years."

"An underground society created from being thrown out into the Wilds?" Xan breathed out, impressed.

She sighed. "Well what did you think, boyo? Some are built from tough stuff. You didn't think you were the only one that survived the Wilds, did ya? We watched you, you know…scurrying through with that creature of yours."

Xan's eyes widened. *They were there shadowing me when I was trudging through the Wilds, helpless and scared? How can she berate me for my rage-fuelled mistakes when she sat back and let a petrified child wander alone in a strange land?*

Before he could say something to that effect, she went on, "But oh no, we wouldn't dare cross that beast. You were nothin'. Could've taken you in. But I wouldn't cross the *Mika Tikaani*: one of the fiercest of 'em all, y'hear."

Xan had seen Qilin's ferociousness but thought it was only reserved for defending him.

"Anyway, we've lived mainly in the underground, in the darkness, doin' what we could to keep ourselves alive." Her last words were tinged in sorrow, washed in the dead dreams of her people.

Xan pressed, "How do you know about us and what we're doing?"

Miami's laugh, instead of dismissive, came out as a shrill cackle. "Us and the general, well, we go back and forth, talkin', plannin', tryin' to sabotage as much as we can. But, we found out when he green-lit that plan with you, even though it was...not...handled well." She eyed Xan sheepishly. "We knew that this'd be our greatest shot to set things right."

Xan glared, deflated as his body sagged. Juniper crossed her arms, seething through clenched teeth. "Handled well is an understatement, don't you think? Your pissant buddy ol' pal the general just neutralised Qilin, like she didn't even matter—"

"I get things didn't go as planned, and I'm sorry for it," Miami interrupted softly. "I don't condone what he did to ya creature friend, but we all do things out of character when desperation takes 'old of us."

Xan lowered his eyes. It was clear this was her way of giving him the benefit of the doubt, but Juniper had more to say as she stamped her foot, sending a loud crack echoing across the dusty walls. "Desperation was certainly in his actions as my whole crew were slaughtered before my eyes. I was kidnapped and tortured. Yet here I am, on this path of bullshit. So, if I'm here, willing to push things aside for the moment, drop the way you're lecturing Xan like he's the monster. Bit fucking hypercritical when the general planned his disgusting acts of violence while Xan acted purely on emotional impulse." Her green-eyed glare beamed into Miami. "Ask yourself who the real monster is then," she spat with disdain.

Miami shifted uncomfortably, as if considering the weight of Juniper's words. They seemed to linger upon her. "I can understand you're 'urt. I'll let those words settle. In time, maybe the gravity of them will...make me feel different." Tears welled, but they shrank behind the masquerade of sadness and it was resolve that replaced it. "I won't apologise for 'im, for every time we stood by and didn't raise a hand for injustice, but I'll look to move forward with ya, to do better. No more judgement for any of us, y'hear?"

"So, okay, you live in the underground, basically employing guerrilla tactics and doing some of the dirty work to finally expose Madame Bleu?" Juniper started a slow clap. "Good on you. It's really made a significant difference." She rolled her eyes, sarcasm heavy enough to weigh her down.

Balfour returned with the guard Juniper had killed at his side. She had snapped their scrawny neck near enough in half. But there they were standing next to Balfour, alive and well.

Xan and Juniper didn't know where to start. "How the blazing fucks did you resurrect someone?" Juniper stammered, hand now cradling an open mouth.

"This copycat tech was banned from Gemarine, along with its creator. When Madame Bleu decided it was a threat, of course," Miami explained. "She seized it for 'erself and banished Dryno, the inventor. He's old now, but he rebuilt what he'd created and now we 'ave our own way of infiltrating the system a little deeper. The guard that stands before you is one of us. 'er name is Voilani."

Xan eyed Voilani, the person who had taken on the appearance of the guard. Amazement hidden by the thoughts whizzing inside his head. *This is amazing tech. Replicating the exact physical features of another person is extraordinary. I need to find this Dryno and learn from him.*

Juniper crossed her arms, pouting. "Why wouldn't you use this to basically replace all the people who are doing the wrong thing on the surface?"

"Genocide ain't really our thing," Miami levelled.

Juniper scoffed. "Yeah, good one, bitch, you know that's not what I meant. It was more like dig out the evil roots and let the other trees spread out."

Miami composed herself. "We've limited resources, and our mantra's about choice and movin' on the right path. So if we did dig out those evil roots without tryin' to fix it first, then I guess we'd be the same as Madame Bleu."

The guard, who was actually Voilani, interrupted, "How long do I need to maintain this appearance for?"

"We'll check back in a week and give ya a breakdown of where we're at. But this might be a long-haul mission 'cause this is our best shot, y'hear?"

"For the right path." Voilani nodded resolutely.

"For the right path," Miami mirrored her, then watched Voilani as the Sytheract guard moved to the door and disappeared to live her new life for the foreseeable future.

Juniper sighed, and Xan noticed another glint of regret pass across her eyes. A deep breath seemed to steady her but he wondered where her thoughts were. *Is it that this poor girl is being sent to be something she isn't because of us? Or, is it because of the guilt of killing someone for me?* His shoulders sagged, the guilt still plaguing him, too.

"Listen," Miami said gravely, "you should get movin'. I can try to delay the general from makin' any ahhhh…rash decisions like using someone else as bait like before. I really think you should leave as soon as possible."

"What do you mean, bait?" Juniper snapped.

"Oh, dear child, you're already angry with me, I—"

Juniper raised her hand, commanding Miami to cease babbling. "You mean to say, *you* were the ones who sabotaged Captain Larrsen?"

Miami scratched her neck and grimaced. "He was a bad character, Juniper. We selected him for a reason."

Juniper's scowl was murderous and Xan reached out to place a palm on her back, whispering softly at her side. "Let's figure out who needs to pay later. She's right in saying we need to consider our next moves, though."

"This isn't over. You owe me one big fuck of a favour to make up for all this bullshit – I'm telling you now," Juniper conceded.

Xan suddenly remembered that they couldn't test any of the substances. "Wait, Lilianna was meant to be here with the kit, but something must have happened."

He realised then that she could be in danger. *Oh fuck, what have I done? Sending her off into the unknown when people might be watching us. What if something's happened to her, as well?*

As if reading his thoughts, Juniper reached for his hand. "She's stronger than you think. If anything has happened she'll have found a way out."

"Either way, you need to get movin'," Miami warned.

Xan and Juniper looked at one another, pained expressions and sorrow sifting between them. They knew what was needed.

A tough decision.

A decision to leave without Lilianna by their side.

"I know you don't want to hear this, Xan, but sometimes you need to make a sacrifice for the greater good. We aren't leaving her for good or anything, but we need to move, right?" Juniper rationalised.

Xan frowned. "I don't particularly want to hear your war-tactic rationale right now."

Juniper squared her shoulders and glowered. "Well, as a leader you need to make tough choices, sometimes. Welcome to the war of heart versus mind – where no side ever really wins." She shrugged, all traces of pity in her tone gone.

Xan turned from her and faced Miami. "When she gets here, please let her know we couldn't wait for—"

"It'll be done." Miami held up her hand, halting his request. She bowed with reverence.

Xan and Juniper left the underground crew behind. He should have been feeling better being closer to a resolution. But as Xan imagined Lilianna's face when she learned of her abandonment, he couldn't help the twisting of his gut, wishing there was an alternative solution.

CHAPTER 28

Laser rays sailed over their heads, bright and bold like intermittent flickers of sun behind migrating clouds.

Juniper, Boorak and Edaline had been crouched in a deep trench, caked in mud for hours, now. The unrelenting onslaught carried on around them. "Where's that airstrike I ordered?" Juniper screamed as she waved her battered Cranston ray gun in front of Edaline's face. "You relayed the order, didn't you?" There was a hint of accusation in her tone.

Edaline yelled back, "Of course I did. It's not my fault they're taking their time!"

A deep growl rumbled from Juniper's throat. She detested lying there, useless as a girthy dick on an oaf that knew nothing about how to please a woman.

"Look," Boorak shouted, pointing to the skies blanketed in bulbous clouds of smoke.

223

The squadron of Windbreakers appeared overhead. A low roar ran across their jungle kingdom, ravaged in the throes of battle. Ejector racks released multiple gravbombs and they tumbled from the sky.

A battlefield bathed in ominous silence was a shelter without a roof. It wasn't right.

Juniper pushed up out of the mud and yelled for the soldiers in the trenches to follow her. She pointed the ray gun in her left hand and held aloft a boronium sword in her right. She charged, mouth open in a ferocious cry of the untamed.

Edaline followed closely behind. Close enough that flecks of mud kissed Edaline's cheeks as they searched for Cryptoborgs clinging to survival after the gravbomb strike. Boorak in turn followed Edaline, as he always had. From clan members to the battlefields under Juniper's leadership, it was seldom that separation tore between them. As it was, despite Juniper being occupied with her cardio workout of 'Running To Enemy 101', she knew Boorak's priorities were:

Giving Edaline lustful eyes.

Why he looks at her back that way when Edaline can't see, is fucking idiotic.

Defending the rest of the squadron.

It was unfortunate, but she acknowledged that each and every member of her squad had their weaknesses and strengths. Boorak was not one for team loyalty but he brought wrath and rage in equal parts. And when the call of battle rang out across undefended lands, one needed someone with a charcoal heart from the inferno of grief.

Upturned plates of rock and sediment were strewn across the landscape. Torn limbs and severed heads in helmets were lush fields of flowers in the reaper's playground.

The half-mangled body of a Cryptoborg crawled across the ground, their dark metallic laser gun shaking in hands the colour of mauve. They pointed at the warrior in the first line of defence. Juniper pounced, sword swinging like the quill of a manic poet. Ink absorbed into pages pungent with perfect prose.

She lopped another head clean off their shoulders, the Cryptoborg's abnormally large mouth wide in a silent scream of anguish. As the helmetless head slammed into the field of mud, its sharp compact teeth snapped shut like a metal trap. Turning quickly, Juniper thrust a blade into another's fading heart. On their knees, the Cryptoborg's spherical helmet made of forged gold tipped off their head, exposing long flowing white hair, broad oval eyes completely black and soulless, blinking in shock. Juniper pulled back the blade, and the Cryptoborg whimpered with sorrow as they fell. Their vibrant mauve skin was a contrast atop the deep umber of their battlefield grave. Blood branded Juniper's armour with the insignia of impenitence.

Ray gun blasts started up again. The incisive bitter stench of a burning forest, stinging her nostrils. Through the window of smoke rapid laser fire looked like shooting stars, emerging from the void. One fizzed past Juniper's ear, slamming into the chest of a Sytheract behind her, who had a name she couldn't recall. *The records will remember his sacrifice.*

Edaline didn't falter as she fired into the distance, followed closely by orange bursts from Boorak's ray gun. The shroud of smoke parted, and her soldiers laid eyes on the enemy advancing toward them in haste.

"Boorak and Edaline, take opposite flanks," Juniper commanded. "Slay those fuckstains!"

Edaline smiled. "With pleasure!" A coarse scream followed, and the demonic pulse of the hyperblaster cannoned into the flank of the approaching army.

Boorak hesitated as he watched the famished fog consume Edaline until she was but a symphonic medley of wild screams in the distance.

"Get moving, you fermenting glob of dick cheese," Juniper yelled at Boorak, then she, too, faded into the mist of battle to deliver her scorn.

Juniper threw her helmet on the ground, exhausted. Scanning the horizon under the setting sun, silhouetted mounds dotted the landscape like rocks that had settled over time. It was an ocean of dormant ships, each anchored to a piece of the planet forbidding their departure.

But if one would wade through that ocean, they would find the ships were thousands of slain corpses, drifting toward the penultimate wave that would wash them away forever.

The helmet stared back at her with hollow eyes, searching for justification for the bloodshed. For the tactics employed. For the loss of life.

Her armour was crumpled in a heap beside the helmet. The under-garment of black linen – ripped and serrated underneath her breasts – flailed in the bitter draught. Defined abdominal muscles painted with flecks of fuck knows what, heaved as she ran her dirty fingers through matted hair.

It appeared they had won, but at what cost? She shivered, not only from the cold, but from the questions that stormed the fortress of her mind.

No matter how many times she led soldiers to their demise, she couldn't help but fracture a little within, as the humanity she was meant to possess ebbed further away.

The Cryptoborg bodies too. In death they were peaceful figures, but weren't we all peaceful when greeted by death? Almost like the pain of living is expunged upon our entry into the boulevard of palliative care.

Do the Cryptoborgs deserve such a horrific death?

What makes Gemarine the pinnacle of all existence – that we need to keep slaughtering them over and over?

She started to question why.

As a soldier, 'why' was harder than blind acceptance. 'Why' got you thinking and 'why' got you exiled.

It was an ancient war with ancient beginnings. But all in all, it was just another scenario of kill or be killed. So, she resolved to defend Gemarine.

To slaughter those who would come to cause harm to her planet, to her clan, to her friends, to Qilin and Xan.

It was settled, then. Her mind could rest.

The taste of battle was now in her mouth; the iron of blood, the salt of beaded sweat, the thief that was adrenalin, stealing all the moisture. Across the wasteland before her, a figure strode with rage nipping at their heels. It was Boorak and he held his arm out as if transmitting on his MPD. The look on his face was wrath tarnished with a sullen smattering.

"They took her!" he hollered in Juniper's face, spittle sprayed onto burning cheeks.

"Back the fuck up," she said, forcefully placing open palms onto his chest and pushing him away. "Now that I can't smell the stench of your stale ass breath – do you wanna try again?"

"They took her as hostage, Juniper. They took Edaline."

Juniper's demeanour sank. She knew what this meant. Boorak appeared as though he didn't. Although the fury in him was evident – chest extended, fists balled and a scowl that could shatter glass – there was a hopeful air about him. Juniper was the god and his presence a prayer. Piety was pitiful, but it allowed one to cope.

Boorak gestured to the MPD. "They want to talk with you."

Juniper breathed in deep, rubbing circles into her forehead and pausing long enough to foretell the events before they would occur. An internal tear shed into the ether. Grief was premature perhaps, but realistic resignations were ballistic vests in the armoury of the heart.

The Cryptoborg leader appeared in holo as if she were on the muddy tracks in front of Juniper and Boorak. Edaline was bound and on her knees, flanked by two Cryptoborg soldiers gripping both her arms. She was gagged with a torn piece of ragged cloth. Black ringed her eyes and beneath her short-cropped hair, a halo of dried blood cradled her head.

"If you want this one back," the Cryptoborg captain said with a wide stance and a proud chest, "you will meet me at the road of the fallen and we will discuss our trade."

Despite knowing exactly what needed to be done, Juniper's stomach roiled in dread. She braced herself, and knew release would come later. When the eyes of her soldiers weren't boring holes into her back.

Boorak hovered over her shoulder and she felt the steam rise from his body. It wouldn't end well for any of them. In particular, Boorak would never accept what was to come.

"We have nothing of worth here for you. Return her and I will call an end to this battle and spare countless lives." Juniper spoke with confidence, allowing the idea of mercy to weigh upon their conscience.

The Cryptoborg captain took off her helmet of gold, throwing it off camera – the darkness of her eyes was disconcerting. The mauve of her skin glistened with battle fatigue and thick locks of wavy white hair grasped her shoulders tightly. "Your leader has something of worth. We believe it will help to mend the fractures in the galaxy."

Juniper frowned. "Do you think I have tea parties with Madame Bleu? I don't know what she has or care, for that matter." She adjusted her stance. "What I do care about is injustice, and right now your prisoner has done nothing to deserve death."

"If you fight only because you blindly accept instructions from your leader, then you are simpler than we thought." The captain scoffed. "Do you even know why we fight? Why Gemarine is so important to us?"

"My interest is not in politics, my interest is in protecting my people from threats. You are a threat. If that's simple, then I don't give a fuck. My conscience is clear."

"You have much to learn, Captain," the Cryptoborg snapped with finality, clicking her fingers to the soldiers holding Edaline. Juniper's second in command was brought to the front of the holo cam. The pain in her eyes was unbearable; she knew her own fate. When hope dies, it casts a shadow across dreams of the future. Where there was once radiance, therein lay ailing gloom.

Juniper wanted Edaline to know her value, to know she would conjure rage. So, as the silver sword pressed against Edaline's neck, Juniper growled, "If you do this, I will find you. I will slay everyone you love."

Boorak grabbed Juniper's arm and pleaded with her. "You have to go and meet them."

Shaking Boorak off aggressively, she whispered into his face, "Do not beg me to do your bidding. You know what must be done."

"You're too proud to even sacrifice yourself for a soldier who loves you. Shame on you and shame on Gemarine. You are the executioners of the galaxy so you deserve your own treatment," the Cryptoborg captain scolded, biceps flexing under the weight of her weapon and the anger in her heart.

She dug the rusty blade into Edaline's throat, the controlled cruelty evident in the way her biceps flexed as she hacked deeper, manically. Blood spurted through Edaline's gurgled wail. Pupils dilated in horror and shock. The blade cleared the jungle of flesh and wrenching hands grabbed hold of a tuft of Edaline's hair and put her on display. Jagged rags of tissue protruded from her swinging neck. The white sclera of her eyes, a crypt shielding this demonic desecration of her body.

Juniper watched the holo feed in disgust.

Tears simmered behind her eyes. Ire built steadily behind twitching muscles. Each flicker of pain transferred to the vats of emotional storage within. She would use them later when she enacted revenge.

Boorak sank to his knees, crying with the desperate wail of a broken man.

There were tactics in war. There were mind games tugged by emotional strings. In all her training, these were the tactics that never changed.

It made sense to her in the learning centre, and it even made sense now.

Sometimes, the sacrifice of one ensures the safety of many. Juniper knew that if she'd made that trip to the road of the fallen, she would have been killed along with the soldiers under her watch. The steadfast rule was always – if a hostage is taken there will be no exchange.

Instead, she exchanged her soul in return for an eternity of self-flagellation.

CHAPTER 29

Lilianna ran through black. The chill of the night air bit into her pale cheeks, staining them red. Heavy footsteps cracked into the silence, resounding off the stone buildings laden with aesthetic displeasure.

The mobile kit thumped into her awkwardly as she struggled to keep it strapped to her back and run with purpose. Run toward the only illumination that was a sweltering sword through the night. Run toward the ship readying to take off. Take off into the air without her.

"Stop!" she yelled, frantic and panting, cheeks flushed. But there was no use; no one could hear her and their ship hovered for a moment as the thrusters engaged.

In desperation, she clutched Zondini's Cranston ray gun attached to her hip and yanked it from her utility belt. The first thing she had ever stolen was a Cranston ray gun from the inner circle of their tyrannical ruler. *Pretty bold for a novice thief.* In fact, all her recent actions went against who she was. Drugging someone, stealing his weapon, letting his disgusting tongue inside her mouth. She shuddered at the coiled snake of regret, striking out at her with venomous intent. The memory would fade in time. At least, that's what Lilianna hoped.

Aiming the stolen laser at the ship, she groaned. Lilianna had never shot a Cranston ray gun before. But if she didn't get on that ship, they would be going to the general without any evidence. Truth would still be hovering in the clouds, brewing a storm. Lightning would crack, thunder would howl. The sun would never again smile against the pale blue sky.

They'd be going to save Qilin and then what? The whole thing would be purposeless.

Squinting through one eye, with vision hazy and jolting, breathless and shaking, Lilianna aimed the barrel to the left of the ship and squeezed the trigger, clenching her jaw. A counter zap beamed through her arm, and she cried out, recoiling her hand as the laser smashed onto the ground. Another shot bounded across the street and slammed into an older building.

The ship dispatched its weapons system coldly, pointing at Lilianna with a menacing, metallic smirk.

She opened her mouth, terror written upon her face in wide-eyed cursive. Dropping to her knees, tears fell as she resigned herself to doom. But the weapons retreated and the stairs lowered, instead. Xan's athletic silhouette beckoned her onto the ramp and into the safety of the Comet 8.

"Lili, hurry!" he screamed above the deafening strain of the ship. "Get over here now!"

Lilianna pushed upwards, shaky and unstable with the weight of the backpack. "I'm coming!" she yelled, joyful tears now awash on her cheeks. The ship's lights highlighted her features, creased with exhaustion and relief.

Lilianna gripped Xan's strong hand and she let him guide her into the twisting bowels of the ship as the engines roared and Juniper took off into the sky. The kinetic thrust threw Lilianna forward into Xan's chest. A place where she could make her home, lock with a key so only she could access all the rooms, trinkets and wonders. His muscled arms cradled her close and she slowly found his grey eyes boring down into hers, hungry, worried and safe all in that flickering glance.

"Are you okay?" His breath tickled the point of her nose and he smelt of warm honey and the sweetness of tonka bean.

Not, where the fuck were you? Not, why are you so late? Just, are you okay?

She finally let herself feel, tears spilling onto his chest; a part of her trying so hard to seep into his heart. But skin was love's armour, deflecting all she was to the ground below. She knew Xan understood though, as he took the time to hold her in the midst of emotion thick in the atmosphere.

"What the fuck took you so long?" Juniper yelled from the front of the ship.

Lilianna started to laugh, wiping away the last of her tears. *Of course, she would say that.*

Lilianna pulled back and Xan smiled at her as she rolled the mobile kit off her back and onto the floor.

"Also, great way to draw attention to us in a stolen ship, on a covert mission, trying to take down the overlord," Juniper continued, heavy sarcasm undulating in her voice.

"I don't know," Lilianna yelled back at her, "I was desperate." She pleaded with her to understand.

"Well, all I can say is lucky you knew how to use it." Juniper scoffed.

Lilianna's voice quivered with a burst of embarrassment. "Um, I didn't."

"Holy shit. Well let's fuck our lucky stars we're still alive," Juniper hissed.

Xan fumbled around with the portable testing kit and made his way into the piloting area as Juniper was about to ruin the warm atmosphere by engaging the hyperdrive for the space jump.

"You guys might want to strap in for the next few minutes," she warned.

The ship rocked and shook. Lilianna closed her eyes, but somehow even the darkness moved. The pressure inside her head increased and she strained against the discomfort. At once, a calm silence settled over the cabin.

She opened her eyes and the expanse of space spread out before her, stars twinkling like jewels in blackened sand.

Juniper unclipped, the autopilot setting switched on. "`Cruising on fixed path`," it notified the trio.

"Thank you, Oh Wise One," Juniper sneered with that playful glint in her eyes.

Lilianna heard Xan's buckle clip come off. He then reached around to her side and unclipped her buckle, letting it nestle against her hip. She stared at him, wondering why. He answered the silent question.

"Let's do this together," he said. The weight of all she had experienced up until this point surged within her. The harrowing experience of being bound in chains, seeing the Valkor ship splattered with blood, caught red-handed alone in the lab, drugging a member of the inner circle, using seduction as a tool for freedom and finally nearly missing the ship as it prepared to take flight.

But as Xan took her hand, leading her toward destiny, she didn't allow the terrors of regret to ravage the present. Time would no doubt pinch her at various moments in the future, reminding her of such indiscretions. But there was a part of her pleased with the way she could adapt for a cause. The way that even though her morals screamed for mercy, she killed them with love.

The testing kit lay open on the floor. She looked at Xan as he bent down, and knew at that moment her self-sacrifice was all worth it for him.

"Juniper, pass me the samples, please," Xan said, extending his empty palm toward her.

Juniper handed over the clear, sealed containers, each with three samples used to power Gemarine.

He placed two of them into the testing kits and handed the final one to Lilianna. "Did you want to test this? It's from Sytheria." He shook the tube back and forth in front of her, as if it were a simple object without any power to alter the whole course of their lives.

"Do I follow the same process as other tests we've run in the field?" she asked, worry shaking the curiosity in her voice.

"Yes, but the importance of this test is selecting the 'purple' function, which will tell us whether the source was mined from a dead planet or a live one."

Juniper interrupted, "What do you mean by 'dead planet'?"

"Well, I guess it's not as easy as saying, the planet is dead or alive – it will analyse the sample and determine nutrients, the presence of microorganisms and cross-analyse against previous samples of planetary data in the system when we knew the planet was thriving. There are also certain elements buried in deep layers closer to the core. If any of these are detected, no planet would be able to survive invasive mining on such a level."

Lilianna chimed in, "Any reading below a combined category three will indicate extinction-level variable nutrients or elements of subcore mining. We can hope for a category four if the planet is dying but anything past that, well, we know that it's over."

Xan tacked onto her train of thought. "And in that case, we will know that Madame Bleu is as the general says she is."

They shared a collective look of concern.

"Well, won't I feel like a fuckwit if all this turns out to be real?" Juniper spoke with the heavy set of bitterness in her tone.

"You were being held captive. You didn't have a pleasant introductory information session." Xan spoke with anger lacing his breath.

Juniper looked downcast, as if recalling the blade against her skin or Serarra dying at her feet. "None of us did."

The silence was permafrost set within the expanse of their anticipation. Lilianna stared at the one tube lying in her palm. It was her home in her hand. It weighed hardly anything at all, but she somehow felt it quivering, afraid of what she would find.

She left her family so they would thrive. Older than most to make the decision to leave, her twelve-year-old heart broke upon hearing the words from Derrison, when he came for her. *"You will break this world. If you want your family to live, then you must leave."* She couldn't even recall if at that moment she'd asked Derrison, *"What will I do? How could I possibly cause the end of the world?"* She remembered his convincing display of time manipulation, of an explanation about her future soul bond and his terrible influence upon her. It seemed fear was a tool for manipulation. Like so many worlds across the galaxy she had researched, Earth and Dracia, so very close to home, had had their timelines altered by influential leaders or organisations using fear to satisfy an appetite for desirable change. But it was also other sentient worlds they admittedly knew very little about, but were still operating in similar capacities. The Rectilians on Marzuka and the Pyrgamies on Pyrothius. They were all ruled by fear-based regimes that ensured widespread citizen compliance. The Thractotians on Gorloth 7 had something similar to Gemarine, which appeared lovely and utopian on the surface, but Lilianna now doubted whether that was genuine.

Lilianna loved her family enough to sacrifice herself, her tether to them and to her former home. That might be why she never fit into the Gemarine ways. Instead, she continued reading about soulmates, dreaming of fictional scenarios where true love was a thing. But it wasn't fictional where she belonged. On her home planet they mated for life. Soulmates existed.

She could never have that now, but those dreams would be tinged with bitterness if the realisation of a lost civilisation came upon her.

"Alright, let's get it done." Xan handed one of the kits to Juniper. They both pressed the button and set the vial down, looking at Lilianna expectantly for her to do the same.

Lilianna took in a deep breath and pushed the button down. Holding out hope but knowing hope wasn't something that reached back for anyone, rather, it shimmered like a distant aurora flare, promising warmth without providing any feeling at all.

CHAPTER 30

LOCATION: GEMARINE
YEAR: 116 (2 YEARS AGO)
LILIANNA – 20 YEARS OLD

The lab was quiet.

Qilin was asleep, curled up in her usual spot, dreaming of all the things *Mika Tikaani*s do. Which, obviously, Lilianna didn't know. No one knew enough about them, anymore. The slithers of knowledge were scattered over torn pages of ancient texts scanned to the cloud database. She could pull up all the data on her MPD at any time, but information about Gemarine before the colonisation of Topaz City was sparse at best. The Celestials who maintained decorum in this particular quadrant of the galaxy were said to have used this as their home base, but then mysteriously fell out of existence, presumably dispelling into the ether, bodies expired or moved on to further life elsewhere.

Xan shuffled to and from the desk strewn with holo formulas, to the readouts on the computer screen, to the microscope x in the corner.

It was a flurry of activity because as soon as they arrived back from Yarmandor, Lilianna and Xan were both eager to check the results in order to find out why Qilin went haywire.

The documentation on *Mika Tikaani*s never described them as having access to elemental powers. They were depicted in paintings with the Celestials, but as far as any special abilities went, nothing was ever scrolled.

Lilianna and Xan both had had a restless sleep, but here they were the next morning, brightened by the promise of discovery.

As they collated the data, trying their best to interpret the results, the door creaked open behind them and in strode Ranjit.

Xan spun across to the desk, swiping away all the holos so the information would remain private. He then crouched over the desk, chin on the palm of his hand, casually contemplating.

Lilianna frowned. It was unconvincing.

"Morning, you two! You're in early today," Ranjit exclaimed. Deep brown eyes flashed from behind dark-rimmed glasses perched atop his aquiline nose. A soft hand swept thick grey locks into the undulating waves atop his head. A Human originally from a place called India, he was a resourceful, intelligent kid once. Unfortunately, he lived in the poorer communities called slums, so stellar opportunities hadn't presented themselves. In came the Gemarine escort when he was ten to whisk him out of the slums and onto a planet in desperate need of engineering solutions. Although it took him time to develop those skills, he became a key engineer for the city.

Once Xan's department grew, Ranjit transferred over to expand upon his versatility. He possessed a double degree in planetary xeno-biology and engineering so it was almost serendipitous that he would help run the biobase; the sanctuary for all the creatures. Today was his day to work from the lab.

"Just studying some samples from Yarmandor," Xan said, with a tone as bland as he could muster.

"Oh goodness, the sulphur there," he exclaimed, turning to face Lilianna. "It wasn't pleasant, was it?" His cheeks swelled with a hearty laugh.

Lilianna's face twisted in annoyance. "Not particularly." She recalled the horrible stench and turned to face the window in case she might throw up from the memory.

Xan changed the subject quickly. "Before I forget, we need to go over construction projections for the biobase. I'm looking at about four expeditions in the next month and we need the workers aligned with the schedule."

"Xan, you worry too much. Have I ever been one to neglect the timeline? Have I ever let the workers dally?" Ranjit crossed his arms, the sleeves of his sage green coat rolled up, exposing fluffy grey hairs speckled across dark skin. "No I have not!" he answered himself with a firm voice.

"Hey, you know me, Ranjit, I do the fun exploring stuff, you make sure they, you know, continue to live!" Xan laughed.

"You do a lot more than that and you know it." His right eyebrow arched, the distinguished grey moustache bristling against his top lip. "Isn't that right, Lili?"

Lilianna smiled. Xan did do a lot. Sometimes too much. Researching, planning, exploring. Then, during 'off' weeks, all three of them would work at the biobase administering vitamins, ensuring microclimates were operational and training the rest of the staff under the keen eye of the operations manager, Duffington – a large gender-neutral Aranther, blue-hued and muscley, with the capability to balance all the many moving parts.

The biobase was magical. Every time Lilianna hovered up on a transpo, it sent waves of reverence through her. Clear hexagonal honeycomb pieces moulded into one another creating large domes spread across miles of wilderness beyond the city gates. The sunlight glinting off each domed structure, unnatural but still glorious flowers blooming among the weeds.

Appearance was not everything. As a heart beats inside the body, the heart of the biobase stretched out capillary fingers giving life to all the living things within. That was most impressive.

Galactic creatures were united, each in different habitats. Alongside one another from different worlds fighting against a common enemy: extinction.

Ranjit's engineering feats deserved more than accolades. He found a way to keep creatures from different temperatures, atmospheres, environments, climates all in the same central location.

A viewing platform cut through the middle for the general public to view and appreciate the diversity of the galaxy. The exhibits operated on a seasonal, limited basis like the artifactories on Sytheria where they would display various artworks, sculptures or ancient weapons borrowed from one region and shared around the globe. On Earth, museums did much the same.

Instead of the creatures remaining in captivity, Xan released them back into their environment with spawns from the breeding programs or an opportunity to continue the line with another of the opposite gender. Xan worked harder than anyone else at the centre, but it was his project from the start. He delivered the initial proposal to Madame Bleu after he had achieved his Gemlevels, which meant he had the most responsibility. Madame Bleu didn't initially love the idea, but with media support and galactic backing, Xan was able to get the biobase over the line.

Xan tensed slightly, indicating the need to resume his work. "Alright, Ranjit, I gotta—"

"I know, I know." Ranjit rolled his eyes behind the distinct frames of his glasses, preferring them to the regen eyesight corrections most Gemarinians opted for. "You're busy, you have to get back to work." He laughed, swatting his hands at Xan as he moved into his section of the lab, laying out his devices to start work of his own.

XAN
22 YEARS OLD

They stared at Qilin lying there, curled into a compact bundle, the spikes on her tail smoothed over so her blue and black fuzzy fur cushioned her chin.

The results that flashed on the screen were unfathomable. Xan leant on the desk, jaw agape, staring at Qilin then back to the results. She had been his companion the whole time he'd been on Gemarine and it was like he was seeing her truly for the first time.

Aside from the way in which she could interact with matter on a subatomic level, the most alarming discovery was that there was an expiration date to these 'interactions'. It appeared that each time she expelled this energy, it brought her closer to that expiry. The summation was she had possibly one or two elemental anomalies left before she would flitter into dust.

Qilin as dust.

The thought brought him to the verge of tears in an instant. A persistent ache crawled through his veins like the seedpods of a tree germinating in the soil of regret. He had forced Qilin to use this power twice. He was contributing to her demise. His desire to explore, to locate, to save — it made him a liability to Qilin's existence. Her loyalty was imbued to his well-being, and if he continually put them both in reckless situations, she wouldn't survive.

Was it time to let Lilianna go on expeditions by herself?

No. She just wasn't ready. The last expedition had taught him she still had a long way to go. Maybe he would need to cut back, and take extreme caution henceforth. Make sure every expedition was a huge information dump of training so that Lilianna would soon be competent and confident enough to take over control of saving the galaxy's most vulnerable creatures.

He sighed. The exploration was part of him. He was King of the Wilds, as they said. He was the 'Extinction Extinguisher' – a more recent headline cast across the network.

Wouldn't it mean that that part of him would be lost? A worthy part to eradicate for the survival of his favourite companion, he conceded.

When a cherished friendship makes one feel whole, surrendering a fraction of oneself is no sacrifice at all.

CHAPTER 31

LOCATION: GEMARINE
YEAR: 118
XAN – 24 YEARS OLD

The second to last vial stood stoic among fallen comrades. Soaked not in blood, but in the red haze of the testing kit, it showed them all a catastrophic result.

Below category three.

Earth was dead.

Sytheria was the final one.

As it slowly turned from violet to vermilion in death, a solitary tear fell from Lilianna's eye, draped in the sorrow of her past and the future she was denied. She had cried enough lately, and it appeared her body would give no more.

"Okay, well, that fucking sucks," Juniper said, her voice soft and sombre.

"Understatement of all time." Xan bowed his head, strands of hair swaying across his mournful eyes.

Lilianna looked dejected, her slender hands folded neatly in her lap. "Now what?" she asked.

"We go get Qilin, obviously, see what the general proposes and then we go about trying to fix this," Xan directed with confidence. A hint of despondency claimed his usual positive disposition.

"Listen to another monologue from that asshat. I'd rather chew off my other hand." Juniper feigned a ravenous feast on her remaining fingers.

Lilianna stifled a laugh, but Xan thought, *At least when darkness flows around us all, it's lessened by the light of humour.*

In fact, in the small, silly comment that Juniper made, it was clear to him that united, they each held something special. It was as if they fit like carbon and hydrogen atoms, and when fused together they created a diamond; faceted, sparkling light, exuding beauty. Each quality they lacked as an individual was made up for by the collective's strengths. Their bond was more important once they realised their home planets were gone. Their homes were now within one another.

"Unfortunately, General Asshat knows a lot more than we do, so I guess we need to get ready for the show." Xan rubbed his hands together, balling them into fists and then back again.

Lilianna eyed him with expectation. "How can we even save our worlds or change what happened, though?"

"That's the thing we don't know. I mean, thinking of all I've studied, it can't be possible." Xan scratched the side of his cheek, sprinkled with stubble.

"But you've been concentrating on biology rather than physics," Lilianna said matter-of-factly.

This is true, Xan thought. He moved his hand down toward his chin.

"At least you'll both be able to understand the concepts when we figure it out." Juniper moved back toward the pilot seat. "I, for one, am useless and have no idea about that science shit."

"You have other strengths," Lilianna voiced with admiration in her tone. She blushed immediately, as if realising revering Juniper made her weak.

Xan quickly said, "And in fact, each of our separate strengths will have to be utilised if we want to get ahead of this."

"Alright, well, here goes another one of my strengths." Juniper keyed in coordinates. "Are we all ready for this space jump?"

Xan and Lilianna exchanged a glance and in solidarity they both spoke deeply and with decisiveness. "Yes."

The jump threw them into the middle of space, stars blinking around them as if they were waking from a dream built from the echoes of serenity. The expanse of blackness spread out before them across one side, but as Juniper pivoted their worn and rusted Comet 8, they were faced with a demonic shadow that stretched across the void. A Valkor ship, eerily similar to the one Juniper was tortured in and where Xan massacred innocent civilians.

A planet rotated in the distance, orange and purple hues blending in violent effusion. It was hard not to marvel at the vibrancy; the colliding colours burst like a rainbow's slaughter. Beauty suspended in space, designed for aesthetics alone.

As they were pulled into the dock, Xan had to remind himself the spectacle wasn't just for his eyes. Life swirled beneath those clouds and gases, chaos ensued and intensity reigned, but it looked oh so beautiful from their viewing platform.

This time as they lowered the hatch, General Heronicus stood flanked by two armoured soldiers, the shimmering lens of a pixelated shield protecting them.

"Can't be too cautious these days." Heronicus eyed Xan with disdain.

Xan ignored the pot-shot, swallowing the hatred down, as he saw Qilin in a chamber lying on her side. He held his breath for a sign from her. The rise and fall of her fur confirmed it. She was alive.

"It wasn't…expected that I would have taken exception to your methods," General Heronicus snarled. "I expected something like that from the unhinged one," he gestured to Juniper, who blew him a kiss and mouthed *fucking loser*, "not from you. I almost ended that majestic creature, but you would never have complied without her."

"Damn right," Xan snapped. Anger swelled - something he thought he could quell, but it soared on the crest of a wave. "Now give her the antidote and once I've determined her health…we can talk." The last three words uttered with the gravel of a man who took no prisoners.

"Very well." Heronicus made a whistling sound, created with friction between his tongue and lips, and one of his offsiders brought forth Qilin to the general.

Heronicus produced the vial and inserted its contents into Qilin, closing the door before handing her over to Xan. He made eyes at Lilianna, but she swiftly avoided his gaze.

Xan scanned over Qilin with his MPD and it detailed a report to him. Vital signs were all fine. Physical markers were all tracked to her DNA, scheduled to awake from unconsciousness in ten minutes.

"Satisfied?" the general spat.

Xan gave him a filthy scowl. "I tell you what, mate, how about you get to the point of this whole mess now that we're here."

"I wasn't the one who massacred—"

"Don't you fucking dare put that on me." Xan's voice was thunder across darkened skies. "I'll take responsibility for the way in which I reacted, but you can't absolve yourself of the blame, for if you instigate a riot then fade into the shadows, all blood spilled should still be weighed against you on the scales of judgement."

Heronicus considered this, then went to answer.

"Honestly, don't bother answering that. Get on with it," Juniper encouraged with fierce confidence, standing in Xan's shadow but operating as an extension of him.

"Very well," he said, gruff lining his voice. "So, you now know the fate of the befallen worlds; the way in which these worlds were destroyed is not something I shall divulge now. Maybe it is something you will learn on your own." He shifted and scratched his neck, searching the horizon wistfully. "But I shan't digress. Miss Juniper must be appeased, of course." He bowed with feigned grace, and she narrowed her eyes as if a black hole closed suddenly.

"This mission appears to be our last hope and you have been selected not just by me — but the universe, it seems, has also given its stamp of approval. I attempted this before our race was exiled but I was only able to obtain one part. Another part lies with Madame Bleu and the last remains lost to an ancient poem. I'm hoping the cogs of fate will turn when I give this to you and you will be able to fulfil what I could not."

"So, what is it we need?" Xan pressed impatiently.

The general was given a rusted metal box by one of the armoured guards. It opened slowly and expelled a gentle whine as if fate herself winced with a foreboding sense of doom.

Cushioned inside lay a stone. The stone was a silky grey but pulsed with bright blue flecks, energised by the blood thrumming through Xan as he stared in awe. It was stunning.

"This is the Crystal of Fate." Heronicus motioned as if selling the item at auction. "There are two other crystals — the Crystal of New Life and the Crystal of Time — that need to be found and pieced together and placed into a portal. At this moment, no one alive has ever been to the planet of Periah, which is home to the portal."

Juniper looked ready to throw her hands up in frustration. But Heronicus held up a finger as if to delay another tantrum. "Don't despair. There was no need for anyone to go to the planet without the crystals."

The general's offsider handed an ancient text to Xan. The leather-bound cover was charcoal, faded and scuffed. The pages were preserved by what appeared to be a shimmering forcefield blocking infecting bacteria and the decay of time.

"All the pages have been fortified and are protected from the elements. This text is the only record in the known universe of not just the portal planet directions, but the key in which to open them," Heronicus said.

Juniper's tone was mocking. "*The key in which to open them.* You fucking clown, just say the combination of three crystals."

Heronicus continued, ignoring Juniper's outburst as if she were an insect buzzing across his periphery on a humid day.

He walked across the platform with hands clasped behind his back, boots clanging across the metal grates, narrating to no one in particular. "Gemarine granted us access to its society because we possessed this ancient text. Madame Bleu wanted it. She wanted the ability to effectively own the galaxy; own time, fate and new life. But she never got her grubby little hands on it," he snarled. "So, she never actually got the directions to anywhere or found *all* the crystals."

Xan scowled at the pages, turning them over slowly.

"You can read more when you depart." Heronicus flicked a hand at the Comet 8. "It will give you information that I cannot right now. But as long as you go to page forty-three – the poem is there to be deciphered."

"A poem, now!" Juniper finally threw her hands up in all her flailing glory.

Xan tried to focus. "What does the poem refer to?"

"It will help you figure out where to find the last crystal. Although be warned, the greatest minds we have known have never been able to decipher it."

Xan wasn't sure if he would match the greatest minds the galaxy had known. He was definitely confident in his own ability, but this was a mystery that had stood the test of time. Instead of dwelling on the impossible, he tried to discuss the best plan of attack once they'd finished this idle chat with the general. "So, how do I know what to do first?"

Heronicus now stood stationary on the platform, rubbing his chin in contemplation. "My advice would be to split up. Find a way to get the crystal from Madame Bleu, while the other group works on solving the poem."

Xan found it hard to believe the clock of fate wasn't ticking against him. "There's no time limit on this?"

"No, but I'm not sure how long you can get away with working against Madame Bleu. She has a way of finding traitors and making them pay," Heronicus warned.

"She sent one of her inner circle to investigate the lab. I was there and I only just slipped away." Lilianna spoke up for the first time. "So, even though there's no time limit, I'd say we have mere days before she figures something is amiss."

Xan turned from Lilianna to General Heronicus. "You've put our whole crew in danger by forcing us to act in such a reckless way." Xan was bitter. Not about the predicament they were all in, but at how they'd already put themselves in danger by stealing, breaking into a fortified area and Lilianna being pursued by a member of the inner circle. He pursed his lips and a shadow of wrath passed across his gaze. "Every one of my expeditions is planned meticulously. I could have done the same thing here."

Heronicus shook his head. "The fate crystal pushed me forward. It practically forced my hand and made me do this," he reasoned calmly. "I get that it's not ideal for you, but neither was getting my home world blown apart in front of my own eyes for the sake of understanding Madame Bleu's true intentions. At least you have a chance to save yours."

Xan was puzzled. "Wait, I don't understand how we can do anything if all the worlds are gone."

"The portal is a gateway to parallel timelines," he said flatly. "You will need to go back to various key moments in time and make sure that each world does not fall into ruin."

"Go back in time?" Lilianna whispered, as if to herself.

"Madame Bleu ensured apocalyptic conditions in all three worlds by taking out influential figures. When those worlds finally fell, she took what she needed from each planet. Mining resources closer to the core where the minerals were rich and life-sustaining for Gemarine."

Xan thought the task would be immense, but time travel was unfathomable. "Time travel...is impossible," he said slowly.

"Yes, indeed it is, if you are a mere mortal. But the Celestials were not. Their essence lives on in those crystals. They are the guardians of this galaxy and they have ensured its protection."

"I have so many questions," Xan spluttered.

"I'm not going to waste time giving you a lesson in quantum physics when things are clearer in there." He pointed to the leather-bound text. "You've already been gone long enough. Go back to Gemarine before they realise where you are. If you need anything from me – you can contact Miami and she'll relay the information."

Xan understood the ancient text was worthy of careful study and would better provide him with a blueprint with which to use time travel to fix the broken worlds. But the bitterness wouldn't abate. The fact that Heronicus would sit back and watch while others did his dirty work didn't sit right with him. "So, you'll recline on your golden throne while we do as you please?"

"In the final battle, I will be there. I will finally enact my revenge on Madame Bleu. But until then, all I can do is let fate's music swell to a crescendo – I'll be moved by its lingering melody, and I'll be carried by its rhythmic purpose, but I won't feature until the cadence beckons."

Juniper rolled her eyes again and Xan imagined another tirade blasting through her mind: fuckwit, loser and over-the-top piece of shit, in particular, coming to the fore. "How do we know you'll be there when it counts?" Xan stepped forward, shoulders squared.

"I get why you think the worst of me, but I want my planet back as well as wanting the best for your planets too."

"I'll never trust you. But I'll fulfil this mission if it means we can reverse what Madame Bleu has done. However that may be."

"Well if this works, I'll be indebted to you forever. And I solemnly swear I will be at your beck and call." General Heronicus saluted him with esteem.

Xan saw the pitiful salute and registered the sworn oath. He would never call the general for anything. If Heronicus turned up at the final battle and fought side by side with Xan, then the moment Madame Bleu lost, he would spill the general's blood all over her putrid corpse. Two power-famished fools, united in death.

"Qilin is stirring, Xan. It's time we got back," Lilianna called, a concerned look softening her face.

Xan stared at the general, not knowing how to leave it. He ended up not saying anything at all, turning on his heels and trudging toward the ship, the crystal weighing heavily in his hands.

CHAPTER 32

LOCATION: GEMARINE
YEAR: 118
JUNIPER – 24 YEARS OLD

Juniper piloted the Comet 8 away from the Valkor carrier, its foreboding frame diminishing as she accelerated through space.

Crystals that open portals, time travel, ancient celestial texts, portal planets. This is some crazy ass shit.

An enemy who approached her, weapon in hand, didn't stand much of a chance against her skill; unmatched prowess and the killing-with-a-smile mentality. This, however, was anything but a simple enemy who could be met with a brutal finality. This was convoluted. This was outside of anything any one of them could have imagined.

"What does it say in that book?" Lilianna's voice was heavy with worry, as she stroked Qilin behind the ears. The poor creature was still groggy from her ordeal, fighting to stay awake.

"It's going to take me a while to figure it out, Lilianna. Maybe give me a bit of time here and I'll see what I can come up with."

Juniper recognised Lilianna's helplessness as her shoulders slumped. "Come here, Lili." She flicked the ship to cruise mode and said, "Have a seat and loosen your suit a little at the neck."

Juniper shifted in behind her, setting her fingers gently on the bare skin of her shoulders, massaging with deep, flowing movements digging into flesh. Unknowingly, her pent-up desire inadvertently controlled her actions. "Let the big old scientist boy figure it out." Lilianna was tense beneath her fingers. "Besides, when was the last time you slept? Let it go a little. You feel so tense. Here, try this."

Juniper flicked a vibrating switch on her exohand, which she often used for other types of massage, and moved it across Lilianna's shoulders, diving into knotted muscles, as well as skimming across her skin.

Lilianna let out a sigh. "Oh gosh, how good."

"I know, right? You must have been through some crazy stuff over this last week. You deserve a moment here." Juniper sounded like she was trying to sell a product, but it was simply relaxation she was selling, and Lilianna was buying up all the stock.

Lilianna shifted again at the mention of having a tough week, and Juniper assumed something had happened that she wasn't comfortable discussing.

Juniper's tone changed as well as her demeanour. "Listen, you don't ever have to let me in on anything you're thinking or feeling, but I'm always…around." She was going to say, here for you but that exposed too much heart, atrium walls and all. That wasn't acceptable.

Lilianna lay back more comfortably and her golden glance set itself upon Juniper. "I don't often say this to you, but…I…am grateful for you. In more ways than you'll know." She moved her gaze to what was beyond the window before Juniper could acknowledge anything more than genuine affection, but she thought there was something else there.

I think she feels something for me, too. Is that possible if she's so wrapped up in Xan?

Juniper let the thoughts sit with her as she massaged across Lilianna's shoulders, and realised the idea excited her deeply. She'd always wanted

Lilianna in a sexual way, to warp the steel walls that bound her tight, to truly see light as she stripped away the layers of darkness. *Maybe this will finally happen.*

"How about you catch a quick rest in the quarters and I'll wake you when we have to get off the ship." Juniper bent low and kissed her on the cheek, continuing, "You might not hear it from me ever again, but I appreciate you, too." Lilianna blinked the shock from her face, cheeks glowing a dusty shade of pink as Juniper lingered a little too long at the side of her face.

LILIANNA
22 YEARS OLD

As Lilianna gathered herself awkwardly and hurried off to the shared quarters she wondered if Juniper was trying to seduce her.

Her forehead creased. *No, no, surely I'd know rather than have to question it. It's Juniper.*

She was breathing hard as she stumbled to her destination. Xan was studying the ancient text in the corner. His back was against the wall, knees up with the text resting in his lap. Tasty biceps flexed as he massaged his neck, twisting it from side to side. Veins thrummed in his jugular, trailing past stocky shoulders to the lush pastures beneath that zipped suit he wore. Rather than continue rushing to her quarters, Lilianna stood biting the top of her forefinger, staring like a psycho.

Juniper and Xan together would be an interesting...experiment. I've never done anything like that — she slammed her thoughts shut. Cross with herself for considering such a thing. But her thoughts immediately returned to what was beneath that suit and she felt something again, crawling across her inner thighs like an insect. An insect that had a venomous sting that hurt ever so good, that beckoned the colony to ravage her. Sweat dripped across her brow, cheeks flushed and her chest heaved. She was losing herself, but maybe it wasn't the time to mourn. Maybe, it was a time to start anew and build the Lilianna dream, not simply fall in line with the Gemarine one.

JUNIPER
24 YEARS OLD

Climbing over to her seat, Juniper sank down into its jaws, letting it swallow her into its belly. She closed her eyes and breathed deeply, stifling her need: her desire for what felt like the hundredth time in the past week. Insatiability was not something easily contained.

Even in horrible situations, once the adrenalin had dissipated, the carnal need remained. During the war, the soldiers embraced it. During stressful training drills at the academy they embraced it.

She didn't give a fuck about embracing the human in her; she was an animal too. *If an animal wants to fuck – she takes what she wants.* Juniper wanted to snarl, to gnaw, to roar, to stalk on her hands and knees. But tiredness overcame her as if lack of sleep and the gravity of their task attached hooks to her eyelids, sealing them shut. There was nothing to do, but drift off with the fading roar of the animal within.

XAN
24 YEARS OLD

Xan had felt Juniper's eyes lingering and he knew that look all too well. Heat radiated off her even at the most inappropriate of times. She sank into her chair, exhaling a large sigh of frustration, and then must have fallen asleep.

It was up to him, now. The pressure was immense. Doubts about his intelligence gnawed, but he considered all that he had built over time. Contributing to the development of the different atmospheric pills, the functioning capability of the biobase, researching and cataloguing alien species from across the galaxy - these were no easy feats. So, maybe he could do this. Maybe his mind *was* one of the sharpest the galaxy had seen. Could he find the Crystal of New Life? Unite each of the crystals to control new life, time and fate?

He read over the cryptic poem in the text again and again.

A fire burning in the sky
Consigned and cloaked in white
Beneath the veil you will see
The fire burns eternally.
What appears so dense can be broken through
Exiom delivers, carbon true.
A constellation mourning loss
The heart of all embossed
Three moons converge
That fire always burns.

He thought it through. *Is it pointing to the direction of a white planet? 'Cloaked in white'. So maybe it's a frozen world they'd need to find. But then how can a fire burn on a frozen planet?*

Xan wore what felt like a permanent scowl, eyes narrowed, staring inwardly.

Well, I know it's a carbon planet, so that's a start. Oxygen-based, but it has exiom? That doesn't make sense. Exiom is toxic to most carbon-based lifeforms, so if there's any trace, it wouldn't have been explored by us, or by anyone really. So that means I'm trying to find a planet we probably thought was uninhabitable considering our technology can't counteract exiom in the atmosphere. Thoughts buzzed without breath inside his mind.

Xan called out, "Phineas, can you give me a list of all planets with exiom atmosphere, white in appearance, large planet density."

Phineas returned the results and its synthetic voice beamed, `"There are seven planets that have been categorised with such results, each deemed unliveable by Human standards."`

"Keep the results of planets with three moons," Xan levelled, looking into the distance as he thought of the possibilities.

Phineas returned two results. A planet called Jurda V in the Prynva System and Nixronamas in the Ortegan System.

Xan studied the readouts of both planets. They were nowhere near one another and in totally different galaxies, but that wasn't the point. He still hadn't been able to comprehend what the constellation clue might point him to.

Mourning loss? Why would a constellation mourn loss? What would it lose?

Xan studied the text, but his sight wavered. He slapped his cheeks.

This is not the time to fall asleep.

But the hands of time wrapped him in a steady grip, and rocked him gently. Angelic voices sang, harmonising in major thirds, pleasant and consonant. Constellations spanned across his mind's eye. Asterisms flickered and dropped out of his orbit. The declination of planets north or south of the celestial equator spread out before him. A grazing occultation, but the distant planets waved at him, beckoning him to acknowledge. The answer was in that brain of his somewhere, but his body begged for respite. It was time to rejuvenate and so he let himself fall; gravity can't pull you down in dreams.

CHAPTER 33

The stage that Madame Bleu spoke from was expansive, but not as expansive as the backdrop. The cliffs of Untiqua were dull red like the onset of flame. Bright green moss and lichen crawled across its face; the stain of new life infused with fire.

Madame Bleu stood behind the audio duplicator, which sent her message far and wide across the gathered crowd, hanging off her every word.

"Good morrow, family, and welcome to the Pinnacle Star Festival." Her hands were outstretched, her smile wide. A tuft of grey hair curled high, rising atop her head like a wispy crown.

Massy turned to Xan and yelled into his ear to be heard above the noise of the crowd. "Do you have any stardust on you?"

"Juniper's carrying some tonight. We were going to take it when everyone flamed on," Xan yelled back.

Massy's face drooped, a cantankerous sulk imbuing his aura. "I don't particularly want to listen to the same old speech I've heard since I sprouted my reproductive organ."

Juniper burst around the corner and draped her arms around Xan affectionately. She turned to Massy. "So, last week?"

She and Xan giggled, while Massy's face turned sour and he produced a fake laugh at her expense.

"Sorry, couldn't help having a laugh." Xan brushed his fringe back.

"Just kidding, fly boy." Juniper adjusted herself and stood in front of Xan, resting against his solid frame. "So you want some of the good stuff early?" Juniper winked, producing a small clear packet filled with the stardust drug, glittering in gold.

"Yeah, seriously, Juniper – I love this festival but I don't want to sit through the Madame Bleu speech, then the re-enactment of the shooting star, *with streaks of flame across the sky*." He mimicked the last part. They'd heard it recited near enough a thousand and one times. "Ya boy is up for a good time." Massy started dancing, hands at the back of his head thrusting his pelvis forward at anyone in the vicinity.

Juniper flexed a look of disgust and pointed toward his nether regions. "Firstly, watch where you point that thing, you fucking vaginal hazard." Massy continued dancing more vigorously to counter the barb. Juniper ignored it. "Secondly, you better listen to my commands, boy, or no stardust for you."

Massy's sulk returned as he stopped dead, frowning at her. "Why you gotta do me like that?"

"I ain't doing you like anything, Massy." Juniper's face creased, repulsion coursing through her. "Behave yourself, and you might get lucky…"

Massy's face lit up.

"Not with anything sexual, you fucking peasant. Just the drug!" Juniper sprayed her words like spitting venom.

Juniper turned her attention to Lilianna, who she'd met a couple of weeks beforehand. "Lilianna, how are you feeling, honey? Wanna head up to Rakour Rock with yours truly?" Juniper turned to the golden-eyed Sytheract who was confined to her thoughts, listening intently.

"Um, yes, I'll come," she said tentatively, flashing an uncertain glance at them all.

XAN
20 YEARS OLD

They all bustled through the crowd and jogged to Rakour Rock, laughter bristling between them. Carefully, they climbed the rock wall, concentrated alcohol lining their pockets in compact liquid bags, swishing as they made their way to the top. Reaching the pinnacle, they peered out.

"We can still hear and see everything, so it's no biggie, but fuck, how good is the freedom?" Massy yelled, with no one around to hear him. He spun around several times with a gigantic smile on his face, black knotted hair trailing with his movement.

Xan had to admit, it was nice not to be squashed together like soldiers in a trench. Not that he would know personally; Juniper had given him all the gory details of battlefield ethics. Suitable physical distance was certainly not one of their concerns.

"I love all those sweaty bodies up against me," Juniper purred, winking at Xan.

He shrugged, grabbing a seat and peering out across the festival and the coastline beyond. "We're not still talking about being on the festival grounds, are we?" Xan's smile was cautious, but playful.

"Hoe life is the only life for me, baby." She whooped atop the rock, but it was swept across by the wind into the noise of the crowd, dying among Madame Bleu's shrill voice magnified by the audio duplicator. A black garment flowed behind Madame Bleu's slender body. Her frame was enveloped in a dark nebula, ensuring she was the only visible being on the stage.

"Juniper, let me get into that stardust, would you?" Massy preened, his hands taut as he bounced up and down like a delinquent denied the chance to administer chaos.

Juniper skipped over, licking and dipping her finger into the glowing powder. She held it up to Massy's nose as he closed one nostril, inhaling sharply.

"Mmmmm," his head lolled back in ecstasy, "that is nearly as good as a little Sytheract honey bouncing on one end while an Aranther meat stick entertains the other." He licked his lips, swaying on the spot, eyes still closed.

"Not all Sytheracts are honeys, Massy," Lilianna argued.

"Oh, Lilianna, you have no idea. You're wasting what evolution gave you, girl." She frowned. "But, you do you." Massy put his hands up and backed away, then resumed a spinning dance routine on his lonesome.

Juniper scooted over and put an arm around Lilianna. "Massy, I will not stand for the objectification of *my* Lilianna."

He flicked his wrists at her dismissively. "When you're in the highest ranks of the military then come take me down, otherwise watch me slay at Fusion."

Juniper laughed with genuine wickedness. "You slay in the regular rooms, but get to the premium rooms with me someday and, um, we shall observe the slaying you actually do."

"Nothing can bother me now. Fly, shooting star, fly away." He flicked his wrists again, gesturing to her to depart Rakour Rock.

Juniper laughed and cuddled Lilianna closer. Xan was particularly glad they got along relatively well. They were both the most important people in his life and if they couldn't coexist, it would have broken his heart.

His clan wasn't the most loving group. It might have been because he was older upon entry into the planet that they hadn't really developed a deep connection. These people - Lilianna, Juniper, even Massy, the fool - were his true clan. Maybe when he earned clan sire status of his own, he could submit the application for it to at least contain these four.

"Did you want some?" Juniper asked, holding up the bag of glowing goodies.

Lilianna looked sheepish. "I haven't had any before. I never knew the right people, I guess."

Xan was about to step forward and protect her from any pressure, but there was a small glean in her eye.

"If it's safe, I'll try some," she said, exhaling nervously.

Xan was surprised. The personal conversations they'd shared led to him to make certain assumptions about other parts of her life. He was aware of her aversion to Gemarinian promiscuity, holding out for depth of emotion with physical contact. Having grown up on Earth, he had experienced both ways of life and much preferred the free spirit of Gemarine. However, he understood she was seeking a stimulation of her essence rather than just her clitoris.

But drugs? He thought that aversion to wilder ways might extend to them, too. He was clearly mistaken.

Juniper took a small bit out on the end of her pinkie, and with the other hand brushed Lilianna's hair behind her ear.

Lilianna sniffed the substance into her nostril and her eyes went wide. The effect was instant. She immediately smiled and breathed out deeply. "Oh, wow."

"Give it some time, honey. You'll feel delicious." Juniper kissed her on the cheek, then skipped over to Xan who stood arms apart from his sides, a smirk sliding across his face. Juniper jumped up onto him and wrapped her legs around his waist.

"Want to share?"

"Yes, please." She sniffed her own portion, then prepared another for entry into his nose.

He sniffed and then she kissed him in that primal way he recognised. Every inch of her kiss groaned with hunger. No, not hunger. Complete starvation. Xan was the food of desire and Juniper had forsaken her diet.

Stardust swirled inside him, clarity of sensation ensured, the sensitive nature of touch compounded upon oneself. The pleasure centre in his brain glowed with animation, pulsing with each moment Juniper wrapped herself around him.

She let go and dismounted, but whispered in his ear, "When the flames soar into the sky I want you to rip a hole in this outfit and I want you inside me."

"It would be my pleasure." Xan's deep voice resonated against her earlobe. "Correction, our pleasure." She winked, teeth digging into her bottom lip, then she danced off toward Lilianna who was transfixed, watching Madame Bleu's speech on the stage.

Massy was yelling at his flight crew buddies on the MPD holo sphere. "Get up here, you Derricks, come get bent with me."

As he cheered at the top of his lungs, Xan took it to mean more guests would come to their spot atop the rock. He much preferred the close-knit company; Massy's fly buddies could be a little…off. But what was the worst that could happen?

Xan caught the end of the mantra he knew so well after five years watching the same festival.

"The star was not lost, it took flight across the sky, it fused into our hearts, to bring joy far and wide. And we shall never mourn, for it shares in our lives, the birth of its journey, allowed us to unite."

CHAPTER 34

LOCATION: GEMARINE
YEAR: 118
LILIANNA – 22 YEARS OLD

Lilianna and Juniper bent over Xan and exchanged a glance.

"I mean, he's hot enough when he's awake but for some reason I'm even feeling him when he's asleep." Juniper flashed a cheeky smile at Lilianna.

Lilianna giggled and shrugged. "I'm not going to argue."

Juniper reached out her exohand and placed the cool boronium against his open palm. Xan stirred and squinted through tired eyes. "Oh comets, what happened?"

"It's okay, rockstar, we're cloaked on top of the levels. We figured we'd go to yours and rest before getting stuck into everything tomorrow," Juniper said, effortlessly in command.

Lilianna recognised that Xan was about to protest, to push through his pain, but he let his shoulders slip and relented. "Yeah, I guess we all need it, don't we?"

Xan sat on the couch with the text on his lap. He was frowning and muttering to himself. A glass of alcohol was placed on the clear table next to him, a condensation ring bleeding moisture onto its surface.

Lilianna's glass was nearly empty. Juniper rocked her head back, sending the murky remnants of her third drink down her throat. She let out a sigh of satisfaction and then raised her eyebrows as if to instruct Lilianna to do the same.

Reluctantly, she tipped her head back slowly and copied her barbarian mentor. A shiver crept over her as she stifled a wince with a lopsided smile.

"Another one, yeah?" It was evident Juniper expected only one reply.

Lilianna nodded in agreement, the swirls of inebriation slowing her movements.

Juniper then took her by the hand and guided her toward the kitchen. "Do a shot with me, babe."

The protest hadn't even left her mouth as a glass was thrust into her hands. "To us."

They clinked glasses and the liquid sailed into the channel of her throat, into rough waters ahead. Lilianna grimaced, looking at Juniper through one eye. She had her tongue poking out playfully, jade eyes glinting with mischief.

"Let's get old man river to join the fun, shall we?"

She took the bottle and swigged it, splashes trickling down her neck, soaking into the material where her assets were contained. Lilianna had an urge to lap at where the liquid fell, but she swayed and stumbled after Juniper instead, mildly aware of her inhibitions being as lost as the last crystal they were searching for.

Juniper snatched the text off Xan, and he protested mildly as she laid it on the table next to the couch. Juniper straddled him with the bottle and said, "Open your mouth, sir."

"Juniper, this isn't the right time," Xan said crossly.

"Oooh, such a big, gruff man when he's busy being a nerd." She swivelled her head and faced Lilianna, who swayed softly on the spot, amused. "Lilianna, don't you want Xan to let loose just a little bit?" The dare in Juniper's smirk caused Xan to eye her curiously.

"He deserves a break, I guess." A feeble voice escaped Lilianna.

"That's the spirit!" Juniper held the bottle aloft, saluting no one in particular, then turned her attention to Xan. "Open wide, babe."

He remained passive, so she pushed the bottle to his lips. The liquid disappeared as he looked at Lilianna over Juniper's shoulder with the radiation of a supernova burning in his eyes. Juniper abruptly kissed him, licking the remnants of the alcohol off his lips, tantalising and slow. Lilianna expected to feel jealous, but it was a jealousy associated with desire, not attached to emotion. She wanted Juniper's lips on hers as much as she wanted Xan's. This surprised her greatly.

Was it because she was drunk, or drunk with lust? Or a symbiotic relationship between the two?

Lilianna's lust and desire didn't come from nowhere, though. It came from years of repression, of forcing the need down, quelling its consumption of her. But it festered and grew, and now she didn't want to keep pushing it down. She wanted them both to push her down and ransack her body's compartments until she was bare, filled with something more.

Juniper unzipped her outfit and poured the contents of the bottle across her own breasts, splashing across her dark skin. First, it pooled in their laps, but tentative beads inched down until Xan's tongue curled across them, holding them captive in the cage of his mouth. He swallowed, then devoured her exposed nipples, erect with excitement as Juniper's head reared back, a pleasure-filled smile on her face.

Lilianna walked forward slowly, unaware that she was doing so, her bottom lip bitten by ravenous teeth. She sat down next to them as Xan and Juniper relished a forceful open-mouth kiss, groaning into one another, absorbing the sound with passion.

Alcohol stung the air, but she couldn't care less – she wanted to taste. She wanted to not just feel her passion, but the passion of someone else driving into her. Juniper turned and faced her, sensing Lilianna's radiating presence on her left; their bodies magnetised, embers fusing to scorch the smooth red velvet couch they were fixed to.

Lilianna licked her top lip, breath catching as Juniper leant forward, more than aware the movement was for her. A strong pulse thrummed in her neck as a fervent tongue explored the inside of her Sytheract pointy ear, trailing from the lobe all the way to the tip.

Xan watched with love-drunk eyes. Fever prickled across Lilianna's skin, but an overarching, steady hand of excitement soothed her. She had never strayed a thought to being intimate with another woman. But Juniper, she was different. The way she held herself; the way she commanded a room. Those thoughts would usually fade, drift to the valley of the ill-conceived only to dwindle in the shade of those more sustainable. But ill-conceived thoughts would have their time. Their time was now.

Juniper's fingers caressed her lithesome neck, drawing a path along her jawline until they rested on Lilianna's quivering bottom lip. Lilianna's body, it seemed, was more attuned to the moment than her mind; she was finally letting it do the talking. The excitement pulsing throughout her was bolder and she opened her mouth, wrapped her tongue around Juniper's finger. Juniper smirked with wicked deviousness and licked Lilianna's bottom lip softly and slowly. Lilianna responded to the tease by pushing forward hastily, hungrily, allowing Juniper's tongue to merge with hers in a fight for lust's medallion.

Lilianna became breathless as her sane mind returned briefly, reminding her that a woman's lips had not yet graced her own. But desire was rampant as her care shrank away, and she savoured the softer sensation, the gentle but lascivious writhing of Juniper's tongue over hers.

Juniper broke the kiss and her once frosty jade eyes were alive like sparkling emeralds touched by the sun. She had firm hands fixed to Lilianna's cheeks, and she forced her head to the left, lost in Xan's grey eyes, swirling like smoke in a field of burning flora. Her imagination had designed this moment as soon as their eyes locked for the first time, but it wasn't like this. Juniper hadn't been there with her wicked smile, gently coercing the embers to grow. It was always Xan and her, fusing as one. Part of her heart creased with disappointment but the heat inside her skin betrayed that whimsical heart. It hurt her, but it was a delicious ache.

Xan moved his face forward slowly, but instead of a careful, ardent introduction to his touch, Juniper grabbed the back of Lilianna's hair and bunched it into a knot, holding her still for him, in submission. She gasped at the ferocious treatment, shocked at how the pain excited her, and as she did, Xan's lips engulfed hers. She couldn't breathe; she felt alive for the first time. His tongue reached inside her mouth, searching for passion and finding it; spinning it in circles, driving it down into waters steaming with molten rock.

A moan escaped her, uncontained, followed by a deep groan from Xan. It gave her permission to let go a little more and he pushed in deeper as she folded into his embrace. The weakness of emotion spread throughout her. As much as the desire coursed through her, a murmur of love and expectation remained.

Juniper clawed at Lilianna's zipper from behind as she licked slowly and purposefully up Lilianna's neck once more while Xan occupied her mouth and her mind.

When the zipper reached past her navel, Juniper reached over Lilianna's shoulders and slid her palms across the dunes of her chest until her hands cupped both breasts with amorous intent. Lilianna had never submitted like this before. Every part of her body bristled with excitement and an insatiable desire for more, so much more.

They explored the uncharted territory of her body and awakened parts of herself she never knew existed. Juniper grabbed Xan's hair and forced him onto one of Lilianna's breasts, and while Juniper squeezed and pinched one erect nipple, Xan licked and sucked at the other. Eyes fluttering, she groaned again. Involuntary noises emanated from within that she couldn't control, but she didn't care now that she finally had Xan in her grasp.

She sank long fingers into his hair and grunted with longing for him; for lust explored. Her nails dug into his scalp but he didn't cry out, he bit down and sucked harder, almost daring her to come undone.

She felt Juniper over her shoulder, forcing her to crane her neck for another soft, sensual kiss. She was surprised what Juniper evoked within her. Desire didn't dampen. As Xan ignited perpetual fires, Juniper fanned the flames.

Juniper whispered in her ear, "You love this don't you, you little slut." Lilianna heard the words and tried to respond, but she couldn't. Her response was written all over her body and she couldn't believe she had this in her.

A slut? Hardly a slut. But to act like one in this moment made her delirious, and she realised she really did love it and she wasn't afraid anymore. She wanted to listen to her body, she wanted to let the moment change her.

Lilianna was losing control as Xan pulled the zipper down, further exposing her glistening self to him. She looked at him and almost couldn't breathe, lungs seized as if caught underneath a frozen lake, staring up at sheets of ice, so close to fracturing. Juniper almost snarled, but louder this time, "Tell me you fucking love it, Lilianna. Say it, you little slut."

Xan crawled down between her thighs and lovingly slid his tongue inside her, slowly advancing upwards, dancing in circles in the right spot. "Yes, I fucking love it," she screamed, voice shaking.

"That's my girl," Juniper breathed in a low, commanding voice, as she squeezed Lilianna's nipples, watching Xan work his kiss around her inner thighs, teasing. Gripping her thighs, he spread her legs wide, and this time as he lowered himself toward her, worked his fingers and tongue in tandem, making Lilianna shake and whine and writhe in pleasure. Lilianna unzipped the rest of her uniform and touched herself in front of him.

Xan stared at her, massaging himself, and licked his lips, ready to taste her again. He pushed forward, unable to contain himself and she felt his tongue work above her fingers. Forceful, pushing up against her, swirling and spinning in concentric circles, while she pushed her fingers deeper. Sweet sounds of ecstasy filled the air and it took Lilianna a moment to realise they were coming from her. She craved to be pushed to the brink and her high-pitched screams made her needs *very* clear. She stopped touching herself, instead holding onto Xan's head, practically ripping at his hair as she convulsed, begging for more.

Juniper was now naked; the bronze in her dark skin glittered in the faint light as she roamed behind Xan and grabbed at him as he stood up, facing her. Lilianna could see how responsive he was, and she watched as Juniper pushed and pulled off the top of Xan's uniform so he could command action soon. He turned to Juniper, his mouth a wet smirk. His eyes screamed pure desire and he moved forward and kissed her with force. She reached down and released him from the confines of his pants, hard and perfect for the taking. Lilianna was still wrapped in ecstasy, but he drew her up by a clump of her hair.

"On your knees and open your mouth," he said with a gruff forcefulness she had never heard before.

Lilianna obeyed and Xan directed himself to her waiting lips as Juniper knelt next to Lilianna, and then shared him between both of their salivating mouths. As Lilianna struggled with Xan in her mouth, Juniper plunged her fingers deep inside her. She gasped and released Xan as she gripped him tightly and moaned at the movement inside her.

"Don't you fucking stop, Lili. Be a good girl, now."

Her feelings swirled. She wanted to please him, so she embraced her own pleasure and then concentrated on his. His moans and grunts told her she was doing a good job, and Juniper whispered in her ear, "That's a good little slut."

The more Juniper said it, the more excited Lilianna became.

Without prompting, Lilianna pleaded, "Take me now, sir, please take me now." Xan pushed Lilianna down onto the floor while Juniper spread her legs.

Xan entered her slowly, and she felt every beautiful part of him filling her up. She held her breath, savouring the raw pleasure of him inside her for the first time. He drew back, and pushed inside again, this time with a hint of more force. She moaned again, responsive to him. She reached up and brought him closer, allowing him deeper and they kissed passionately, moaning into one another's mouths.

Juniper's tongue was on her neck, moving to her earlobe, and Lilianna sank into the pleasure they both gave her. Xan pushed back off her, placing his hands lightly against her throat and thrust his hips with dominant force, pushing deeper and harder into her. Juniper whispered in her ear as she played with her nipples. "Tell him you love it." She moved her fingers down her body and found Lilianna's sensitive spot, rubbing it expertly while Xan pushed inside. Lilianna groaned, unable to speak. Juniper kissed her but she couldn't kiss back as she screamed for more, her eyes sealed shut, all her buttons being pushed.

She reached out and grabbed hold of Juniper's hair, grunting. Juniper responded by pushing harder upon her as Xan applied more pressure on her throat. "Look at me, Lilianna."

She opened her eyes. His muscles were coated in a sweaty gloss, reflecting the twin moons peering through the window, envious that a third companion would never share their pocket of sky. Veins thrummed against his neck like a flooded dam spilling down to his shoulders, unyielding, strong; an unbreakable wall.

She was losing herself. "I want you to cum," she said in a commanding voice she didn't recognise. "I want you to lose yourself all over me."

He thrust forcefully as Juniper pressed harder. Lilianna convulsed uncontrollably, heat spreading from her core to her fingertips. She never knew she could feel like this, that *they* could make her feel so good. Juniper squealed with excitement, "Yes!"

Lilianna forgot how to function in her blissful state, but she felt Xan's strong arms pick her up and flip her over. Juniper positioned herself in front of her and buried Lilianna's face in between her thighs, hungry for a taste. Xan entered Lilianna from behind and bundled her hair in his fist and pushed her face deeper into Juniper. Lilianna was surprised the taste was sweet, and she followed the outlines to where Juniper's fingers were deep inside herself. Lilianna used her tongue to apply more pressure, wanting to please Juniper, now. Xan pulled her head up and moved his lips next to her ear. "Tell me how much you love this." He increased his tempo to the point where she saw stars. Juniper squeezed her nipples.

"I—" was all that came out. Xan thrust even harder, twisting her neck and making her look into his eyes. "Say something, now."

"I love this. I love being a little slut for you." He kissed her then, groaning into her open mouth. She was coming apart again. She yelled out, "Fill me, Xan!"

Juniper's fingers circled with the same intensity that Xan slammed into her. Her eyes rolled to the back of her head. She screamed as a burst of pleasure shot throughout her body, her legs shook as Xan and Juniper held her tight. Xan let out an almighty roar beside her right ear and she felt him release inside her, each throb of his perfect cock giving her body another burst of spasms.

She fell forward, unable to hold herself up, and Xan lay on top of her. Juniper stroked her hair and whispered, "You're such a good girl, Lilianna, such a good girl."

She didn't feel like a good girl at all. She felt bad, but it was good, so so good.

CHAPTER 35

LOCATION: GEMARINE
YEAR: 118
XAN – 24 YEARS OLD

Xan leant against the door watching Juniper and Lilianna sleeping in his bed. Qilin curled her tail around his leg and waited patiently for him to stop musing, but he couldn't help it. The spikes at the end of her tail brushed against him gently, a feeling he had come to enjoy over the years.

Fusing with Lilianna had always plagued his lustful thoughts and to have shared that moment with Juniper was so special to him. But in the throes of passion, often feelings are forgotten, and in that sudden moment of clarity – watching them sleeping, arms draped around one another – he wondered if maybe he did the wrong thing. If by chance, Lilianna would soon wake and swim away, desperate to escape the flood of her own ethos.

The love I have for her might not be exactly what she needs from me, but I care deeply for her and that should be enough – shouldn't it?

He turned away, Qilin playfully nipping at his heels. Xan's laugh was as true as the beams of sun inching through the small cracks in the light blockers. Xan had missed Qilin's presence, the way her innocence brought him unfiltered happiness. Thankfully, she was behaving like normal, now. Phineas had confirmed there were no side effects.

Qilin skirted around the kitchen as Xan prepared a breakfast for when his company awoke. He decided to combine Human ingredients with some local delicacies. A Borork egg omelette, similar to a quail egg, sprinkled with the Philox weed, which had the potent flavour of garlic. He cooked rice with soy sauce from the Human fermenting plant in the industrial section of Topaz City. He garnished the dish with chopped Yishu spores, an interesting pink and grey fungi, and Firenzes – from the bright orange, fiery, chilli-style plants.

Aside from his mother's congee recipe, it was something that always reminded him of his split identity. The Gemarine side and the Earth side. Other Humans from western countries had perfected their own equivalent of bacon and eggs but in Hong Kong, his family always preferred the Asian Fusion as opposed to simply assimilating.

He threw Qilin some of the abundant spores and she gobbled them down with abandon.

Xan skipped down the hall toward the sleeping quarters carrying the delectable feast he had prepared, and placed it on the bedside table as his two scantily clad companions continued to doze.

A holograph shimmered of the Pinnacle Star Festival – Juniper on his lap, Massy and his fly buddies roaring with laughter and Lilianna smiling meekly atop Rakour Rock – the constellation in the background missing its perfect star.

Xan straightened, and a flicker of hope burned inside his mind.

A constellation mourning loss.

The Pinnacle Star had fallen from the sky. It was rumoured that the Celestials had caused the star to fall. It was said to have been a beacon for their kind. Once it departed, so, too, did the Celestials.

Why wouldn't there be some correlation between the Pinnacle Star Festival and the ancient text?

He recalled the poem recited by Madame Bleu at each ceremonial opening of the festival:

"The star was not lost, it took flight across the sky, it fused into our hearts, to bring joy far and wide. And we shall never mourn, for it shares in our lives, a birth of its journey, allowed us to unite."

The star took flight across the sky and landed elsewhere. Where did it land?

He burst out of the room without waking Juniper and Lilianna, Qilin on his heels, and placed a call to Phineas in the hallway as he ran to the text open on the couch. "Send me a holo projection of the night the Pinnacle Star departed."

`"Sent."`

It flashed on Xan's wrist. Qilin swatted at it with her paw.

"Show me the path it was said to have taken once it fell."

`"Xan, I hope you do know stars don't actually fall, they—"`

"I'm no idiot, Phineas, now show me the path!"

Xan's excitement made him rude. Phineas obliged without hesitation, as a glowing trail plotted the course of the departing star.

Xan murmured to himself as Qilin snapped her teeth at the moving dotted lights in the holo sphere. "That's the Hydroxyl Constellation."

He raised his voice now to Phineas. "Tell me if one of the planets you listed before is in the Hydroxyl Constellation?"

`"Jurda V is in closest proximity."`

A wry smile snaked across Xan's face.

Jurda V it is.

JUNIPER
24 YEARS OLD

"Tell Ryker? Are you serious, Xan?" Lilianna raised her voice in the kitchen area.

You awaken a sexual demon and all of sudden she finds assertion as well? Well, I'll be damned, Juniper mused.

"You don't know him like I do. Why won't you trust me?" he said forcefully, crossing his arms.

"Xan, you know I trust you with everything I have, but I'm...anxious about bringing in other members of the crew, especially the nephew of our apparent enemy."

"The thing is, you have never got along with each other, so right now you have prejudice, seeing through repurposed glass."

"He is her nephew!" she yelled in annoyance, in disbelief.

"This is Gemarine. Our family is found here and I'm telling you he is ours." Xan slammed his fist against the wall, stamping out any replies.

Lilianna threw her hands up, exasperated. Her eyes then burned into Juniper's, who stood cross-armed and listening carefully. "Don't you want to pipe up with an opinion? You always have one, but all of a sudden you're silent."

Juniper's eyes went wide with shock. "Lili, speaking of piping you should pipe the fuck down. Just because we shared a bed last night doesn't mean you can speak to me like that."

Lilianna's cheeks flushed and she crossed her arms against her stomach and looked away.

Juniper sensed she'd gone too hard, too fast, so she changed tact with a joke. "Secondly, I don't want to interrupt your new-found marriage. Y'all can enjoy that archaic Earth bullshit as a dynamic duo." She scoffed, laughing boldly in the faces of the two people she'd fucked the night before.

Lilianna scowled with the angst of what appeared to be a whiny little bitch, frankly. And Xan was...the same. Two whiny peas in a bitch pod.

Clearly her joke hadn't landed well. In a discussion about battle tactics and the maiming of assholes, she most definitely read the room. She didn't even need a bottle of lube 'n' go. It was all natural, baby. But in emotional arenas…a budding artist known for capturing texture and terrain might paint a grim, monochrome landscape of a barren wasteland.

"Listen, I get you're anxious and unsure. But the magnitude of this particular space jump cannot be managed by me. We need a bigger ship and that means Massy, straight up."

Lilianna interrupted, "Massy is a harmless oaf and—"

"Ba-ba-ba, I'm not finished." Juniper raised her voice and Lilianna's shoulders shrank again.

"Massy or anyone else on this crew can't repair the ship or monitor what it needs like Ryker can. I don't really know the kid well, but we can't do this without them. It's a risk, but probably a risk we need to take, hun." She softened her tone with a term of affection and it seemed to work as Lilianna let her arms fall by her sides.

Xan spoke again. "Exactly, and I'm so afraid that things can go wrong. But we will only tell them what they need to know. We decide what is vital to share. Anything too deep is reserved for us three only."

Juniper moved to Lilianna and placed her real arm around her. She flinched ever so slightly, but then relaxed into her embrace, as if remembering it might be okay to stop being wound so tight.

Xan came forward also, kissing them both on the forehead. Juniper saw Lilianna's arms reach around to Xan and then felt her hand sliding toward her own back. She couldn't help but feel warm. A part of something more.

"I'll keep an eye on Ryker." Juniper gave them both an easy nod, her chin high. "In fact, in general, I'll keep us safe," Juniper said with complete confidence.

CHAPTER 36

LOCATION: PRYNVA SYSTEM
YEAR: 118
LILIANNA – 22 YEARS OLD

"**W**ell that speech was one for the ages. Rousing, arousing – it had it all!" Massy breathed with fire. He held his dominant fist aloft as he easily navigated the cosmos with one hand on the controls of the *Attenborough*.

"Give it a rest, this is serious stuff," Lilianna said from the seat beside him.

"Serious stuff, like finding a magical crystal on Jurda V? Or reciting poetry about fallen stars?" He stood up and waved his arms about as if performing on stage. But then his face turned grave. "Or having to lie to Madame Bleu, who is keeping a close eye on us, that we're collecting crystals now, as well as creatures?"

Lilianna recalled Xan's retraction of the vital information. As far as Massy knew, they needed the crystals to help with various creatures at the biobase. They had read some ancient texts and the Crystal of 'New Life' could be found on Jurda V. It would help with bringing creatures on the brink of extinction back to healthy populations.

"This work goes hand in hand, Massy. If you remember, our mission has always been the same. We fly into the darkness, we wrap our hands around the most vulnerable creatures, we pry them out with nothing more than hope, sometimes."

"Well not only hope, you literally use your hands too." Massy wiggled his grubby fingers in front of her face.

Lilianna tried to stifle her annoyance at the level of insolence. Massy was usually a nice little A5 chew – a sweet, tasty dessert-like treat. A nice change from all the protein-heavy chews. But when there was more at stake, she realised her patience waned. *I wonder, if he were told the full story, would he still be as dismissive?* Though she acknowledged that in one's life there were a multitude of individuals that enhanced an existence. There were the friends you would share the most intimate of details and who would shed equal parts blood and sweat for you. You felt that in your bones. Then, there were the friends who would play on simple moments to bring surface-level smiles.

So, she smiled *surfacefully* at Massy. "Look, think of it as, we deal in creatures and now we deal in crystals, too."

"But the crystal part is secret. We're like jewellery smugglers riding through the galaxy about to make a fortune." He spread his arms wide, mimicking wings of a ship, skipping around like a child.

"Whatever helps you understand it better, buddy." Lilianna put her head in her hands, exhausted. When she took them away Massy had stopped pretending to be a ship, his face now right up against hers – the black and yellow circular birthmarks inches away from her eyes, now wide in surprise.

He whispered to her, "It's fine. I have no morals. I'll be a thief or a smuggler – whatever lets me have the most fun. But you." His finger met her forehead with a delicate touch. "You wouldn't do this for anyone but Xan." A satisfied smirk was plastered on his puffy face.

"Massy, c'mon. I do this for the creatures, you know that. Besides, Xan is my boss." She tried to leave it at that but Massy wouldn't let it go.

"No, but seriously, I know you've thought about it. The way you flush pink when he stoops low to pick up a cage – getting a glimpse of that sexy bot bot in action. The way you avert your big eyes whenever he throws you a mild compliment. It's so obvious."

Lilianna remembered the night before and the swell of fulfilment as he was inside her. It was suddenly as hot as hell in her suit and she squirmed to adjust, giving him nothing. "Well, I won't deny I haven't thought about it," she admitted, looking at the ground in haste.

"Well, haven't we all? I've seen him in his prime at Fusion, and if he didn't have such a stringent no fucking with work colleagues policy, I'd be getting around whatever he offered." Massy shrugged.

Lilianna changed the subject quickly; Massy was a little too close to discovering what happened the previous night. "Well, either way, I'm glad we got clearance for this mission."

Massy rolled his eyes but seemed to understand she didn't want to linger on the topic. "Yes, yes, but the flight path cleared is not the one Xan told me to fly." He tapped his forefinger to his temple. "Uncle Massy is loving Xan's cute little reckless streak…and I'm so here for it."

Juniper lumbered up behind them before Lilianna could say a word. "Talking reams and reams of shit again, Massy?"

"I believe that is written in my job description, just as 'being an annoying bitch' is written into yours." He flashed a smile with yellowing teeth.

Lilianna left them bickering to search for Ryker. It made her nervous that Juniper had abandoned Ryker surveillance, but it seemed Lilianna's own misgivings about him plagued her judgement.

When she reached him, Ryker was browsing on his MPD and looked up, startled. She'd never seen him truly smile before, but once he realised it was her, the tiniest of movements flexed across his lips.

Is that him trying to smile? If so, I've seen an insect show more happiness.

Lilianna could still hear Massy and Juniper arguing like a clan leader and one of their delinquent children. *No prizes for guessing who plays what role.*

She wanted to be more than hateful glances and barbed words thrown heedlessly. Softening the disquiet within, a pleasant tone materialised across the space between them.

"What are you working on?" she mustered.

Ryker seemed surprised that her tone was soft, her expression neutral. "Oh, um, I'm concerned about the exiom. I know Xan has done the calculations, but nothing has been attempted like this before, at least that I've known." He broke off, tense as he twisted a screw to repair a damaged part of the *Attenborough*. "It's just...if Xan is wrong, well..." He reached down beside his foot and picked up a small papertallic bag. He placed his lips to the small hole that had bunched up at the end. As he pushed air inside, the bag began to inflate. The very moment it swelled large enough, he slammed his hands against it and a booming crack reverberated off the walls, startling Lilianna. Torn tufts of the papertallic bag drifted like leaves in their autumnal genocide, descending to mass graves of comrades already fallen.

"I mean, that performance was...sublime," Lilianna teased.

Ryker shrugged. "Hey, you got the idea though, right? Exiom comes into contact with us, we get crushed to a pulp. Simple."

The awkwardness at being in Ryker's presence shifted a little. "Look, I'm worried too, if that makes any difference." She hurried the last few words.

For a moment Ryker looked unsure, almost wary of the pleasantries, but decided to speak. "Everyone around here is all gung-ho most of the time. Bravado encroaching upon stupidity."

At times I feel like an outsider; like I'm different and I can't relate to them either, Lilianna thought, but sharing an affinity with him felt odd.

"I'm not particularly enjoying this whole experience. Over the last few days I've found myself doing things I wouldn't normally do," she admitted.

"Well isn't it horrible when you have to forget yourself to be remembered, you know?" He ruffled his own greasy black hair and let it fall across one side of his face, the darkness of his eyes sewn with a lingering sadness. There was a deep melancholy that attached itself to him like the *Vampiris Vetra*, a blood-sucking insect from the Khulor Quadrant.

Xan came around the corner. "Yes, but also, we're remembered for navigating the space outside our comfort zone for a cause greater than our own."

Ryker said with a sneer, "Last I heard, eavesdropping was rude – even for a boss."

Xan ignored his comment as his hand went to Ryker's shoulder. "It will all be fine. I might not be able to wield a sword and lead an army, but I am sure of how to lead with my mind."

"Well you better be, because if you're not, our ship will crash onto jagged rocks of death, our corpses toasty and warm under all those flames." Ryker's sarcasm was dry, aided by a dead-eyed stare.

"Always such a positive Pete." Xan chuckled, brushing past Lilianna. As he did so, his hand swept across her back tenderly. And in the midst of panic, she felt a craving for more of his touch. The events of the previous night were still very much in the periphery of her mind. It wasn't necessarily a moment where she had murdered her morals, because she loved both Juniper and Xan in different ways. There was no way she would have let it happen with just anyone at Fusion, that was for certain. But still – would they ever be able to give her what she craved? Or was it about finding some kind of compromise? Whatever the solution, it would not be found within. Anxiety circled as she realised with dread, she would need to talk with them both at some stage.

Xan called out, "How long until the space jump, Massy?"

"My fearless leader, I'm powering up the boosters and we shall be gone," he yelled back, fiddling with buttons and knobs.

Xan turned to Lilianna and Ryker. "Buckle up, looks like this is it."

Ryker shared a worried glance with Lilianna, but she plastered a confident smile upon her face to steel him. She called upon her innate quality of seeing good in others, doing so by trusting Xan's calculations with her life as well as his instincts with Ryker being loyal to their group.

She moved to her seat next to Massy then looked over her shoulder at the papertallic bag in pieces on the floor. "Readying space jump," Massy bellowed as an overexaggerated wink made the circular birth marks on his forehead waver.

JUNIPER
24 YEARS OLD

The ship shuddered violently for a number of frantic seconds. And then they were there, staring at the white mass that had rebuked other carbon-based explorers who had come before them.

Xan assured them it was okay.

Juniper knew her strength did not lie in determining the why and the how; she had lived her life with Xan bringing complementary aspects to a partnership. So it wasn't anything new for her to trust him so deeply, but it was always said, if your ship collides with exiom, the end was far from spectacular...for continuing to live, that is. The density of it was much thicker than air and if matter came into close contact, it reared its volatile gaseous head.

She thought back to so many moments in her life when Xan had saved her; the battle of Tardonelle when first contact with the Apezoids didn't go so well. When she lost her arm against the Cryptoborgs defending the western border. Even when a tactical training drill on their own base went wrong, and on her watch several cadet soldiers had been maimed.

They were all huge moments in her life where she'd put her faith in Xan and he'd come through. Every time. It was no different here.

"Keep those trusty buckles fastened, my friends. This is where we find out if Xan is the smart cookie everyone believes him to be," Massy sung, evidently masking his worry with idiotic jokes and an apathetic disposition.

"Please, Massy, I'm not one cookie, I'm a planet full of desserts." Xan's rumbling voice was heavy with playful confidence and Juniper giggled to herself, thinking, *He's been hanging out with me for way too long. That kind of shit's from the Juniper playbook.*

Massy laughed with wicked resignation and pushed the throttle, grabbing the yolk and heading through the white wall of exiom death that had shielded Jurda V since it sprouted into existence.

The opalescent blanket was nearly upon them. It was like an unassuming fog, creeping slowly, causing only mild concern for optics. As they were absorbed by the planet's gravitational pull, the ship moaned in resentment. The exhale of winter's breath filled the periphery as they hit the atmosphere. The ship's low moans turned to ear-splitting screams, as the hull convulsed in fits of shock. Lights flashed alarmingly on the dash, and even though Juniper knew her way around the control panels, Massy – with sweat flying off the long strands of his black hair – appeared to have several hands as he tried to soothe the ship with a maternal touch.

Juniper was starting to feel light-headed as the tremors increased. White was all around them now, like purity herself smothering them in a pitiful death grip. In an instant, the ship lost all power, and the interior lights aboard died. The gloved hand of darkness cushioned the chaos. The calm was more disconcerting. The calm invoked the fear. The bile brewed, and it was bitter in Juniper's throat.

Was this the end? Splashed with white.

The silence screamed.

CHAPTER 37

LOCATION: JURDA V
YEAR: 118
RYKER – 21 YEARS OLD

Ryker's skin was clammy and his pallid complexion wore the shell of the moon. The ship floated like a cloud, but the atmosphere tugged at its core. If it drifted for much longer the pressure of the exiom would crush them all.

He unbuckled himself and immediately fell to his knees. The artificial gravity felt like it had doubled, but he crawled desperately to the hatch that housed the heart; where he as the surgeon would slice, dice and splice.

Ryker's immediate thought was that the exiom had knocked out the core reactor, and he needed to switch a bezel to the connector pathway to get it firing again.

The bezel would act as a defibrillator on the dead organ of the reactor. Sending shocks into the combustion chamber to get a reaction, to get movement once more. The longer they let the hands of exiom close around their throats, the less chance they had of ever breathing again. The bezel was really the only hope.

As he stumbled into the small space, the crushing sound of metal was enhanced by Massy's bellows of help. "Ryker, what the fuck is going on?"

Lilianna's shallow breaths were the frightened hands of a clock as it ticked through rusting gears.

Before, in the heat of the Valkor exchange, Ryker and Massy had abandoned the crew because the fight wasn't theirs. Any notions of heroic redemption were stalled as a cushioned coffin beckoned them in.

He wasn't doing this for them, was he? He was still doing it for himself, saving his own skin.

Ryker's grip was vice-like on the pathway brace. The ship groaned as rectangular metallic shards snapped off into space, swallowed by the exiom – famished from years of starvation. Ryker navigated the line, whispering to himself, guiding his spindly fingers to detach the bezel. As he removed it from its shell, to his dismay, he realised it was fried, or at least the orange wire was. The most important wire.

He snatched the welder from his utility belt and charged it with the flick of a faded button, holding it up in front of his face. The light beamed across his arched nose as he sniffed, smelling charred wires, electrical burns. Heart pounding, he began splicing the orange wires together, while the ship crumpled. Warning lights flashed, ripping metal screeched with pain in the cockpit.

The bezel flickered, giving Ryker a hopeful indication of life. The first audible breath of an infant emerging from the womb. Only now he needed the bellowing cry to declare, *I am of this world, I will claim my place among the others.*

It flickered a second time, so he continued to weld as if it were his own life wire tethered to the core of the galaxy. He was desperate to secure himself to something. Desperate to feel as if he wouldn't float away flailing and falling into nothingness.

Sweat dripped down the arch of his nose, sizzling against the burning flame. Ryker's heart thrummed throughout his entire body, the death knell of steady beats.

The bezel glowed orange, a crescendo of electric buzz met his ears. Without hesitation, he smashed it back into the slot and yanked the lever down with force. The ship immediately pulsed with energy and accelerated through the torrent. Ryker pitched backwards inside the small space and his head crashed against hard metal. As he fought consciousness, the image of his aunt, Madame Bleu, filled his mind. A promise that fell from his lips as she stared down at him.

"Good, my boy, very good." Her whisper the hiss of a serpent.

He couldn't help but wonder where his loyalty belonged.

Had he chosen the right side or was he doomed to float the chasm of madness unappreciated? A weakened pawn for the powerful.

Instead of reliving the memory, he floated in blackness for the time being, unable to discern right from wrong.

XAN
24YEARS OLD

"He's a little genius," Massy yelled, pushing the throttle down and adjusting the yoke.

"By my calculations we should break through in three, two, one." Xan couldn't help but exhale with a mighty breath mixed with equal parts relief and wonder.

The white occlusion parted and his hypothesis became real, laid bare in front of them.

The lifegiving hues of greens and blues stood out among the copper cliffs that dotted the landscape. A gushing waterfall pounded into a chasm that fed lakes and tributaries spanning off like a network of capillaries toward the heart of this planet. The density of exiom was a lie, it was a filter for the sun to pass through in speckled delights as a breath of life; as a golden chalice distributing nutrients across the periphery.

Xan shook the awe from his state, and called out to Lilianna, "Can you check on Ryker, please?"

She, too, stared awestruck out at the world below. Her golden eyes matched the light that reflected in sparkles radiating off the water's surface.

Lilianna unbuckled and it appeared she now registered concern. Determined footsteps thumped onto the boronium floor toward the back of the ship.

"Xan, he's injured," she yelled, panicked. "Bring some regen gel."

Xan raced across to where the medic gear was stored without delay. He ripped open the seal and ran to where Lilianna crouched over Ryker who groaned in pain.

Ryker was sprawled in a heap, his matted black hair soaked with blood. She cradled his head.

"You'll be okay, mate, you did good. Real good." Xan squeezed his shoulder as Lilianna applied the gel to the gash at the back of his head.

"Boss, you better get up here. I think I've found the crater," Massy said, sounding dumbstruck by the sight before him.

Juniper added in, "Holy fuck," for good measure.

Xan glanced at Lilianna, asking her if she could manage looking after Ryker. She smiled and nodded, and held a clean rag to the back of his head with bloodstained hands, stemming any flow.

Xan rose and walked slowly toward the large window with the panoramic view of the planet's surface below. There was an almost perfect circle of the lightest blue, speckled with flecks of gunmetal grey. The dappled light that came through the clouds allowed them to view the deepest depths of the lake before them. It reminded Xan of the cenotes, sinkholes that filled with crystal-clear water over time. And it seemed it would be harder than simply hiking into a crater and digging out a stone. The crater was now filled with water and at the centre would be the crystal, puncturing the planet's surface like meteorite years ago. They'd have to dive deep. Who knew what was in there?

LILIANNA
22 YEARS OLD

Massy landed the ship by the lake, and they stepped out into the open air, breathing in pure and beautiful oxygen.

Lilianna held out the pills to both Massy and Xan. "Okay, so take these, now. It will help you withstand the pressure of diving so deep."

They each took a blue pill and swallowed.

"According to our tests, the water doesn't contain any nasties that will poison or infect, so you should be good to go." She gave them a thumbs up and then swung her hands by her side. Juniper gave her a look that inferred she was a nerd and then some.

Xan attached a shield across his face so it would help him see clearer and give him a breathing backup in case the pill didn't work as well.

"Why did I agree to this?" Massy whined.

"'Cause we called the hero line and you answered. Although, I would've thought you were the receptionist," Juniper quipped.

"Why don't you have the pill then, goddess of heroes?" Massy's voice turned nasally behind his face shield.

"If I stripped down in front of you, your little prick wouldn't be able to handle the excitement."

Lilianna stifled her giggle as Juniper strutted back onto the ship. "I'm checking in on the real hero, and seeing how his head is doing. See your asses soon enough."

Massy grumbled some inaudible nonsense and turned to face the lake. Lilianna was submerged in water to her ankles, and reached out for Xan's hand.

"Be careful," she said. Her eyes met his and then drifted away shyly.

"You don't have to worry about me." He winked, turning toward the lake and without a hint of trepidation, dived in.

"Hey, wait for me!" yelled Massy and as his toes hit the surface an almighty high-pitched shriek tainted the serenity of the lake. "Ouch, that is some cold shit." His face grimaced in pain.

Qilin whimpered from beside Massy. She held a paw above the water and then she limped, squelching back to rest at Lilianna's feet. It looked like she was hurt, so Lilianna reached down, sifting through the coarse blue fur to locate the source of the issue. Qilin's chin rested on Lilianna's shoulder, afraid of what caused her discomfort. Her wispy breaths merged with hushed cries, which would've sent an arrow into a heart forged with boronium. Lilianna was desperate to quash the pain from the *Mika Tikaani,* and as she rummaged through the strands of fur, she finally saw it. A black and bright green worm-like creature feasting on her flesh.

"Yuck," she squealed, pinching it between finger and thumb and throwing it away from them. Qilin bolted after it and put it between her sharpened teeth. As she crunched down, a burst of blood trickled down her jaw.

"Oh, Qilin, that's so gross," she complained, smiling at the lack of embarrassment creatures felt.

Massy squealed as he submerged himself into the cobalt lake.

Qilin instead galloped forward and sat upon the ground beside Lilianna. She licked Lilianna's face with all the innocence that a creature could possess. A beautiful, blissful existence, without the weight of emotions, of expectations, of worlds and galaxies held together by crystals.

"Ah, girl, life is weird, isn't it?" Lilianna asked as she scratched behind Qilin's ears.

Qilin answered with a gentle, satisfied snort.

CHAPTER 38

Xan waded through the crystal-clear water. If he weren't so anxious to find the final crystal he would have regarded this as one of the wonders of the universe. It was a catastrophic discharge of beauty. The Crystal of New Life had done wonders already. Evolution would evidently take longer to produce large aquatic life, but still, small marine creatures floated by, coral networks beamed with vibrant splashes of colour, seagrass undulated, gently caught in the wheels of time.

Xan wanted to document every aspect of this journey. Usually, he would press record on his MPD, scan the site taking holographic renders so when he sat on his couch, staring out from the living area, it would be like he was reliving this memory. Beautiful moments on loop when the shadows of the night came crawling.

But in this case, his determination overcame his wonder, quelling it with a deathly strike to the heart. As it died softly, he searched with

Massy – their MPDs shining a fluorescent beam of light following the topographical map plastered on their screens.

Floating toward the centre of the map, Massy called across the MPD, audio communications wired into Xan's inner ears.

"Is it getting hot in here, or is it just me?" Massy waved his arms, and through the pulsating flexes of the water, Xan recognised his confusion.

"Stop being silly, Mass, we have to find the—"

"I'm serious, Xan. Do you not feel hotter?" Massy's eyes widened in panic.

Xan didn't feel as out of breath as before, his muscles no longer numb. A quick readout on his MPD showed that the water temperature was in fact, steadily increasing.

How is this happening?

"Locate source of the heating water, Phineas, now!" he yelled, bubbles billowing around him.

"Detections of low ambient pressures building toward the northern point of the lake. Proximity of magma combined with pressurised water ensures that there will be a hydrothermal explosion in approximately eight minutes."

If Xan hadn't been submerged in water, he would have been submerged in sweat. "Eight minutes!" he repeated incredulously. "How?" Kicking his legs with purpose, he was determined to get to Massy.

Phineas responded to the question, even though it was a bewildered remark. "I already explained how the hydrothermal—"

"Shut the fuck up, Phineas," Xan shouted, frustration flowing in waves much like the surface of the lake.

"Okay, acknowledged," Phineas responded, emotion devoid in his AI programming.

Xan reached Massy, and it didn't take long to understand the situation was dire. They both fought through the water resistance.

Xan explained to Massy, "We need to kick hard, cup our hands to slice through the water and propel ourselves forward and get this crystal fast!"

Massy nodded then faced forward, kicking hard in the direction of the centre of the lake.

"I'm an aquatic genius," Massy bragged as they followed the map on the MPD.

They made it to the centre of the map and although it was only two minutes of intense swimming, it felt like an age. The timer on their MPDs counting down to the hydrothermal explosion mixed with the prophetic doom that spanned the horizon, didn't particularly help the situation.

A pulsing glow had gathered beneath the sand. It was the Crystal of New Life practically signalling them, desperate to be unveiled.

Massy dived down eagerly and was soon lost in a haze of sediment as he scratched the lakebed, disrupting the visibility and clouding the clear water around him. Xan stared hard at the silt swarming like locusts. Brittle wings carved out confusion in his perception.

Phineas chimed in his ear, "`Five minutes remaining until hydrothermal explosion.`"

Xan didn't know whether it was his mind playing tricks, but he felt flustered. Not from the certain possibility of being the contributing flavour stock in this cosmic soup, but from the definite increase in water temperature.

"C'mon, Massy, what the fuck are you do—"

Out of the disrupted silt, a silhouette emerged burning with an orange glow. The silhouette became a body, rising toward the surface. It was Massy, but he was weighed down by a large crystal with three distinct columns, facets shimmering like the sky catching the tears of a setting sun. His cheeks puffed out and his jaw was set tight as he attempted to bring it up. Like a frog, he bucked his legs and strained his body to give grace to his spluttering movements.

Phineas was calm; Xan was not. "Four minutes remaining until hydrothermal explosion."

One of the larger aquatic creatures that looked like a lizard swam in front of Massy, startling him. The crystal slipped from his grasp and started to spiral toward the bottom.

Xan responded quickly, diving down and kicking his feet frenetically to intercept the crystal before it was camouflaged in a colourful coral forest.

The crystal was heavier than expected, but then again, what weight did new life carry? Cells, organelles, atoms and molecules all packaged in a crystalline lattice, carrying with it the promise of an Eden resurrected. But, was there more to life than those base components? A spark of inimitability. The vehemence of intuition. The saccharine taste of desire. The breath of idle contentment. Each of the components are that which cannot be measured effectively.

Despite what new life it could bring, it would need to save Xan and Massy, somehow. He swiped at it several times, slipping through his fingers, until he jerked his body forward, allowing his hand to cup the base before it sank away from sight. Tucking it under an arm, bicep bulging, his legs swayed with poise, propelling him toward the surface of the lake.

As Xan and Massy both emerged, breaking the surface with a splash, Xan spluttered, "You nearly lost it!"

"It weighs a tonne. I thought I could manage."

"Next time, wait for me and we'll do it together." Xan's breathing was still rapid, but his mind was attuned to recognise his distaste at Massy's penchant for heroics.

"Ummm, I will literally never have to dive into a lake for a crystal again." Massy's voice was a rotting tree branch absorbing a burning ray of sunlight.

Xan kicked beneath the surface, struggling at the constant treading of water. "Can you dismantle your MPD and clasp it around the crystal, set it to the buoyancy feature so it can handle the weight?"

"Why mine?" he whined.

"Are you joking? I'm clearly struggling. Hurry up." Xan hardly ever turned sour, but exhaustion and stress can turn mindful Zen warriors to demons in seconds.

"Shit, okay, sir," Massy replied hastily, eyes wide in amusement.

Phineas came through once more, "Three minutes remaining until hydrothermal explosion."

Massy unclipped the MPD and fixed it to one of the crystal columns and it automatically adjusted to its girth. He keyed in the commands and then the crystal was weightless in the water.

"Let's push this back to the shore. Hurry!" Xan called out, frantically kicking on the surface of the lake, crystal ahead of them. The shore seemed so far away. Possibly too far to survive.

Phineas was there again. A reminder of his impending death. "Two minutes remaining until hydrothermal explosion."

Massy screamed beside Xan, "We're going to fucking die here!"

"Keep pushing. We're going to make it." Xan said it for positive reinforcement, for belief. But could words propel them closer?

Xan sweltered in his suit. The temperature had risen, turning his cheeks pink as he pushed through the water, the edge calling to them with fresh allure.

Massy huffed and puffed. "Fuck, I don't think I can do this."

Xan stole a glance at him. Massy was struggling to breathe. He grabbed his suit with his other hand and tried to heave him forward.

A rumbling started from what sounded like far away, but near the cliff edge, steam rose and bubbles began to form, rippling to catch them in its net of melting death.

LILIANNA
22 YEARS OLD

Juniper lounged in Massy's chair with her feet up on the control board. "Look at those oafs," she remarked at no one in particular, but Lilianna swivelled up from where she was grooming Qilin's dark fur, tufts of blue and black floating inside the cockpit. The vibrations of Qilin purring against her thigh calmed her.

Xan and Massy splashed and flailed unceremoniously in the water. She hadn't noticed the steam rising from the lake like a caliginous wraith, bearing down on them as their faces distorted in anguish and desperation.

Swimming isn't that difficult, is it?

The crystal bobbed in the water ahead of Xan.

They appear to have the crystal in tow, so why do they look like death is chasing them?

Juniper yelled back, "Looks like they got the cryst—"

The ship jolted without warning, sinking, shaking – the sound of metal crunching. Qilin screeched, high-pitched with an ethereal air.

"What the fuck!" yelled Juniper. She hastily activated her MPD. "Give me a report on what's happening."

"I detect a large unknown species attempting to consume the ship," the AI said.

Lilianna and Juniper stole a despairing glance at one another.

"Consume the ship?" Juniper bellowed incredulously. "I've been hungry before but, what the fuck?" She clipped up her bootstraps and ran down the hallway to the weapons store closet.

A huge explosion sounded out across the lake, adding to the intensity of the situation.

There was no time to look back; they needed to concentrate on their current predicament.

"What are you going to do?" Lilianna shouted after her.

"What I have to!" she yelled back, breathless, spiralled hair bouncing atop her head.

Qilin nipped at Juniper's heels, bounding to the weapons closet with her. The *Mika Tikaani* was her little general, waiting to wield a weapon in between clenched teeth.

Juniper grabbed two Cranston ray guns, holstered them, and her determined eyes narrowed as she scanned the rows for anything else with fire power.

Grabbing a hyperblaster off the shelf, she sped off as she called to Qilin, "C'mon, my girl, lets fuck shit up." Lilianna steadied herself against the wall as the ship rocked with another surge. She watched the *Mika Tikaani* and her Human mother run off to defend the *Attenborough*. Lights flickered in the hallway like an ailing breath. At once, Lilianna was alone.

CHAPTER 39

Juniper and Qilin climbed onto the top of the ship, and the sight halted them in their tracks.

What appeared to be a gigantic, parasitic worm was slowly consuming the ship. Its skin was a dull grey. Glossed and wet, it dripped in mud and sludge. Blotches of bright green throbbed angrily on the surface of its bubbly skin, and as it inched its way forward squelching and slurping, muscles throughout its body quivered, ingesting more of the ship down into its throat.

Qilin snarled, but the worm-like creature didn't seem to react or have any awareness of its actions. It was simply acting upon instinct. Gulping – crushing the metal with force, swallowing further and then repeating the same action.

Juniper turned to Qilin. "It's okay, girl – hopefully this works."

She cradled the hyperblaster like a doting mother, pumping the forend slide with affection. Curls of her violet hair jiggled in front of her eyes, so she flicked her head swiftly and the hair swished atop her scalp. Plump lips pursed as Juniper took aim, and her tongue circled her top lip as if this somehow gave her a feeling of sexual gratification.

She was clearly in her element. Which might have been concerning to some, as her element was all manner of violence. But throughout her life, she'd never turned away from shades of grey. In fact, she completely embraced the colour spectrum, letting the vividity and monochrome blend together, sprinkled with a healthy smatter of crimson droplets.

As the forend slid back into place, the hyperblaster buzzed, gathering its strength. Upon releasing the trigger, it sent an almighty bolt of intense heat into the heart of the creature.

A circular burn appeared, kissed by a rim of orange sparks, dwindling almost instantly to a blackened stain. Metallic crunches continued as the alien slug seemed to relish the taste of charcoal at the back of its throat.

Juniper howled with the serrated sanity of a sadist, pressing down on the trigger with a wild rage that grew with each chaotic blast as it thumped into the creature. Her green eyes were wide, an untamed forest swathed in an eerie embrace. Mouth agape, teeth bared in a malicious snarl, veins on the side of her neck thick like dunes rolling across a war-torn wasteland.

Qilin sprang forward, using her claws to tear at the gelatinous flesh. Perforated skin, with a pale green ooze trailed across the top of the ship, but the alien slug kept on eating, unfazed by the disturbance at its dinner table. Nothing seemed to work.

Juniper's hyperblaster billowed trails of smoke into the air, framing her as a fearsome soldier in distinguished slithers of grey. A scratching noise startled her out of warzone mentality and as she turned, she glimpsed slender fingers grip the edge of the ship. He pulled himself up to face her, the white bandage around his head flailing as the wind coddled him, attempting to soothe the intensity of the moment.

The feral Juniper subsided and the grim credentials of her other 'soldier' colleagues hit her like a punch to the urethra.

What the fuck does this skinny ass bitch Ryker think he's doing?

Before she had a chance to yell at Ryker for disturbing her transition from crazy bitch to mega crazy bitch, Qilin pounced forward, catching her eye. The *Mika Tikaani* slashed at the slug again and again, swiping across its skin with the thorns in her tail. The blue in her fur was alive with fury, shining as if anointed by light passing through an exiom cloud.

At least she was a soldier worth celebrating.

But still, nothing Qilin tried could put a stop to the swallowing.

XAN
24 YEARS OLD

Massy threw the crystal onto the shoreline and dived onto the sand, ripping off his suit like a madman.

Phineas had warned them of the inevitable hydrothermal explosion and luckily thirty seconds after they lumbered up onto the shore, blistered and raw from the rising water temperatures, the catastrophic crack rumbled beneath the surface.

A jet of steam rose swiftly from below the arching cliffs and bubbling water expanded across the surface in a mass-heating event. Xan's skin was already tender and he shuddered to think of the damage, had he been exposed to the water in its current state.

"Well, that was an anticlimax," Massy said, puffing with exhaustion.

"It all happens deeper down, Massy. I guess it's like the analogy of a duck. Looking calm, gliding across the surface but their legs are kicking frantically beneath in order to stay afloat."

Massy's face screwed up in puzzlement. "What the fuck is a duck?"

"Uh, I honestly can't be bothered right now," Xan said, energy depleted.

A feral scream tore through the soundscape, echoing off the cliffs surrounding the lake. Xan's and Massy's gazes snapped toward the ship and they were shocked into submission. A gigantic alien slug was eating the *Attenborough*.

"Are you kidding me right now?" Massy slammed his fists against his thigh. "When are we going to catch a break?"

A hyperblaster rattled off a foray of shots. Xan didn't respond, but once every now and then, his Aranther buddy talked a morsel of sense. It was one of those times when he found himself wondering, if there was a break to catch, why weren't they dexterous enough to seize it?

RYKER
21 YEARS OLD

Juniper's MPD exploded with a crackle. "What is that?" Xan's voice was tinged with fear and confusion.

"I'm no professional xeno-biologist like you, but it's a beastly worm slug thing that seems a little…hungry, so I'm trying to keep us off the menu," she yelled, sending another blast aimed near the mouth. A piece of its lip melted off and stuck to the *Attenborough*'s crumpling body.

Ryker held a hulking metallic tool in his hand called a cooler yield; it had a spherical dome in between two boronium columns, flowing purple with a liquid that often cooled the ship as neurons fired and the reactor surged with life.

Lilianna and Ryker had quickly deduced a theory before he climbed atop the ship to try and help Juniper. He didn't have much experience in heroism, in fact, he had more experience running away with flailing arms and shrieking at the top of his lungs.

But now he stood atop the ship, as a guardian angel to this crew of misfits. A bandage halo kept the hair from his eyes. His wings were his tools and he would use them to fly toward the alien slug, who was having a grand ol' time ruining all of his decent modification work on the *Attenborough*.

Overtly heroic he may not have been, but without him their missions would fail. The tinkering behind the scenes ensured the ship sailed the turbulent waters of space. In many ways, they took him for granted. By doing something outlandish, would it make him more valuable to them?

Massy must have been back in the cockpit below as he felt the power surge across the ship. Moments before, Lilianna had screamed at him, "When Massy powers up the ship, that will be your cue."

Juniper yelled, "What are you doing, kid?"

He didn't answer. Instead, he stomped forward to face the alien slug. Its dark, hollow eyes were vacant. A sticky mass of saliva drenched a quarter of the ship. Steadying himself, he couldn't help but falter.

If I throw this into its mouth, who knows if it'll reach the stomach?

The plan was that once the alien slug swallowed the cooler yield, its stomach would distribute coolant and dry ice throughout its system. If it didn't die, it most certainly wouldn't want to consume anything further, which would mean Massy was free to fly off into the sunset.

Ryker thought he heard Juniper's MPD crackle with sound. He held up the cooler yield with the intention to throw it into the alien's open mouth, but before he could, Juniper snatched it from his grasp. She dived midway through the air, turned to face him and saluted with a wry smirk. Landing on her shoulder on the top of the ship, she slid across the sopping wet goo and disappeared down into the alien's mouth.

Qilin darted forward, and recognising her intent. Ryker dived with desperation and latched onto her before she could follow Juniper's path. The usually friendly *Mika Tikaani* turned to face him and her eyes glowed burning red.

CHAPTER 40

LOCATION: GEMARINE
YEAR: 98–118 (RYKER'S MEMORIES)
RYKER – 11–21 YEARS OLD

Half of Ryker's clan had died in the battle of Asriade. A sentient species called the Blinkens attacked a party of explorers on a resource-gathering mission to Asriade. Unfortunately, his birth parents were also not spared. A war ensued and Gemarinians never ventured there again.

Clans were integral to the social cohesion on Gemarine as they ensured each child of Topaz City grew with access to not only loving parents, but other important life skills.

A clan was made up of individuals who, together as a team, could provide stable access to a plethora of emotions, skills, knowledge and creativity to feed off one another. And, in looking after a child or children, enrich their lives in a way that two parents could not. It was the 'you need a village to raise a child' mentality in action.

The strength of the blood connection was still strong, and Ryker was a true child of Gemarine. Born of a Sytheract mother and a Human father, he was one of the first interspecies children who grew into greatness. It

302

just so happened that Madame Bleu was the sister of his mother, a former noble Sytheract explorer who helped to colonise Gemarine. There was a group of Sytheracts who opposed soul bonding and when they first contacted Aranthers on Dracia, they sought a planet where they could build from their own ideals.

When his parents died, Ryker was eight years old. The pragmatists in his clan remained but the empaths and the emotionally tuned ones were gone too, so he tried to turn to Madame Bleu. Warmth did not guide her movements; instead, icy tendrils seemed to feed her soul, and each breath of love was tinged with the mist of misgiving.

Naturally, out of reach, he tried even harder to make her see him. But at the learning centre, everyone was too afraid to befriend him because of who he was. That was until, Lambastian. A beautiful dark Aranther male who was bold and brazen, but warm and unabashedly accepting. Ryker soon found he didn't particularly care for any females, he only cared for Lambastian. But Lambastian crossed a line, and was found to have disrupted the last of the three sacred rules.

Gemarine was founded on the principle: 'Contentment through unity, peace through protection'. The three sacred rules were developed to ensure this way of life was truly upheld.

We are all one kind and no judgement shall come between us.

We are to strive for peace to protect our community.

We must do what is best to preserve the unity of the planet.

Ryker never got a chance to say goodbye.

Instead, Madame Bleu sat him down one evening, smugness in her face, and said, "Lambastian has been exiled." Her voice was the colour of royalty. "He paid a price for being a disrupter and no blood of mine will follow that path, or fraternise with those who create those fading footprints of an attempted revolution. Isn't that correct?"

Oh, I'm your blood now, am I? he thought bitterly, as silver tears burned his dark eyes.

"That's correct," he murmured, gazing upon the floor.

"In fact, it's important you comply with everything I set." Madame Bleu crossed her legs, straightening her posture. "I'm making you a special deal."

His head pricked up, hurt still creeping through his blood, emanating from a newly torn heart.

"What would you have me do?" Ryker's voice was feeble. It seemed this interaction in particular highlighted his propensity to shrink inside himself, to run from conflict and accept blindly what others laid out for him, even if it broke him.

"Well, you'll simply continue at the learning centre as planned. But…" She paused, grabbing his jaw in a deceptively strong grip, squeezing so his eyes stared only into hers, wide and, frankly, evil. "You will be my eyes. Catching any insubordination at its most basic level." She released her grip aggressively, and his neck spasmed with the sudden lack of pressure. "Maybe you can help prevent further exiles by feeding me information." Madame Bleu looked off into the distance, caressing the sharpened tips of fingernails absent-mindedly.

Begrudgingly, Ryker nodded. He knew no other way. The only bit of freedom he tasted was on the tongue of a beautiful boy, who was gone now. But Ryker's heart was exiled too, and it didn't feel like it would ever return.

At Fusion years later he followed the strong Aranther boys, asked them to fuck him rough, sometimes string him up and punish him. Sexual masochism gave him some relief. He was able to release the demons of his past and it made him feel worthy. Still tortured over his exiled lover, blurring the lines between pain and pleasure made it easier to continue on without him.

Last night in particular was certainly no different in the usual sense, yet it was very different indeed. After a foray with a gentleman Human, he was taking some time away to refuel. Among the crowd of bodies, he spotted Lilianna bustling out the door. Running, tears streaking her cheeks as she fled onto the street, into a transpo and sped off into the night.

She never comes to Fusion. It's a well-known fact she doesn't believe in it. So why is she here?

He could no longer focus on the men brushing up against him, hands gripping his throat in a playful show of dominance. Lilianna turned over in his thoughts and that was enough to soften any chance of an erection.

Madame Bleu buzzed his MPD.

This is a surprise.

"Ryker, meet me immediately."

There was not even the hint of a question, just a demand. It sickened him that he was just a tool for her. He was a tool for everyone, he realised sullenly. A tool using other tools to maintain a ship.

What a fucking waste of a life.

"Of course I can. May I ask what the problem is?"

"I'm concerned about your little crew. We need to talk."

He inhaled with the scent of pink peppercorns and danglewood sprouting on the sidewall beneath the club. The breath filled Ryker, but all his confidence escaped him.

Trapped once again.

CHAPTER 41

Xan climbed onto the roof of the *Attenborough*, to the hub of activity. His wetsuit was zipped down to his navel and then tied around his waist, exposing his torso.

Ryker was holding onto Qilin desperately, and after noticing Xan's presence atop the ship, yelled out, "Help! Her eyes!"

Xan stumbled forward, hair sopping, skin clammy and damp. Dropping to his knees, he crawled, levelling his face against Qilin's. "Don't do it." His tone was deep and enchanting. "Not yet, girl. Not yet."

He stroked the thick fur behind her protruding ears, the calm within him destroyed. His hands rubbed feverishly. The red eyes dwindled like a leaf from a Tanadar tree faded by the sun. Xan's pleading appeared to convince her that she didn't have to use her power.

It was unknown how many times she had left until her expiration. Xan ruminated on this fact every day. What would make her finally give up the last of her essence? He didn't sing praises to the stars or plead for their guidance and interference, so he did everything in his power to soften hers.

"I didn't do anything, Xan, she…" Ryker shook his head as if clouded by an incredulous memory. "She just changed when Juniper jumped into the alien's mouth."

"Trust in Juniper," he said soothingly to Qilin, closing his eyes as she closed hers, letting her pupils settle into submission, returning calm to her stare.

Xan turned to Ryker. "You did do something." Ryker looked uneasy, seemingly fearing the worst. "You saved her." Xan's features softened, and brittle tears were thawing sleet as winter waned. He cupped the underside of Ryker's chin and their eyes locked, a well of appreciation passed through their stare, deep and dark but theirs alone.

The MPD on Xan's wrist squeaked with life. "I don't know, Xan, the darkness is endless, the walls are closing in, I'm not certain this is right."

Right on cue, the alien slug stopped consuming. There was a sudden recoil and a belch that sent a putrid gust of air toward Xan and Ryker, signifying that maybe it was working.

The ship catapulted forward as Massy manoeuvred the throttle in an attempt to escape from the alien's grip.

Xan, Ryker and Qilin tumbled off the ship. Qilin landed on her four feet like a feline warrior. Ryker crunched his shoulder into the ground and Xan held onto the wing, only to slip off into the lake with a subtle splash.

The ship stumbled and hovered across a shallow part of the lake, water fizzing as its thrusters came close. Xan popped his head up out of the water and the cool breeze was a kiss on his sweltering skin. He watched Massy struggle to keep the ship from diving deep into a colourful graveyard of vibrant blue coral. His breath was muted under the strenuous situation, but the ship steadied briefly as Massy pulled hard to the left and settled across a patch of reeds not too far ahead.

The Crystal of New Life glowed at the edge of the lake and Xan pushed hard through the pain to get to it. Although the lake had cooled considerably since it had reached boiling point, Xan knew his skin would not look the same as he exited the lake.

Qilin greeted him, licking his face as he clambered up onto the shore, crawling to the crystal as it lay against the sand. Ryker, streaked with mud, a bandaged head and a dislocated shoulder, still lay flat on his ass while the alien slug belched deep, coarse spittle into the air.

Xan recalled a line in the ancient text. 'The Crystal of New Life, orange glow burning bright, incantation "per cai per rei, secum xe norve"'.

Xan hugged the crystal to his chest and closed his eyes, optimistic that 'new life' also meant regeneration and healing. Hopeful whispers of the ancient words trickled out of his blistered lips.

Qilin lingered beside him, purring worried prayers into his neck. A coolness spread throughout his body, like the first snowflake of winter coming to rest upon his nose as he walked under the jacaranda tree in Hong Kong. It brought excitement and wonder. It made him feel alive when all around him seemed dead. Brittle branches, trails of smoke across the tops of houses, grey clouds stooping low.

As Xan opened his eyes, he glanced at his hands. His skin glowed with renewed vigour. It appeared the damage caused by the high temperatures of the lake lingered no longer. As he exhaled a breath of relief, a muffled message came through on the MPD.

"Xan, I can't get back out. I'm suffocating in here. I'm going to have to blast my way out." Juniper's voice was strained, panicked.

Xan recognised she had tried not to kill the creature to appease him; he didn't have to warn her to act in that way. But it was either she be lost to the unpleasant darkness of an alien's inner tract, or she blasted her way to freedom.

A burst of green blood shot from a burn midway through the slug. The exoarm came first, ripping at the slug's sticky flesh, then Juniper's head emerged, caked in viscous liquid. She bellowed with frustration, her hyperblaster sounding off three more times as the rest of her body emerged, green blood bursting like a fountain fed by a sewage canal.

Juniper yelled expletives in a screech that would rival the most ferocious beasts in the galaxy. As she flicked the frankly disgusting green jelly balls of slug filth from her skin, Xan strode forward. The Crystal of New Life lay in his outstretched hands, and he moved toward the alien slug writhing in pain from the perforation in its belly. The crystal burned bright with the ancient incantation melodically retrieved from his mouth. He passed Juniper, who wiped her eyes so she could at least see. She could handle herself.

As the alien expelled painful groans, even though it may not have been aware yet, it didn't deserve an ending like this, at their hands. He approached the wound as the green goo tumbled out, flowing like molten lava. He began the incantation and the orange of the crystal glowed brighter. Pressing the crystal to the wound, he finished at "… norve." The wound sealed itself, repairing the damage to the broken skin, then suddenly the slug stopped groaning. Xan took a moment to take it all in. The healing power of the crystal. The fact that such a potent power existed. But then an intelligent thought thumped him harder, like a slap across the back of the head.

Vacate the area before the slug decides to eat something else, maybe a tasty leg or two!

He turned on his heels and ran, calling to Juniper as she stared with an open mouth at the crystal's power. "C'mon, She Hulk – let's get out of here." He didn't wait for her reaction; she probably didn't understand the reference. Footsteps behind him were laden with a squelch or two as she followed him to the mangled, but functioning ship.

LILIANNA
22 YEARS OLD

Even though Massy's yellow and black marks across his forehead were basically a coating of hair or fur of some kind, there was a sheen of nervous sweat settled across it.

"We were too close to being a submarine." His exhale, fraught with adrenalin, smelt stale and acidic.

Lilianna was still breathing as if flying through hyperspace. Her words were stuck behind a wall of fear. "I…can…hardly speak."

"Hopefully the crew didn't take too much of a terrible fall, then. I'm glad I was in here." Massy loosened his shoulders.

Lilianna desperately searched the ship's external cameras for signs of life. All four of them were heading toward the ship in various ways. Qilin bounding with a heedless gallop, Xan, water dripping off his shirtless body, with the orange crystal alight in his hands like a flare. She swallowed, feeling flustered watching him scantily clad, remembering the beauty of the night before. But all that faded as Juniper came into view, doing her best to skip along the surface, wet with green sludge all over her body and a scowl on her face.

Lilianna's jaw dropped and she had to double-take, stifling a giggle.

"What the fuck is that?" Massy pointed to the screen.

"Don't, Massy, she'll kill you."

"If looks could kill, yeah, I take your point."

Xan climbed onto the ship with Qilin first, Ryker just behind looking poorly. "I'm taking him to the regen chamber to clean him up." Xan was all business, purposefully striding past Lilianna as she bent down and scratched behind Qilin's ears, receiving a loving lick across her cheek.

At least I've got affection from this one, she thought as Qilin nuzzled into her.

Juniper's heavy boots smacked hard upon the metallic floor of the ship. Massy stared while Lilianna did anything but will him to stop.

"What the fuck are you looking at?" she seethed, glaring at Massy.

"You look like you've been jizzed on by a fat goblin cock." He broke out into waves of laughter crashing onto a quiet bank.

She didn't say anything, just took determined strides toward him and swiftly sent her boot into his private parts with a crunch. As he doubled over, her knee flew up into his nose and he reeled backwards, ending up on the floor in the foetal position. She dragged a hand across her hair, accumulating a pile of gelatinous green goo and shoved it into Massy's open mouth, rubbing it all across his face. She stormed past Lilianna. "I'm having a shower. Tell that ball-less fuck bag to get us in the air and on course by the time I return."

Massy spluttered on the floor, and Lilianna peered over at him. "I warned you," she said simply.

Through pain and clenched teeth he revealed, "It was worth it," as a pained smile graced his idiotic green-stained face.

CHAPTER 42

Madame Bleu burst into her level amidst a flurry of colourful words, ignoring Ryker playing in the corner. Her grey bob of neatly cropped hair bounced as she fetched a drink from the cabinet, poured it into her chalice of choice and took a hefty swig. Her blue eyes closed and her thin mouth pursed with pleasure.

Her eyes opened and settled on Ryker, her breath nearly returned to normal. He held a crisp white crystal in his grubby little hands, scraping it along the floor; a soldier in his battle fantasy.

The chalice fell fast, a stone from a tower. Her screech startled the young boy and he dropped the crystal immediately, looking at her with a befuddled glance, eyes glassing with a plunge into a meek puddle of woe.

"You insolent fool. Never, ever touch this again."

A clawed hand flashed across the crystal, seizing it. Her ceremonial black coat flicked menacingly out toward Ryker's face, as Madame Bleu turned and bounded toward the other end of the office.

Madame Bleu dialled on her MPD. "Maraudar, I need you to come up here, now." Her tone was a frayed wire.

"Do you require…servicing, Madame? If so, will it be me, or Thaspina and Zondini also?"

The anger in her subsided. "I need you for another matter concerning the crystal. You are my most trusted and loyal member of the inner circle; this matter concerns you and you alone."

"Thank you, Madame, I will be there shortly," he replied with an undisguised level of pride singing in upper registers.

"And as for your question, now that you have brought it to my attention, bring your A-game for servicing post-task."

"As always, Madame."

The call ended. "Ryker."

"Yes, Madame."

"Go to your room and play there. Aunty has some work to do."

Ryker watched through a crack in the door several weeks later. His dirty fingers swept oily raven hair over the top of his head so the wispy fringe didn't obscure his vision.

"I'm going to prepare my move in the coming days, and Ryker can go back with his clan. I can't have little ones around poking into my important things. That crystal incident was the final straw."

Maraudar nodded. "I understand."

"This will be your level now and you will guard the crystal with your life. Nothing is more important. Keep the passcode safe and hidden."

"You can trust me, Madame." Maraudar stood unflinching and resolute.

"I know I can." She moved forward and kissed him. Their tongues fought against one another. Ryker wanted to look away, but he was fascinated.

Why is she touching him like that? She's his boss…that doesn't seem right.

The kiss was over, but the tension between them reeked. Ryker didn't understand it then; didn't know the difference between heartfelt passion, acting on urges, or simply releasing tension to clear the mind. But he could recognise the balance of power was askew here.

"Is there any other way I can serve you, Madame?"

She pursed her lips and her greying fringe, like a scythe, caressed her cheek. "You will serve me well tonight," she said, her voice deep with desire.

"I live to serve." He got onto his knees and kissed her feet.

"Kiss higher than that, you little fuck boy." Her voice was gravel on a garden pathway.

They exchanged eye contact, but Ryker didn't understand the look.

She lifted her leg and her flowing cape exposed her warmth to him. Maraudar dived into her, and she arched her head up, moaning.

Ryker's stomach somersaulted and he looked away, opting to stare into the darkness of the room instead. Before he tiptoed across the floor to his bed, he heard Madame Bleu's voice deep and raspy.

"Now call Zondini and get him to bring those two Aranthers and the Sytheract males we often use. I want you all to worship and pleasure me all night. Hurry up, servant boy, meet me in the room when you're done."

RYKER
21 YEARS OLD

Everyone always underestimated Ryker. Even the crew he was very much a part of. They had never lauded his qualities, never placed him on a pedestal with deafening applause as his theme song played. But it worked to his advantage. He observed, learned, and stowed all the secrets away.

Secrets were a currency in their own right, and he had to wait for the right moment to cash them in.

This was one such moment. The passcode to the vault where Maraudar kept the time crystal had been etched deep into his brain for years now. Maraudar thought it safe and hidden, but secrets come alive if you look with great intent.

The passcode pattern he used was that of the astrological chart the Pinnacle Star took as it fell from the sky. Maraudar couldn't see how reckless it was to use the departed star's constellation pattern. But obsessions have a way of bleeding into the subconscious of even the most stalwart of individuals.

Whenever Maraudar would run yet another errand for Madame Bleu, Ryker would type the pattern in and handle the time crystal. He loved looking at it, but he also loved the allure of something forbidden.

The day had come when he realised it wouldn't be so easy anymore.

Look at how fancy this new input is.

Maraudar curled his bicep while pointing, as if he knew aesthetics were his only hope.

Ryker rolled his eyes as he walked over. Sweeping the long fringe behind his ear. The input had an additional security measure.

"The vault entry is now configured to accept my DNA or something along those lines. I'm no scientist but, hey, you can't fault extra security, right?"

Ryker despaired. A pathway to the time crystal was closed for good. Or so it seemed.

CHAPTER 43

LOCATION: GEMARINE
YEAR: 118
LILIANNA – 22 YEARS OLD

After Juniper had showered and taken some R and R in the regen chamber, she looked a trillion credits once again. Lilianna was almost annoyed at how her beautiful dark skin shimmered like sand dunes bathed in dusk. How many times had she wanted to be Juniper? Not just shed her own pale skin and bask in the artistry of Juniper's, but strut through streets exuding self-confidence. Envy was not an accomplice in the pursuit of self-acceptance, so she repressed that feeling, in hope that present company and time would help her see the beauty in herself rather than dream of what she was not.

Flicking her wet hair across the top of her head, Juniper caressed the floor purposefully with dainty feet as she made her way toward the gathered group, her delicious body veiled in ivory casual attire.

Xan was fully clothed again, which was a shame to all who crowded the deck. Ryker was newly repaired after time in the regen chamber, and

Massy had used a heavy application of regen gel to his broken nose and broken package.

Xan, with the Crystal of New Life beside him, laid out the foundations for what was to come next. First, they needed a quick detour to an off-world Thractonian sanctuary that housed the feather of the *Perutonian Ridge Crested Joloulos*, ensuring Madame Bleu would have a gift upon their return to Gemarine.

Lilianna now stood in front of Madame Bleu with the feather of a *Perutonian Ridge Crested Joloulos*. Rocking on her boots with nervous energy, she smoothed out the vibrant feather before twirling it in front of Madame Bleu's dark eyes, inspecting every inch.

Lilianna waited while Madame Bleu held her neutral gaze on the feather. She was about to spout off with useless information about the *Perutonian Ridge Crested Joloulos*, much was her nervousness, when a thin, satisfied smile swept up across Madame Bleu's sunken cheeks. "Well, it seems your little crew has come good in the end. I do appreciate this gift."

"It is such a rarity, Madame, and something I hope will bring you joy and prosperity." Lilianna's tone was bubbly and bright, but the quiet in her pulled loudly, wanting her to return.

"Yes, well I should think it is reparation for the damage your crew caused." She finished her scalding words quickly, as if they were too hot on her tongue. Shifting her demeanour, Madame Bleu arched an eyebrow. "Where is Xan, by the way? I much prefer gifts of magnitude coming from...hmm...shall we say, leaders in their field."

Lilianna often didn't need to bite her tongue but she could have severed it in two at that moment. She was extremely disappointed at the way in which Madame Bleu continued to devalue her. Her only respite was in the knowledge that Juniper would be in the midst of breaking into the vault to steal her precious time crystal.

Lilianna settled for, "He should be here soon to present you with the final gift."

"Well I don't particularly enjoy waiting around for—"

Xan burst through the door and Lilianna's jaw dropped. He was dressed in ceremonial garments. Tapered light forest green pants, a fitted beige collared shirt and a dark abalone cape that sparkled with silver trimmings depicting bursts of stars.

Honestly though, he'd look good in a colourless sheet with a hole cut out.

As she caught her breath and followed his stride into the room, there was a definite presence he exuded, even before Madame Bleu herself.

"Nice of you to join us." Her tone was sardonic.

"My apologies, Madame. I had to make sure this tingsha was correct and capable of providing you with the radiating qualities that you deserve." He presented her with a deep aquamarine bottle.

"Oh?" She held her nose high, regal and arrogant. "What will this do?"

"Well, it was steeped in the feathers of the *Perutonian Ridge Crested Joloulos*, so it will have taken on the radiating and immunity-enhancing qualities. You can combine it with a base moisturiser or alternatively mix it as a tea to consume." He lowered his voice and produced an apologetic smile. "But it doesn't have the sweetest taste, just warning you."

"You underestimate me, Xan. Often one needs to take the hard line to achieve the simplest of rewards. In this case, I believe health and well-being is a reward that shall bear the sacrifice of an acrid taste."

"You have been warned." He chuckled with ease, and Madame Bleu joined in with him, casting eyes to Lilianna, who forced a smile. She didn't have the political nuances to endure a conversation like this, and marvelling at how easy it was for Xan.

"Please sit, sit, we shall indulge in a small sharing of plates." Madame Bleu's tone was now lukewarm, encroaching upon motherly. "Thaspina, please fetch our meals from the preparation room. It is time for a Gemarinian delicacy – none of those chews for us this evening."

They sat in their seats at an ornate blackened-wood table, carved from the twisted tree forest. It was long. Too long to create any intimacy in the setting, but it was clear that Madame Bleu, who sat at the head, preferred distance between those who she deemed 'beneath her'. Which, as Lilianna realised, was basically everyone else.

"So, Xan, King of the Wilds, why call upon me for this formal meeting? Why not you and I in an intimate moment instead?" Her eyebrows raised slightly with the innuendo.

Xan's laugh was a burning candle, warm and fragrant. "I haven't heard 'King of the Wilds' in a very long time. Isn't it funny how on Earth or Gemarine, the sensationalised story headlines are all the same?"

She chuckled, too. "I wouldn't know about Earth, dear." Silence landed as the laughter died. Lilianna shifted uncomfortably in the chair.

"So, tell me, Xan, why are you here?" Madame Bleu eyed him with suspicion.

Xan appeared taken aback slightly and he swallowed, then composed himself, and if Lilianna saw it, so did Madame Bleu. "It's true, there is another reason to meet. I have a request to make of you."

She clasped her wrinkled hands atop the table. "And what might that be?"

"I would like the Valkor prisoner we captured to be released into my care."

She threw her head back in manic laughter. Once she let out the last wheezy chuckle her head snapped back into place, her face adopting a serious masquerade. "You have to be joking."

Xan found composure in a neutral, confident stare. "I'm deadly serious."

"Why the hell do you want that useless mute? He hasn't said a word in captivity. In fact, I'm not even certain he is an intelligent being."

"I want to leverage some of the knowledge he might possess for new fauna."

She laughed again. "You want to take responsibility for a mute, because he might be able to point you in the direction of some new creatures? My starlord above, Xan, I've known no one else like you."

"Well, I'll take that as a compliment."

"Don't." Madame Bleu's voice was flat and her easy smile was yanked from her face in an instant. "You come here as a teenager, tainted by Human traits and qualities, then you demand a nice, cushy job swanning around the galaxy, getting all these insignificant little creatures and putting them on display. Poking, prodding for everybody's entertainment. You're lucky I still permit this madness."

"The madness you permit, is sustainable to Topaz. In fact, it is profitable. It not only turns the wheels of credit, it gives you a green handprint, that all Gemarinians respect you for. I basically make you look good. Yes – it fuels my passion, but it also fuels this city."

Xan flexed his fists and the veins in his neck quivered in anger. Although he was meant to be putting on a show for a distraction, this was real for him. Those words were a reflection of what he believed in. Still, was he treading too close to the water's edge? Would Madame Bleu attach weights to his legs and let him sink to depths unknown?

"So what will this oaf bring to you?" She rolled her eyes, her wrist bent as she ripped a piece of spiced bread with coarse hands, shoving it into an open mouth.

"Look, all I'm saying is – I need another member of my crew regardless. The strenuous demands of running the biobase, conducting experiments, researching expeditions and captaining the field trips – I'm strapped for time. I need someone who can be trusted in the field, and as a lackey who won't talk back."

"Well, you definitely won't have that problem." Her smile was mocking.

Xan ignored it. "Exactly, and I think, why have a capable body wasting away, when we could be putting him to work?"

"That I can agree with, but what makes you think he will want to join you? You slaughtered all the Valkor on that ship but him. Part of me thinks you want him out to finish him off." She swished the fermented amber alcohol in her glass and Maraudar inched forward from a darkened corner to offer her more from the bottle. It made Lilianna catch her breath. Maraudar was the keeper of the time crystal and the longer he stayed in their company, the less chance they would have of being caught.

"I'm not about extinction regardless of the incidences. I would like a chance to redeem myself."

"Oh, right, so it is all about the world liking Xan once more." She coughed in that condescending tone.

Thaspina came out with various plates. "Here is poached panetti with an aroma of fillias herb, infused with corte blanche." Without a hint of warmth, she mechanically placed each meal in front of Madame Bleu's guests.

"So what if that's the case? I'd rather be pushing for the cleanliness of redemption than sullying my hands further with the grimy darkness of apathy." Xan picked up a knife and fork, cutting into the pink meat of the panetti, and looking a little concerned as he didn't usually eat dead animals.

"What will you give me if I permit this?" Madame Bleu took a slow mouthful of the panetti and the sticky corte blanche dripped down her chin. Lilianna grimaced.

"The tingsha and feather weren't enough?" He tried to lighten the mood with a wry smile.

"Hmm, I thought that was a bit of bribery to get you back on your missions. Nothing to do with Valkor boy."

Maraudar's MPD flashed and he moved into the adjacent room to take the call. Lilianna's palms were sweaty and she clasped them together for comfort beneath the table.

Why is he receiving messages? Is something going wrong with the break-in on his level?

Xan's eyes followed him as he disappeared into the next room, but his features remained calm as she chewed the panetti.

"Let's cut to the chase, Madame. What is it that *you* want?" Xan placed his knife and fork down beside the plate, giving all his attention to the conversation.

"Crystals." Her lips pursed and her eyebrows arched, highlighting her smugness. Xan's hand shifted toward his thigh, a blade peeking out with hungry eyes above the waistline.

Is she asking about crystals because she knows we have them?
Is this plan already ruined before it's even begun?

CHAPTER 44

R*yker and Juniper; the dream team. What a fucking joke*, she thought. *Will this plan find ruin before it's even begun?*

She shook her head.

Gotta make do and hope that pastie little silkworm doesn't spin a web of shit.

"Hey, kid, you got this, right?" Massy almost read her thoughts.

Ryker squinted. "Yes, yes. I've known Maraudar my whole life. He's essentially been a really shit caretaker. I can do this."

Massy paced the foyer of Maraudar's building, deep in thought. "The DNA is the thing that does me in. What if that doesn't work?"

"Jeez, Massy, shut the fuck up. We're already all on edge. We have to have faith in the plan. If he calls him down at the right time, I'll get in position and administer the serum. It's as good as done," Juniper levelled confidently.

"Alright, alright. But if things go to hell, I'll throw you both under the bus quicker than you can swallow ten loads. I don't give a shit."

"Lovely, Massy. Just lovely," Juniper puffed out of the side of her mouth.

They reached the opening to Maraudar's level through the motitubes one by one. Massy was to be stationed outside the door to warn of any oddities. If there were any, they would immediately cease what they were doing, and hide.

Ryker entered the code via the keypad lock, and knowing the number sequence, he breezed through. He pointed to the vaulted safe through the main room. "It's in there. Just remember the pattern is this." He started to draw the long combination in the air.

Condescending little asswipe.

"Ryker, I'm not an insect. I remember what I'm meant to do." She pushed through into the room aggressively. "Focus on your tech bullshit and don't worry about me."

Ryker angled his head toward the server room, and with the MPD as his weapon, focused on manipulating the surveillance so they left no trace.

Juniper stood in front of the safe and took in a deep breath. There were twelve pages of potential pattern combinations and although she feigned confidence with Ryker, she needed a steady hand and a clear mind. There was a restart available if she got it wrong once, but the second time was a complete shutdown; boronium bars would descend from the ceiling, alarms would blink and scream, a whole orgy of security would descend upon her. She liked orgies, but not that kind.

The first screen materialised and she consulted her MPD with the outline, saved as a simple photograph on the local storage. With her fingers slick with sweat, she drew the first pattern across the pad. A blue light confirmed the correct pattern, instantly moving onto the next screen.

Okay, Okay. Fucking owning this shit. She exhaled with a relieved smile.

RYKER
21 YEARS OLD

Ryker came in tentatively, rubbing his hands together with nervous energy. Juniper was bent low, sweating over the keypad.

"What are you up to, now?"

He heard the shakiness in her voice, something he'd never once attributed to Juniper. "It's number nine, so I've got to keep…moving—"

There was a loud beep, low and sudden, halting their conversation. Red flashed across the screen and locks clicked back into place, as the display unit returned to the start.

"Fuck," she whispered with the ferocity of stinging needles. A clenched fist slammed against the boronium door of the safe.

"Did you do it right?" Ryker asked, afraid of her answer, as well as the repercussions.

"I thought so," she replied, clearly annoyed, running a shaking hand through the curls of her hair.

"Just breathe and go from the top," Ryker let out, almost immediately regretting it.

"Ryker, if you start giving me Zen breathing techniques, in a second I'm going to shove my whole exohand into your anal cavity and set it to expand."

Ryker swallowed. "I'm trying to give you encouragement."

"Well, all I need from you is the right patterns," she said, her voice sharp like thorns hidden within a sweet-smelling hedge. "Actually, let's hope they're the right ones and I messed that one up. Otherwise, we're fucked."

CHAPTER 45

LOCATION: GEMARINE
YEAR: 118
XAN – 24 YEARS OLD

Are we fucked?

Does Madame Bleu know we have two out of the three ancient crystals in our possession?

"You want us to find crystals for you?" Xan exclaimed. "I told you I was finding it difficult with the workload. Now you want me to excavate a bunch of gemstones?" He scoffed, choking on the fear of what she may have discovered. He clasped the dagger at his hip. "I know you have a penchant for opulence, but this seems unnecessary," Xan chided. But he immediately regretted it, worried he'd overstepped the mark of banter into disrespect.

Thankfully, Madame Bleu valued a challenging back and forth. "Xan, you disappoint me. For a man of deep intelligence, you've narrowed your focus too much on creatures and now you're missing the wonders of the galaxy." Madame Bleu smirked, chastising him. "Even your golden girl here would know of the rumours." Her eyes turned to Lilianna, seeking recognition there.

The light caught Lilianna's golden hair, swaying as she chewed her food, a pink flush creeping across her cheeks. The whole time they'd been there in the grips of fear, he was able to control himself, control the room. But not now. He could only will Lilianna to be calm enough.

Words finally escaped Lilianna's lips. "I have heard...some things over the years."

"What things, child? Impress me." She flicked her fingers in Lilianna's direction.

Lilianna sideways glanced at Xan, seemingly unsure of how much information to divulge. "There was said to be a number of crystals capable of housing immense power. But as far as I'm aware, it is only a whisper now of what once was shouted across the galaxy."

"Very poetic. I suppose you somewhat know your stuff." Madame Bleu's pointed nose twitched, and she shifted her determined gaze toward Xan. "I want these crystals. I want this power," she said flatly, her hands clasped and resting on the table. "I have a crystal division working on ancient texts, interpreting directions, formulating theories, but as much as it pains me to admit, the team members are...useless. I want intelligence, I want devotion and I want the best of the best following leads."

"But why can't they—"

"Do not interrupt me," she exploded, her jowls turning grey with the flare of fury.

Xan remained composed and let the silence hang.

"You may have your Valkor oaf, but as a result, each mission you go on to nab your dirty little creatures, you must explore any surrounding planet in its vicinity looking specifically for crystals. Not just any crystals. *The* crystals. I will provide you with two other crew members of *my* choosing." Xan was about to protest but she held up a finger and he stopped short. "This is a take it or leave it offer," she replied with finality.

The awkwardness hung stale in the air, like the vinegar essence of the tingsha that dulled in the room.

Xan didn't need time to think anything over. "I accept," he said, stone-faced and brazen. It would only take moments to set a course in motion to start searching for the crystals. But if all his plans went well this evening, he wouldn't need to go on an expedition at all. He thought about the Crystal of New Life and the Crystal of Fate relaxing together in complete serenity back on the ship. Once he had all three of them, he would do as the ancient text said, and unite them on a distant planet. Only then could he fix what Madame Bleu had broken.

"Very well." She extended a slender arm and clicked her fingers in annoyance. "Maraudar!" she yelled.

He did not come. Thaspina came instead. "Madame, he was called to other business, as you may recall."

"Ah yes. Fetch Zondini and both of you can bring the mute Valkor to this table. Xan here has adopted a son." She fought the laugh that clawed behind her quivering lips. "Good luck in your journey to fatherhood. May it be fulfilling for you." A devious smile ate half of her face.

Xan nodded, stifling the urge to roll his eyes.

Madame Bleu abruptly pushed her chair back and it squeaked loudly into the cavernous hall, startling Lilianna as she jolted out of her chair in fright. "I must take leave for a moment or two. I've many errands to run." She discarded her napkin distastefully on the half-finished plate in front of her. "The heathens in the crystal division will send word to you of proposed missions to take over the next segment of time." She half turned to leave, her cape threatening to envelop her shadow. Her voice lowered so it was deep and threatening. "I'm expecting results, Xan, or we may have to rethink the long-term plans of your sanctuary or biobase – whatever those cubes of shit are called."

Before she departed the room she looked over her shoulder. "Lilianna, you're growing on me. Maybe it's because of your subservience, but if you ever want something more than working for a fool, I am open to discussion."

CHAPTER 46

LOCATION: GEMARINE
YEAR: 118
JUNIPER – 24 YEARS OLD

There was no discussion between Juniper and Ryker. Her sole focus was on making sure the pattern would be correct this time. She had made it to the seventh screen, sweat beading off her forehead. In high-pressure situations on the battlefield, sweat wasn't an issue; overconfidence was really the only thing that may have hindered her. She would spill blood with the slice of her exohand, each of her finger blades shining with the sheen of vibrant death. Her Cranston ray gun, smoking with a wispy exhale of an executioner.

But here, staring at a screen, waiting to see if meticulous movements caused pain or gain was essentially torture. As she completed the seventh screen, her MPD pinged with an alert. Massy had sent the emergency signal.

"What the fuck?" She spun around with pupils bulging, pure shock sewn with coarse stitching into her face.

Ryker looked at his MPD hastily, and flicked through to the live feed in the hallway.

"Shit, Maraudar is coming now!" His eyes were alight with anxiety, knees knocking together as if caught bare in a blizzard.

"What, why?" The wavy curls on top of her head bounced in fright as she searched for somewhere to hide.

I thought the inner circle were all at the feast with Lilianna and Xan?

The cogs in Juniper's mind turned and took her on a winding journey through painful memories of her own. Coming to a halt at the dire possibility of betrayal.

She hated to draw that conclusion. But how else was Maraudar about to catch them in the act?

Not bothering to wait for Ryker's reply she went through the logical steps. "Okay, I'm going to figure this out." She breathed out calmly, but then, catching herself, whispered hurriedly to Ryker, "Quick, hide somewhere."

Ryker twisted and searched desperately around the room. The only place it seemed, was under the couch. It was as cliché as it could get, but it would have to do.

He dived underneath.

The door handle wiggled.

Juniper unzipped her top so her cleavage was on show. Sitting on the couch, she crossed her legs and welcomed a sultry seduction to her stare. The reduction of her womanhood to simple physical manipulation irked her. She was a lot more than that, and there would be a time to show them more than just tits and ass.

The door flew open.

Maraudar looked upon her, furious and puzzled at the same time.

"You!" he said with a deep growl. "What the fuck are you doing here?"

The screen to the safe was on the eighth incarnation, waiting for her to continue with the pattern. It was on her mind, but she was careful not to bring his attention to it. She needed to really draw out the seduction.

"Finally, you're here! How long does a girl have to wait around?" She brushed a rogue curl from her forehead behind the ear, eyes rolling in feigned annoyance.

"You didn't answer my question," he said with menace as he trained his Cranston ray gun upon her.

She laughed with ease, throwing her head back, and settling deeper into the couch. Her arm tucked behind her neck, pushing out her breasts.

"You know, I saw you the other day, while I was being *interrogated*." The way she said interrogated was laced with sarcasm. "And well, I'm not the type of girl that waits around for anything really. If I want something…I go get it." Standing up, her slow, purposeful footsteps were for him. The confidence and demeanour made sure his stare climbed from her boots, taking in the bridges of her legs to the heavenly destination worthy of a pilgrimage. Juniper reached him as he stood with his mouth salivating, pushing his gun wilfully into her chest.

"Now put away your laser, and show me the only gun I'm interested in."

He let her seize the laser and place it on the side table next to the door. She gripped his hand, leading him to sit on the couch.

"You wanted me?" he asked, unsure, the doubt weaving through his formerly aggressive tone.

"Why wouldn't I?" Juniper matched his incredulity. "The darkness in your stare, the firmness of your arms, the power in your position, the way you threw me onto the street." She bit her lip. "It's fucking hot."

Maraudar considered this for a small moment. "No one has ever said this to me."

Her fingers drew intersecting lines across his thigh. "It's because you're hardly ever out of Madame Bleu's clutches. Imagine if you weren't only servicing her. Imagine if you could take control." She lowered the zipper to her navel, then traced her skin, looping across her breasts with a dainty caress of a finger. "What do you want, Maraudar? You can seize the moment."

He reached out tentatively, pulled back her bodysuit tenderly, exposing Juniper's shoulder first and peeling away until one breast was on display. He stared for a moment then moved his hand across it, a delicate caress at first, and when Juniper's eyes closed and her breath caught, he pushed harder.

Her hands groped for any thickness across his pants, and she found it, rubbing hard against its rigid outline as he ripped open the other side of her suit and sucked feverishly on her nipples.

It was exhilarating, despite the precariousness of the situation. A searching male's fierce tongue on her body again. Juniper had missed this, and she'd take as much as she could get right now, knowing that soon she'd have to try and subdue him with the anaesthetic needle fixed to the side of her boot.

Maraudar trailed his indulgence along her neck, then he met her plump lips pursed for the persecution of his libido. Tongues flashed wildly as she gripped his masculinity harder, wanting to feel it pulse in her hands.

The next part happened so fast.

A sharp stabbing pain shot through her side and she clamped her teeth down hard on his tongue. As her neck muscles jerked, she felt it rip, severing it in two. One part limp in her mouth, she spat it across his shoulder and he bellowed in a deep roar, blood flicking onto her face as she turned to the small blade fixed in her side.

She swayed.

That little motherfucker stabbed me.

A deep rage gripped her. The brain interpreted her instructions carefully as she set her exohand to finger blades and stabbed her forefinger into his jugular, tearing across. Eyes were no longer a dim, soft green as darkness, hate and the strength of a woman reflected in Maraudar's bulging pupils.

Women were often touted as inferior on planets other than hers. She would dare them to come and lecture her about being less than. No one on Gemarine wanted to fuck with her. This was why.

The sounds that came from Maraudar immediately ceased. Silence fell, only disturbed by the barely audible pulsing of his blood spurting across Juniper's mouth carved into a snarl, her naked breasts heaving with hate. His hands moved to his throat and he rolled onto the floor, blood molten lava pooling around him, viscous and slow.

RYKER
21 YEARS OLD

Maraudar dropped to the carpet, blood flowing from his throat and mouth. Legs twitching as his body sought the finality of death.

Ryker peered out from underneath the couch, recognition in Maraudar's fading stare confirming betrayal with that knowing look. The dark eyes were wide with a final breath, stained with the deep maroon that covered his jaw like a mask.

Ryker wanted to whisper that it wasn't his fault. He wanted to reach out and touch his hand, he wanted to comfort him with a memory of their smiles. But in reality, he stared back at dead eyes. The dead eyes of a man who'd practically raised him.

This was his fault.

Death on his hands; a tombstone in his open palms, painted red.

CHAPTER 47

LOCATION: GEMARINE
YEAR: 118
XAN – 24 YEARS OLD

The Valkor's eyes widened as he glimpsed Xan who stood from the table, bowing to welcome him into the room. It wasn't customary for Xan to bow, especially to a prisoner, but he wanted to make him feel as comfortable as possible. The memory of his blade smiling as it split flesh brought a jolt of self-hatred. Repression was a tool to dispel the guilt, making damn sure of its impermanence. If he let it, guilt would ravage him until a husk of his former self remained, extinguished by the zephyr that fluttered through brittle branches.

Thaspina deactivated the laser shackles and they dropped to the ground with a hefty click.

Madame Bleu strode through the large, dark wooden doors, an ashen insignia burned and crusted onto both panels, and returned to her seat at the table. She sipped casually from a frosted glass, then spoke. "Valkor, you are now released into Xan's custody." She extended her arms toward

Xan as if presenting him to the stunned Valkor. Then, losing interest, she relaxed back down in her seat. The plates and napkins had been cleared from the table while she was gone as if by magic.

The former prisoner inched forward, scratching nervously at his wrists. Lilianna stood, acknowledging how difficult it must have been for him, and moved to meet him with an open embrace. "I'm so pleased you will join us, Dallis," she said, using the name he gave her earlier, conjuring warmth from her golden eyes.

The creases at Dallis's mouth strained into a thin, forced smile and his eyes flickered from Xan to Lilianna, to Madame Bleu, and beyond.

"Don't waste your breath, Bright Eyes. He's as dumb as they come," Madame Bleu said without the hint of an apology.

"Lilianna, take him to the ship and make him feel at home please." Xan's voice was the rumble of a stirring volcano.

"As you wish." She bowed with grace. Xan could have sworn all trace of fear had escaped her, replaced by a look of sexual energy, much like he'd seen in Juniper before. Was it because of the way he commanded her? Did she feed off that? Did it bring back memories of the other night? Did it mean she wanted more, perhaps?

He watched them both leave the room, Lilianna as animated as he'd ever seen her, trying to make Dallis feel comfortable enough to engage with her at least.

"She takes orders well. I bet she's a good fuck, if you're into submissive little sluts, that is," Madame Bleu cooed seductively, taking a gulp from her chalice and holding stoic eye contact that suggested she preferred to adopt a dominant status while fusing.

"I've trained her well in every aspect of *work-related* business. Let's leave it at that." He shrugged, determined not to disrespect Lilianna's new-found sexual appetite.

"I bet you have." She looked him up and down, licking her lips as if he were the decadent dessert slapped on a plate in front of her.

Xan's stomach churned – not at the dessert, that was wonderful – however, Madame Bleu's look was a mouldy dollop of cream, tainting the otherwise lovely indulgence. Xan was more forceful this time and chose to ignore her subtle advances. "As I said," he adjusted his cape and rolled his broad shoulders as he returned to his seat, "she does extremely well with business-related matters. You should consider taking her more seriously."

Madame Bleu's nostrils flared as she drained the last of her drink, slamming the empty glass onto the table as if expecting an instant refill. "Oh, you're so boring. Wound tighter than a Sytheract still searching for a soul bond."

Xan took a final spoonful of the chocolate-based twin moon cake, licking it clean. He considered her for a moment. "Majority of the time, maybe so." He pursed his lips then readjusted his posture, easing his back into the seat. "I guess that's what happens with being a leader, as you would know. The relaxing moments are hard to come by because you've always got the weight of so many lives cupped in shaking hands."

Madame Bleu snorted dismissively. "The comparison between what we do is laughable. For one, you are a leader of a bunch of creatures, some of them literal maggots, and we're not even talking about your crewmates." She waited for a reaction, but Xan purposefully held eye contact, waiting for her to continue.

"You wouldn't know the first thing about true leadership," she went on. "Being the surrogate mother to a complex swathe of species on this planet, ensuring they stay alive, ensuring they thrive, ensuring they are content and protected." Xan cringed internally at the way she recycled the words of the insignia. "You wouldn't know the sacrifices I've made to ensure the balance is kept."

I do know, you psychotic genocidal, maniac. I know all about these 'sacrifices' you've made.

Madame Bleu bowed her head for a moment, and for a small second silent reflection appeared to distil her bravado. Her eyes met his, glistening with memories he couldn't possibly comprehend. "The weight of the decisions and those sacrifices would be enough to break some people."

Xan considered for a moment that maybe she cared about the worlds she destroyed. Poor innocent souls that were heedlessly forsaken. But as if those painful memories were at once exterminated by an internal blast, the steely resolve returned to her gaze. Her jawline tightened, and her cheeks became angular with the pout of thin lips. "But I will never be broken. That is a promise."

CHAPTER 48

LOCATION: GEMARINE
YEAR: 118
JUNIPER – 24 YEARS OLD

Juniper helped Ryker out from under the couch. He seemed broken and vacant, dazed at the gruesome scene before him.

Ryker stared at the splatter of blood across Juniper's breasts, as well as droplets still trickling down the sides of her mouth. There was a piece of pink flesh; Maraudar's tongue, discarded on the grey casing of the couch. The copper scent of blood permeated the recycled air.

"Are you okay?" Her voice finally reached his ears, and he turned across the couch, emptying his stomach with violent lurches.

Juniper looked frightening as she caught sight of herself in the reflective panels surrounding the level. A massacre masquerade marred the beauty of her face. Papules of blood dotted the skin on her forehead, spray from Maraudar's spurting wound. A cascade of blood ran down across her breasts, still tacky to touch. Not even she liked bathing in the blood of her enemies. That was a little too morbid. She quickly zipped up her suit, stained and shivering, then focused on dragging Ryker to the sink. "Drink water, now," she commanded.

Ryker stood with an effort, swaying to the haunting melody of guilt. Leaning over the sink, he retched and then threw up again. Juniper reached past him and switched on the tap so he could sip at the water when he was done.

Juniper pulled back, allowing Ryker the time to bring colour back to his face. *Who knows what colour actually means to this poor, pale bastard.* She punched in a command to her MPD and dialled Massy. "Hey, Dingus, get in here. Now."

Massy barged through the door, but halted as soon as he surveyed the gruesome scene before him. Juniper caked in blood, Ryker white with sickness and Maraudar's dead body still twitching involuntarily on the floor.

"What the fuck, Juniper?" he stammered, the terror in his voice undulating.

"Don't 'what the fuck' at me," she shrieked in a whisper. Her thoughts were a mess as she scratched at her arms, trying to peel off the blood. After a moment or two, the composure she was famous for returned. "Go find me something to wrap the body in, and do it fast."

Massy's mouth hung open still, but he eventually nodded meekly and scooted off, searching throughout the level to find something.

Don't freak out was the mantra pulsing through her. She didn't want the blood on her. She didn't know the extent of the wound at her side; they were the worst parts. Juniper had killed before in battle, she had maimed, she had seduced when needed. But she had never ripped off someone's tongue, tasted the blood drip down her throat as she sent a needle through a thrumming jugular, his cock in her other hand.

What a fucking weird scenario.

Juniper breathed in and the soldier took over. It was all about the mission. A solution was required. Xan and the others were relying on her to fix this. But how could she?

She worried someone on their own crew had betrayed them by signalling Maraudar. But he could have been coming to his level for any reason. It's not like she could interrogate a corpse now, could she? So the truth would stay guarded by the reaper.

So many people relied on her. Xan, Qilin, Lilianna, the three worlds hanging in the balance, the underground.

Holy shit, the underground. A light bulb effectively switched on in her head. She dialled 'Miami' using the designated scrambled signal on her MPD.

"Juniper, I wasn't expectin'—" She stopped short at the sight of her. "Holy gravbombs, what happened to ya?"

"You know how I said you could make up for all the bullshit you did with a favour?"

"Yeah, what're ya thinkin'?"

"Do you have Maraudar's DNA stored anywhere?"

"Yeah, lovey, we have all those inner circle asswipes. Why?" Miami was confused as she twirled a long grey streak of hair around a finger.

Juniper swallowed as the tension in her shoulders loosened. "We need him replaced."

CHAPTER 49

"**O**kay, Ryker, they'll be here any moment. This hinges on you." Juniper held both his hands. She looked awkward and disingenuous, but comfort was not her thing. "Are you good?"

Ryker stared at the woman who had killed Maraudar, smudges of blood smeared across her bodysuit that water could only distil, not completely rid. It was clear she was trying to be supportive.

"Yes, I can do this," he tried to say confidently, but he felt another burp rise from the pit of his stomach.

Massy paced nervously behind him, waiting for the underground crew to arrive. "Okay, get going then, kid. You got this." Massy clapped him on the back, a gesture of bravado between mates, but Ryker hated it and grimaced.

Ryker turned to look back at Juniper and wasn't sure he would ever be able to look at her again without remembering her half naked and caked in blood.

How could a good man like Xan be enamoured by this unhinged psycho?

JUNIPER
24 YEARS OLD

As Ryker took the motitube up to Madame Bleu's level, the man in the body of Maraudar knocked at the door, and was greeted by Massy.

"Holy fuck. What is this, witchcraft?" he breathed, disbelief caught in his stare.

Juniper shoved him aside. "Hey, thanks so much for coming."

"No need for formalities. Miami was happy to help you," replied the man posing as Maraudar.

Juniper huffed out a breath. "I bet she was happy."

Massy couldn't stop staring, moving his head one way and the other until he burst out, "I mean, it's uncanny."

Juniper ignored him again. "The body is on ice in the tub wrapped in sheets, but the couch and all the blood we—"

He held up his hand. "Say no more. We'll see to it that it's fixed. I'll send someone on my way to the inner circle level. As much as it seems so intense right now, this is actually a blessing."

"How so?" Her voice was flat and uncertain, regret settled in like an old acquaintance.

"We now have a seat next to Madame Bleu. This is an important position."

Massy turned to Juniper. "What is this guy on about and is someone going to explain to me what is happening?"

"Massy, shut up – let's get through this first and you'll know whatever I want you to know afterwards," Juniper said, with caution in the forefront of her mind.

"I won't waste anymore time," the new Maraudar said. "I'll meet Madame Bleu now and maintain this cover until we hear something from you." Before Juniper could even ask for his real name, or better still, express a heartfelt thanks for the swiftness in which the underground's support was delivered, he left abruptly with confidence in his footfall.

Juniper turned to the vault, intent on finishing the final screen and getting access to the crystal. After all that madness, it still wasn't in her possession. What was, though, was Maraudar's DNA.

After inputting the final pattern, the screen glowed blue. It flicked to the final authentication mode where it asked for a sample of DNA, as well as a pupil scan.

She turned to the body on ice, and with her exofingers, hacked around the eye socket, pulling out an eye streaming with vessels like a comet hurtling through space. Massy leant against the door frame about to hurl. "Get the fuck outta my way, you little bitch." Juniper shouldered him as she walked by. Her frown was toxic and Massy backed away in complete submission.

"You are something else," he groaned with distaste.

As she picked up the discarded severed tongue, she replied, "Even though you're being facetious, I'll take that as a compliment." She jogged over to the vault screen and pushed the tongue down into the DNA reader and held the scavenged eye up to the scanner to open the vault. Massy turned away, as it appeared too difficult for him to watch the gory details.

Juniper tapped her foot impatiently. She'd waited long enough and wanted this ordeal over and done with. Massy's lingering presence and unspoken judgement were doing her in. She wanted to get the goddamn crystal and fuck off back to the ship for a shower, punch a wall or two in rage and maybe get Xan to fuck her senseless so she could just forget.

The screen flashed blue and the pressure of the door released. Its bulky boronium frame swung back, revealing the time crystal in all its glory… which was nothing really. It looked like a shitty clear rock with flecks of amber and turquoise. Pretty to some, but a rock to others.

Juniper snatched it and stuffed it inside her pack.

Finally satisfied, she turned to Massy. "Remember, you need to meet Xan now, so get to the ship. I'll go and clean myself up and be there ASAP."

"Damn right you do," Massy said, straight-faced. "How can you…do that and not care?" he spat.

How fucking dare he?

A scowl developed at the slightest inclination of anger, but she decided for once not to bite back, remaining composed and at a stretch, demure.

"Massy, there's something a lot bigger at stake here – that's all you really need to know." She shrugged with an air of politeness and then stormed out, leaving him to survey the room alone and breathe in the stench of an idiot.

CHAPTER 50

LOCATION: GEMARINE
YEAR: 118
XAN – 24 YEARS OLD

The door swung back open and Maraudar came into the room, straightening his garments and shifting his hair.

"Where the hell have you been? Errands don't take that long." Madame Bleu tapped her foot on the dark polished floor.

He blinked several times, as if perturbed, unsure of what to say as he stared up at Madame Bleu. Xan started to see a mixture of not just fear, but loathing and a smattering of discontent all rolled into one.

"Well, speak, you fool!" she shouted, the wrinkles on her forehead like the scars of tillage on a willing patch of land.

He stuttered, "I...I...was checking on a prized asset, Madame."

She rolled her eyes. "Fucking make yourself useful and go into my bedroom, get on your knees and get ready to lick my cunt." Her voice was sharp and decisive.

Maraudar swallowed, thrusting a quick, worried glance in Xan's direction, and then shuffled toward the room as Thaspina and Zondini watched him, baffled at his behaviour.

346

Something's off, Xan thought. *Did he catch Juniper and she threatened him?* He was eager to find out.

"Anyway, unless you want to join these three in servicing my nightly needs, I believe this concludes our business." Madame Bleu looked hungrily in the direction of her bed, as Zondini and Thaspina took their cue.

Xan stood up and began to bow, readying himself to leave, but suddenly Ryker burst through the door looking flustered.

"Ryker, what are you doing here at this hour?" Madame Bleu asked impatiently.

He stole a cautious look at Xan, then back to Madame Bleu. "I need to ask you something in private. It's a family matter."

She turned to Xan. "I should have accepted your payment as taking this fuck-up off my hands for all those years." Xan was about to protest, but thought better of it.

"I'll take my leave then, Madame. Thank you for your hospitality and enjoy this evening with the inner circle."

"I will. Xan, if you change your mind, you're welcome to return." Her lips bulged as she kissed the air in his direction.

Xan feigned a smile, feeling ill and a little sorry for the air who had to endure her kiss.

"Maraudar! Get up off your knees and come take Ryker into the sitting room for a discussion. Get him a change of clothes, he looks like he hasn't washed in days." A look of pompous disgust overcame her.

A flicker of stinging recognition crossed Maraudar's face as he laid his eyes upon Ryker.

"Maraudar, wake up and get your ass into gear. What is wrong with you tonight?"

He blinked twice, steadied himself and moved toward Ryker, who had seen it too and looked confused. "Ah, let's go...son." A deep tone encompassed his voice. It was authoritative and assured.

Xan turned to leave, closing the door as Ryker went to talk with his aunt.

CHAPTER 51

Juniper walked down the corridor of the ship after the rejuvenation of her shower. The Crystal of Time was nestled in her pack.

She passed by Ryker making final adjustments on some of the fittings in the maintenance hull of the ship. He looked more sullen than usual. After he had returned from Madame Bleu, he and Massy refuelled the tanks, preparing for the next epic journey. Xan hadn't divulged any information about their destination, yet they knew it would be an important trip.

As far as Juniper was concerned, she wasn't sure about laying all plans bare with each member of the crew. She still had a sick feeling about the Maraudar situation. Not the feeling of his limp, severed tongue in her mouth, but the way in which he came to interrupt their thieving experiment.

Was someone sabotaging them from within? Or was it a bit of a bad coincidence?

A coincidence is just a way to validate fate's scornful laugh in the face of hope.

Trust was a big thing to her and for it to be broken by someone in the cohort was a decidedly low act. The darkness within her quaked as if the foundational plates clashed against one another. Usually, the quake would rumble until a fully-fledged storm laced the skies with bright blue strikes of lightning, atmospheric pulses that cracked and split seams sewn tight. But she had to quell the hurt of being lied to, and channel it into a path of exploration, a magnifying glass that examined clues to find the person she needed to bleed dry when the time was right. She had done it before the last time she was betrayed.

Ryker had proved his worth, though. Massy couldn't hurt a space mite and Lilianna's emotions were as easy to interpret as a fresco artwork on the ceiling of a chapel. Dallis she didn't really know too well. But would he have been able to trigger an alarm upon release from containment so soon? She didn't think so. Then there was Miami and her crew – would someone of the underground be in a position to sabotage them?

Either way, she needed to confer with Xan. He was the person she knew the best and the leader of this troupe of misfits, so he might be able to shed some light on her train of thought.

As her boots clanged onto the floor of the ship, Lilianna found her, a look full of wonder. She couldn't tell if it was because she wanted to fuck her again or if she was excited about seeing the crystal. Juniper gave her a nervous smile, garnished with a hint of 'don't fall in love with me and become some clingy bitch, please and thank you'.

Massy was checking the neutrometers and flipping the different coloured switches readying the ship, and yelled from his seat, "Is that the time crystal bitch I hear coming aboard? C'mon girl, show Daddy what it looks like – I didn't even get to see it." He twisted around with a great big smile on his face. In the harsh internal light of the ship, the regen gel couldn't go all the way to fixing the damage she'd caused to his nose. A faint scar, a constant reminder of his idiocy.

Seems like he's shaken off his shock of the Maraudar scene quick enough. Such a little bitch, trying to avoid confrontation.

"For one, you don't have the presence to be anyone's daddy and second, ew, I'm not your fucking girl. Show me respect or I'll crack your nose in half again." Juniper smiled sweetly and batted her eyelashes at him.

"Ah man, she can never take a joke—"

"Actually, *she* can very much take a joke, but *she* refuses to be undermined and disrespected. So, try again," Juniper interrupted, pointing her exofinger in the air.

"Meh, I won't bother." He turned away, back to his controls, sulking as Lilianna hovered next to her like a little pet waiting for a pat. Juniper hoped it wasn't because she'd opened her legs for her, then all of a sudden a whole bunch of emotions rushed inside and she now wanted to soul bond like lame-ass Sytheracts on their home planet.

The only thing that came inside me was...

"Hey, so," Lilianna began.

Juniper got ready to jump through the glass window just to get away from anything remotely emotive.

"I'm actually curious as to what this particular crystal looks like compared to the others." She pointed to Juniper's pack with a smile that didn't seem crazy at all, just warm and cosy.

A relieved exhale seeped from Juniper; she wouldn't be picking glass out of her skin for days.

Xan burst in before Juniper could give Lilianna an answer.

"Juniper, bring it to me please." His was voice, deep, commanding, sexy. *Stop it, Juniper. Just commanding.*

She skipped over, handing it to him with a wink. He was uninterested in her, evident in the way his eyes zeroed in on the crystal as he held it aloft. The light danced off each facet, sending radiant sparkles into the ship.

"I can always trust you." A husky whisper in contrast to the controlling tone he used a moment ago. He reached out and squeezed her hand.

Resistance was futile. Without a tether, her smile flailed in open space. But he enacted the gravity, so it would always return back to him. A true smile, for a true friend.

Juniper caught a glance of the Valkor over his shoulder and unpleasant memories rushed back. She had pushed them into the dark corners of the mind, willing cobwebs and dust to settle. But through an open window dust might swirl, cobwebs could clear. Here was an open window she needed to close steadfastly or get used to the slight chill.

Narrowing her eyes at the auburn-haired Valkor, Juniper mustered a nasty stare of death to invade his worthless essence, but he perked up, sapphire eyes twinkling with hope, flashing a brilliant white-toothed smile as if he couldn't grasp negative body language.

"Hello, Miss Juniper. My name is Dallis." He bowed and knelt with a jerky, awkward movement. As a Valkor, he might have been as graceful as a white-tailed bird in flight, but as a creature of Gemarine, she would score him a two out of ten.

"Hello, Dallis," she said slowly, her eyes remained fixed and wary, her voice like dry tinder, crackling on the crest of an ember breathing life.

"Ahhhh," he stammered, eyes flickering, "might I apologise on behalf of our people for my role in—"

"Dallis," she said evenly. She couldn't handle the soppy bullshit any longer. "Words cannot conjure souls to return. Words cannot erase hurt that was caused. But actions and loyalty can strengthen a broken bond. If you pledge your allegiance to our cause, then consider yourself absolved."

She flicked her hair and trudged toward her quarters. "Wake me up when we're at the portal planet – whatever the fuck it's called. I've had enough for one day."

Dallis was left with an open mouth as Xan chuckled to himself.

CHAPTER 52

.

Juniper stormed out of the room with Qilin on her heels, while Dallis scratched the back of his head nervously, mouth agape. The man who'd been seconds away from slaughtering him had taken him into his care, and his race had kidnapped and killed Juniper's crew, putting her whole career in jeopardy. The only friendly face was Lilianna's, and his eyes found hers like a hopeful beacon in the midst of a blackened void.

She smiled, knowing pity was etched into the curves of her mouth, but unable to hide it.

Xan noticed the exchange, and moved away from Dallis toward his captain's chair, calling back, "It's going to be tough, Dallis, but at least you're free." He turned to Massy and sat next to him, plotting the course to the Periah: Planet of the Portal.

Lilianna moved forward to Dallis's side. "As much as it doesn't feel the best right now, you'll come to see the good in everyone here." She reached out and placed her hand on his.

He flinched and looked away, and she immediately withdrew.

"Sorry, I...Valkor seldom engage in physical contact other than for, ah...copulation." Dallis flushed with embarrassment.

Lilianna winced inaudibly. *Copulation? Oh my, so not sexy.* But who was she to think that? *This is probably how the others think of me. Some little pristine princess afraid of physicality.*

Flashes of Juniper's tongue caressing her nipples, Xan's length pounding inside her, that burst of light, of purity that flooded her when...

"Although I can permit it through my desire to become one with your customs," he finished, brushing his long fringe away from his bright eyes.

Lilianna realised quickly her face felt hot, and she'd ignored what he was saying, remembering she was no longer a 'pristine princess'.

"It's a show of comfort. Something to let you know I have your back." Her smile was kind and reassuring.

He spun around twice, nearly falling over himself. "My back? What happened with my—"

Lilianna couldn't stifle her giggle. "No, no, it's a saying. Oh gosh. We have a lot of work to do."

Dallis looked sheepish. "Oh, of course. Please accept that I will take time to adapt." His voice was robotic, but he placed a large hand on his robust chest as if swearing an oath.

"We all do, and further to that, hopefully you'll see the good in us quicker than it takes you to adapt to everything."

"Oh, I think that the perception of good must flow both ways. I am a representation of every Valkor who has come before me and thus, I must show you the strength of our character and not the strength of our vengeance."

Lilianna took a moment to consider this, although he might not have been particularly adept with customary nuances, he was an intelligent being and he would find his way.

"I am looking forward to getting more acquainted with you, Dallis." Her smile was warm, and his eyes met hers then shifted away quickly as Xan spoke.

"Are we all ready to go now?" he yelled, then nods and yelps followed by everyone within earshot.

Switching to his MPD he called out, "Ryker, are you on board and is the ship ready to go?"

"I'm working on the mechanics with some final tweaks," he said flatly.

"Okay, so making a quick announcement. Because this is in a little-known system, we have to be extremely careful. We're going to do the hyperspace jump and then navigate manually through to Periah, keeping at a steady speed so that radar cannot pick us up."

The MPD crackled, "I thought I told you not to wake me until we were there." Juniper's voice crumpled like a thick blanket.

"Stop being a little brat." Xan breathed fire into the MPD.

"Make me," she replied, then cut comms abruptly.

Xan rolled his eyes and turned to Massy and winked at him, giving him the go ahead. Massy nodded and the engines roared, the hyperdrive murmured in anticipation and he eased the throttle so the ship rumbled as she climbed into the skies.

Xan's MPD crackled again. "Hey, Xan, I know you're busy right now, but please come and see me when you have a chance. Thanks, love."

Without taking his attention off the flight path he said, "Yeah, sure." Uninterested but compliant to Juniper's request.

Lilianna guessed what she wanted from him. It wasn't necessarily jealousy that zapped through her. There wasn't really a word for wanting to be tangled in both of their embraces again. Whatever that word was, that was what she felt. But instead, she got comfortable in the seat and ruminated over her complex feelings. Societal standards on Sytheria promoted soul mates and life bonds, Human culture was a less stringent version of that, Gemarine was a free-for-all, but what she was gearing toward was unique.

A part of her didn't want to admit or recognise it, but the other part screamed at her. *I want to be with them both.* And not just physically; she needed them both. She shuddered, gut churning at the thoughts that betrayed what she believed to be her core values. She'd given her body before, but not in the act of simple pleasures – there had been her heart behind her intentions but seemingly never theirs.

As Massy jumped through hyperspace, she wondered what they might find.

A flash of light, and that familiar nausea spread through her instantly as they materialised on the other side. The blackness of space speckled with tiny twists of pink and purple ahead of them.

"Navigating through the asteroid field ahead," said Massy. His serious tone, almost like a foreign entity, was present in him.

"Alright, you got this, buddy?" Xan asked with a hand on Massy's shoulder.

"Of course, boss." Massy was more focused than Lilianna had ever seen him. Lips stuck together, hands gripped tight on the controls.

Xan then walked toward Juniper's sleeping quarters, brushing Lilianna's shoulder as he passed. She turned and looked longingly at him as he disappeared down the hallway. Maybe she was jealous. Not jealous of the relationship they had per se, but she felt a niggle. It was, she realised, a desire to be included.

They might be talking about something trivial and, sure, they might even fuse to release some tension, but she wanted to be viewed by both of them as worthy enough to know secrets, to know them past their barriers.

As she turned back, she caught Dallis staring at her and he quickly avoided her gaze.

That's weird, she thought. But then again, Lilianna wasn't used to identifying the longing glances from another.

CHAPTER 53

LOCATION: PERIAH
YEAR: 118
XAN – 24 YEARS OLD

With the planet over his shoulder, shimmering with a golden aura, Xan told the crew to gather in front of him. And each one of his favourite individuals in the known universe stood – or in Qilin's case, sat – watching him expectantly, tense about what lay ahead.

Juniper had told him in her sleeping quarters: "At any rate, I normally would've just fucked the shit out of you until we reached our destination, but I have grave concerns someone out there is working against us."

"I don't believe you," Xan said, flatly refusing to acknowledge her.

"How do you figure Maraudar barging into the level like that?" She gestured hysterically with her arms, but her tone suggested he was an idiot.

Xan recalled Maraudar walking away from the dinner table and speaking into his MPD. "He received a call at the dinner."

"Exactly!" Juniper slammed her hands down on the table beside the bed. "I didn't even know what happened at the dinner – yet I suspected some weird

shit went down." She tapped a finger against her chin. "Was Lilianna or Dallis with you?"

Xan thought hard. "Yes! Well, at least Lilianna was there when he received the call. She escorted Dallis out a little bit later on, though."

Juniper raised her finger as if to say something, but Xan quickly came in over the top of her. "If you start accusing her of being in on 'it' — whatever 'it' is — I'm actually going to spit in your face."

Juniper then smiled in that wicked way, and Xan rolled his eyes. She quickly reverted to the matter at hand. "Look, I'm telling it like it is, Xan. I'm like, ninety per cent certain someone is working against us. I had an inkling when I left Maraudar's level in disarray. But with more time to think since then, I'm sure now."

As Xan searched outside the window into the darkness beyond, he didn't want to believe it.

He pulled up the camera feed from inside the ship: Ryker was casting a hateful glance out the window, tired eyes, bent and tense; Massy was scratching behind his ears — deciding on sniffing it, then recoiling in disgust. Dallis searched in Lilianna's direction, dipping his head every so often so that his auburn fringe veiled his lovestruck gaze. Lilianna wasn't clear on the feed but he pictured her in memories, searching him with expectation, like he would carry all her dreams. And of course Juniper was in front of him in the flesh, arms folded across her breasts, wearing a smug smile like she knew it all. Knew that Xan was about to go against her recommendations. As if to reinforce that belief and hope in others weigh heavier than the burden of trust.

Xan stood in front of the crew, Qilin at his side, chest raised, shoulders squared and head held high. "Friends, most of us have been together for quite some time, and I never would have anticipated that this would be our calling." He looked to Qilin at his heels and took a deep breath, steadying himself. "Life has taken a complicated turn and so I, on behalf of this crew, have decided to follow this path." A slight pause increased the anticipation. "Some of you have heard the stories of the ancient crystals, and what they can do. But this planet we're going to, Periah, holds a portal of great power. With the three crystals combined, we will be able to open the portal, go through and...fix some mistakes." Xan was unsure of how to phrase the repairing of the timeline, without asking for ridicule.

Massy spoke first. "Sorry to interrupt, sir." All traces of silliness erased from his demeanour. "What mistakes do you mean?"

Xan's worry lines grew, and his feet shuffled on the spot. "It's hard for me to say more than that, because sometimes the fear of failing means the bridge built from sheer determination will crumble before we ever set foot on it." He then smiled, carefree, eradicating the negativity from his mind. "But before setting foot on this path, we must know *why*. We must have a reason. That reason has never been clearer to me. But because I believe in you," Juniper caught his glance, and looked unimpressed, "I wanted to discover it together."

He held out the time crystal, the one stolen from Madame Bleu. "This is the time crystal and it holds the key to finding out the next part of our mission."

"I know you wanted these crystals for a purpose – but what – now we're going to go back in time?" Massy was agitated, his voice cracking at the end of his question.

Xan ran fingers through his dark hair. "I've studied the ancient texts thoroughly now. The Celestial Guardians put this...failsafe in place, so that if any extinction-level events were razed across the galaxy – whoever could put these crystals together would be able to fix what had been broken."

"Why is it our responsibility, though?" Massy asked, as he cracked his fingers one by one.

"Some of you believe in the stars. Believe in the guardians of the previous age. Some of you don't." Juniper crossed her arms, looking away. "But the Celestials gave us the means to do this, and the stars may have brought us together to fix what has been broken. So I'll answer your question with rhetorical ones, Massy – is it right to watch as we fell trees, only for the wood to be used as excess commodities? Is it okay to walk past someone who stumbles and falls, not even offering a hand? Is it our fault when we stand, passive, behind a tyrant who pushes a button labelled extermination?"

Massy's eyes shifted to the floor where dust gathered. The same dust that blows out into the vacuum of space when the door opens, exterminated, extinguished from their world. He didn't utter a word of resistance this time.

Xan continued, "We take on this responsibility, not because we caused it, but because we have the means, the power, the will to fix things. The sins of our ancestors can be absolved if we invest in a fortuitous future for all."

Dallis exalted, "Hoorah!" His face set with determination: serious and resolute.

A moment of silence followed, then Lilianna burst out laughing, dispersing the tension for everyone else as they roared together. Qilin's tail wagged and thumped against the floor. Dallis with a bemused, dumbstruck look tried to join in without knowing he was laughing at himself.

Xan finally resumed. "Thank you, Dallis, for your...mild support." It was encouraging that Dallis could be roused by a speech and forget that Xan had nearly killed him. He hoped it was the start of earning his trust back.

Ryker had been quiet and solemn as he listened, but finally he asked a question in a soft voice. "So, what are the next steps?"

"The ancient text highlights an incantation. We must say it at the same time we hold the time crystal. The crystals need to absorb the energy from different parts of our bodies," Xan said. "It will then transmit a glimpse of the future into our collective minds."

"Wait, so we basically all need to be touching it at the same time and then we'll have some shared vision?" Juniper finally produced something positive to the conversation.

"Yes. From what I can understand about the text, it will give us an idea of where we need to go and how we can possibly fix it," Xan explained.

"Gather round folks and let's rub a crystal. The genie of time is acomin'." Massy rubbed his hands together.

Juniper didn't say anything; it was Lilianna that piped up. "C'mon, Massy, this is serious. Not one being in known history has done this. It's time to shape up."

Eyes glassy, he stepped up as contrite as he'd ever been. Comedy was a defence mechanism at the best of times, and Massy, who had been through some harrowing times, relied on this to push him forward. But he extended his hand and gripped a part of the crystal.

"Repeat after me, uno mindrasi, ino candente. Yrtedi fin focal, xuriphus an optor."

Then, flashes in the screen of the mind's eye, moments of time shooting through at lightning pace, caught in a web of desperate visions.

Xan stands beside a short professor with dark square-rimmed glasses, wisps of grey hair combed across the shine of his balding head.

The formula for combating the climate crisis scrawled in Xan's own hand on a tech board.

Experiments successful.

Tears streaming down smiling faces.

The professor, a proud mentor.

Xan, his student who had saved the world.

In the face of a bloody war many decades later, Humans are divided into factions.

Red, green and grey colours distributed as totems for each faction, as far as the sun's reach.

Juniper stands atop the crumbling steps of a parliament building.

She is flanked by a loyal commander in chief, with dark features and long flowing hair the colour of burgundy wine.

Contentment passes through their stare after years of turmoil.

Juniper closes the door to an office with the symbol of an eye and the text 'The Watchers' scrawled beneath.

Lilianna's soul bond clasping her hand tight.

Their golden coats swaying as they walk across a rocky desert into the horizon of a setting sun.

The discovery of an abundant natural resource capable of producing energy for fuel.

Ships propelled in bursts of fluorescent green.

Cities bathed in spectrum light from a large, connected power source.

Marvest the Aranther and his fraternal twin, eyelids shut and perspiring with concentration.

Minds interlocking through meditation.

The oneness of a deeper consciousness, the connectedness of achieving a shared spiritual plane.

Tribes once torn apart by differences finding common ground through a common mind.

The collapse of the civil war, enlightenment reigns over the planet of Dracia.

The intertwined minds of the crew separated, wrenched from the warm embrace of the other. The visions evaporated into the stark reality of the present moment.

All of the crew stumbled back as if an unknown force pushed them away from the crystal. Disorientated, they clawed the air for something solid to steady themselves.

Xan held onto the captain's chair and closed his eyes. The light in the ship burned his retinas, headache swelling, breathing ragged.

As he squinted through the slits his eyes would permit, he observed the rest of his team in similar predicaments. Indistinct bodies sitting or lying on the floor, others still stumbling or braced against the ship.

"Ohhh God," whined Massy, "a little disclaimer next time please." As his stomach contents were splattered across his boots and the deck where he stood.

Qilin galloped over and gobbled up the contents before Xan could object. She then plonked down on her rear end, looking satisfied. Xan shook his head.

"No next time thanks," wheezed Ryker, sprawled out on the floor, frozen as a snow angel.

As one by one they pulled themselves together, Xan spoke again, slowly this time and with considerate effort. "As intense as that was," he paused, swallowed and burped unapologetically, then continued, "it gave us a glimpse or snapshot about what we need to focus on."

"So, that was an alternate timeline, I'm guessing?" Lilianna said from the floor, as she hugged her knees to her chest looking ghostly.

"Well, according to the text, the time crystal will show us the timeline we were taken out of. Seeing and understanding what happens in that timeline will help us navigate to those specific time markers that we saw. We need to make sure all those events actually occur, without our present selves enacting them."

Massy shook his head from side to side. "My brain hurts."

Juniper, warrior woman, was sprawled across the floor face down. She lifted her head up and said, "Who knew he had one?" Then her forehead met the deck of the ship once again to the sounds of Dallis laughing.

"Time travel sounds like a hoot," Ryker suggested, now sitting up craning his neck this way and that. "Explain it again, for the present denser cohort."

All eyes looked toward Massy and he began to protest but relinquished his right. "Yeah okay, I have no fucking clue, so I'll cop that."

Xan straightened his bodysuit and stretched his arms across his chest, encouraging circulation in the muscles. "What we saw were moments in time that weren't allowed to flourish. This was because Madame Bleu took key people out of the timeline."

Massy nodded. "I'm with you so far."

"Those worlds fell into ruin because she took the key people out. The course of time needs to be corrected once again, but instead of us being a part of it..."

"We need to pass the information to the next in line." Lilianna finished his thought.

"Exactly. Then we'll be able to merge the broken timeline with the corrected one." Xan smiled. But a part of him was rocked by the veracity of the vision. He was the person who combated climate change. It was something to be immensely proud of. But the other visions made him both proud and a little envious. Envy wasn't something he was used to feeling.

There was a competition for places in Gemarine, sure, like select spots for various occupations or an expedition being rejected because there were too many ships patrolling that quadrant of the galaxy. However, there were always opportunities to explore alternatives.

But what had him feeling hot all over was seeing the likes of Juniper and Lilianna flourishing in a world without him. He didn't like that. He liked being *their* person. The withered stalwart tree in a forest of saplings.

An unease spread over him.

What will this mean for us if we tamper with this parallel timeline? He needed to research more to find out how General Heronicus and the Celestials believed this interference with time would work.

Will I wake up one morning on Earth forgetting about my life? Qilin, nowhere to be found.

The unease turned to sickness.

That would be a nightmare.

Qilin sat at his feet, her tail curled around his right leg. A protective, but affectionate gesture – almost like she was holding him steady with love itself.

As much as romantic love didn't enter his thoughts on Gemarine, he loved his crew and it broke him to think he might have to lose them to win the war of their worlds.

Ryker encouraged him back to the present discussion. "So, the next in line for Xan was the professor. Juniper had a commander in chief. Lilianna, well, um…" He couldn't finish, his elbows were bent and he scratched his hair at the back of his head awkwardly.

Juniper finished what he was saying flatly, "With her soul-bonded mate."

Lilianna flushed.

"Who was the Aranther guy?" Ryker asked.

"I know him." Juniper spoke confidently, now on her feet and looking more alive. "His name is Marvest and he guards Soldier Headquarters."

"Pardon me for my intrusion," Dallis said, "but why wasn't Ryker or Massy shown in the time visions?"

Ryker perked up. "I was born on Gemarine, so even though I'm part Sytheract, I've never actually been there."

Dallis nodded then turned to Massy. "And you?"

"I guess it means that whatever I would have done, might not have been on as large a scale as fixing the climate, finding alternative energy sources or creating peace across the world," Massy said.

"Just an average Joe." Juniper smirked. Massy clenched his jaw, fuming, but he didn't say a word. Often that was worse.

"Joe, which one was that?" Dallis asked seriously.

Juniper giggled and said, "Never mind," then turned to Lilianna. "This guy," thumbing in the direction of Dallis, "is a comedic genius."

"Look, it's all very confusing," Xan said. "And something we didn't necessarily sign up for. But here we are, with the tools to fix a large hole in the fabric of time. We have to at least try." Xan's voice found intensity in that last moment, which roused Qilin. She pounced on him, wrapping her front legs around his neck, trying to nibble at his ears absurdly. Xan play-fought with her amidst hearty laughs, ultimately ending on the floor with Qilin in his lap.

Juniper came to his side, kneeling and resting an arm at Xan's back, the exohand ruffled Qilin behind the ears. "I'll follow you through time, through water and even through the intestines of a giant alien slug."

Dallis chimed in, "That is quite a specific example but I shall, too, face the wrath of alien slugs on this quest." He raised both arms into the air, biceps bulging.

Massy rolled his eyes. "At least I'm not the dumbest fuck in this crew anymore. Yes, yes, I'm in. Let's fix time and all that." The sarcasm was defined in the haphazard way he waved his hands, pretending to be excited.

Xan said, "Alright, so we go to Sytheria first. I want to find that natural fuel source there. We'll need it if we want to navigate through time and space efficiently." He got up and started to move with intent. Pressing buttons, beckoning Massy over to the controls. Then he turned to the only Sytheria-born Sytheract in the room. "Lilianna, you will need to take point."

LILIANNA
22 YEARS OLD

As they blasted into orbit and through the atmosphere, Lilianna's heart hammered. What she'd seen completely threw her. A glimpse of the life she could've had, cruelly taken from her. A soul bond so complete and wholesome. It *was* hers.

Her home now was a world that often didn't feel like it even had a soul. But Gemarine did have a lot. It had freedom of choices, it had no judgement, it had Qilin, Juniper, Xan.

She glanced at Xan. His brow was creased, attention focused on the horizon, or rather, what lay beyond it. The sculpted arms, the defined jawline set hard, the veins in his neck, thick with the blood that coursed through him, through his heart. The heart she loved more than any other physical attribute.

Juniper was by his side, staring just as intently at the planet ahead. Steeled by years filled with battle; wars raging on around her and within her. Scars bit down hard across her skin. Her chest heaved with controlled breath, touching the many branches of her lungs; distributing the fierceness throughout her body. It was the same fierceness that pushed Lilianna to be more than a withering mess.

For the first time since she was a child, Lilianna would waltz back onto the planet of her birth, where her family was, where her apparent soul bond was. But when would it be? There was a date that flashed on the screen in her mind. But for her that would be five years ago, for her planet – which was already ravaged and dead – it would be a lifetime ago, thanks to physics and the quantum entanglement of space.

Her older sister, Fleurah, would be twenty-one, which would make her younger. Time dilation was a crooked branch on the sprawling tree of life.

It all blew her mind.

Seeing Fleurah would surely be too hard.

She would need to avoid the family home at all costs.

CHAPTER 54

LOCATION: PERIAH
YEAR: 118 (THE PRESENT)
XAN – 24 YEARS OLD

Following the coordinates, they approached the clifftop, straddled by silver and sandstone rocks. Spilling off the top, rushing water frenzied into a pure white froth, plummeting into a vibrant aqua pool. The pool was surrounded by greens of life – growth nurtured by a sun who cared, giving the best of itself to the planet when it wailed for sustenance.

They landed atop the cliff, as nubile stones underneath quivered with fright before they were crushed by the weight of the ship. It wasn't difficult for Massy to locate the portal frame. Aside from the ancient text providing its approximate coordinates, it was twenty times the size of anything else on the planet – large, foreboding and made from a completely different material. Ancient symbols were carved onto the surface of its circumference – a halo covered in the rust of neglect and weathering. But it beckoned for use, like an eye full of sorrow, weeping for a wounded soul. It almost buzzed with an energy wafting out from the core of time itself, willing repair.

Xan was first off the ship with Qilin, Juniper right behind them, peering across the landscape, neck craned, whole body tense and on edge.

"Where are the inhabitants of the planet?" she said, alarmed.

"In all the reading of the text I did, there were portal guardians thousands of years ago, but they're all gone now. The retreat of the Celestials most likely drew them to other places," Xan explained, as Qilin matched his footfall across the springy surface.

"How many pages of that old-ass book did you read?" Juniper asked, keeping her guard up despite the casual nature of their conversation.

"All of it." Xan shrugged, as if it were child's play.

"Honestly. You are the biggest nerd burger on the menu." She laughed, and it echoed across the valley below. "When did you even have time?"

A confident smile materialised. "When I fucked you and Lilianna into a satisfied slumber, the real work began." He bumped her on purpose, making her stumble off course.

"Please," she said, her voice rising, dragging out the syllables. "The only sedative I needed was you talking about guardians and portals. It *bored* me into a deathly slumber." Juniper poked her tongue out and threw rude finger gestures into his face, which he swatted away with a grin that masked the enormity of what they were attempting.

The rest of the crew joined the trio as they made their way to the portal opening, close enough to make out the intricate markings across the large circumference. They each spent time scanning the symbols, heads back, mouths agape in awe.

Qilin made her way over to the far corner and scratched at the portal, trying to get Xan's and Lilianna's attention. A loud, high-pitched squeal alerted everyone in the vicinity and Xan ran over to her quickly to stop her sharp claws from producing the worst music that Periah had ever known.

Her spikey tail wagged against Xan's leg as he knelt to study the deeper indentations on the side of the sturdy frame. Tracing his finger across, he realised it was a slot for the crystals. Right beside the slot, retractable from the frame, was a glowing orb, with eight numbered slots beneath it.

Xan wondered for a moment about the makeup of the glowing orb. It didn't appear to have any technological qualities, but he deduced from the numbered slots, this was where they must key in the dates.

"I've found it," he called across to the others who were still slowly taking in the massive structure.

Dallis, more so than any of the others, seemed to be completely engrossed in the beauty of the natural surroundings. Kneeling next to a bubbling brook, he let the water run over his hand as he skimmed its surface.

Xan was pleased Dallis was with them. He may not have been the mute Madame Bleu saw in the confinement cells, but he had a reticent innocence Xan found charming. More importantly, he reminded him of how prudent it was to garner self-control. To ensure that even if emotions were to overwhelm him, creatures and other species deserved a chance to prove they were good. Dallis would be a constant reminder of why he did anything – giving new life and giving second chances.

At Xan's call, the crew gathered close by. Dallis's fascination with the brook came to an end as duty called. Juniper stayed vigilant, stalking around the portal, investigating shifted rocks or branches that may have been carried downstream.

Xan brought the crystals out of his pack and into the light. Refracted rays of the sun were trapped in their facets, spilling beautiful patterns across their faces. The collective group stared intently as Xan placed the Crystal of New Life into its designated spot. Once he'd inserted it, a rumbling and shifting of plates within the planet trembled throughout their bodies. Everyone looked down at their feet as the soil shifted, then up at the portal gate as it cracked and threatened to burst with life. But it was only a little hint of what it could do.

Xan took a deep breath and placed both the fate and time crystals into the portal slots in quick succession.

JUNIPER
24 YEARS OLD

As Xan placed the final crystal into the designated slot, the rumbling beneath the surface of planet ramped up, knocking Juniper off balance so she was standing with her arms out to the sides, steadying herself. Looking down, Juniper caught sight of a footprint in a muddy section of moss gathered near the stream.

She knew that print well.

Her heart's tempo increased, the conductor of her life flailing wildly. Her voice was taken, as if shouting into a blizzard. Breath was condensation, and the inhale ensured the chill curled internally, nestled in her gut.

Turning to the group, she frantically searched around them, waiting for a confirmation, waiting for those fears to be realised. Her Cranston ray gun was drawn now, a muscle memory from years in the trenches, stalking this prey. Eyes now spotlights searching the trees beyond the portal gate, zooming in on every tiny inconsistency.

But her mind flashed with harrowing images of war; the smell of her own burning flesh as a laser sword sliced off her arm and cauterised the wound, the freezing mud caked across her body, shivering as she tried to sleep beyond enemy lines in a darkened forest, the taste of blood as it dripped into her mouth, twirling swords and bodies pirouetting to the sombre, imperfect cadence of death.

As those memories faded, a ray of sunlight glinted off a tree – which wasn't possible, not unless the tree was metallic.

They'd given themselves away.

She yelled, "Cryptoborgs!" as she released a cannon pulse from her laser, aimed at the tree. The Cryptoborg staggered away from the trunk and fell, injured or dead, she couldn't tell.

XAN
24 YEARS OLD

Xan hurriedly clicked the time crystal properly into place, and the ground rumbled as the portal surged with life. A glowing blue wave of light spanned from the energy of the crystals across the entire area, bubbling, fizzing – inviting them to push through.

Lasers sang short, sharp, high-pitched melodic motifs overhead. Bolts crashed through the portal as it absorbed each hit. Twenty Cryptoborg soldiers hidden in the ridgeline streamed down toward the gate and the crew took cover behind anything they could find. Massy and Dallis cowered behind granite boulders, ducking out either side to fire on the enemy as they swarmed across the landscape screaming their famous war cry.

Juniper leapt across rocks, spinning and evading the laser scorches that zinged off the granite. She reached the first potential victim, and with her ire blade, sliced across their neck without a flicker of concern. The Cryptoborg's head rolled down the hill, tumbling end over end with a wheel of blood spraying the rocks the colour of war. Another charged and she threw her battle sword into the air directly above her, letting it float like a majestic dragon as magnetised blades shot off her exohand, lodging into the eyes and throats of the pursuers.

She caught the sword again as she felt the presence of another over her shoulder, and twirled, decapitating the soldier with a swift glide of her wrist. The finger blades returned to the vacant space on her exohand. All her children tucked warmly into their blood-soaked bed. The sound of war was dissonant. The splitting of flesh, the clink of metal, the gentle hiss of a dying breath. The climactic roar of pain, who demands a rousing ovation.

Juniper knew pain well. A masochistic acquaintance who bestows suffering, not only unto the casualty but also the inflictor.

Another Cryptoborg soldier approached but Juniper swiftly met the dirt in a skid, slicing upwards, the crunch of sword through metal from the groin across to the shoulder resulting in yelps of anguish and a smattering of blood. Two halves of the Cryptoborg fell opposite one another, mirrored in death.

As Juniper continued to fell an army, Xan screamed coarsely, "Get to the ship, everyone. Run!"

Lilianna reached for his hand. She didn't speak, and she didn't need to.

"I'll be fine," he breathed, "I'll always come back to you."

Lilianna's eyes spelt pure terror in the language of innocence, but his calming words gave poetry to her soul.

Qilin put her paw on Xan's foot, and he knelt so his face was level with hers. "Now, you, my beautiful girl, need to go and protect Lilianna." Her ears were pricked up, listening to his every word. Xan pointed at Lilianna, as if his body language would reinforce his request.

Qilin wasn't a normal creature operating from regular fight or flight mechanisms. She could manipulate the elements, she had illogical understanding of emotions and so must have sensed the danger they were all in. Her blue forked tongue left the sticky residue of love on his cheek. Not for the first time, the amber eyes of the *Mika Tikaani* he'd met in the Wilds a decade ago, looked as if there were something more within. A degree of comprehension and understanding way more intricate than he might ever know. The stare was severed as she turned on the heels of Lilianna.

They both followed Ryker toward the ship as Massy and Dallis fired off haphazardly, covering Xan. He punched the time, date and coordinates into the number slots, and a blue light pulsed within the orb as if asking to confirm. A high-pitched noise jammed Xan's senses, and he dropped to his knees.

As he looked to the horizon, the setting sun silhouetted Juniper in the dance of combat. The Cryptoborg soldiers began to surround her, magnetised to the greater threat. Xan hadn't experienced war, but he knew its tactics from historical data of all three worlds. He was Juniper's honorary counsellor after she'd recounted battles and missions over the years. He knew that first, one must identify the biggest threat and eliminate them. Right now, he needed to recall his training with Juniper and ensure his intervention counted. There was a lot at stake: his Juniper.

He clasped the Cranston ray gun tight and fingered the trigger, blasting lasers across the developing crowd.

Strong and severe though she was, a pack mentality tended to overcome a lone warrior. He stumbled as he rose to his feet. Nerves tingling, hands shaking at the thought of losing her. Thinking of all the times she had saved him, he pitched forward to repay the favour.

JUNIPER
24 YEARS OLD

Juniper's ears burned but she kept focused on the kill, on the evasion, as well as figuring out her strategy of combating the herd of dick-munching Cryptoborgs. Who was she kidding? She was beyond feeling overwhelmed.

As two attacked her at the same time, a blade entered the flesh on her bicep. In a flurry of action, she turned, jade eyes radiating emerald with fury. Exofinger blades were sent flying across the Cryptoborg faces devoid of gold helmets. One snipped a female's crooked nose and nearly took it off along with the top of her ear. She dropped to her knees howling, her own dark blue blood threatening to gurgle down her throat. Gathering herself, she rolled behind a tree, denying Juniper the pleasure of finishing the job. Xan's laser burned holes through several unassuming Cryptoborgs up ahead. They had been too focused on encircling her; they hadn't bothered about the rest of the crew. As the purple Cryptoborg oafs dropped motionless onto the rocks, Juniper was thankful for the days and nights she'd tutored ray-gun-o-phobe Xan. She was pleased her methods of persuasion had been intrusive.

Juniper parried a blade that slashed across her chest and ducked under a heavy punch that came close to crunching her jaw. Her exoblades returned and she clawed with them, stinging a Cryptoborg male like a scorpion scorned. But he lashed out, grabbing her wrist with a locking grip, crushing her exoarm. Before he was able to get the upper hand, she thrust her sword into his bowels, weakening his grip. He let go, sighing with bitter resignation, so she rammed the sword through to the hilt, drawing her face right up against his, and spat her own blood to mark him as another victim.

"Die, you fuck!" She violently shoved him to the ground, revealing her sword sheathed in his defeat.

"Time to go." Xan grabbed her arm but she flinched in pain. Her bicep was perforated, her strength waning. Adrenalin propelled her forward as she registered Xan's instruction valid. They set off running toward the ship.

Massy burned through the starting engines as Xan and Juniper ran through exhaustion to reach them. It felt like forever, legs burning, lungs crying out for oxygen, as the ship hovered, moving ever so slowly toward the portal gate. The hatch lowered. Massy or Ryker must have been monitoring the cameras. They both jumped onto solid boronium. Tripping and sprawling across the floor of the ship, they held onto the groove of the hatch as it moved upwards, sealing it for the journey through the glowing portal gate.

CRYPTOBORG SOLDIER
27 YEARS OLD

They didn't see her latch onto the outside of the ship. They didn't know that Cryptoborgs could magnetise their space suits to a ship made from boronium and titanium.

Her nose and ear were haemorrhaging blood from when Juniper, the famous Gemarinian warrior, had sent exoblades to slice her face. She was wearing her gold helmet now, and it was a tray storing all her discarded fluid.

A small price to pay to change our fate.

She whispered the mantra out aloud to steel her resolve. "We are the hands of fate. Right the wrongs."

EPILOGUE

YEAR: 118 (THE PRESENT)

Long hair the colour of charred remains blew in the fragile air generated within the ship.

Prying open the portal and fighting off the Cryptoborgs was intense enough. But now the real fun began.

MPDs were fried and useless after going through the portal gate, so there was no way to communicate properly with Madame Bleu. Sabotage was the only option.

There were agents positioned in different time periods on Earth, Sytheria and Dracia, ready to be activated if Madame Bleu needed them. She wasn't daft enough to burn the memory of several planets and leave these things to chance.

Was Xan that stupid he didn't know someone was working against him in the crew?

The numbskull was a sucker for love, trust and honesty. Where would that get him when he's maimed and lost in time? Even though he'd survived the Wilds of Gemarine once with a creature that was practically conjoined to his leg, it wasn't going to happen this time.

376

Time would swallow him. Flesh withered in minutes, bones ground down in hours, the memory of him a stumble in the heartbeat of the galaxy.

It wouldn't be easy though. Juniper had smelt the noxious gas of betrayal creeping through the ship. Her walls were constructed quickly as her eyes turned cold with suspicion. No doubt she had warned Xan, but luckily he had insisted on giving them all access to the time crystal. It showed what their route would be – which meant there was a means to formulate a counter plan – the ultimate sabotage. So he knew what he needed to do. To ensure that Gemarine would prosper, dominate, be the indisputable force of the galaxy.

He would play his part. He would make sure he took his rightful place next to Madame Bleu. Everyone would see him then, as a hero. Not a simple sidekick. It was his moment to shine.

By the end of it, time wouldn't just swallow Xan. It would devour them all.

THE SECOND BOOK OF THE GEMARINE CHRONICLES *"BTBOT"* – WILL BE RELEASED IN 2024.

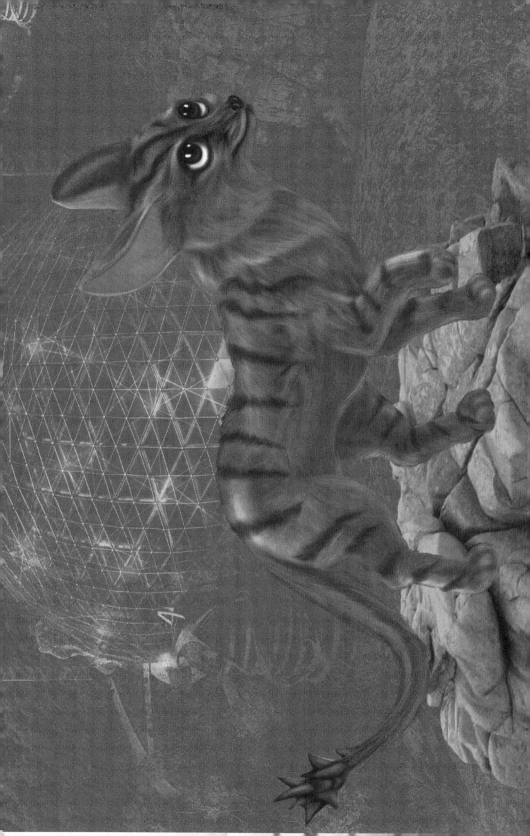

ACKNOWLEDGEMENTS

I would like to start by acknowledging the Traditional owners, custodians and Elders of the Darug Nation, both past and present. Most of my writing occurred on Darug land and I wanted to pay respect to all Darug community members living on and off country and show my support for the Darug Nation and its people.

Firstly, thank you to you for buying this book and for continuing to support my author journey. Secondly, this section is dedicated to all the people who have been helpful over the last year, specifically related to the composition of this work.

To my developmental editor, Emmie Hamilton – normally words encapsulate so much; we are writers and readers because we believe this. Unfortunately, in the case of how much you have influenced my writing, how much you have fixed my writing, how much you have helped me grow as a writer and most importantly, how much you have been there for me a friend – words ain't no thang. This piece of work would not be what it was without you and I'm so very grateful that you leant me the tools to succeed, and bolstered my self-belief. I'm incredibly lucky to have known you and so thankful that you continue to endure my idiocy each and everyday. I look forward to many more years of friendship and writing partnerships with you.

To my editor, Louise – thank you for being able to uphold my voice and find ways to ensure that this story was told correctly. You gave BFW a meticulous polish that has allowed it to really sparkle and shine.

To my beta readers and proof readers Zane, Liz, Nick and Leaha - thank you for providing valuable feedback that gave me a much stronger manuscript. You didn't let me down when I needed you.

To the supportive team of readers and friends who have made a huge difference to my confidence as a writer: Renee, Issy, Gus, Tanya, Connor, Alyssa, Jessica, Vie, Chase, Scott, Jenna, Matt to name a few. To the fellow indie author community who have been kind enough to not only show support but continue to be a source of inspiration for me. I would like to name some of you who have been on another level with your cheerleading and consistent encouragement – Shana J. Caldwall, Liv Evans, Nikki Minty, LJ Duncan, Kate Schumacher, Jessika Grewe-Glover, Meagan Johnson, Gabriella Margo.

Thank you to the bookish businesses who have been supportive of my work thus far – Book Addiction, Ariel @ No Shelf Control, Social Book Tours, Read it with Whiskey Podcast and Indie Author Maxx Podcast.

To everyone in my extended family – thank you for always being the first in line to rave about my creative endeavours. Thank you for understanding the pursuit of the ruinous, writer path as there are always many challenges to overcome. To my daughter, thank you for giving me purpose.

To the heroes of conservation that helped inspire Xan and Qilin's friendship – Sir David Attenborough, Forrest Galante, The Wildtimes Podcast, Bradley Trevor Greive and Dr Jane Goodall.

To my sources of writing inspiration - Pierce Brown, Kathryn Barker, Emily St John Mandel, John Wyndham, JRR Tolkien, Gregory David Roberts, Ray Bradbury and Stephen King. Thank you for the words, the truth and the stories that gave me strength to find my own voice.

CONNECT WITH JP MCDONALD

Website: www.jpmcdonald.com.au
Instagram @jpmcdonaldwrites
Tiktok @jpmcdonaldwrites
Facebook @jpmcdonaldwrites
Email: jpmcdonaldwrites@gmail.com

Call to Review:

If you enjoyed this piece of work, it would lovely of you to consider leaving a review on the various review sites and/or your social media accounts to assist in reaching more hearts and minds.

Made in the USA
Monee, IL
23 December 2022

23404716R10231